# Ties of Smoke

*A Novel of the Djinn Chronicles*

**Claudia Herring**

For Barry, always

"She felt that small shiver that occurred to her when events hinted at a destiny being laid out, of unseen forces intervening."

— *Dorothy Gilman*

**1**

*1811, the garden of Bramley House, twenty miles from London, England*

The deafening boom stopped the birdsong. A sluggish coil of smoke from the pistol lingered, a tracing of chalk on the air. In an instant, the noises flooded back. The birds' warning cries shrilled in her head, the snap of their wings like brittle sticks hitting flagstones. Frantic stragglers dodged her and winged after the flock.

Lavinia stood there, frozen in panic. She had been caught, found out, and her husband Peter had shot Yasir. Her breath came in ragged bursts. Yasir's confused expression when he couldn't heal himself alarmed her almost as much as his wound. The djinni slumped, his voice fading, "Send me to the urn."

She had commanded Yasir to take her with him. Would his magic fail again in his weakened state? Before this, she had suffered from Peter's violence. Her husband had an even better reason now.

Lavinia ran, bloodied skirts in her hand, the gravel of the path sinking at the pressure of her footfalls. Fear made her fleet. If the djinni could not help her, the garden ended at the wood's edge. After the woods there was a road. Then what? And where?

She kept her pace even when the pull of the djinni's magic made each step lighter. Even when the garden blurred as she was swept away.

❖ ❖ ❖

*Later, the djinni Yasir's urn*

*I should have vanished when Lavinia's husband lurched from the shrubbery, aimed his pistol at me and bellowed, "Get your bloody gypsy hands off my wife!"*

*Hesitation is not a trait of the Djinn—neither do we tarry where we are not wanted. I stayed because of Lavinia, my Lavinia.*

*A shoulder wound. A trifle really, minor even to this human form I have assumed. And for me, a djinni, only a few moments of blood and pain.*

*How wrong I was.*

Lavinia squeezed her hands together as she looked over the odd-shaped instruments aligned precisely on the brass tray. Things she had never seen before. Things sharp and frightening. Yasir had become so weak, he had sent her to fetch these. How could he use them? And on himself?

She lifted the tray, sagged from the weight, but braced herself and hurried over to him. He hadn't moved, and lay sprawled on the magnificent carpet, smudges of lavender under his eyes. Removing his bloody kurta must have left him exhausted. She set the tray down and knelt beside him. Blood still oozed from the wound in his shoulder.

"Yasir."

His eyelids fluttered.

*Lord in heaven*, he'd said before that he could heal himself. If so, he would surely have done it here, of all places. She looked frantically about, barely registering what she saw in her anxiety: a grand bedchamber opening onto a spacious hallway rather than a dark, cramped space.

She was *inside* the urn. A tremble shivered through her, but she ignored it. She wouldn't let fear render her helpless.

She bent over him. "Yasir."

He moaned and opened his eyes. Golden as the setting sun, they never failed to entrance her.

"We must call a physician." She stroked his dark hair, his curls entangled in the loops of intaglio gold earrings. In his flared nostrils, straight nose and strong jawline, the beauty of the feminine mingled with the strength of the masculine.

"I cannot . . . summon anyone." He took a shallow breath. His eyelids slid shut. She pressed her cheek against his. Hot, fevered. Her chest tightened. He couldn't be worse, please, no. With him in his human form, she could try and do the things she knew to help a fever, and hope he would react the same as a human.

"If something happens to me . . . you . . ." Yasir raised his arm in a wobbly sweep, indicating the urn. Lavinia glanced around, blinking tears away. Her heart banged against her ribcage. *Saints and angels*, he was telling her his wound could be fatal. That he would . . . He would die . . . She would be left in the urn.

Alone. Forever. With his body.

She took his face in her hands and leaned closer. He opened his eyes—those eyes that had seen centuries and countless magic, that spoke to her in ways more eloquent than the strum of lutes and the rhythm of poetry. She could barely speak as she held back her tears.

"Y-You . . . daren't suggest that. You are strong. This is merely a small setback. The wound doesn't look infected." She sat up. A few crimson rose petals stuck in the blood caking his shoulder. With a delicate touch, she removed them.

"I will need herbs, a pot and water. Is there a hearth or kitchen of sorts in—"

He pressed his finger to her lips, took her hand and placed it on the tray. She shivered. No. Surely he didn't expect her to use the odd instruments. Why, she had never—

"Take the short, thin silver wire with the loop on the end." He watched her. "No, not that one."

He sounded stronger. Perhaps her little talk had imparted vigor. She put her hand on another wire contraption that looked nearly identical.

"That one . . ." His voice faded. Yasir closed his eyes. His chest rose and fell as he caught his breath and looked at her, his golden eyes as dull as tarnished brass. "It will attract the lead shot. You will feel it attach. Insert it straight into the wound."

Lavinia held the wire over the round bullet hole—still oozing blood. Her hand quivered. She would have to push this metal instrument into his glistening wound, force it through living tissue. Yasir should at least have some brandy or spirits of some sort before—

"Now!" Yasir's voice was a snarl. She winced. Held her breath to steady her trembling hand. And pushed.

"Uh . . ." he gritted his teeth. "Push . . . it . . . farther. SLOW. STOP."

She held the wire steady, sure that it had bumped against a solid object. Something moved the end of the instrument, like a fish tugging. What was this thing that could curse a djinni? In her mind she tried to envision the inside of his body: imagined the bullet pulsing in time with his heart, alive within his muscle and sinew. Saw it contorting into an ellipse as if trying to flee.

She startled as she felt something yank on the wire.

"It attached." Yasir's voice strained. "NOW. Remove it." He squeezed his eyes tight. His complexion tinged gray. "HURRY."

Trying to keep her hand from wobbling, Lavinia pulled the instrument out. The ball surfaced through the bullet hole with a vile sucking noise that turned her stomach. She held the wire up, the shiny bullet stuck in the loop, dripping blood. She swallowed hard, keeping down the nausea. This had hurt him. She had hurt him. If only . . .

Yasir paled.

His body thinned as though it were a cloud. Solid, then translucent. Through his chest she could see the patterns on the carpet, dulled by his dusky flesh, more vivid near the wound. Lavinia clutched the wire, fighting the limpness of her grip, the dizziness that swirled through her head. *Lord in heaven,* had she killed him by her own hand?

"Yasir! No, no. Come back." She lay her hand on his arm, careful to keep her touch light. His skin warmed as he grew opaque, solid under her palm. Then he faded, his body almost transparent, like ancient, wavy window glass distorting what lay beyond.

"Yasir? Yasir, stay with me." She put her face next to his, the wire and lead shot tight in her fist. "What can I do? Just tell me. Please. I can help."

His body solid now, he eyed the bullet with horror. "I fear the bullet . . . is poisoning me." He stifled a moan.

"The bullet from Peter's gun?" She recalled the split-second flash of terror in Yasir's eyes when he couldn't heal himself after Peter had shot him. The image stayed with her: the djinni's pupils growing from tiny vertical slits full of mirth at Peter's insignificant attempt to harm him—then, with Yasir's realization—into huge black pits of horror, eclipsing his bright gold irises, staring that awful dread into her.

"This is no ordinary wound." Yasir's wavering voice sounded almost unrecognizable. "Does your husband have . . . connections with . . . conjurers, sorcerers?"

"Peter? No, nothing remotely magic. He's a model antiquary, facts and evidence." What facts and evidence would he have presented against Yasir, against them both? *Thank the angels in heaven* they were here now. And safe from Peter, no matter his inclination. She pictured him, pistol pointed at Yasir, face contorted with fury. The boom of the gun vibrating through the garden, through her, shattering all their lives.

"The bullet has a strong curse. He must have found out about me. Try to recall."

"A curse? From Peter? Why he . . ." What did Peter know? He had acted suspicious, but Yasir spell-cast him to forget.

Yes, Peter caught her in the garden embracing Yasir, but mistook Yasir for a gypsy. Peter had no idea he was master first, that Yasir had been his djinni. Yasir's spell made Peter give her the urn. She pressed her lips tight. She would never forgive Peter for this. She would never forgive herself.

"But Yasir, the bullet can't affect you now. It came out clean." She had kept her voice steady, hadn't she?

His eyes changed, pupils huge and dark with a fear so potent she turned away, her chin trembling. If such a powerful creature were afraid, what in the name of all saints could she do to help him?

"I am trapped. I have not the power to leave this body . . . to assume another form. I do not know this . . . mortality." His breath came in great gasps.

She tried to keep her voice soft and confident. "You will recover. The bullet is out. See." She held it up. Her hand shook. She hoped he didn't notice. "A small piece of metal. Harmless now."

"This weakness. I never . . . Through the centuries, I have seen humans die, secure in the knowing it could not happen to me. Where do they go? To hell and damnation that some prattle about? Is it true? They burn for eternity?" He clutched her hand.

"Yasir." She stroked his forehead. His flesh burned with fever. "They go to a heaven more beautiful than the Sultan's garden. But you will stay here with me. We will make a life. I can see you are better already." That look he gave her. Unfocused. Indulgent.

He didn't believe her.

"T-take the bullet away." For a split second, Yasir's face contorted into a horrid grimace, then his body faded, becoming a swath of mist on the carpet. "I feel it still. The curse is in the bullet. I worsen as long as it is near. *By the Djinn,* take it away."

Lavinia tore a wide strip from Yasir's discarded kurta and wrapped the silk tightly about the instrument and ball, tucking the ends into a secure bundle a little wider than her clenched fist. She pushed herself to her feet, the room spinning about her. Staggering, she grasped the back of a nearby chair. She let go, made sure she stood steady on her feet, and stepped farther away from Yasir. The smudges under his eyes vanished. She had moved the bullet only a short distance from him and already he was improving.

Clutching the bundle, Lavinia rushed to the door, glimpsing to her side a tall chest shining with inlays of ebony, mother-of-pearl and gold. A jeweled coffer glittered on its polished surface. As if her glance animated it, the box opened, spilling richly garbed miniature figures of ivory and silver. They called in piping voices, "Laa-vi-nia, Laa-vi-nia," and raised their tiny arms, reaching for her when she passed by as if they wanted to stop her from saving Yasir.

She swerved from them, almost colliding with a huge shape. As she backed away, her eyes traveled up the golden coils of an enormous oil lamp in the shape of a cobra, its hood expanded into a cape of winking gems high above her.

Feeling she had run a gauntlet, she paused at the threshold, the furthest she could flee, yet still be able to see and hear Yasir.

He fixed his eyes on her, blank, as though he wasn't sure who she was or why she was standing in his chamber. "Thalia, *min ra terk nema kened,* do not leave me." He spoke low and soft, each word a weight to be borne. She imagined him embracing her.

Lavinia curled her fingers around the bundle. Her heart sank. *By heaven,* had he become delirious in such a short time? He had called her Thalia once in a moment of passion. He claimed *she* was Thalia, his first and only love, reincarnated from centuries ago. Thalia, whose father, Rakhshan, cursed Yasir to the urn in a fit of rage and jealousy, attempting to separate them forever. At first, Lavinia refused to believe the djinni when he revealed she had been reborn as this woman. But he had shown her. The visions. The memories. The feelings. She was Thalia. Here, for him, at last.

"I can't, Yasir. I can't stay."

*No matter how much she wanted to, how much she loved him.*

"I have to take the bullet away. Then I'll come back."

*She had to save him. She would save him. God help her, she would save him.* She meant it to be a strong thought, but it came out a prayer.

Yasir's eyes cleared and he seemed to recognize her. Did he know they were in this time, this place?

"Go to . . . the great room, after the hall splits . . ." He rose up on his elbow. The muscles in his arm trembled, but she stopped herself from rushing to help him. If she were nearer, the bullet would surely make him worse, and she was afraid to let go of the accursed thing, afraid to set it down in his room for fear it might further harm him.

"On the marble table, a jade vessel. Place the bullet inside. Close the lid. Tight." He waved her away. "Make haste."

She turned from the door. How could she leave him there suffering so? What if he—

"Wait!" Yasir sat up, swaying, his eyes bright.

"Beware . . . the Guardian." He thrust his arm in her direction and looked deep into her eyes, struggling to form the next word. "You . . . must say it. *Anetshar shashh.* Say it when—"

The whites of his eyes turned to gold, glittering like a doubloon. He dropped to the carpet.

"Yasir!" Lavinia stepped into the room, reaching for him, but with the bloodstained bundle in her hand she couldn't go to him. She stood for a moment, staring. He lay so still, the carpet's colors swirling about him like ants disturbed from their nest. Then a small rise and fall of his chest, then another. He breathed.

She sagged against the threshold, suppressing the urge to run to his side, to cradle his head in her lap.

"*Anetshar shashh,*" she spoke the phrase aloud, trying for the exact slur of the "r", the long drawn-out "sh", trying to fix it in her memory.

Say it . . . But say it when?

*The next day, Bramley House, Peter's study*

Lord Peter Bramley poised his quill over the two sentences he had written on the thick cream-colored foolscap. The precise script, each letter perpendicular as if lined up by a ruler, read like a confession: *I took the Scottish Dress Pistol from my Desk. Suddenly I was in the Garden.*

Peter stared glumly at the words. A drop of ink fell from the nib and bled into the paper fibers, a dark stain fanning out like some virulent pox. He set his quill in the gold palm tree penholder and closed the top of the pyramid inkwell. Why the deuce couldn't he remember?

He read the words again: *I took the Scottish Dress Pistol from my Desk. Suddenly I was in the Garden.* Then what? What on earth did he do before the servants found him? He rubbed his fist on his forehead, but the dull ache starting at his temples remained the same.

Dobson, his butler, and Stevens, his valet, had each gone over the scene with him several times. Their patience had to be admired. They heard a gunshot, a woman's scream. They ran into the garden calling his name, his wife's name, but no one answered. Fearing the worst, they summoned more of the staff and combed the paths and greenery until Lavinia's maid found him. "God help us. The master's dead," she screeched, and fell into hysterics.

The servants had surrounded him as he lay unconscious on the gravel path by the Lady Banks rose. The tiny white flower petals settled on his body like a dusting of snow. He had no wounds. His pistol had been fired and lay several feet away. Five paces towards the lilac bushes, rose petals of an impossibly rich crimson were arranged on the ground in what looked like the outline of a body. None of the gardeners could identify the rose.

He put his hand to his temple and flinched at the ache pulsing with the beat of his heart. The pain increasing as he thought of Lavinia, pale as a corpse. *Dear Lord please . . . Bring her back to me.*

# 2

*H*er legs as unsteady as her thoughts, Lavinia drifted to the side of the urn's never-ending long hall and leaned against the wall, the lead bullet hard against her fingers through the bundle. She had kept a fast pace and put some distance between the vile object and Yasir, surely far enough for him to be free of its curse. But with all that had happened since this morning— She closed her eyes, her body still, her mind quiet for a moment.

She had left her home, her husband, everything she knew, to be here with Yasir. How was it possible for Yasir to be cursed, still suffering from that dreadful wound? She stifled a sob and raised her head. The high ceilings of the hall dwarfed her, the tall sweep of space terrifying. At every doorway, every direction she dared turn, shadows flickered and darkened as if someone lurked just out of sight. Her insides churned in panic.

The hard marble wall seeped cold through her gown. Her hand curled like a claw around the silk enfolding the instrument and bloody bullet. She was inside the urn. Inside a djinni's urn.

What had Yasir told her? *Best not to think overmuch on it. I have seen madness take some.* At this very moment in her room at Bramley House, the urn sat on her dressing table amongst her bottles of perfumes, her jars of cream and powder.

She had held it in her hands.

Now she was *inside* it. When she attempted to assimilate the two images, she felt her brain might burst. She squeezed her eyes shut, unable to put together a coherent picture. One more moment to gather strength, then she would hurry.

The rigid stone lost its chill. In a heartbeat, it grew soft as a sponge and rippled ever so slightly as though it were breathing. She jerked away and stared at the shimmering surface, yellow blending into the gold of apricots, thousands of speckles reflecting the light like an amorphous sea creature. That feeling of eyes upon her. Someone, or something—she squinted at the wall—was watching her.

Was the urn a sentient being? She tottered, then steadied herself and tried not to think about the breathing wall, about Yasir's bleeding wound, about the cursed bullet in her hand.

"I am here with my beloved Yasir. I am his master. I must save him." She stated the words aloud in case the urn could understand, her voice thin and reedy, but even so, it brought her back. Her chest rose and fell with her even breath, the surface of the floor firm beneath her feet, as though she had plunged back into her body after a bout of delirium. Grasping the bundle in her fist, she hastened to the great room to find the jade vessel and secure the bullet inside. Then Yasir would be well.

Passageways opened off the hall, dim and eerie. Between them, evenly spaced arched entranceways held forbidding doors, ornate with gilded carvings and inlaid with sparkling gems. Sensing movement behind her, she stopped. She held her breath and turned. An overriding silence. The only motion a flickering light from the open door opposite. Something near. Low.

She looked down and groped for a handhold as the colors of the floor tiles surged and rearranged under her feet. Before her eyes, countless multi-colored squares formed a mosaic of a fierce dragon breathing scarlet flames into a blue sky. She peered down the hall. The scarlet tiles extended into the shadows. No one was stalking her. But someone, or something, was trying to communicate.

She had no time for these puzzles—she had to go on. With trepidation, she followed the mosaic of the dragon's back, then the long stream of fire from its mouth into the cobalt sky. Depictions of stars winked from the glossy bright porcelain squares, disorienting her with the eerie feeling of walking upside down in the darkness of the heavens.

After some distance, she paused where the dragon's flames receded into the deep blue of the floor. The hall branched into two passageways, dim and cavernous like giant open mouths. Yasir had said the great room was after the hall split. But which way?

Anxious for a clue, she looked down. The blue of the tiles lightened as a wave of color rolled over the surface and a path of bright orange lit the floor of the hallway to her right. This direction? But what if the other way— She caught a flicker of red from the corner of her eye. Fire? She whipped her head in that direction. She would have to return, tell Yasir . . . The passageway glowed as if lit by flames. She moved closer. It grew warmer. No smoke or flames, just a sinister radiance. She stepped back, her breath shallow, and turned away.

The orange light in the other passageway shone brighter on the tile closest, then dimmed. The next tile lit up, dimmed. And the next, on down the hall, as if a figure walked the floor, its footsteps marking the way.

She looked behind her and squeezed her eyes shut at the heightened red glare. Closing her fist tight around the bundle, she followed the orange trail down a wide hall until it ended at a silver archway inset with glowing jewels.

Before the threshold, she stood staring at the impossibly high ceiling, a glittering white marble sky over a room as expansive as a sweeping meadow.

She stepped inside, glad to leave the eerie hall behind. Craning her neck, she took in the vast heights. Foliated onyx columns, their capitals formed of fanciful creatures, soared like tallest trees. The ceiling ascended above the columns, reaching into the very heavens. At the far end, a rainbow shimmered into view, the lucent pastels arching over statues of gold and jewels that dwarfed the crowded furnishings.

The room, so huge, so cluttered.

Which direction?

Overwhelmed, she collapsed into an ivory chair, nestling the bundle in her lap and stretching her arms above her head with a little moan. Soft daylight permeated the great room, light that in any other chamber would filter through windows. But there were no windows here. Would the floor show her the way again? She eyed the tiles of porphyry, mother of pearl and wondrous gems glittering and inert in the odd light.

How could a simple jade canister stand out in this opulent disorder? She would find it. She had to. She must not fail Yasir, yet she had never felt so alone, so abandoned. Feeling sorry for herself didn't help. She would take this cursed bullet to the jar and go back to a healthy Yasir. Lavinia reached for the bundle. Scrabbled in the folds of her skirt. It wasn't in her lap.

*Angels in heaven!* The bundle.

She searched the floor around her. Next to her chair sat a tourmaline coffer overflowing with luminous pearl necklaces. A clasped silver orb near her foot wobbled desperately as if something inside were trying to escape. The orb's crystal stand lay beside it in shatters, sharp fragments glinting. Where in heaven's name was the bundle? She dropped to her hands and knees and looked under her chair. Something dark and lacy skittered into the shadows. She recoiled, stumbling as she rose.

How could she lose the bundle? How? She hadn't moved, only stretched. She hugged her arms across her chest, her insides hollow, as a thought seized her: could the bullet somehow return to further harm Yasir? Was the curse that powerful?

From the corner of her eye, she caught a flash of white slipping around a bulky silver chest. She sprang after it. The narrow turn between a pair of painted screens led to a long, golden half-wall shimmering with reflections. A blurry smear of white rippled in the bright surface at the far end. She picked up her skirts and raced forward.

As if it had seen her, the bundle soared into the air and fled over a silk rug, disappearing into an immense wooden couch, the sloping canopy carved into vines and trees lurking with exotic jungle creatures.

Eyes and teeth and tongues painted lifelike. A twisted vine swung as if rocked by a breeze.

Lavinia crept closer. Dark green leaves rustled, moving aside to reveal a glimpse of orange and black. A soft growl vibrated the wood.

She backed away. Yasir had warned her: *Beware of the Guardian.* At first she thought he referred to something about the bullet. She never dreamed it could flee from her. Or perhaps he meant that an entity inside the great room might cause her harm. And the phrase, she repeated the words aloud, *"Anetshar shashh."* Could the words cast a spell? If she pronounced them wrong would she cause some unintended consequence, some ill to Yasir?

Nothing stirred in the canopy. Did the words have an effect? She might have imagined the wood moving, the sounds. She searched for a glimpse of white. The bullet could be anywhere in that wooden jungle. Or it might have slipped out the back, escaped from the side. "If I have to return and tell him I lost the bullet ..." She closed her empty fist. "I will not be the death of him."

As she walked to the back of the huge couch, a flutter of white caught her eye. There it was, sitting pretty-as-you-please on a bright green banana leaf. Of all the nerve. She edged nearer, her hand poised to snatch the bundle, but it vaulted into the carved foliage.

She squinted into the deep wooden jungle. At a movement in the shadows, she jumped. A tiny pink face with glistening bug eyes peeped from the stiff leaves.

With a piercing screech the creature leapt at her. Lavinia shrieked, flinging her arms to protect her face, but the furry beast clamped onto her forearm with its bulbous fingers. She tried to shake it loose. The creature dug in, hanging on, the bundle clamped in its pointed yellow teeth. She lowered her arms. Why, the animal resembled a baby monkey, orange and pink, as small as a doll.

Lavinia seized the cloth in its mouth and pulled, enduring the monkey's ineffectual slaps. The creature's hind feet, rubbery and hard, dug into her chest as it pushed off in a flying leap and landed on a life-sized bronze statue of a harem dancer. Hopping from foot to foot on the dancer's outstretched arm, it took the cloth from its mouth and spat a stream of yellow-green saliva. She looked at her dress, a putrid green streak over Yasir's dried blood.

"Why you little imp!" Lavinia kept her eyes on the monkey and picked up a sandalwood cane resting against the couch.

The creature swung by its striped tail from the dancer's arm and squealed, jagged teeth in a fierce grimace as it shook the bundle in its wrinkled orange fingers. She brought the cane up slowly behind her, dodged another streak of foul-smelling saliva, and aimed for the cloth. The cane thumped on the monkey's tail and bounced off the dancer's arm with a startling clang.

Howling, the beast fell to the floor, the bundle landing at Lavinia's feet. She scooped it up, dropped the cane and dashed away.

Behind a thick sandstone column, she stopped to catch her breath and pressed the bundle into her skirts. Skirts dark and stiff with dried blood. Yasir's blood. It seemed years ago, when it was only— yesterday? No, at best, an hour ago that Peter shot him. Why did she have to carry this ghastly reminder? If only the blood could be gone and Yasir's horrible wound healed. She craned her head around the column, searching the cluttered area.

The monkey was nowhere in sight, but she could hear squeals and squeaks of its angry chattering in the distance. She fumbled with her skirt and looked down in surprise at the soft billowy folds. The stiff dried blood and sticky saliva had vanished into pristine blue and white stripes, the fabric as fresh and clean as when she first donned the dress this morning to impress Rose, Peter's sister. Yasir's doing? Or the urn's? Did this mean Yasir was healing? She must hurry and finish her task.

From inside the bundle, she felt a flutter, like limbs stretching. Stifling the impulse to scream and fling it aside, she kept a tight grip and whispered, "These are objects of metal. Not living things." And for good measure she said, *"Anetshar shashh."*

She pictured what the jade vessel might look like as she walked by another column. If she kept the image in her mind, something might lead her to it and then she could leave this disturbing room. She followed a path between stacks of rugs and came upon a sitting area with couches and tall-backed chairs. Which way? She sniffed the smoky atmosphere. The soft musky scent of sandalwood. Ahead, rows and rows of curvy brass vases bristled with sticks of incense. Smoke curled into the air.

When she waved her hand, the smoke cleared for a moment, and she startled at the huge elephant head on the golden statue looming above her. Four human arms arced in a frozen dance from its portly human body. Its human legs were draped in folds of cloth, left foot firm on the jeweled dais. At the front of the dais, a plaque of lapis lazuli displayed an inlay of mother-of-pearl calligraphy, the strokes like tracks of an exotic bird. The writing reshuffled into familiar letters. She made out the word *Ganesha*. Eyeing the elephant head, its giant trunk curled close to its face, she walked under Ganesha. The statue's long blue shadow fell on the billowing clouds of smoke.

Had the arms moved? Her shoulders stiffened.

*Her imagination had become overwrought.* Just the effect of the odd light, or the smoke floating upwards, wreathing around the statue's huge head.

Clutching the bundle, she kept her eyes on the mosaic floor. She wouldn't look at Ganesha. Looking made things come alive, made them pursue her. But why? This was Yasir's urn and she was doing his bidding. She stopped. Was the monkey trying to help her? The bullet skittering away to show her the right path? She pressed her lips tight. She couldn't accept it.

The pad of her thumb flicked against the back of her ring, and she looked down—her wedding band, not the ruby ring from Yasir on her right hand. Was that somehow significant, or was she desperately putting meaning to these random happenstances? She focused on the floor and put one foot in front of the other until the scent of sandal-wood faded.

What if she had passed the jade vessel? She raised her head slowly. She wouldn't *dwell* on things, just glance.

Before her, smiling as if they dared her to try their acrobatic positions, life-sized figures tangled in the nude, their shapely legs and muscular arms in impossible configurations. What were they doing? She moved closer. Carved in high relief on the edifice wall, the women, ample breasts draped sensuously in jewelry, hips accentuated with thin golden girdles, were enjoying their revelry as much as the men. Scandalous.

Studying a curious grouping, Lavinia inhaled sharply. The tangle of legs and arms and plump, high breasts were actually three women and a man. Why they were each— Lavinia could feel her cheeks burning. She reached out to touch the life-like figures, their flesh painted dusky amber, their jewels gilded. With full lips tinted red, kohl-lined eyes heavy-lidded with desire, they looked as if they would come alive and rebuke her for watching. Lavinia backed away, breathing hard.

A tap on her arm. She let out a cry. With a shudder, she slunk from the stout golden fingers groping for her. Holding the bundle close, she ran between the fluted columns of what looked to be a temple and hurried through a darkened doorway. Inside, her back to a chill stone wall, she mouthed the word Ganesha. When she had passed under the statue, the arms *had* moved. It wasn't her imagination. Now they were seeking her.

Keeping to the dark shadows, she stole a look from inside the thick sandstone portal. Long golden arms slithered around the weathered surface of the temple like a huge serpent. She squeezed her eyes tight at the scrape of the gold on the stone blocks of the building.

What did Ganesha want? She had walked underneath him, but hadn't touched anything, merely stopped to read the writing on the pedestal. And the script had shown itself in English. She peeked outside again. The wall opposite held the lascivious carvings, a hand grasping a voluptuous breast, thigh touching thigh—

A blur of motion. Lavinia pulled back inside the doorway, trying to shake the image of one of the figures detaching from the stone panel, its rough arms around her, pulling off her clothes, forcing her to join them until Ganesha came for her. *Looking made things come alive.* She gulped down her breaths to stay quiet.

At a faint whiff of sandalwood, she stiffened. In the silence, the *skrish skrish* of the statue's arms brushing against the outside wall sounded unnervingly close. She glanced behind her. The temple foyer led into a large passageway. If she went deeper inside she would be harder to find. The bundle firm in her hand, she stole down the shadowy corridor towards a black obelisk lit with muted light from above.

Her footsteps rang on the marble floor in the murky rotunda. Rays of light filtered through the crystal cupola crowning the dome, flickering over the obelisk like ripples in a brook. Did she see eyes, a face, in the dark surface of the stone? The loud echoes of her footsteps, the wavering arcs of light, the dank shadows, like being underwater. She could hear her breath rasping. Keeping the obelisk in sight, she stepped away until her back pressed against the shallow carvings in the wall.

A dull, swarm-of-insects thrum vibrated into her, prickling the back of her neck. Sharp cracks snapped through the clammy air in rhythm with the light undulating on the obelisk. A bright, blinding flash leapt from its surface. At a puff of dust inches from her foot, she jumped aside, dropping the bundle just as a loud boom rent the close air of the chamber.

A second flash. The smell of something burning. "Dear Lord!" She snatched the bundle and banged it against the floor. The tiny flames started up again, bright yellow in the gray smoke. "Stop, stop!" She rolled the cloth through the dust on the floor until the curls of smoke faded.

There. The brightest archway. When she reached the long corridor's end, a kind of grand foyer, she sat stiffly on a stone bench next to the multi-columned entrance, her fist tight around the scorched bundle. With a sharp inhale she straightened. A woman sat opposite her, staring. *Lord in heaven,* who was she, and where had she come from? She studied her.

The woman didn't move. Odd, she had the same dress, the blue stripes on white, her hair, black and—

Wait. Lavinia raised her hand. The woman raised her hand. It was her own reflection, as clear as in any looking glass. Yet the wall had the rough surface of the other stone walls. She craned forward, and clapped her hand to her mouth. This odd mirror also showed the door next to her, revealing the courtyard beyond.

Shimmering in the reflection stood a black marble table. In the middle sat a jade vessel, glowing like a pale green moon.

# 3

*L*avinia brushed her cheek on the pocked sandstone of the doorframe. Grimacing, she put her hand to her face and studied the courtyard. Remarkable, a whole temple complex set inside the great hall. The marble table sat far away on the rough stone pavers, a lustrous black slab with the jade jar a looming presence. Cocking her head, she stood still, listening. Strange how many noises she heard. A series of escalating squeaks, a poor creature caught, then killed? A distant rushing sound like trees in the wind or cascading water or the statue's arms sliding over rough stone.

At her next breath, the noises died as if someone had clamped a bell jar over the temple and its grounds. The air heavy, still. The table and vessel sat waiting for her out in the open courtyard. There was no place to hide. She would have to deposit the bullet in the jar and flee before Ganesha found her. Was the Guardian lurking nearby? Could Ganesha be the Guardian?

She glanced over her shoulder, but the room, the halls extending deep into the interior, stood silent and empty, a place for ghosts.

Lavinia took a deep breath and crept outside. Teetering at the edge of the portico, she peered down the worn stairs—steep and narrow. She hadn't realized she was so far above the courtyard. Her foot rested safe in the middle of the first step, the bundle tight in her fist, the bullet and wire still, thank God. She took the second step and picked her way down, a bit faster as she became used to the narrow width of the tread, the unusual height of the risers. It seemed forever until she was almost to the end. Sighting the jar glowing brighter as if it were expecting her, she placed her foot firmly on the second-to-last step, and missed.

Flailing for a handhold, she grasped at the air. Falling. *Oh Yasir,* she was falling. And nothing to break her fall, save hard stone.

Her hands, fingers splayed on the irregular stone pavers, were empty. She stared at the uneven gray paving. This close, the pocks and nubs were magnified: bits of shining crystal, flecks of deep black, a vein of pink. Her knees throbbed. An increasing ache settled into her hip. She raised her head. Squinched her eyes shut in pain. Her head spun. The courtyard tilted, everything at a blurry angle, then righted, and tilted again. In front of her, the singed cloth of the bundle fluttered, as if the fall had stunned it as well.

*Grab it before it escapes.* Her body stayed leaden and still, even as her mind screamed commands. She set her eyes on the bundle. Gritted her teeth.

Clumsy as an infant, she lurched forward on hands and knees, scraping her palms and fingers on the scarred stone pavings. She reached out, her arm wavering with the beat of her heart. The cloth vibrated as if it might take flight. She closed her hand around it.

Hands and knees aching, she staggered to her feet and focused on the table looming yards and yards away. She stumbled ahead. Clutched the silk cloth to her chest. Swung her arm out to hurry, and almost toppled to the pavement. One step. Another. She hobbled to the vessel, praying to herself, to Yasir, to the good Lord.

The table came to her chest, the top a thick octagon, its dark surface reflecting like a mirror. She moved now with a sureness of purpose, her limbs warm, the pain a distant ache like a bad experience suppressed. On tiptoes, she stretched her arms over the cold surface, wiggling her fingers towards the vessel as her double did the same upside down.

The bullet pulsed in her hand, faint, a foreign heartbeat.

"You're almost home. Be still," she whispered. The glowing green jade felt warm to her touch, like the urn. She pulled the vessel to her. Her fingers tingled: from excitement? Fear? The vessel's magic? At last, she held the jade jar in front of her.

Feeling lighter somehow, she exhaled as she removed the lid. The wide mouth opened into a deep dark interior. She held the bundle closer. Did she see something move inside? She wrinkled her nose at the faint stench of an unemptied chamber pot, replaced so quickly by the cloying fragrance of gardenia that she must have imagined the fetid odor.

She lined up the bundle with the jar's opening, almost dropping it as a long, slow hiss filled the air, reverberating in the jar's insides. She jerked her head around. Nothing was in the stone courtyard. She squeezed the cloth. The bullet and wire stayed motionless. The bullet had always been silent, but perhaps at this last minute it had protested.

She loosened her hold and dropped the bundle into the jar. With a thrusting twist, the cloth glanced off her hand and lurched from the table. Lavinia grabbed for it, but the bundle slipped through her fingers. She whirled around. Glimpsed a blur of white. A muted thud. The scrape of something scuttling behind her.

Not now. Not when she was so close. She spun sideways to follow, overbalanced and staggered into the table, tipping it backwards. The vessel tilted. Lunging forward, still gripping the lid, Lavinia caught the vessel just as the table leveled itself. She set the vessel down, replaced the lid and brushed at something on her arm.

Like a deep sigh, a slow "sss" emerged from her thoughts, swelling into consciousness until she knew it existed outside of her, knew she had heard it from the very beginning. Her scalp tingled as the sound vibrated like the naja snake's rumbling growl. Out of nowhere, a searing pain radiated up her arm and ripped through her. Gasping at the intensity, she stared, disbelieving, at the segmented monstrosity, all sticky legs and pincers, creeping up her arm, hissing.

With a scream she thrashed, swatting madly at the creature. She knocked the vessel sideways. The jar appeared to float in the air for a moment, the jade glowing in calm serenity. The vessel rose, wobbling. Then, as if an invisible hand thrust it downward, the jar crashed into the paving stones, shattering into jagged shards.

"No!" Lavinia stared at the pieces. Front pincers opening and closing, the ghastly creature stood erect in front of the ruins of the vessel. As she backed away it hissed, and Yasir's warning played in her head: *Beware, the Guardian.*

What was the phrase? A— *shash.* No. *"Anet shash."* No. *"Aents—"*

The creature jumped straight at her. She stumbled backwards. It waved its pincers and ran up the surface of her skirts towards her chest.

*"Anetshar shashh. Anetshar shashh. Anetshar shashh."* She shrilled the phrase. Brushing at her clothes, she shook her skirts and flailed at her back. Was the monstrosity on her still? Her arm throbbed. She could barely lift it. She stepped backwards, holding her skirts away from the ground, and turned, searching for the creature. She stamped her foot. She would stomp it to death, she would . . . She glanced at the broken vessel and drew in her breath, elbows pressed into her sides, her arm weak, pulsating in pain.

*"Anetshar shashh."* The words came out almost silent on her breath. The phrase had taken effect. The creature splayed itself over the jar's remains, pinchers closed, the jade paling against the glossy black of its spiked exoskeleton. Its tail unfurled. The barbed stinger on the end curled down, bunching the jar's fragments close. The creature extended its thousands of bristly legs over the shards as if it could pull them together again. Its beady eyes glittered at her, antennae twitching, head turning side to side.

She let out her breath. Of course, the Guardian. Yasir had tried to tell her, but had lost consciousness before making it clear. If she'd only thought to say the phrase when she opened the lid, perhaps the creature would have taken the bullet into its lair and all would be—

She whipped her head around. "The bullet!" Only a few minutes had gone by since she last saw the bundle skittering away over the short pillars separating the temple from the enormous room. Even with her arm throbbing and hanging limp by her side she would have to manage—

With a cry, she fell forward, gasping at a blow to her back. Something latched onto her waist and lifted her into the air. She struggled as she was propelled away, the menacing Guardian on the glowing jade shards blurring into oblivion.

Before she could make sense of it, she was level with the gigantic elephant head, staring into its unfathomable diamond eyes. She had never seen diamonds that large. They shone like the noonday sun on rippling water, hiding what was beneath. As she looked, a kind of glimmer passed over them, as subtle as the shadow of a cloud, and they stared into her and through her, more alive than her own eyes seen in a mirror.

She shrank at the flaring light. Before her, in a glowing nimbus stood Yasir, magnificent in a cloth-of-gold kurta, his headband glittering with diamonds and rubies, his golden eyes shining with schemes. Yasir, healed!

The image faded. So this was how Ganesha communicated. "Put me down. If he's healed, I have no need to be here." Pushing on the statue's golden hands at her waist, she glared at the other two hovering above her. She swallowed hard, her limbs weakening as the courage drained from her body. Those enormous hands could crush her and no one would know what happened. Not even Yasir.

The statue glowered at her, the creases in his face shining with precious jewels. Spirals of fragrant smoke curled around him. Incense offerings. A pagan idol? What would he gain by crushing her out of existence? She gripped at his hands as they moved her through the air. Would he drop her? She looked down. The floor came closer. She closed her eyes.

Ganesha set her gently on the floor and released her. She swayed, but managed to stay upright as she watched his giant trunk draw up to his face, the smoke swirling around her.

*Run!* Her whole being screeched, *Run!*

She set her feet to take off, but the smoke thickened, closing in. Again the image of Yasir appeared. She stared, confused. He was in bed, eyes weak, reaching out to someone, arms trembling. She craned her head and looked far above, trying to see the statue's expression, but his trunk curled stiffly in front of his face. What was Ganesha trying to tell her? Yasir healthy, then ill. She knew that. This was useless. She had to find the bullet or Yasir would get worse and—

Mouth open in a howl, the monkey came at her, tiny pointed teeth gleaming. Lavinia recoiled as it jumped over her shoulder. She looked down only to face the hissing Guardian, its legs working in unison as it skittered straight for her, disappearing before it scrambled onto her skirts. She peered through the smoke, seeing nothing but billowing white smoothing into a silken texture. The bullet burst through and fell to the ground with a thud. On her hands and knees, she clutched the bullet in her hand, its weight hard on her palm. Yes! She finally had it. Gloating, she opened her fist to a ball of black smoke.

Phantoms.

Not counting the bullet, they were the creatures that had threatened her. So they were all acting to help the bullet, acting against Yasir. Was Ganesha the mastermind? If so, why did he want Yasir dead? She looked up at the statue, his jewels glittering through the incense smoke. Did he want to rule the urn?

The rigid gold of Ganesha's trunk softened and unfurled. She felt firm hands grip her waist again. She stayed still, holding her breath. His trunk came closer and closer until the two protuberances at the end trailed along her injured arm. The pain. Tears rolled down her face. If she moved, said anything . . . The trunk ran up her flesh to the blackened welt from the Guardian's poison. She shrieked in agony as sharp stings pierced her skin, worse than when the repulsive insect pricked her.

"Stop. Please," she begged.

Curling like a caterpillar, Ganesha's trunk rose above her. With her good arm, she pounded one of Ganesha's hands. He let go of her waist. His other hand dropped away, hovering next to her. If she moved he could seize her, crush her with a clumsy grasp.

The bullet. Had it scurried back to Yasir? Was it working its curse on him now? Ganesha bent his great elephant head. Pieces of her jagged reflection looked back at her from the hundreds of facets in his gleaming eyes. What was he going to do to her? She should run, get away, but she stood trembling, tears brimming.

Ganesha's golden eyelids closed in a slow blink as he opened his fist, revealing a small box of red-fading-into-green jade in the middle of his lined palms. An impossibly long lifeline was etched into the gold of his hand. He unlatched the ebony clasp and lifted the lid.

Her lips parting in astonishment, Lavinia looked up at him. "It's not possible." Her voice cracked. Perhaps this odd creature truly was a god. Inside the jade coffer, in a depression just its size, lay the bloodied bullet.

Squinting, she bent towards it.

The bullet jumped at her.

"No!" She leapt backwards and turned to run, but two of Ganesha's four hands fastened upon her arms, pulling her towards him. Lavinia writhed in his grip. One of his hands closed tighter on her wound and she shrieked from the sharp burning pain.

"Yasir! Yasir! Help!" She tried to slip from Ganesha's hold and he swung her around to face him. "Let me go. The bullet. The bullet!" She struggled, her eyes on the bullet now sitting still in the box. Inanimate. A shimmer. Just the light? A wobble. The bullet leapt from the box again, straight at her. She jerked to the right, but Ganesha held her fast. Her muscles tightened. She curled into the statue's hard hands. Squeezed her eyes shut. Would the bullet poison her like it did Yasir, or just kill her outright? *Lord in heaven, please don't make it hurt like the Guardian's sting.*

The chill from Ganesha's hands made her shake. It would all end here in the urn.

She wrinkled her brow. No horrific pain had slammed into her. All was silent. The fragrance of sandalwood strong. She opened one eye. The bullet hung in the air an arm's length away, straining in her direction as if against an invisible wall.

"Put it in the box." She twisted against Ganesha's firm grip. He rapped her on the head with his trunk. "That *hurt.*" She eyed him with a nasty glare. Did a smile flicker on those fixed golden lips? He waved his trunk over the quivering bullet. In a slow, wavering trajectory, the lead shot wobbled back to the box and settled into the depression in the jade. She scowled, waiting for it to spring at her again, but the bullet stayed still.

"Shut the box," she said. She glanced up. Ganesha's trunk came towards her again.

"Don't touch me. Shut the box," she said in as fierce a voice as she could muster, the pain in her arm making her voice weak. Would Ganesha let the bullet hurt her?

"Why are you working against Yasir?" Her voice gained a bit of strength as she spoke to the statue. She wouldn't be afraid of this gold abomination anymore.

The end of his trunk hovered over the bullet.

"You don't understand. Yasir is good. He is master here. No, I am master here," she said. "I order you to—"

Ganesha brought his hand in front of her, the box nestled in his golden palm, the bullet quivering.

"Please. The bullet has done enough harm." Could she move fast enough to shut the lid before the bullet could react? If it reached Yasir, that would be the end of him. She reached out. Sprang her hand at the box. Her fingers slapped the lid, but it stayed open.

As if shot from a pistol the bullet leaped at her. She was too close. A fire roared through her hand. Slid up her forearm. A sharp sound trilled in her head . . . was she screaming? She felt her bone shatter. Burning agony mixed with her screams. *My God!* Her good arm, her good arm! How could she help Yasir now?

She sank, limp, but Ganesha held her upright. Her arms: one blackened and swelling, the other shattered and bleeding. The Guardian's sting. The bullet's curse. How long did she have? She couldn't tell Yasir goodbye. She couldn't go near him.

Ganesha settled her gently on the floor. She moaned. "You must let Yasir know I didn't fail him. That I tried. I tried . . . "

Ganesha shook his huge elephant head. His hands curved around her, two on either side. The misty smoke, the glittering gold, the thousands of her reflections in Ganesha's diamond eyes staring back at her—stretched thin, squashed fat, or in pieces—fitting together every which way as if she were inside a kaleidoscope. She envisioned Yasir waiting, watching the door to his room. Happy to see it open just a crack. The bullet flying inside, piercing his body, all because of her failure.

The great room grew dimmer. Clouds of incense smoke gathered around her, mounding thicker and thicker, blocking the light. Ganesha's trunk trailed along her bleeding arm, then slid up her other one. She flinched, expecting pain, but only felt a light tickle. She forced herself to look and gaped in surprise. No bullet wound. No blackened, swelling skin.

The smoke thinned. Ganesha set the box in front of her, the lid closed tight. Again, his stubby fingers flicked the latch open. She sat up, hands braced against the floor. What horrid thing did he have in store for her? Ganesha opened the lid. The bullet sat in the same depression, now surrounded by a golden cage, the wires embedded in the jade.

"So you *are* with Yasir." Lavinia rubbed her arm where the bullet had entered. It felt normal, smooth and soft, unscarred. "And now you know that I am also."

Ganesha's great head gave a ponderous nod.

*Finally, some acknowledgement.* "Yasir is safe. I must get back to him." She rose, quivering, but buoyed by a joyous energy. Ganesha's eyes clouded, and she could see only gray in the hundreds of facets. Wispy smoke twined thicker around him, dulling the glow of his gold. She couldn't explain how, but she knew he was sad.

"Yasir. He will be well? Since the bullet is now contained. He—"

The statue raised all four hands, palms up. His trunk spiraled down, dispirited like his eyes.

"What then? What?" Her voice ended in a piercing timbre and she stared at Ganesha, her body taut. The bullet was locked in the box. The *jade box*. Yasir would be restored to health.

The two soft fingers of Ganesha's trunk touched her forehead. Inside her mind a deep placid voice spoke: *He is suffering. Is there no help for him?*

Lavinia felt her body droop. She was weary. Weary. One of Ganesha's hands gripped her waist. In her mind she answered silently. *You* are asking *me?*

# 4

*G*anesha's long magical arms wound through the djinni's urn, his huge hands overlapping the span of Lavinia's waist, transporting her back to Yasir. What would have been an ordeal became a thrilling journey.

As they left the great room she saw nothing familiar. Passing by a wall of hammered gold hung with terrifying masks, she shrank into the elephant god's sturdy fingers and tried not to look at the mouths open in screams, the serrated teeth bloodying protruding tongues. Dark pupils of silent glistening eyes, open wide in pain and horror, tracked their progress.

Ganesha slowed his pace in a library of books bound in gem-encrusted onyx, populated by a grove of straight, thin-trunked trees. Their mother-of-pearl leaves reflected in a still pond of what she suspected was solid crystal, until a silvery fish flopped out, splashing a rainbow of diamonds into the depths. From the corner of her eye she glimpsed shadowy figures closing in.

"Hurry." She grasped the elephant god's fingers, fearing the figures might somehow waylay them. At last they passed the threshold out of the great room and wound through the long hall. The statue's hands gently nudged her past the gilded doors into Yasir's room. She had envisioned Yasir waiting at the threshold, sweeping her into his arms, enveloping her with his amazing magic. Her stomach suddenly cold and heavy, she steeled herself for what she might find. "Please help him. Help him to be well," she whispered to Ganesha who carried her farther into the room.

Yasir lay in bed, propped in a reclining position on fat pillows. He looked up, his eyes so golden, so weak. He reached for her, the jeweled rings dull on his fingers when they used to sparkle as if lit within.

"Lavinia."

How good it felt to hear him say her name. She parted her lips, but no words came. She blinked back tears. No blood marred the fresh bandage on his shoulder, yet he wasn't healed. His pale complexion and labored breathing told her that.

If she had shut the bullet inside the jade vessel, Yasir might be whole now, his magic restored. Perhaps she should have brought him a fragment of the jade as a healing talisman, but she would have had to deal with the Guardian. She rubbed her arm and shuddered at the thought of the creature's barbed tail, its agonizing sting.

Yasir's expression brightened. "I see you were rewarded with assistance." Yasir studied the elephant god's hands on her waist, then bowed his head and placed his right hand over his heart. "Sri Sharanam Ganesha, my heartfelt thanks."

Ganesha released her. His hands came together into a prayer, then vanished.

"You . . . you sent help? How?" Lavinia stood over him. This close, she used to hate the way his magic absorbed her, made her do whatever he wanted, kept her from speaking her mind. But now, now she wished it back with all her being.

"When I became conscious, much time had passed. I realized I had not explained fully about the Guardian, but then you had the charm."

Lavinia cocked her head. He hadn't given her a charm.

"The incantation, the phrase I gave you—*Anetshur shushh.*"

"But you didn't tell me when to use it. What it means. I—"

"It means simply, 'release the vessel.' But, of course, it is a charm, so the words carry the weight of magic to which the Guardian responds."

*Lord in heaven,* if only he had been able to tell her. It would have . . . all the hurt . . . the fear. Yasir pulled her to him and she sat beside him on the bed. She felt him flinch from his wound.

"Forgive me. I did not prepare you properly," he murmured into her hair as he caressed her. "I put you in danger."

"I-I was so afraid. So lost. It isn't what I thought, this urn. Your home." She raised her head. "I w-wonder if I even belong here."

His finger trailed warmth as he ran it along her cheek and she blinked at his radiance, dull as it was. "My *delara,* there is no place else you belong. If . . . When I am well, you will see. It *is* everything you thought, and more."

She nodded, words silent inside her. Because of her, he had been shot. Because of her, he was suffering. Yasir watched her for a moment, then said, "I feared for you, Lavinia. The Guardian is serious about his task. There were other forces. I sought Sri Ganesha's protection on your behalf."

"With the bullet farther away, I was much stronger." He held out both hands and looked down at his body, the silk sheets rumpled around his legs.

Lavinia touched his cheek. "You were stronger then, but now?"

He put his hand on hers, pressing her palm onto his skin. His magic flowed into her, then faded like a drop of tincture in water. Weak, so weak. His seeking help for her had reduced him to this. He had contacted the elephant god *before* the jade vessel broke, before Ganesha had put the bullet in the jade box. Yet he hadn't gained any strength. Had all she'd done been for naught?

A slight movement in the tall silk curtains gathered at the side of the bed caught her eye, and she froze at the sight of a figure in the shadows behind the heavy brocade. Lavinia took Yasir's arm and lowered her voice to a soft murmur.

"Yasir. A man." Keeping her eye on the figure, she fumbled her hand along the bedside table, clutched a silver drinking horn and raised it to her shoulder.

Yasir managed a grin. "Lavinia, I have not yet lost all my senses. Let me introduce you to our guest, the physician nah-Quah."

The figure stepped from the shadows: small and wiry, his narrow eyes dark almonds set askew under pale yellow eyebrows. His skin was surely a play of the light, but as he bowed, his complexion remained a dull chartreuse, thankfully less garish than his gaudy lime green headpiece.

To summon this doctor, Yasir had used more of his power. So the jade box *had* worked in containing the bullet's curse. Yet Yasir was now weaker than ever.

"I'm so glad you are here." Lavinia held her skirts and dipped in a shallow curtsey to the doctor who had hurried over to greet her. If he had magic she couldn't feel it. Nah-Quah spoke rapidly in what Lavinia at first thought were indecipherable chirrups like a bird, yet she gradually understood.

"Ah . . . I am honored to be in the presence of the Great Djinni's paramour." He bowed again. Lavinia caught her breath at this indelicacy. She stood with her back to Yasir and couldn't see his reaction. With a polite smile, she brushed a streak of incense ash from her torn skirt, shuddering inside at whether she looked at all presentable after her ordeal in the great room.

Nah-Quah straightened, his eyes round with alarm.

*She couldn't look that bad.* But he stared past her at Yasir, who had struggled to a seated position. Lavinia turned and put her hand to her mouth as his bandage splotched dull red and he slumped. Nah-Quah peeled the linen dressing from the djinni's shoulder. The bullet hole gaped, inflamed, leaking blood and pus. The doctor tossed pillows to the floor and pushed Yasir onto his back, his swift fingers arranging the old bandage like a dam around the wound. In a continuing motion, he unlatched a heavy brocade bag and slid out a compact wooden box of miniature drawers and doors with incised gold hinges and red-fringed pulls.

From inside his high-necked tunic he pulled a silken cord with an elaborate brass key, inserted it into a door at the bottom and lifted out a gilded box with a large opening at the top covered with an ornate screen. He set it by Yasir and swung the tiny door open.

Long spindly legs on segmented bodies tapped out of the box and trailed through the sticky mess on the djinni's shoulder. Lavinia rose partway from her seat, her hand to her mouth. Struggling to keep her composure, she squeezed her hands together and sank back into the chair. All ten of the iridescent insects gathered around the bullet hole, uncurled their orange proboscises and stuck the ends into the wound. The dull sucking sounds grew louder.

She had seen leeches used to bleed those with fevers, and shivered at the thought of the slimy black worms. But leeches were silent. Lavinia's arm started to throb and she looked away for a moment. She'd had enough of insects today, and in a place where she'd never thought to find them.

Spindly fingers splayed on her arm. She jumped. Nah-Quah drew nearer, his round head level with hers, his fingers thrumming on her skin. For Yasir's sake, she was glad she didn't shriek.

"Beneficial. The So-che-chee saliva mitigates impurity and has a curious effect, ah . . . on spells." The physician smacked his lips, sounding eerily like his insects.

"Curious effect?" Lavinia took a deep breath and tried to look polite. Perhaps this doctor worked in a laboratory and saw few patients. A sinking feeling took her at the thought that the insects were merely an experiment. Had Yasir, in his weakness, summoned the wrong doctor?

"Ah . . . the So-che-chee can scare bad magic." Na-Quah put his fingers together and moved them against each other in rhythm with the insect's sucking.

"Just what is needed," she said, hoping to keep the uncertainty from her voice. She wasn't sure about the effect of leeches, and these insects inspired her even less.

Yasir, his eyes dull, stared at the So-che-chee as though this were an everyday occurrence. His pain must have lessened, for he lay stretched out on the bed, more alert, arms relaxed.

Her fingers glanced over his wrist, his pulse running so fast and hard she couldn't detect spaces between beats. When she had first noticed his heartbeat—*the heartbeat of a djinni*—it varied wildly, sometimes so far apart she feared it had stopped, but then the thud would come, weak like an afterthought. Perhaps this was normal, but Lavinia met nah-Quah's eyes and placed the physician's hand in the exact spot on the djinni's wrist.

Nah-Quah repositioned his fingers several times, eyes averted to the ceiling, mouth moving as though he were counting. Or praying.

The physician kept his fingers on Yasir's pulse and pursed his lips. She thought he might whistle, but instead he emitted whirs and clicks that mimicked cicadas. The So-che-chee raised their shiny heads, red eyes directed at nah-Quah as their proboscises curled into hiding. They scampered into their cage, leaving Yasir's shoulder clean, the wound smaller, thank God, but still open.

Nah-Quah put the puss-filled bandage in a waxed cloth sack and handed it to Lavinia. "Please take this into one of the many rooms and place it in anything metal, ah . . . brass, bronze. It is not necessary for the vessel to have a lid."

Not another quest. Refraining from rolling her eyes, she took the sack and opened her mouth to ask a question.

Nah-Quah wiggled his fingers at her. *Six. He had six?*

"Please go now. It is best to keep tainted fluids away from our Great Djinni." He motioned her away as though he were scattering chickens.

Lavinia held the sack in her hand. Something wasn't right. She stared at him and he looked away. This nah-Quah, what was he up to?

She rushed out the door. After all, Yasir had chosen this physician. It only made sense that she follow nah-Quah's instructions. The doctor's statement rang true that proximity to the residue on the bandage could hurt Yasir. And she had seen many metal vessels on her way to the great room when she peeked through the open doors flanking the hall. She would be back in a few minutes; surely they wouldn't do anything foolish before then.

Yasir closed his eyes at the sharp stinging. Nah-Quah unwrapped the next paper packet and sprinkled lavender powder onto his wound. Yasir winced.

"Ah . . . hurts, but not overmuch," Nah-Quah said, unfolding the paper rectangle. He tapped red powder over the bullet hole. The empty papers on the table curled and crackled like twigs in a fire as they grew smaller and smaller, vanishing with the feeble pops of a soap bubble.

"Master Djinni, she is Thalia, is she not?"

Yasir's voice came out a whisper. "Yes." His eyes followed the physician's hands as he sprinkled black powder. The strong smell of anise rose from his wound.

"Master Djinni, ah . . . forgive my impertinence, but she is with child?"

Yasir's voice strengthened. *"My* child." His spirit soared for a brief second.

"Master Djinni, of course." He peered at Yasir. "There is, ah . . . an ancient legend. The child of the Princess Thalia and the Great Djinni will conquer the diabolical magician." He stopped, a knowing look in his eyes.

Yasir raised his hand. "We must not speak his name or talk of the prophecy. Not with this curse on me. Put it from your mind." He poured energy into his answer, his voice deep and strong. This secret must be kept. At last, he had his long lost love, Thalia, come back to him through Lavinia. Now there was the baby. Nah-Quah had seen it. Yasir prayed Rakhshan had not. The magician possessed powers far beyond what a human should.

"If I may speak . . . " The physician blinked as if he could bat away the curse with his thin eyelids. Yasir inclined his head. Steepling his hands, the physician cleared his throat. "The injury carries dangerous magic for one such as Master Djinni, for a being of many, ah . . . spirits. The spell is intricately wrought." He shifted his gaze to the wound, inflamed and bleeding again.

"To save Master Djinni, I must call a magus." Nah-Quah met Yasir's eyes, his domed forehead creased by one irregular furrow in the center. "When the magus travels, all know, even those who could have cast this spell. Alas, there is no other way." His hand hovered over Yasir's shoulder. "We best not tarry."

Yasir clinched his jaw. He had guessed as much. He could feel the curse taking his strength, bit by bit, spoiling his magic like a virulent pestilence.

"Master Djinni, may I ask permission?" Nah-Quah's voice, so gentle before, now had a gruff quality. Sweat beaded his upper lip.

"What choice do I have? Either way I risk death. Or worse." Yasir met the physician's gaze and scowled at the pity in his expression. Nah-Quah knew the magician Rakhshan's reputation. Knew what he had done to Yasir—torturing him, imprisoning him in the urn. No doubt the physician could recall it in detail. His kind had ways to see the past, even if they had not experienced it.

Nah-Quah grimaced, but in the next second hid his expression. Taking that as a sign, Yasir gathered his crippled powers and delved into the physician's mind. Just as he suspected—nah-Quah had found a vision of Yasir being kidnapped by Rakhshan's soldiers. Weakening, Yasir turned away and left the vivid images running through nah-Quah's head. He would not relive it. The torture. The humiliation. Cursed to the urn.

He stared past the physician, seeing into another age, another place where he was once happy. But now he endured a double-curse—the poisoned bullet, as well having to live his life as a slave to whoever opened the urn—just when he and Thalia were together, when she was carrying his child, his hope.

He shut his eyes. The blood pulsed in his brain. In this human form, the poison from the bullet tainted his reasoning, yet he was stuck in this shape, his magic too weak to let him change for a significant amount of time. His head sank further into the pillows, his shallow sigh fading into the silence of the chamber.

Yasir summoned his strength and looked at nah-Quah.

"Proceed. Call the magus."

He would use what magic he could and fight this. He stared at the aquamarine ceiling, the translucent luster of inlaid mother-of-pearl mimicking fluffy clouds. How he wished for the boundless blue sky and ever-changing clouds of Lavinia's world.

He had his Thalia. His son flourished in her womb. The son that would save him. Oh, but he knew of curses—the hourglass sands ever flowing, never depleting—relentless, eternal.

# 5

*T*he gilded door stood ajar, and for the second time that day Lavinia slipped inside Yasir's chamber. She laid her palm on her waist. Only a short time ago Ganesha's strong hands had held her there, and gently nudged her into the room. There had been no sign of the elephant god as she roamed through the hall, searching in the chambers for a metal container.

She pressed against the wall, glad she hadn't burst in announcing that she had rid them of the foul bandage. They were up to something. She could see Yasir, sitting in bed, eyes focused on a pillar of cold blue light streaming from the ceiling, his face rapt in wonder. Shading her eyes with her hand, she squinted. On the other side of the shaft of light, nah-Quah, spectral in the hazy blue glow, tilted his head upwards, arms raised as though he were embracing the eerie light, or perhaps calling it down into the urn.

*Why, the little sneak.* The bandage, the bit about tainted substances— just to get rid of her so he could persuade Yasir to let him do what he wanted. The ultramarine glow lit the furrows of nah-Quah's frown, tinting his yellow-green skin a ghostly aqua.

A tall thin shape wavered inside the light and grew into the semblance of a human figure, the chill blue giving it an appearance of something raised from the dead. A cold draft touched Lavinia even this distance away, and she clasped her arms over her midriff, hugging her elbows as an unpleasant smell enveloped her, musty and decayed like the odor of Peter's shrouded Egyptian mummies.

She should quit this room, this malevolent cold radiance. *But who would protect Yasir then?*

The being inside the column of light arced in Yasir's direction and gestured in a blurry arc. "Salutations to the illustrious son of the magnificent Djinni Zamyad al Din, Pearl of Sovereigns." The voice, in fits and starts, grated like an iron wheel scraping for purchase on loose gravel. Raspy breathing filled the silence after the creature's strong greeting.

*Was it a man or woman?* Lavinia studied the figure through the eerie light, but its shape changed like a cloud, seeming substantial but transforming before her.

Yasir nodded his head. *"Taobor,* Magus Ir-A, Mistress of Time and Space and All Therein."

"Revered One, Great Djinni, even that short greeting siphons your strength." Ir-A's voice creaked. The being stepped from the brightness, her smooth gray robe rippling like water.

An icy frisson crawled up Lavinia's body, rising with the level of the blue light filling the room. Her skin prickled. Shivering, she fought the impulse to turn away, and started when the magus faced her, eyes glimmering in the shadowy depths of her hood.

The magus walked to Yasir, her tall skeletal shape poking angles from inside the voluminous garment as if a bat-like creature were trying to escape. Halfway to him, she stopped, legs settling from their unwieldy gait, then, in a burst of sudden speed, she glided forward, appearing to be blown by a strong wind gust. She stood silent beside him. Ir-A raised a hand, gloved in the same smooth gray, and dropped the robe's hood, which bunched like folds of skin around her shoulders.

Lavinia strained to see. Hundreds of wrinkles, like ridges etched into sand by an outgoing tide, lined the magus's pale face and neck. Under stark white brows her eyes were lost in deep creases but for a faint flicker. This being must be hundreds and hundreds of years old.

Ir-A peered at Yasir's bare chest. "I see, Revered Djinni, a grievous wound." The magus dipped her head down, down, her body bending in impossible ways, her bones protruding into her flowing robe, making it resemble a misshapen tent. She sniffed the wound like some animal, the wrinkles on her face drooping, and jerked her body up so fast that Lavinia let out a small cry, but no one seemed to notice.

"We have little time," Ir-A said, her voice cracking. Was she overcome by emotion?

Lavinia stared hard. The magus's wrinkles almost imperceptibly vanished into a smooth dewy complexion, her wiry white hair changing to a glossy yellow, her rheumy eyes now healthy gray and shining with apprehension. A slim, graceful maiden.

Ir-A slid one of her gloves off and held out her delicate white hand. The lead bullet gleamed in her palm. Lavinia sucked in her breath. How could Ganesha betray them? Or had the magus stolen the bullet? This could kill Yasir.

Lavinia hurried to him.

Ir-A whipped around. Her clear gray eyes flashed, then collapsed into ominous dark slits buried in an avalanche of wrinkles.

Lavinia instinctively ducked, but the magus only eyed her as one would a bird that pecked at the ground. Lavinia stepped closer, insides quivering. "P-put the bullet away. It was secured, safe with Ganesha." Her voice came out thin, strained through her horror. She looked from Yasir to nah-Quah. Both stared reverently at Ir-A.

*Did they not feel it?* Lavinia put her hand to her chest. Her heart pounded. Something wicked emanated from this magus. But how could she believe that, for Ir-A was here by leave of nah-Quah and Yasir.

Ir-A spat on the bullet. With a hiss, it ballooned into a black sphere, filling the magus's palm.

"No!" Lavinia rushed over and clutched Yasir's arm. He looked up at her, then at Ir-A, who set the sphere on the table beside his bed with a metallic clang.

"Remove it. At once." Lavinia glowered at the magus and reached for the sphere. She would take it to Ganesha, make sure it was locked in—

Yasir swept it up. "This is meant for me only." The black orb rested in his hand, radiating malice into the room, into Yasir.

"But, Yasir. Something is not right. She—"

"Lavinia, it is as it should be. This will cure me." The orb burst open in his hand, the black hull falling away, revealing three golden rings crisscrossing one another at their centers.

He and nah-Quah were surely deceived. How could the orb, sprung from the very bullet that cursed Yasir, heal him? This Ir-A, she had an ulterior motive. Perhaps she even put the bullet in Peter's gun. First, the disgusting insects, and now this impostor, foisted upon Yasir by nah-Quah. And Ganesha, giving the bullet to the magus? A conspiracy? But why? How could Yasir not suspect?

She looked closely at the intersections of the rings but couldn't see the bullet anywhere. The sphere wobbled, its unsteadiness becoming a slow spin, twirling faster and faster until a blur of bright gold vibrated in Yasir's palm, dazzling with its pure brilliance.

Lavinia moved closer to Yasir. His eyes, still dull from the bullet's spell, reflected the golden light. He wasn't healed. She shook him, but he remained transfixed. Nah-Quah also, staring at the sphere.

Ir-A sneered at her, or had she imagined the magus's upper lip curling in triumph, her sunken eyes cold and hard?

"Yasir." Lavinia put her face next to his, looking into his eyes, but he stared straight ahead. "Look at me."

He didn't respond. The seductive glow oozed malevolence. How could they not feel it?

A blaze of blue flared in the center of the orb, like a match igniting, and faded away. Then, with no warning, a ball of blinding luminescence erupted in a silent explosion. Squeezing her eyes shut, Lavinia turned away. She could swear she breathed the faintest whiff of what must be fire and brimstone. When she dared look, a dark shape had materialized in the waning brightness. Three misshapen legs. Crooked tail. Owl eyes. Shaggy mane.

*Angels save us.* A demon.

If she could knock it out of his hand, he might yet have a chance. Yasir, his face limned in light, stared at the creature growing in his palm. He hadn't even looked at her.

Lavinia dove for the orb. A rough hand grabbed her shoulder and pulled her backwards. Her stomach lurched as the room blurred past, but she slowed and floated to the carpet like a soft cloud settling onto a grassy lawn. Ir-A loomed over her, the wrinkles in her face sagging into a leer.

"Do not meddle with this." Ir-A's rasping voice hit her like a brisk slap. The crone bent down–down–down until her soggy breath fell on Lavinia's face. She cringed at the magus's closeness, and held her breath at the foul odor. Ir-A's wrinkles smoothed into the fresh face of a young woman, her placid gray eyes boring into Lavinia.

"You interfere where you do not know. This is a healing light. I will take care of him, and you will have your djinni back." Ir-A's creaky voice became silvery, and surrounded Lavinia like a soft blanket muffling her resolve.

Lavinia sucked in a great gulp of air, surprised at the fresh smell, and pushed herself off the floor. "I see your young face. But I know what you are." She backed away from Ir-A and stumbled to Yasir. The golden rings in his palm shone, duller now, still entrancing him.

Inside the rings, bathed in light, stood a minuscule woman, chin raised in the way of royalty, her head encircled by a sparkling jeweled crown. Pink feathers instead of hair sprang from under it and spilled to her waist, the downy soft ends fluttering like blooms of mimosa. Her ivory skin glowed unearthly against her shimmering silver garments.

Lavinia followed a blur of motion behind the woman. A tapered, curved appendage whipping back and forth. A tail? Bending forward, she focused on the lady's right hand, which curled around a golden scepter. A cobra entwined the staff, coiling around the lady's arm, and fixed Lavinia with soulless eyes, the diamond in its forehead shining in place of expression. In the woman's left hand, a tiny black orb pulsed like a dark heart.

The gems in the woman's crown shone bright and Lavinia half-closed her eyes against the glare. A soft rainbow arced in the space between them, bathing the woman in muted colors. Lavinia stared through the translucent hues. As the lady raised her golden scepter, the cobra opened its hood. Glowing in her left hand, the now-opalescent orb sent a shimmering halo around her.

A little queen, a demon, then a beauty. Like the Magus. Ir-A, transformed into a wrinkled hag, appeared next to Yasir. Lavinia kept her face expressionless.

The little queen, standing calmly in Yasir's palm, moved her mouth, but Lavinia couldn't hear. He brought the orb close to his face and peered intently at the tiny woman while Ir-A hovered over them like an overly protective mother.

Lavinia could steal the orb. Save him. She reached for Yasir, but he turned towards her. "Ir-A will heal me," he said. "This is to keep you safe." He raised his hand and passed it in front of her. She tried to lunge forward, but her arms and legs stiffened. Curse the stubborn man, she would slap him out of his stupor, but she couldn't move. Clever of Ir-A to give him a boost in his powers, deceiving him into believing the demon in his palm could restore his health.

Lavinia attempted to speak, but the words stayed inside her head: *Release me. Let me help you before Ir-A works her final spell.* Yet, Lavinia stood motionless, a pillar of stone, while Yasir reclined and laid his hand on his chest, holding the little queen next to his wound.

*Oh, Yasir what are you doing?*

The tiny lady waved her scepter and Yasir's palm glimmered like white-hot metal. Lavinia could only watch as the luminance cloaked his hand, his arms, his chest, until he was swallowed in a brilliance as fiery as the sun.

She flexed her arms and legs, loosed from his spell, but she could do nothing now. "Yasir?" She peered through her fingers into the glaring light that swirled like raging fire, obscuring all in its midst. "Yasir, don't leave me." Lavinia bent towards the light, but a grip strong and firm wrenched her away. She whirled around to face Ir-A.

"Do not fear." The magus tightened her grasp, her voice gentle, smooth and young. "He will survive this."

"You! You mean him harm." Lavinia let herself fall towards the fiery light, if she gained enough momentum the abrupt pull on the magus's hold would free her. But Ir-A jerked her back. Her wrinkled fingers, cold like the blue light in which she had arrived, sank into Lavinia's flesh.

She peered over the magus's shoulder. "Nah-Quah. Help." The physician gestured, motioning her to come to him.

"This is not for humans." Ir-A's voice had changed. It boomed with strength. Lurking deep in the furrows of her face, her eyes shone with an odd cast. Was she desperate to have Yasir in her power? To destroy him?

"Let me go. You can't have him." Lavinia struggled, scowling at the magus. She reached towards the bed. "Yasir," she called into the fiery mass. It boiled and seethed in silence. Wincing, she thrust her hand into the swirling brightness, expecting the scorch of flames. To her relief, it felt cool.

The magus dragged her backwards, but the light expanded, creeping over Lavinia's arm. She felt a slight tug like a wave pulling as it recedes from the seashore. The magus lifted her partway out of the brightness at the same time the luminous mass heaved and sucked her in.

"La-vi-nia!" Ir-A cried out her name, each syllable a sharp needle sliding into Lavinia's flesh. She flinched from the pain as she landed on the soft mattress. Worth it to be free of Ir-A. Surrounded by the effulgence, Lavinia could barely see her fingers in front of her, and she thrust her hands out, feeling for Yasir, when the firmness under her knees dissolved.

"She-s hss mubflx." Ir-A's voice shrilled from over Lavinia's shoulder. Nah-Quah's excited commands intertwined. "Gubth. Garbtat!"

The bed jostled from their weight. A hand glanced off her arm. Fingernails raked her skin. But no one caught her as she tipped into the nothingness at the center of the light.

"Yasir!" Lavinia shrieked. She tumbled over and over, the icy air blowing by her as she plunged into the void.

# 6

"Yasir. Where are you?" Lavinia's words tore from her mouth before she heard them, as she plummeted through the light. The wind stung her eyes. Her hair whipped her face, snapping like flags in the wind.

She forced her arms out, trying to right herself, but something banged into her foot and she veered to the side, instinctively adjusting her limbs like rudders. In an instant, she leveled out, falling slower, and managed to look back.

Ir-A hovered above her, arms reaching like crooked branches, white hair flying behind her. The magus scowled in grim determination, her wrinkles shadowed in the harsh light. *That disgusting creature wouldn't catch her.* Lavinia faced forward and kicked, propelling herself faster, but clammy fingers clenched her ankles and jerked her backwards with a grip as unforgiving as a pair of manacles.

Lavinia glanced behind as a shadow swirled over the magus. She turned her head for a better look, and met a man's cunning eyes, his hooked nose sharpening on his dusky face as his shape refined. With inhuman speed, he took the magus in a stranglehold. Lavinia felt Ir-A's grasp loosen. She kicked hard. Free! But she spun in circles, and by the time she was pointed in the right direction, the man had vanished.

Ir-A floated, indistinct and shadowy. Her eyes locked on Lavinia. In a heartbeat, the magus became sharp and vivid, as if Lavinia's presence had brought her into clarity. Ir-A sped towards her, white hair flowing behind her, a malicious grin lighting her pale complexion as she focused on Lavinia.

Ir-A had won.

A crosswind gusted hard, pushing Lavinia sideways, closer to the magus. Raising her arms to straighten her course, she miscalculated and rolled headlong over and over. Lord in heaven, she couldn't stop. In a rush of nausea, she retched, toppling like a rock, the light around her fading into darkness.

Lavinia ran her hand over smooth black upholstery. Her fingers slid down plain shiny silver legs. One minute she was falling . . . now she sat in row upon row of peculiar chairs. People in eccentric tight-fitting garments carried knapsacks or pulled trunks on wheels as they hurried past. Others sat in the chairs, trunks and satchels stacked nearby. Waiting for a coach or carriage?

She looked at her hands, her arms, her legs. She wasn't injured. No pain anywhere. She thought hard. She had been in the urn, had tried to find Yasir through the bright light. Her stomach fluttered as she relived the horror of the mattress giving way, the terror of falling. Ir-A chasing her, closing in . . . And now she sat here in this place. But how? She felt the cool, smooth upholstery of the chair.

With a hard twist she pinched the skin on her forearm and flinched from the pain. She stamped her velvet slipper on the shiny stone floor—solid beneath her feet. This was like waking from a dream, but instead of waking into a familiar place . . . She looked around. A decidedly different place, a place that—

She jumped at a crash, and looked down at a bulging bag dropped next to her.

"And where art thou headed, milady?" The young man burst out laughing. She looked up, eyes blazing. *Who was this, to think he could talk to her without an introduction.*

"Oh, sorry. Thought you were, you know, playing around. Are you going to a Renaissance festival somewhere?" He cocked his head, his hair tousled as though he had jumped out of bed without a thought to his toilet.

If she answered him, he might leave sooner. "Why no. I have just recently arrived," she said.

He widened his eyes. "Man, you sure have the accent and mannerisms down. You'll kill 'em." He rubbed his fist across his unshaven face, plopped into a chair a few down from her and plugged his ears with white wires. She frowned at the rips in his dark blue trousers, but he ignored her and leaned back, shutting his eyes.

"Lavinia?"

She turned her head. In front of her stood the djinni, haloed by the glare of bright rectangles in the lofty ceiling.

"Yasir." She jumped to her feet. "You're better." She took his hand, an anchor in this foreign place. His magic surrounded her. She had forgotten how it took her so out of herself.

"I—you—you weren't in the bed. I *fell* into the bed." Lavinia gaped at her surroundings. She could see so much more when she was standing above the sea of chairs. Huge, this palace. Lighted letters flashed red, blue and orange. People on silver stairs glided up and down, but stood still on the steps, clutching the plain banister. *So much of silver.*

Yasir led her to a vacant area across from the boy, who gaped at them and pulled the wires from his ears. A shrill sound burst from behind her. Lavinia snapped her head around just as Yasir yanked her from the path of a stunted hackney coach on fat black wheels. *Ugly and plain, not like the grand carriages at home. And driven inside a palace, through crowds of people.*

"Where are the horses, Yasir?" She followed the conveyance with her eyes until the crowd closed behind it. He turned her face towards him.

"Do not be distracted by this place. Why did you follow me, Lavinia? Ir-A was to keep you safe."

"Ir-A," she whispered the name. A wave of apprehension shivered through her. *Was Ir-A here?* Lavinia glanced over the area: rows and rows of seats filled here and there with scantily clothed people; floor-to-ceiling windows sans curtains exposing them to the outside darkness dotted with orbs of light; a group of fat elderly men and women in tight trousers and brightly patterned shirts tromping doggedly down a great hallway. *Had the magus gone back to the urn?*

"Ir-A is evil, Yasir. Evil."

"She is a great healer and knows much of devilry. Evil can often best fight evil." Yasir put his hand on her arm, drawing her near. He leaned close, his voice low. "You should not be here. *He* could have followed you."

She pulled away, shaking his hand off. "Whom do you mean?"

"The one who cursed me to the urn. For centuries, he had forgotten about me, smug in the idea that I was helpless as someone's slave. Consequently, he does not know the location of the urn. But now, things have changed. He believes I have become a threat. He has reason now to pursue me. And you." Yasir curved his hand above her shoulder. She shrank from the warmth of his touch.

"What reason? Tell me. Why would he be after me? I've done nothing." She tossed her head, eyes hard with anger. "All the better to stay together to protect one another. I'll not go back. I am the master. You have to obey me—"

"Attention!" A voice came from somewhere far above. "A car is parked in the no parking zone at drop-off seven, license number TDX-650. Please move it immediately or it will be towed . . ." The woman's voice droned on and on.

Lavinia clutched Yasir's arm and swiveled her head, looking up. "Where is she? What does she want?"

"Lavinia, many things happen here that you are not prepared to understand. You do not belong here."

"And you do?" She arched her back, tilting her face at him. "Are you truly fully healed?"

"I am to meet someone . . . "

"Oh, another magus? Or a doctor with, ah . . . snakes . . . this time?" She put her hands on her hips, envisioning with a shudder nah-Quah putting serpents instead of insects on Yasir's wound. "I don't see how this—" She paused, mouth open. Silver doors in the marble wall opposite slid open and a small crowd of people spilled out. "—this *peculiar* place can help when—" Lavinia looked past Yasir and gasped.

Yasir turned. "Ir-A, at last." He stood straighter as if relieved of a burden.

Lavinia held tight to his hand. The magus appeared young now, her gray robe replaced by men's black trousers and jacket, blonde hair wound into a tight chignon. The Roman nose supplanted by an elegant straight one, the pale complexion changed to a rosy glow. A simple black reticule hung from her shoulder.

Lavinia's hand slipped from Yasir's. She reached for him, but her fingers passed through his hand. "Yasir?" She could see through his body. See the boy across from them fiddling with the wires in his ears. Then nothing was in front of her but Ir-A. She hadn't just imagined Yasir. He had spoken to her. His magic had reached inside her, his body real, solid.

The magus clasped Lavinia's arm in her cold grip, worse than in the urn. The musty smell of an old woman had been replaced by the fresh scent of spring flowers.

"You know what to do." Yasir's voice sounded strong, his inflection firm.

Lavinia whirled around. The djinni stood behind her. His body solid, his magic pulling at her—stronger than before.

"You'll come with me and be safe." Ir-A spoke with a different accent, her voice soft yet commanding. Lavinia pulled away from her, but couldn't get loose. *She wouldn't be safe, not with this evil creature.*

"I order you to make her leave," she said to Yasir. *Wait, if Yasir obeyed her command, Ir-A could leave and take her back to the urn. Just what they wanted.*

"No, I rescind what I said, I mean—" A heavy hand clamped onto her shoulder. Power like Yasir's surged through her, yet the djinni was in front of her, hands at his sides. She held her breath. She couldn't look.

"Yasir. Ir-A. It has been too long." The voice, deep, melodious and sincere. This must be the person Yasir was here to meet, the healer. Her shoulders relaxed as she exhaled and faced the stranger. The distinguished gentleman looked as aristocratic as he sounded, his perfectly tailored gray suit accented by a red-striped strip of silk around his neck hanging straight in front. With no effort or protest from anyone, he pulled her to his side, breaking the magus's hold.

"I suggest you not worry the Lady Lavinia so. She clearly doesn't want to go with Ir-A." The man stood almost Yasir's height, his thick black hair swept back from a window's peak giving a sophisticated flare to his patrician countenance.

"I recognize you in any form you take throughout the ages, Tarxu Rakhshan." Yasir curled his hands into fists. He glanced a signal at Ir-A, who nodded her head.

*Rakhshan.* Lavinia had to say it in her head over and over for it to sink in. *Rakhshan, Rakhshan, Rakhshan.* He was real. A tendril of dread rose from the pit of her stomach and twined up the flesh of her neck even as she breathed in the magician's spicy cologne. *Lord in heaven,* Yasir wasn't toying with her when he said Rakhshan might have followed her. Was *she* the one who had put Yasir in danger and not the other way round?

"Let go of her, Rakhshan." Yasir spoke in a soft voice, but the threat rang loud.

"You give *me* a command?" The magician made a show of peering around as he suppressed a grin. "Clearly, this time and place has a deleterious effect on you." Rakhshan looked down at Lavinia. If he'd been a cat he would have purred.

"Lavinia, your were my Thalia, my favorite in an age where daughters were less than dogs." The magician's voice held a veiled threat, yet something formed inside Lavinia, an attraction like what one would feel for a nanny or a childhood companion—or a father. She found herself leaning into him. *This man, a stranger to her in this life, and mortal enemy to Yasir. How could he bring forth such sentiment?*

"I gave you more than any princess could want, an education, riches, yet you chose this creature," Rakhshan eyed Yasir in disgust, "not of our kind, not even human." He curled his lips in a smirk. "In your lifetime, after this djinni left us in peace—"

"Hah!" The exclamation burst out of Lavinia. In her memories from Thalia she knew well how Yasir had left them in peace. Her chest hollowed with fear at the image in her mind, the magician imprisoning a horribly tortured Yasir in the urn. She worked her fist. How she wished for Peter's gun, loaded with the cursed bullet. She met Yasir's eyes, but all he offered was a desolate stare. *He knew what she wished. Was he healed enough to risk it?* She waited for the heft of metal in her hand.

" . . . you refused to marry, saying a princess of the blood should remain pure. You refused to speak of your youthful misadventures, yet it appears you never relinquished this—" Rakhshan looked Yasir up and down, "—this, djinni."

In the magician's dark eyes Lavinia caught a flicker of an emotion very different. Rakhshan's body imperceptibly shifted towards Yasir. Could the magician's abhorrence for Yasir conceal some other sentiment? Perhaps an attraction to the djinni's power? Thalia's memories played in her mind: a young Yasir, courting her, creating magic as easily as he breathed. Magic that her father, Rakhshan, brought about in a puff of smoke, the veil of a scarf, hiding his tricks. Magic that he *performed.*

A low hum somewhere far off grew in intensity until it roared into a scream. Lavinia turned her head, trying to find the source as the din absorbed all the chatter and noise of the enormous palace. Rakhshan looked to the huge floor-to-ceiling windows and his grip loosened on her arm. The noise diminished. A chime rang three times, resounding through the massive room as tall as the nave of a cathedral.

"Attention: Mohammed Chung please meet your party at gate number five. Mohammed Chung, please meet your party at gate number five." *That intrusive woman again.* Before Lavinia could make sense of it all she was jerked from her place at Rakhshan's side and stood next to Yasir, his hand firm around her waist.

"What are you here for, Rakhshan? I am ever cursed to the urn, under your power." Yasir enunciated each word, his voice hard like a weapon. The djinni placed his feet apart and crossed his arms. Ir-A stood next to Lavinia. *Please don't touch me again*, Lavinia silently prayed as the magus brushed against her, the three of them facing Rakhshan.

"I am here to prevent my demise. And you know well what I need for that." Rakhshan's mesmeric eyes locked with Lavinia's. "Come." He held out his hand. A tiny golden dragon gleamed on his white shirt cuff.

She shrank into Yasir. *How could she prevent Rakhshan's death? And why should she?* Her head pressed into the djinni's chest. She felt his heart pounding so hard it eclipsed hers. She looked up at him. His golden eyes locked on the magician. *He knows how. He had knowingly put her in danger.* Revulsion for both of them churned inside her.

"You, a mere human, dare face a djinni *and* a magus?" Yasir kept his eyes on Rakhshan and put his arm around Lavinia, pulling her closer.

A man toting luggage and a woman carrying a child strolled by and sat in the seats opposite. The parents arranged their bags while the red-haired toddler wobbled towards them, sucking on something bright orange.

"You have no choice in the matter." Rakhshan leered at Yasir. "Shall I show you?" He flicked his hand as one would bat away a gnat. Yasir sidestepped, barely dodging the magic blow, but the thrust of it wrenched Lavinia from his embrace, straight into Rakhshan's arms. Yasir narrowed his eyes at Ir-A.

A high-pitched shriek made them all jump. The toddler stood next to Ir-A with his pudgy arms held out. "Up. Up," he shrilled. The shiny orange object slipped from his mouth and hung from a cord around his neck. Ir-A ignored him. She focused on Rakhshan and shifted the reticule on her shoulder.

Rakhshan winced and murmured something unintelligible. Lavinia felt his arm tighten around her. Ir-A and Yasir both rushed towards the magician, but the space between them stretched as in a fairy tale. Before they reached Rakhshan, he touched the emerald stickpin on his red-striped cravat. Ir-A fell behind, struggling against something Lavinia couldn't see, but Yasir continued on, then suddenly crumpled to the floor. The child toddled over, touching the djinni's shoulder. "Up. Up."

"Jonathan, come here." The woman's eyes widened when she saw Yasir sprawled on the floor and Ir-A standing beside him with a stunned expression. "Jonathan, don't touch the man." She hurried to the child and scooped him into her arms.

"Can we help?" She shifted Jonathan to one arm and pulled a silver rectangle from her pocket. "I'll call 9-1-1." She started to punch at the surface of the rectangle.

"No need for that. I've just made the call myself. They're on the way now." Rakhshan let go of Lavinia and knelt by Yasir. The toddler leaned from his mother's arms toward the magician and held out his hands. "Go. Go."

"No, Jonathan." The child's mother tucked the rectangle into her pocket. "He does that to everyone."

"Charming." Rakhshan smiled at them both as he lifted Yasir into a chair. By the crafty look in his eyes, he would rather turn the child into a frog than smile at him. Lavinia perused the boy's bare arms and face, searching for warty green patches. Would the child's eyes bulge as he shrank into a slimy, damp creature in his mother's embrace? She leaned close to the woman in front of them who bounced the boy gently up and down.

"Help me," Lavinia whispered.

The woman cocked her head. "But—"

Don't mind my daughter. Rakhshan sauntered to Lavinia and draped his arm around her shoulder. She panics when her fiancé undergoes a fit. An unusual medical condition, you know. But it's mild. And help is on the way

"Oh, okay." The woman frowned at Yasir slumped in the chair. "Shouldn't we try to revive him? Don't you have meds for that? An auto injector? My husband can help. I'll call him."

"We've had experience with this before. The doctors said to let him rest until the medics can treat him." Rakhshan touched the woman on the shoulder. "He'll be fine." Her face went blank for a moment. She blinked, eyes focusing as if she were just waking up.

"Well, I'm sure he'll be fine . . ." The woman gave Lavinia a peculiar look, readjusted the child in her arms, and ambled back to her husband who had piled their bags on a cart. The squeak of the cart's wheels faded as the throng in the main corridor swallowed them.

Lavinia pulled away from Rakhshan, but couldn't wrench free. "What did you do to him? Remove your spell." Rakhshan thrust Lavinia into the chair next to Yasir and sat beside her. She leaned towards Ir-A who had opened Yasir's shirt and was inspecting the djinni's shoulder. "Save him."

"You should have listened to me before." Ir-A shook her head at the yellow pus oozing from the bullet hole and held her hand over the wound. Nothing happened for a long moment, then the swelling and pus vanished.

"Thank you." Lavinia breathed a sigh of relief, but drew a sharp inhale when the wound reddened at the edges and widened. Pus oozed out, thicker than before. Ir-A pursed her lips and stood, giving Lavinia a dark look. She turned to leave.

"Stay and help him, Ir-A. Please." Lavinia clutched at the magus's sleeve. Ir-A paid no attention and eyed Rakhshan as if she were considering bombarding him with a volley of magic, but Lavinia saw the caution in her eyes. The magus walked away.

"Why?" Lavinia faced Rakhshan.

"*You* are why he is in this condition." The anger in his voice made tears brim in her eyes.

She was stuck in this alien place with Yasir's worst enemy and a magus she didn't trust. And Yasir might . . . might. She couldn't think it. He would recover. He had to.

She blurted whatever came into her mind. "*I* didn't imprison him in the urn. *I* didn't make him suffer endlessly all these centuries. *I* didn't put the cursed bullet in Peter's gun!"

For a split second a malicious grin spread across Rakhshan's face. He masked it as soon as it appeared. Lavinia shrank away from him. She had just guessed about the bullet, but his expression confirmed her suspicions.

"You. You!" People walking by stared. A group clumped together frowning, clutching their bags and satchels. "Why did you do this? He wasn't threatening you. He's still imprisoned in the urn." She lowered her voice and tried to stop shaking.

"That too is your doing." Rakhshan took her arm and drew her closer. "You might as well have shot him yourself for all the good you have done him." His deep-set dark eyes gleamed at her, full of blame.

"No. I've only helped him. Not asking for outlandish wishes. Doing what I thought would please him. You can't blame me for your filthy deeds." Lavinia tried to catch her breath and started as Ir-A emerged from behind a massive gray column pushing an invalid chair sparkling with silver. The magus wheeled the chair in front of Yasir, maneuvered him into the seat and buckled him in.

*Why did these magicians and magi make no overt magic here?* They seemed to be trying to be as unobtrusive as possible in this place. A glow of blue light caught her eye and she watched the lone woman across the aisle open a slim box that lit up with moving colored pictures.

"You cannot aid the djinni now. Come with me." Rakhshan held out his hand.

"I'm staying with him." Lavinia wrapped her arms around Yasir, still unconscious in the invalid chair. She shook him. "Yasir, wake up."

Rakhshan took her by the wrists. "If you don't want him to get worse, you will do what I say."

"Help!" Lavinia kicked Rakhshan and shoved away from him, but he seized her. The woman across the aisle continued to view the moving pictures, her face flickering with light. A few people stared, but most scurried by, intent on their destination, punching at small rectangles in their hands as they pulled stubby trunks behind them like dogs on leashes.

"Each time I'm here, I give thanks for the innate apathy of this era." Rakhshan waved his hand over Yasir, who moaned aloud. Purple smudges appeared under his eyes.

"Leave him alone." Lavinia clawed at Rakhshan's face, but he forced her hands to her sides. The red welts rising on his cheek slowly vanished.

"My dear, I warned you. If you want your djinni safe, you must obey me." He put his hand to Yasir's forehead. The djinni gave a soft moan. She watched his skin redden, sweat beading on his face. She put her hand to his skin. Fever, rising even as she touched him.

"His body temperature will keep going higher. He could have convulsions, brain damage. There's no end to the problems that will make him worse."

She caressed Yasir's face, dry and growing hotter. He opened his eyes, only the whites showing.

"Stop it. I'll go."

Yasir's flesh became cool to the touch. He looked at her, his eyes golden again. His lids fluttered and closed, his breathing slow and steady, a good sleep.

"You think you're better than he is, but you're wrong." Lavinia squeezed the words out. A coach empty of passengers meandered towards them, stopping a short distance away to let a throng of people cross in front. Rakhshan motioned to the driver who leaned towards him.

"My daughter isn't feeling well. Can you give us a ride to gate 57?

"Have to pick up a party of two and one other, but there'll be plenty of room provided your luggage is light." The driver looked around them.

"Our luggage is checked." Rakhshan walked closer.

The driver nodded and waved them on. "It'll be a minute before we can go. Have to wait 'til this crowd thins."

Rakhshan helped Lavinia onto the upholstered seat and eased in beside her, effectively blocking her exit. She turned her head. Yasir still slumped in the invalid chair, Ir-A standing behind him staring at Rakhshan as if she had forgotten to tell him something. As Rakhshan faced forward, Ir-A pushed Yasir in their direction. The figures of the magus and the djinni fuzzed for a moment. Lavinia blinked.

The stunted hackney coach lurched forward. Rakhshan flung his arm in front of Lavinia, catching her before she hit the seat in front. She gave him a nasty look. She would rather have a black eye than have him think he was gallant. After the abrupt start, the vehicle slowed to a steady pace and she looked back.

Ir-A had stopped in the shadow of a column, hidden from the crowd, but the angle of the carriage as it moved away allowed Lavinia to see them. Yasir sat in the chair, head to one side, still stupefied by Rakhshan's magic. Something formed in Lavinia's mind while she watched the two of them there. Something that she almost grasped, something important. Then it was gone.

At the blow of a whistle, the carriage halted and a tall man with a pack on his back crossed behind, blocking Lavinia's view. When he had gone, she could still see them. Ir-A had let go of the wheelchair and braced herself against the column. She stood taller, her blonde hair darkening even as Lavinia watched. The magus's physique grew bulky, her hair as black as Yasir's.

Lavinia stared, her brain in a frenzy. *Angels in heaven,* she had gotten it backwards.

In the urn, Ir-A was truly helping. Yasir had tried to tell her. When she witnessed the fight between Ir-A and the black-robed figure she had been mistaken.

Ir-A had not won. Ir-A had lost.

Lavinia clambered onto the back of the carriage bench. She had to save Yasir. The driver moved the carriage forward. She clutched the top of the seat, holding her breath to jump when two firm hands clamped around her waist and Rakhshan pulled her down hard next to him.

She pivoted in the direction of Yasir and Ir-A. Where there had been a slim blonde woman, now stood a herculean man, dark and brooding. "Let me go. I have to warn him. Ir-A is—"

"Do you think I would let my prize get away?" Rakhshan's smirk settled into smug satisfaction. He yanked her towards him.

She craned her head to see them. The man rolled Yasir in the invalid chair at an angle away from Lavinia, his hooked nose more prominent for his wicked grin.

# 7

*L*avinia stood in the garden of Bramley House. Something wasn't right. She felt the cool breeze in her hair, but the plants looked too perfect, the sunlight an off-color orange, the birds chirping incessantly. She looked behind her. Peter lay crumpled on the garden path, unconscious, but with no apparent wound—the same position, the same clothes, the same place as she had found him that morning after he had shot Yasir.

She knelt, laid her hand on Peter's cheek and breathed a sigh of relief. Warm, not cold as she had feared. Yasir had lamented how his spell had taken hold late, at the same time the bullet entered his shoulder. Would the djinni's magic eventually kill her husband?

Peter's eyes sprang open.

She yanked her hand away. Glacial blue irises stared at her, accusing, reproachful. Lavinia drew back, searching the ground for Peter's gun. Did he have another pistol, or a knife hidden in his coat? He had every right. No one would blame him. No one would attend her quiet funeral. He would remarry, have children. She would be relegated to the annals of family scandal, her memory infamous. They would say, *She had no children.* Lavinia placed her hand on her flat stomach. She had no children repeated in her head like a playground taunt.

Peter sat up, eyes blazing. He slipped his hand into his coat.

"No. Peter please—" She lunged for him. Her hand slid through the air as he faded like a shadow in sunlight.

"Peter? Peter?" She'd felt his warm cheek, the faint brush of his whiskers and now he was gone. She touched the pebbles where his body had lain a few minutes before. Cold. She rose from her knees. It seemed to take forever as the air pressed against her, spongy and soft like Cook's yeasty dough. Struggling to stand, she looked for him, imagining those accusing eyes glaring at her from the neatly trimmed hedge, the carefully planted beds. Peter aiming his gun, cocking the pistol. Would she hear the sharp click? Could she flee before he pulled the trigger?

She squinted into the waist-high delphiniums, palest blue like Peter's eyes, desperate to find him before he found her. She turned a corner by the hedge. Gray mist dulled the flowers and fuzzed the foliage, obscuring things only yards away.

If she could just tell him. There was so much to tell him: that he was master of the djinni first, that Yasir caused him to forget and give her the urn. That the djinni came between them. Peter needed to know how alone she felt all those months he was in Egypt. Then when he returned he was so caught up in his artifacts. And the djinni was so attentive, so caring, so . . . Peter should know that she was sorry. So sorry.

He would see what happened. How she was alone and feeling unloved and caught in the middle. She wouldn't die. No one would speak the terrible words: *She had no children.* If he would just listen, everything would be all right.

"Peter." Her voice came out faint and hoarse. If she spoke so softly he wouldn't hear. She foundered in the dense fog. She must find him. Lavinia screamed his name, but heard only an indecipherable croak.

The air felt cooler, as if she had unknowingly turned onto a different path. She groped her way forward. The fog wrapped around her legs and enveloped her arms, turning into bindings inching over her mouth, brushing her nose. She could barely breathe. Flailing in panic, she widened her eyes.

She lay in a strange bed, her arms and legs twisted into the covers.

A dream. A most alarming dream. She blinked the sleep from her eyes. The scent of rich perfume or incense tinted the air. Faint blue light filtered through ornate stone screens in arched windows, limning the curve of a silver vase, glinting off the gold brocade of a silken coverlet.

*Where was she?*

She sat up, wide-awake now.

How did she come here? Where was Yasir?

Only minutes ago she had been in a great hall, rows of black upholstered chairs, silver stairs, silver walls. Rakhshan had pulled her into an ugly hackney coach. She had twisted around. Yasir was slumped in an invalid chair being wheeled away by a noxious stranger. Rakhshan forced her to look ahead as the coach lurched forward, faster and faster, veering straight at a silver wall.

She had shrieked, ducked and thrown her arm in front of her face, slanting into Rakhshan. He wrapped his arm around her, hard as iron.

But she couldn't recall a collision. She had dreamed of Peter and waked to this room. So different from the enormous, stark silver palace.

"Yasir." Her empty whisper gave her a chill. She stared, seeing only this unfamiliar place, feeling a great hollowness inside. Her life, her world.

Gone.

Her men. Disappeared. Yet, the earth spun on, oblivious. She must have fainted when she saw they would collide with the wall. Then what happened? She had no idea how much time had passed, but it had been night at the silver palace.

The faint glow of dawn filled the open areas of the elaborate stonework covering the windows. Birds trilled outside. Even in the dim light, she could see her spacious chamber was lavishly furnished, cluttered with silks, carpets and precious objects.

At a scuffling noise behind her, Lavinia turned, clutching her hands to her chest. The door to her room swung open, creaking on dull brass hinges. If she sat still, she wouldn't be noticed. She held her breath and steeled herself for who or what might come through the door.

The door opened wide. A gigantic man sauntered through, holding a brass tray with dishes covered in gleaming silver domes. He set the heavy tray on a table by the window, his ebony skin patterned in pale blue arabesques of light from the stonework.

"Ya'Qub brings food to break your fast." He looked straight at her.

She tried not to show her shock at his voice, surprisingly high for a man of his physique. He grinned, displaying ivory-colored teeth filed into ragged points.

Lavinia recoiled. He resembled a monster from one of her fairy-tale books.

"Is much food for such a small woman." Frowning, he rubbed his bald head, his hand as large as a draft horse's hoof. He puckered his lips and turned to leave. His back looked as broad as the doorway and she marveled at how he had made it through the first time, when he whirled around and faced her. She gasped at his swift movement.

"Are you wishing for anything else?" He stepped forward, his voice gentle.

Lavinia wanted to scream, take me back to Yasir, but the words rolled around in her head, waiting for a voice to bring them to life. She crossed her arms. Perhaps he would leave if she didn't answer.

"I am Ya'Qub." But he had already said, *Ya'Qub brings food.* He must think she couldn't understand him. And he kept staring at her. She blinked.

The first rays of the sun brightened the room, chasing away the cold blue tints and washing it in color. The man's green vest highlighted his thickset physique. Lavinia shivered at the tattoo transforming his left arm into a sinister golden snake, scales rippling with the movement of his muscles. He glanced at his arm and laughed, a shrill titter that put her on edge along with those pointed teeth in huge red gums.

"Ah, you must thank *Enlil*, Great Giver, Lord of Rain and Wind and Air, for your sustenance." His voice came out clipped, different from before. Ya'Qub eyed her for a moment. "You, you," he shook his finger at her, "must pray especially to *Ga-Tum-Dug*, Great Mother Goddess." He turned abruptly, squeezed through the door and closed it with a loud click.

Lavinia ran over and pressed the handle. It didn't move. He had locked her in. *What if there's a fire?* She wandered the room. Every window was covered in elaborately carved stone screens, beautiful, but an effective prison. Another smaller door sat between two windows on the far wall. She rushed over and found there was no handle.

Lavinia sank into the soft cushions on the divan and, with a sigh, laid her head on a pillow. She had more things to worry about than a fire.

She stared at the tray brought by Ya'Qub. The dishes' silver domes reflected the soft sheen of the morning light. Her appetite had vanished, leaving her stomach feeling like a deflated balloon. *What would they serve for breaking fast in this place?*

The silver carafe, inlaid with bronze designs matching the stonework screens on the windows, radiated heat. She raised the lid and the odor of fertile damp earth and rich peat streamed out on wisps of steam. A strong brew of hot tea.

She grasped the engraved sphere on top of the smooth dome nearest her. At its base curled a metal snake with scales of gold, ruby eyes glaring. She lifted the cover and almost dropped it at the hiss emitted from underneath, but a puff of steam made her laugh at her jitteriness.

A white lotus flower as large as her palm covered the food, its center soft yellow. She bent and inhaled a sweet, fruity fragrance. Her stomach lurched. She turned away and gulped a breath, managing to abate most of the nausea. When she felt near normal, careful not to smell the flower, she ran her finger over the satiny petals. Cold? She checked again, yes, the flower was cold, yet steam had escaped when she lifted the cover.

Lavinia set the flower on the windowsill. In the center of the tray, glistening gray strands dotted with raised circles wound around a silver bowl of thick orange sauce. Chunks of bloody, but charred, meat filled the remainder of the dish. She breathed in the enticing aroma, eyes watering from the sting of hot spices.

She picked up a piece. Moist and warm. Before she knew it, she had crammed two chunks into her mouth. She had never liked

insufficiently cooked meat—the taste of blood made her gag. But now
. . . She dipped a chunk in the orange sauce. Her mouth burned tangy
hot. Warm liquid dripped down her chin—

"I see you haven't lost your appetite, Thalia."

Lavinia jumped, almost spilling the tea she had just poured, and
looked up to see Tarxu Rakhshan standing in front of her, his long robe
so white it shone. His matching turban sported a gold aigrette studded
with an emerald the size of a pigeon egg. She swiped at the dribble on
her chin and half-closed her eyes. Was this dazzling image a vision?

She clutched her teacup and stared, mouth slightly open. Her
shallow breath was the loudest sound in the room. After what seemed
an eternity, she turned away and squeezed her eyes shut. When she
looked again surely this specter would be gone.

"I will not vanish just because you closed your eyes, Lavinia."

She faced him, cradling her teacup in both hands. Rakhshan
looked like a different man than when she first saw him at the silver
palace. In his exotic turban and flowing robe crisscrossed with ropes of
diamonds, emeralds and rubies, he appeared every bit a majestic king,
in contrast to the elegant sophisticate, understated in a tailored gray
suit, his jet-black hair swept back from a widow's peak.

"W-Why am I here?" she stammered as she rose from her chair.

"Surely you know." He looked at her through narrowed eyes, as
though she spoke an unfamiliar language. "A woman three and a half
months along is usually aware she is with child." His voice held a stern
edge.

Lavinia's hand went involuntarily to her stomach.

"I want you here when my grandson is born. I want him safe."
Rakhshan's fierce eyes mellowed. She felt the strongest urge to go to
him and rest in his arms as though he were some benevolent god. Still
dazed by his sudden appearance, the force of his presence, she tried to
review the words he had spoken, but they muddled into a disordered
mass: safe, wanting her here—*where is here?*—you know, you know,
you know, surely.

Her hands tingled. Her fingers seemed to have vanished. The teacup slipped. The piercing shatter of porcelain on the stone floor should have made her flinch. She couldn't move. As if from afar, she watched the dark stains splattering onto Tarxu Rakhshan's immaculate robe. Against the bright white, it looked like blood.

She took hold of the chair behind her and somehow managed to sit, the room swimming at her feet. Head in hands, she collapsed forward, her mind awhirl.

That day, a few weeks ago, when she first discovered she had missed her courses for three months, she had confronted Yasir in her room at Bramley House. *Was the child truly his? Did she carry a magic infant?* These were the questions she put to him. These were the questions he declined to answer.

Lavinia cringed. How Yasir had soothed her, cajoled her. Her mind cleared. She sat up. Her face felt hot. Yasir had told her to keep her suspicions to herself, then caressed her forehead, and she had forgotten. Forgotten she was pregnant. He had deliberately submerged the knowledge of her pregnancy, burying it in the deepest recesses of her mind.

*How could he?*

"I suspected." Lavinia dropped her gaze to the floor at Rakhshan's smirk. She scraped the opulent carpet with her foot. "I was never certain." She looked up at the magician.

He stared at her, his eyebrows raised, a skeptical look in his dark eyes. *Why did it matter if he approved of her or not?*

"So much has happened—" A sob escaped her. She shut her eyes, clenching her fists. Was Yasir still alive? Damn him, damn his schemes and plots and secrets. Yet, with all her being, she yearned for him.

"It is my Lord Bramley's child," Lavinia said brightly. She clutched her hands together in her lap across her taut stomach. She had vacillated between being sure the child was a magical being, to dismissing that as her fanciful imagination. "I'm not magical and neither is Lord Bramley." She tried to look Rakhshan in the eye, tried to make her voice sound reassuring, but his glowing countenance made her squint. "Why would you have the slightest interest in our child?" She attempted a smile to further convince him, but her lips felt as if they had curled into a grimace.

Rakhshan moved closer, his presence confusing. He reached for her. In a heartbeat, she found herself across the room from where she had been a few seconds before, her legs stretched long on the plump divan, soft pillows under her head. Rakhshan stood over her. He had moved her from one place to another and she hadn't had a clue.

"You will be more comfortable here." He covered her with a deep blue shawl of fine silk. As it settled, a numbing complaisance sapped her energy. Her will to keep her guard up became almost a memory. Rakhshan swept two more pillows under her head with his magic.

"Did the djinni not inform you? Everyone knows his kind can see if their women are breeding." He waved his hand and a chair appeared behind him. He sat, tilted forward, and looked her in the eye.

"And, no, the child is not Lord Bramley's. It is the djinni's. Most definitely. He will be half human of our line, with magic propensities, and half Djinn. But more, much more. It is prophesied that the child will bring disaster to our family, to your family. To keep you safe, you need to be here."

Rakhshan patted her shoulder and rose. His chair faded, then vanished. "You must take your ease and rest. You are my daughter, my kin. Be not afraid of me." He put his face to hers, his deep black eyes fathomless. His voice rumbled outwards like distant thunder. "I have not betrayed you like the djinni Yasir."

Lavinia couldn't move her eyes from his, and, for a moment, forgot to breathe. So, her premonitions were correct. It was not her imagination. She cupped her belly with both hands and shrank from Rakhshan's words. A fire of anger threaded through her body. She squirmed as she remembered Yasir inquiring if she had informed her husband of her pregnancy. She had asked him if he could perceive the infant with his powers. *He never told her she carried his child. He never told her that djinnis could see a baby growing inside the mother. That djinnis could know.*

She lifted her chin. Rakhshan stood before her, arms crossed, his arrogance visible in the cock of his head, the set of his legs. This man, this magician, had every reason to turn her against Yasir. He had every reason to lie.

# 8

*S*oft as thistledown or carded wool, under his head, under his legs. Softness pressed against his chest. Even his thoughts came soft and fuzzy. A smell permeated the air, like wine fermented too long. Yasir opened his eyes just a slit. In the gloom, the glow of a window outlined a straight chair. Soft chirps and gurgles flowed into his consciousness.

The door opened, bright light slanting inside. A woman in a sage-green shirt and trousers darted in. She stopped, stared at his golden eyes.

"Oh." She dashed from the room.

He lay there, his eyes adjusting to the dim light, the furnishings of a peculiar style, the smooth shining floor. Cool air wafted from a vent in the ceiling. What Ir-A had called a temple of healing. A place in another time. The magus had arranged for him to meet The Honorable Lord Smyth-Westerhaven at the air terminal.

Yet, Yasir could not recall seeing Westerhaven, could not recall the trip to this house of wisdom. Unusual.

He tried to push himself to sitting, but something tugged at his hands. Soft straps lashed to the metal of the bed bound his wrists. *Why would they fetter him?* A needle had been inserted into the back of his hand, taped there, stinging if he gave it a thought. He raised his head and followed the long tube from the needle to the clear bag hanging above him. A small amount of light blue liquid filled the bottom and dribbled into the tube.

He shook his head, but couldn't clear the fog in his brain. The incessant burbling in the room sounded like voices in a foreign tongue. He concentrated on his wrists. Clouds drifting through his mind broke his focus, but the cloth strips shriveled, and snapped like flimsy threads. *So his magic still worked.*

Yasir struggled upright and dragged his legs over the edge of the bed. A stab of pain in his shoulder pitched him forward, but he grabbed the bed rail before he fell to the floor. He steadied himself as he caught his breath. The cursed wound, still there, worse.

Worse. A cold chill went through him. This place was supposed to heal, to do what nah-Quah and Ir-A couldn't. His hands quivered. The trembling spread until his body shook, rendering him helpless, clutching the rail, which vibrated with a rattle.

In a blur of green the woman returned. "You can't go running 'round hospital with that skimpy shift on now, can you?" With swift, strong movements, she shoved him onto his back and swung his legs straight in front of him as though he were a child. She bound his wrists as efficiently as any torturer he'd had.

"Why am I w-worse? Bring W-Westerhaven." Yasir couldn't remember how to say more words. His mouth worked silently.

"No physician by that name here, Luv. I'm your night nurse. You'll feel better as soon as the meds take effect." The woman fiddled with the hook over his head, removed the deflated bag and replaced it with a full one. He thought to lift his arm to destroy the pouch, but found he couldn't move it.

"No. Help me. I can give you riches, gold—" His hand tingled. Numbing cold spiked inside his arm and burned into his shoulder, speeding through his body, blurring his mind.

"Dearie me, riches." She gave a chuckle. Was she laughing at him? "You can have the gold waiting for me next time. Righto? I suppose you have it stashed right there in your bed." The nurse adjusted the bag, her image fading into black, but her words stood out in his head as if written in white on the darkness overtaking him.

" . . . not any blood type I've ever seen, not in the ABO or Rh group. He doesn't fall into any of the known genotype-phenotype distinctions." The baritone voice in the distinct accent of the Indos wavered into Yasir's burgeoning consciousness.

"You drew his blood?" A woman's voice, cool, aristocratic.

"Of course, Dr. Kushner, it's standard proce—"

"Dr. Senei," her tone flattened. "We have our orders, I went over them—"

"But he-he's not human. I've never seen anything li—"

"It doesn't matter if he's a giraffe. We were told not to draw blood."

"But his condition is worsening. We are *doc–tors.*" Dr. Senei's voice broke.

"This is a private hospital. We are doctors to our patrons. And we do what they want."

"The patient needs help. Do you want him to die? Does our patron want him to die?" Desperation jumped his voice to a higher register.

"Dr. Senei, our patron wants his patient kept alive and drugged. His wound must not heal totally." Yasir heard her take a deep breath. "You said it yourself. This man is not human. And I will tell you what no one else knows." She paused. "He has great powers. If this wound heals, even if he's drugged, he may escape. Our patron also has great powers. Do you want him to find out it was you who allowed his patient to escape, to grow strong enough to use his powers?"

"I-I have never— I am a doctor. I took an oath—"

"You also signed a contract. It clearly states that our oath is subject to our patron's wishes. And he pays you a considerable sum." Her voice was cold. "Perhaps you need a little time to reread the contract. To rethink what you want to do here."

The sweep of the heavy door and subsequent footsteps drowned out the hum of the machines. "Dr. Senei may have breached his contract." The woman's stern voice stopped the shuffling. "We have protocol for that."

"What?" Dr. Senei's voice shrilled above the scraping shoes. The blow of a fist on flesh. "Ooof. My glasses!" The clink and snap of metal.

"I am not a criminal. No!" A sharp cry. "What is in that? You can't drug me. I haven't done any—"

"Here?" Her timbre sharp. "You did it *here?* Can't I trust you?"

"He was getting hysterical." A deep voice suppressed to a hoarse rasp. "Did you want all the doctors and nurses to—"

The sound of someone running. The door banged open. "Did you need help in here?" A silent pause. The machines hummed, smooth and efficient. "I thought I heard— Oh. Dr. Senei. Who put cuffs on him? I don't think he's breath—"

Quiet settled in the room.

*Had they left?* Yasir lay still, listening.

"Your story will be," the woman spoke, her anger reined-in, "Dr. Senei had a drug problem. He overdosed and became uncontrollable, hitting nurse Anderson and knocking her out. Make sure she doesn't remember anything, but for God's sake, don't harm her." A strong sigh.

"Take those cuffs off Dr. Senei. Bring a gurney. We are a reputable—" Short, high-pitched sounds flooded the room.

"The patient is gaining consciousness. Leave now." The woman sounded flustered.

Yasir kept his eyes closed as her words ran through his head like vermin—*our patron wants his patient kept alive and drugged. His wound must not heal totally . . . our patron also has great powers.*

*Eivaellah.* Rakhshan. He was Rakhshan's prisoner.

Someone bumped the bed. The needle in his hand stung. Cold blackness consumed him.

Yasir's muscles jerked, his body coming alive. He opened his eyes. Instruments squawked like a flock of birds, short syncopated beeps and sharp atonal bursts. He thought to cover his ears, but couldn't move his arms. The cursed straps. He was still bound. At least they were not iron manacles. No bloody, raw flesh. Green and red lights flashed their reflections in the window.

The door opened. He squinted at the glare of light from the hall.

Another nurse stood in the doorway. The liquid in the bag she held glinted in the brightness. His poison. A different torture this time. Modern, cool and clean, like the era.

Yasir pulled at his wristbands. Threw a magic spell, then tugged. No difference. Weak. He knew of the drugs of this age, potent and insidious. *Were they destroying his powers? Was that the cruelty of this time?*

"Hullo there. Are we awake now?" The nurse's cheerfulness was made eerie with her over-bright eyes, gleaming at him as though she held a knife behind her back. He turned his head, watching her as she walked to the bank of machines, flipped switches and punched lighted squares. The jarring noises ceased, replaced by a low soothing hum.

His mind cleared in the quiet. He had heard the beeping sound somewhere before. Somewhere he had traveled, somewhere through time. The cart at the air terminal. *Eivaellah.* Ir-A appearing young and sleek in modern garments. Lavinia in her gown from another century, befuddled by the incomprehensible future. Rakhshan intruding, smooth as a huckster in his tailored gray suit and polished shoes, tweaking his emerald tie tack and subtly inflicting a blow that would have killed a mortal.

Rakhshan had taken Lavinia. Yasir curled his hands, but his will couldn't coerce his flesh to make fists. An abrupt sinking sensation drained his strength as if the blood slowly drained from his body. He struggled for his next thought. Rakhshan would keep Lavinia safe through the birth, then steal their son—a djinni's son—and kill him, for the magician surely knew about the prophecy.

Yasir couldn't stop the tears, the warm wetness streaking down his cheeks. His son. Their son. Unborn and doomed. All to naught.

Would Rakhshan murder Lavinia? She was his daughter, Thalia, from the distant past, but she had disobeyed her father's wishes to stay away from the djinni. Her finding Yasir now was tantamount to her murdering the magician. Yet she did not know of her misstep.

Yasir clenched his fists. The needle in the back of his hand stung. He ground it against the metal bar, driving it further into his flesh and clenched his teeth at the searing twist of fire.

*Pain. He deserved pain.* He had not acknowledged Lavinia's pregnancy. His spell caused her to forget. What he did . . . He had intended to keep Lavinia safe. Safe from Rakhshan by not drawing attention to her pregnancy. Safe from Peter. The jealous bastard would have seen through her naïve attempts to hide her unfaithfulness if she had told him she was expecting.

Now she would hear from Rakhshan that she carried a djinni's child, a child of the prophecy. Yasir drove his hand against the bar again. He sucked in his breath. All he had done to try to fulfill the prophecy was not enough, Rakhshan still—

A hand touched his. His body jerked. Behind him the machines gurgled and hummed.

"I need to check your drip." The nurse bent over his hand. A whiff of her flowery perfume, a vulgar imitation, made him long for a real garden, for freedom.

"Lord, what did you do? You're bleeding. The needle is bent." She blotted his hand. "This will hurt."

Yasir gritted his teeth, welcoming the pain. She wiped his other hand with something cold. He breathed in a sour, astringent odor. "We'll have to put the needle in the other hand now. I'll make a note. We'll use something more immobilizing than the strap." She slipped something onto his hand, the soft stretchy fabric covering his palm and fingers, a tight backless glove with a strap. The nurse cinched it tight to the bar. When she inserted the needle he barely felt it.

"Luv, if you do that again, they'll probably put you in a coma. Between you and me you don't want that. Some . . ." She bent to his ear and whispered. "Some don't come back."

Blackness dipped in again, stealing his thoughts, stealing his magic.

Yasir dimmed his powers, slowed his blood flow, and kept his breathing rhythmic, just below the level where humans come into consciousness. He opened his eyes, blocking the mechanics of his waking body from the instruments with simple strength of will. Hour after hour the same blue liquid drained from the bag into his veins. His body was building resistance. He could feel the fog fading from his brain, the synapses flickering and coming back to life. Outside the window darkness leered, a malevolent presence unlike the deceiving interior—clean and scrubbed, innocuous in its sterility.

He paused, checking the strength of his magic, keeping his body constrained.

Yasir projected a ghosted image of Ir-A's gold rings onto his chest. He controlled his breath, siphoned the trepidation from his body, from his mind. The smooth drone of the machines filled the room.

He cast his vision of the orb's queen in the center of the rings and waited. *Would the images absorb his weak magic and become real?* He kept his body's activity to a minimum and focused what he had of his powers, careful to keep them subtle. The spectral queen's tiny feet became solid upon his chest, a silver gown shimmered over her body and she held out her scepter, her ivory skin glowing. She tilted her head and looked him straight in the eye. The pink feathers of her hair ruffled from the cool air flowing through the ceiling vent.

Inside his head he heard her: *Oh Great Djinni, how may Orys, Ethereal born, Queen of Realms, serve thee?*

He sent her the message. *Lavinia has my ring. She is—*

*I know where she is. Do not waste time. What is it you want from me?* Orys glanced towards the noises in the hall, her purple eyes bright with fear.

*Go to her. Save my son. Save—*

Shrill rhythmic beeps pierced the smooth hum of the room. Orys startled and dropped her scepter, light as a blade of grass on his chest. Her message formed in Yasir's mind, but before he could decipher it, the words jumbled. His arms and legs trembled. He felt the blue liquid pumping through his veins—the dosage upped by the machines as they registered him becoming conscious. *Impossible to focus.*

A nurse walked in the door and stopped, staring at Orys shining in the midst of the rings on Yasir's chest. The nurse stiffened, muttering, "Well blow me down with a feather." She marched over to Yasir and snatched Orys, who banged her tiny scepter on the nurse's hand.

"Ow!" The nurse dropped the little queen onto Yasir's chest and stared at her blistering hand, the skin raw. "What did you do to me? Why I'll throttle your little throat—"

Yasir strained his bonds and raised his head, his eyes piercing as his voice filled the room. *"Avarah k'davarah absam cadramysis abreq ad habra."*

The nurse stepped backwards, face blank with fear, and crumpled to the floor, just as Orys vanished. The golden rings collapsed into the diminishing pool of light on his chest.

He broke his restraints and sat up, reeling, the insistent beeping hammering at him as a chill numbness coursed through his veins. If he hurried he had the strength to escape. He ripped the needle from his hand just as a woman in a white coat entered, followed by three hulking men in black suits. She strode over to the machines and switched off the alarms.

"Take him down." Her voice was harsh over the soothing thrum of the instruments. The same cold voice that had argued with Dr. Senei—Dr. Kushner, whose patron was Rakhshan.

Yasir rose to his feet, rage concentrating what little powers he could gather, but the room and the woman blurred, spinning before him. He raised his arm. *"Avarah k'davarah absam cadr—"*

A fist slammed into his face and he fell against the second man who had moved behind him. They forced him onto the bed. The bonds dug into his wrists as they strapped him in again.

*"Avarah k'da—"* One of the men slipped a gag into his mouth and tied it tight.

The doctor hovered over her lackeys. When they finished, she stuck a fresh needle in Yasir's hand, taped it and slipped the bag in place on the metal stand.

"Remove the gag and double-check his restraints." She stood, imperious, watching the men follow her orders. When they finished she waved them away.

"There now, all happy and safe." She looked directly at him. Yasir focused on her pale hazel eyes. He had only a few minutes before the blackness took him. Her jaunty smile faded. She drew back, her face a pallid mask of control.

If only he could steal into her mind, turn her to his will. The pathway opened and he sent a spell just as the doctor clinched her jaw and looked away.

She bent towards him, careful to avoid his eyes and spoke, low and smoldering. "I was warned about you." She pulled a syringe from her pocket, uncapped it and tapped the side with her manicured fingers. The needle slid into his vein as smooth as a caress.

"Just in case," she said as she stood over him, arms folded across her white coat.

The drugs swirled through his veins, bounding like a sea creature in the waves. The image of Orys fading on his chest floated through his mind. His stomach clenched.

He had left out something important, had been cut off before he could say it. He concentrated his magic and his voice broke through the torpor deadening his body.

"Orys, save her also, I beg you. Save my son, but save her as well. Save her . . . "

# 9

*L*avinia peered into the shadowy corners of her room—her prison?—in what she surmised was Rakhshan's palace. The magician had materialized just there, near the window. Would he appear without warning once more, barely recognizable in another outlandish costume—different from his gray suit and swept-back hair at the silver palace, different from the white robe and turban that dazzled her earlier?

She yawned, heavy and sluggish with residues of sleep. She must have drifted off after the noonday meal. The shawl Rakhshan had laid over her slid down her body in an avalanche of blue. She thought of catching it, but her arms—still asleep?—stayed listless by her side and she watched helplessly as the smooth silk glided onto the carpet.

Tarxu Rakhshan could have ordered potions laced into her food. As the thought lazed through her head, she seized upon it, her mind sufficiently roused. If the unfamiliar fare with its myriad spices contained strong concoctions she wouldn't have noticed. She willed her hand to her slightly rounded belly, but only her fingers moved, curving slowly into a claw, grasping air.

Would Rakhshan attempt to harm her baby? He said he wanted the child safe. But he hated Yasir. Did he feel the same rancor towards the djinni's child? Yet, as Rakhshan had talked with her, he seemed less and less threatening, even kind. And Yasir . . .

Yasir had deceived her.

She looked down at her hand, finally managing to cup her firm abdomen. A sparkle of red glimmered. Her ruby ring. She had forgotten about it. Holding her hand in front of her, she sat up, moving normally, to her relief. She hadn't slept so heavily since she was a child and believed her dreams were real. She placed her finger on the ruby and closed her eyes, stroking the gem three times as she imagined Yasir beside her, whisking her safely to his urn.

Nothing happened.

Tears in her eyes, she drew her finger thrice more across the cold stone. Did no response mean Yasir was—

No, she daren't let that thought stay in her mind. When she had last seen him at the silver palace he was still unconscious and Ir-A— Lavinia trembled as a shiver of horror rippled down her spine—Ir-A had transformed before her eyes into a man with a hooked nose, and had wheeled Yasir away in the invalid chair. How many times could the djinni be stricken and survive?

Lavinia spread her hand in front of her, the ruby in her ring dull, yet a golden light glowed between her fingers, outlining her hand in a radiant aura. She covered the ruby, but the golden light remained the same. Drawing in her breath, she turned her hand over. A sphere of luminescence shimmered in her palm, the center a dancing amber flame.

Afraid to move, she stared at the fluttering light. She felt nothing in her palm, no pressure from the weight of the sphere, no heat from the fire. The flame flickered and grew, purple on the outside, then red, yellow and incandescent white in the center, where a dark shape formed.

Lavinia raised her palm level with her eyes and came face to face with a tiny figure. Trying to discern why it looked familiar, she squinted into the flame. *Stars in heaven.* The tiny queen who had appeared to Yasir in the urn stood in her hand. She was as light as a chocolate drop. Lavinia held her breath. This could be a gift from Ir-A . . . or a curse from what Ir-A had become.

But it was all she had.

The queen tilted her head and motioned Lavinia nearer with her golden scepter. Her crown glowed with jewels. Pink feathers spilled from under her crown over her shimmering silver gown like a hazy mist, curling this way and that as if in a slight breeze. The fairy creature opened her mouth and a sound like far-away music burbled into the air.

Lavinia bent closer, straining to hear.

"I am Orys, Ethereal Born, Queen of Realms." The lady let go of her scepter and it floated beside her, the crystal orb at the tip pulsing with a bright blue light. In the urn, when she had first seen Orys cupped in Yasir's palm, a live cobra curled around the queen's arm as it slunk onto her scepter. Now the serpent had turned to gold, an embellishment spiraling the scepter's staff, its staring eyes black pearls.

"Yasir is lost in darkness. With your ring you can save him." The fairy's voice piped as shrill as the chirp of a froglet.

"But it doesn't work in here." Lavinia twisted the ring around her finger. Was this the sum of the little queen's magic? To instruct her to use her ring? What madness was this?

"I am aware of the difficulties." The little queen held out both hands, palms up as if making an offering. "You must use this as well." Lavinia waited for something to appear in Orys's hands, but saw nothing.

"As clear as water, light as air. A vision glass. I will color the glass for a moment so you can see it." A glint of green light reflected from the curved edge, then a green disk came into view, a shallow bowl about the size of a sixpence and as thick as a sheet of paper.

Orys moved her hands apart and the vision glass floated like a leaf down onto Lavinia's palm, settling with a touch so subtle she could scarce feel it. The smooth edge winked a green glimmer as the color faded. If she squinted and it caught the light just so, she could make out the transparent glass's shape.

"Hold the glass above the ruby in your ring. Stroke the gem thrice, count to eleven and stroke the gem thrice more. Then call to your djinni. This will guide him back." The fairy beamed as if she could transport Yasir there that very moment. "Mind, use it at dusk or just before dawn, mystical times, moments of the opening between worlds." She thrust out her hand as if to admonish Lavinia.

"Your djinni is waiting." Orys grasped her scepter from the air and vanished, leaving a faint twinkle, the scent of attar of roses and the vision glass in Lavinia's cupped hand.

She stared at her palm, trying to see the featherweight object. A vision glass? Angling her hand so the light hit the glass at a certain slant, she lifted the disk with the tips of her fingers and looked through it. A pool of blood stained a patch of the green tile floor in front of her.

"Oh." Lavinia moved the vision glass from her eye and the tiles gleamed, clean and pristine. "She didn't say to look through it," Lavinia mumbled. "Best find a safe place to hide it." She lifted the lid of a compact polished wooden box on the ivory table next to the divan, and placed the crystal on the red velvet lining. With great care she closed the lid.

"Perfect, perfect, perfect." She sang a little chorus.

Yasir was alive.

Sun still lit the blue sky—late afternoon, several hours before dusk. Lavinia peered through the *jali* stonework. Close up it was a contradiction in medium, the thick stone carved in impossibly elaborate curlicues as fanciful as Belgian lace. An enclosed garden flourished outside through the scrolled openings. Carefully tended flowers bloomed in profusion, blossoms vivid as fresh paint. She moved to another window. Cool lavender shade pooled under green trees, shadows lengthening as the day neared eventide. From the next window she viewed an emerald stream flowing through marble channels, sunlight sparkling like a song on the clear water.

If only she could walk there until dusk, until time to call Yasir. How could she summon Rakhshan or Ya'Qub to let her out? Pacing the room, she hunted for a bell pull or a bell. She ran her hands over the panels in the huge door, trying to discover a small window she could slide open and summon a servant.

Ya'Qub had locked the door, but she pressed down on the door handle anyway. It clicked. She stood gaping as it swung open. She hadn't heard anyone outside, and they would have made noise when they unlocked it. Perhaps this happened when she had been asleep.

She could leave this place, but she didn't know where she was, or even when it was. This time, this era, this year might exist far in the past or in the future. In her mind, she retraced her path from the urn looking for any clues as to time or place, but her search dissolved into images of Ir-A, the silver palace, and Rakhshan's leering face, solving nothing, only fueling her growing anxiety.

She closed the door and hurried to the ivory table. The wooden box was small. It would suit her purpose. She opened it and checked the velvet padding around the glass, finding it especially thick on the underside of the lid. This would keep the crystal from jostling. She tested the brass latch—it held firm—then put the box deep in the hidden pocket of her skirt. Best be prepared if she found a way to escape.

Taking care to open the door just a crack, she peered out. The hall extended in both directions, wide enough for four soldiers abreast to march under the towering onyx arches. She stepped into the hall, shut the door with hardly a sound, and crept down the corridor. Her reflection watched her from the black marble floors, a ghost of herself.

Footsteps reverberated down the hall from somewhere ahead of her. She froze. With a series of creaks and an abrupt thud they vanished into a soft echo of themselves. She looked for a door that might lead outside, but only encountered endless arched windows embroidered with *jali* stonework, keeping the garden just out of reach.

The bang of a door slamming had her flat against the marble wall, breathing hard. Her hand slipped on the smooth surface and slid down a long thin vertical depression. Following it up, around and down, she discovered a half-sized wooden door painted like the marble wall to fool the eye. Her hands scrambled up and down the door, but there was no handle or depression.

It was useless. There wasn't a way out to the garden. She slumped against the bogus door. She was a prisoner here, a prisoner in an opulent palace, waiting to see what whims Rakhshan had up his sleeve.

The wall behind her sank, taking her with it. *Angels in heaven!* She was falling. Arms flailing, she lurched forward to regain her balance. She whipped around. The door had swung open to the sweetness of fresh blossoms and the musical gurgle of running water.

Lavinia stepped over the threshold and tipped her face to the sunshine, the rays hot on her skin even as the day declined. A docile breeze fanned her hair. She made sure there was a handle on this side, and pulled the door almost closed. Holding it open with her foot, she tore off a strip of her petticoat, folded it and jammed it under the door so it wouldn't lock.

She walked down seven marble steps arranged in a stacked semi-circle and looked back, making sure she knew where to return. The door from the garden proved wooden and ordinary in a wall of gleaming white marble inlaid with vines and flowers of semiprecious stones that sparkled in the sunlight.

She looked around, half expecting to see a guard, or at least Ya'Qub, trundling after her, but saw no one. Perhaps she was merely a guest in the palace, not a prisoner. Birds chirped in squeaks and pips, and a haunting trill floated from a brace of flowering trees. Yet an eeriness permeated the beauty as if it could vanish in the blink of an eye.

Carved stepping-stones led her through beds of fantasy blooms and onto a gilded bridge arched over a winding stream. Across the path, a stone bench in an overgrown alcove offered respite. She lowered her body onto the seat. How could she be so exhausted from such a short walk? She leaned back with a sigh, and found, to her delight, that her view included a turquoise reflecting pond. Fat golden fish lurked lazily in the depths, nosing out from under lily pads and butter-yellow lotus blossoms. The faint rhythmic chirp of crickets had her clasping her hands in anxiety as if each chirp were a clock ticking, never stopping, never resting. Marking the time until she could summon Yasir.

She looked at the sky. Rose-colored clouds drifted over the sun, which had dropped low to the horizon. In about half an hour or so it would be dusk. She retraced her footsteps in her mind. The door wasn't far away. She would have time to do what Orys instructed. She could save Yasir.

A bird burst into song, a loud arpeggio, and fluttered its bright yellow wings, skittering to a landing on the blue tiles at the edge of the pond. Ripples fanned out over the clear water, set off by fish kissing the surface from below and the wind's caresses from above. The soft breeze stroked her face and tumbled through her hair. Gentle like Yasir's hands. She closed her eyes. "Please heal Yasir, keep him safe," she whispered to the wind.

She hadn't been able to tell Yasir she thought she might be expecting, it was so new and strange. And she was afraid. Afraid that the baby was Yasir's. Afraid that the baby wasn't Yasir's. He had embraced her while she cried, but had not spoken. Lavinia felt his arms around her from what seemed so long ago. The words spilled from her lips. "Rakhshan said you knew. Could you see our baby inside me?" Her voice sounded strange out in the open. She hadn't spoken aloud since Rakhshan appeared in her chamber.

As a thread of anger wormed its way through her, she felt her face flush. "My God, Yasir, why didn't you tell me I carried your child? Why—"

"This angry? Bad for the child." Lavinia jolted out of her reverie and turned her head at the husky female voice. No one was there. She looked closer. A dark shadow broke the pattern of light among the trees. The shadow elongated and curved onto dense bulbous hedges, then slipped into the orchard in front of her. It hid in the shade of fluffy white blooms, clouds tethered to the ground by the thin, straight trunks. Was her vision playing tricks? Lavinia stared until her eyes read the play of light and dark as a tall, shapely woman, black as raven's feathers. The woman emerged from the shadows.

Her dark blue skirt hung in pleated, graceful folds. A matching shawl draped across her chest and fell from one shoulder to the back of her knees, rippling in the slight breeze. It was the most elegant costume that Lavinia had ever seen. As she stared, a gold border winked from the deep blue silk.

The woman stood straight, her posture regal. "I have never beheld blue eyes, mmm." Her voice was deep, almost like a man's, but with the lilt and grace of a woman's, a strong woman of refinement. Lavinia stifled an impulse to stand and curtsy to her. In spite of the woman's splendor, she sensed something guarded—perhaps dangerous— behind that splendid facade.

"Who are you? How do you know about my child?" Lavinia attempted a haughty, indignant tone. At home, carrying a baby was not discussed so openly. The lady's eyes shone as black as her skin, pupils obscured. Impossible for Lavinia to read her intent.

"Aside from hearing your angry words," the woman eyed her disdainfully, "everyone knows about the child." She came closer. "Everyone knows, it seems, but you." She walked straight up to Lavinia, knelt down and placed her dark hand on Lavinia's stomach. For a moment Lavinia sat still, shocked that the woman would take such liberties.

"Leave my baby alone." Lavinia thrust the woman's hand from her belly and stepped away from the bench, almost stumbling over her. A flutter, like the irregular flight of a bat, rippled through her abdomen. She crossed her arms over her stomach and looked down. The quickening. This early? What had the woman done?

The dark lady rose, keeping her gaze locked onto Lavinia's. "Is your child who they say he is?" Lavinia bent forward at the sudden sharp pain that rocketed through her. Her fingers tingled. Forks of light flared from the tips, pulsing with the beat of her heart. *Lord in heaven*, what was happening to her?

"What magic have you?" The dark lady stood rigid, then arced her hand in a move similar to Yasir's. "*Caraiite,*" she said, her teeth glistening as she spoke.

A dull force glanced off Lavinia's chest. Not of her accord, her mouth opened. Words spilled out. "Your doubts are unfounded. I am of the djinni Yasir."

*That wasn't her voice. Those weren't her words.* Lavinia put her hand to her throat. Her fingers throbbed as though they might burst. She yanked her hand away. Streaks of light flared from her fingertips and wreathed around the woman.

The dark lady fell to her knees, surrounded in crackling and hissing ropes of light. She struggled to standing, seized one and wrestled it away, only to be pulled to the ground by others that took its place, coiling around her like luminous serpents.

Lavinia stepped back. A low hum vibrated the air, thrumming inside her as it grew in intensity. Her throat convulsed. "Mehadeh, be mindful of what is my father's."

The woman, Mehadeh, held her arms tight against her chest, the light snapping and popping around her as if it would catch her in its teeth. The hum in Lavinia's throat died away in a hoarse cough. Arcs of light from her fingers thinned to slender threads and vanished without a sound. She held out her arms as if they were wings that could fly her away from this place to Yasir. She searched her body. No light anywhere, thank God. A great calm, as still as a sea of glass, expanded inside her.

She took a deep breath and watched Mehadeh rise amidst bursting sparks. Staggering off, the lady never took her dark eyes from Lavinia. Then, of a sudden, the shadows swallowed her.

Lavinia made her way to the alcove by the pond where she had sat earlier. She slumped onto the bench. A burning swath of pain tunneled down her throat when she swallowed. *Did that strong voice truly spill from her? Did she actually strike the woman Mehadeh with light?* Lavinia glanced at the sky, an odd bright purple.

A flutter rippled through her womb. She drew in a sharp breath, the rush of air loud in the quiet twilight. Her child, Yasir's child, moving inside her for the second time this evening.

Then she knew.

The voice, the power, speaking the woman's name, came from the child. This was a babe of magic, special, and everyone recognized it, except for her. But now she understood. "Thank you little one. Thank you for this courage. I promise I will bring your father to safety and—"

Lavinia started at a loud splash in the pond. She whirled around, expecting Mehadeh looming behind her, but all remained quiet. A streak of gold blazed through the water. Ripples cascaded across the pool, now a glorious red and orange reflecting the vanishing sun.

Dusk.

Lavinia hurried towards her chamber.

The outsized brass key from the jewel-encrusted box near the divan was a work of art, swirling with scrolls of intricate arabesques, peacocks, lyre birds and tigers fitted into the curvilinear shapes. Lavinia slipped it into the door lock. The loud click made her feel safe inside, but she paled when she discovered that the rod, which barred the door, was missing. At least anyone who wanted in would probably make some noise: forewarned was the best she could do. She settled into a chair by the window. In the gray-blue twilight, soft shapes and shadows muted the world outside.

"Yasir . . ." Lavinia closed her eyes, imagining the djinni healthy, his magic strong. "Please hear me." She slipped her ring from her finger and wedged it between two small decorative boxes so the ruby faced upwards. Over the stone she held Orys's vision glass—so delicate she feared she might crush it if she gripped it even a bit tighter. She inhaled and held her breath while she stroked the ruby three times. *Next, count to eleven.*

"One. Two. Three. Four. Five—" A rattle came from behind her. Lavinia jerked her hand in surprise. The lock! The crystal slipped from her fingers. She whirled around in time to see the key fall onto the tiles with a clang. Someone hammered on the door.

"Oh no." Lavinia breathed out the words, but the door seemed to hold. The ring had to work. She must summon Yasir. Now. She scanned the table for the glint of the thin crystal against the striated blue marble. When she came to the edge, she stared at the carpet: abstractions of the tree of life, birds of paradise, pomegranates, lotuses. A diverse garden in riotous colors. She flattened her hands on the cold tabletop.

"It can't be lost. It can't." She dropped to her knees on the bare floor next to the carpet and ran her hands over the thick silk pile, her eyes next to the nap, searching in the dim glow from the window. She needed a lamp.

The pounding at the door started again, louder and more insistent. If she ignored them they might leave. She glanced outside. There was still time to summon Yasir. She set her shoe on the carpet, marking where she had quit searching, slipped her ring on, and hurried to light one of the many lamps scattered about the room. The rapping at the door stopped.

Lavinia crouched by the carpet, holding the oil lamp close to the jumbled patterns. She turned in a slow circle. The light sputtered, spreading extended shadows across the walls and ceiling, forming dark, distorted creatures that hovered above her. Her eyes burned. She blinked and focused on each area pooled in the yellow light. The vivid colors clashed. Each curve and angle squirmed under her gaze, the reds and blues and greens melting into gold and orange and purple. She squeezed her eyes shut, opened them and focused again. The task was near impossible.

Placing her hand so it barely touched the carpet, she moved forward one palm length at a time. If she was careful, she might be able to feel the crystal on the surface. The lamp flickered, heightening the growing sensation that someone watched. She looked up. The shadows vibrated as though they held their breath, waiting for her to call the djinni.

"Yasir, how I wish you could help me." Her voice sounded hollow in the lonely room. She exhaled in exasperation and centered in on a new area of the carpet.

A glimmer in the dense pile. Lavinia brought the lamp close. She had seen it, she wasn't imagining. A thin shining crescent arced across an orange and cobalt flower. She set the lamp down, fitted two fingers on either side of the crystal and lifted it with a gentle, but firm, grip.

"No, no, no." A hairline crack jagged through the center of Orys's vision glass. Lavinia checked the window. Dark outside, too late for another try. She would have to wait until dawn.

At the pounding on the door, Lavinia jumped, but held firmly onto the crystal this time. Whoever it was had returned. *Did they know she was trying to summon Yasir?* She scowled at the door. *Were they attempting to stop her?*

If so, they had succeeded.

She put the crystal away, laying it with care on the velvet inside the box, and lit another lamp. The knocking continued. Perhaps they would leave again if she took her time in answering. She walked to the door, and, as she stood in front of it, the pounding ceased. She turned the ornate key and opened it. No one was there.

Lavinia peered into the hall. Voices murmured from the direction of the door to the garden. If she listened closely she could make out a word here and there. She left her door ajar and skulked down the corridor, turning a corner to where she could hear more clearly. Those speaking were several corners away, but due to the peculiar design of the hall, it was as if they conversed nearby.

"I'll wager two darics that he'll keep it," said a deep male voice.

A man with a strong accent replied, "I heard from His Master of the Turban something different." A jingle of coins as if someone checked his purse. "Two darics then, but I say he'll have its throat cut. He—

A child called out from a distant part of the palace and the voices fell silent. Rustling noises and whispers floated down the hall, then the deep voice again. "Another two darics say he won't kill her, unless he finds the djinni alive."

Lavinia slumped against the wall. *Saints in heaven.* They were discussing her and her child.

A cough, a noisy clearing of phlegm. The voice with the strong accent said, "Add two more if he locks her up tonight or tomorrow. That's six for me."

"What? Who is your informant?"

"Get your filthy hands off me." The man with the accent sounded as though he were teasing. He laughed. "Feeling a little unsure about your wager are you?"

"No, I find pleasure in making easy coin."

"Done. I say she'll try and escape," the man with the accent said, then cleared his throat. "Did you hear that Kurush is in the dungeon?"

A gasp.

"He left the door unlocked after he searched her room. I saw her in the garden this afternoon. Unescorted. His Excellency is in a temper. He'll move her for certain."

Lavinia felt the blood drain from her face and flattened herself against the wall, trying to disappear into it. The chill of the marble bit into her bones. She stifled a cry. *Please, Yasir, let the dawn come soon. Save me from this madman.*

# 10

$\mathcal{L}$avinia glanced at the door. The lock would have to do, and it would only delay Rakhshan's guards, if that. Her supper tray, cold by now, waited on the table by the window. Ignoring it, Lavinia sat on the divan. She tapped the carpet with her foot, rose and walked round the chamber again, past her supper tray, past the window, past the box with the vision crystal. When she glanced at the walls she could swear they were closer than before, that the chamber grew smaller with each round of her pacing. Every now and then, she peered through the window at the darkness of the wee morning hours, hoping to see the faint blue that heralded dawn, when she could call Yasir.

But that was hours away.

The darkness pressed into the room. She could barely breathe.

In her bed, she tossed and turned, seeing Yasir near her, then far, far away, calling her name. What would happen if she failed? She was a prisoner of Rakhshan. How could she fight him alone?

A subtle vibration rippled through her belly, like a butterfly beating its wings. Smiling to herself, she placed her hand on her abdomen, the slight flutter tingling into her fingers like a caress. After all that had happened, at least she wasn't alone. Perhaps her son could help with his magic.

She turned her head at a soft knock on the door, didn't move until the baby quieted, then slipped from the bed and crept over.

"Who is there?" Lavinia said in a loud whisper. She stepped back, staring at the door. *How could she have been so foolish?* It could be the guards, ready to carry out whatever evil Rakhshan had commanded. Then she shrugged and, in spite of the fear enveloping her, laughed to herself. Most likely they wouldn't knock.

"Mehadeh." A deep silky voice answered.

A female voice. Familiar.

*Mehadeh?* She searched her mind for the familiar name, for someone to fit the voice and clamped her hand over her mouth. The fearsome dark lady from the garden.

So they had sent *her.* The cold of the tile floor shivered through her bare feet up her legs. She pulled her blue shawl tight and turned away. She did not have to speak with this woman, whoever she was, *whatever* she was. Lavinia swallowed, but her throat had narrowed into a tight dry tunnel, and she managed only a shallow gulp.

Glancing wildly around the room, she spotted a cloisonné candle-holder, short and squat, She picked it up. Tapped it a few times against her palm. Heavy enough to discourage someone.

The knock sounded again and her heart pounded almost as loud. She wondered at the woman's recklessness. The baby had frightened Mehadeh earlier this evening. Surely the woman had learned her lesson. Lavinia put her hand on the small bulge under her nightdress.

"I bring news." Mehadeh's tone was laced with alarm.

A ruse. Lavinia curled her fingers around the sturdy brass candle-stick. She would go to bed, wake early and call Yasir with her ruby ring using the vision crystal. She twisted the ring on her finger. *Would it work?* The jagged crack running through the crystal grew even larger in her imagination.

"I can help you save your baby," Mehadeh spoke through the door. "You want to save Yasir's son, do you not?" She knocked once again, soft but insistent.

So the woman knew of Rakhshan's plot. Did everyone know? Even Ya'Qub?

Betrayers.

The silence of the morning hours settled once more over the room. Lavinia's eyelids grew heavy and almost closed of their own accord. Without warning, Mehadeh pounded hard at the door. Lavinia yelped and lurched forward. The candlestick crashed to the floor, the sound exploding like a gunshot in the quiet of the night.

"If you do not accept my help, you could die here along with your son. At the very least, your son would be the magician's pawn." Mehadeh's words, muffled through the heavy wood, drummed into Lavinia's head, making her thoughts clear and distinct as if the woman stood by her side initiating her dark spells.

Lavinia pressed against the door. Through the thin crack between the door and the frame, she could hear Mehadeh breathing shallow and fast.

"The baby is Yasir's. I do not doubt it now." Mehadeh stated this in a low, firm voice.

Lavinia scowled. Why would it matter to her that the woman believed Yasir was the baby's father? She shut her eyes. What if the crystal, cracked as it was, wouldn't work? Her ring alone could not call Yasir.

"Lavinia, hear me out. At least that . . ."

Lavinia stared hard at the door and drew in her breath. *The woman knew her name.*

The baby kicked. Hard. Lavinia cried out. *So the child will have a say in this.* She shook her head, throwing off the numbing miasma of sleep. This Mehadeh could have easily found out her name. Still, did she really have a choice?

She turned the key in the lock. The clanking of the tumblers banged off the stone walls. She hesitated. Then opened the heavy door and nearly fell backwards when Mehadeh rushed in, shut the door behind her and locked it with a loud click.

Mehadeh pressed her back against the door as if that would keep out any menace, and said, breathlessly, "You are in grave danger. I have come to help you go to Yasir. Rakhshan knows you attempted to contact Yasir at sunset and is opposed to you trying yet again." She surveyed the room, lips pursed.

"He plans to restrict you more than this before dawn." She hastened past Lavinia. "Tonight they will come for you. We must work fast." Mehadeh's cobalt blue garments reflected on her ebony skin, her high, rounded forehead shining like the curve of a sapphire in the light of the oil lamp.

"What you are using—the crystal—cracked. It won't help you now." Mehadeh reached into the folds of her skirt and brought out a ball of glimmering red. "You must use this."

Lavinia goggled at the size of the ruby, as big as a plum. Hundreds of facets covered its surface, reflecting threefold what little light there was.

"This will amplify your ring. The stone will be strong enough to open the path to Yasir that your ring would access if it could work through the power here."

Lavinia crossed her arms over her midsection and studied the dark lady. Somehow Mehadeh knew the powers of her ring. She could be Rakhshan's spy, sent to capture Yasir when he appeared. Yet the baby had his say with his hard kicks, and she had a feeling that the message was in favor of this woman. She placed her hand on her belly. The baby had been silent since Mehadeh came through the door. Wouldn't he let it be known if he disapproved? Still . . .

She eyed this strange woman, a dark shadow holding an impossible gem, so ready to be of assistance, so different from when they first met. "Why are you helping me?"

The woman's smooth forehead wrinkled and she ran her hand over the silk of her garment. She said in a soft whisper, "This should not be spoken of here." Mehadeh's eyes shone —tears?—and she looked behind her, then around the room. "And we must hurry."

*Lord in heaven,* this Mehadeh, so brave and bold last night, was afraid. Was she afraid of Rakhshan? Lavinia took a deep breath. "What should I do?" Once more she prayed she had made the right decision.

"Sit here." Mehadeh indicated the wood and ivory chair by the inlaid table opposite her. Lavinia sat and glanced out the window. Through the whorls of stonework a star glimmered, small and alone in the deep indigo vastness of the sky.

"Place your hand on the table so your ring shows." Mehadeh moved a chair next to her and with a swish of her skirts was seated. Her long dark fingers held the sparkling ruby over Lavinia's ring. A hush fell over the room. Mehadeh sat still, an exotic painted statue, so that when she spoke Lavinia started as though just awakened.

"Rub the stone. No, the stone in your ring." She indicated the ruby in her hands. *"This,* merely enhances the power of *your* stone." Mehadeh rushed her words, her voice concerned and soft, different from her stern, commanding tone in the garden.

"Rub it thrice for Yasir."

Lavinia slid her finger across the ruby in her ring. At the third stroke her breath came strong and heavy. A flicker in her womb. The baby. Lavinia glanced around the chamber but she could find no tell-tale signs of Yasir appearing.

A spark flared in her ring. Both rubies, almost imperceptibly at first, began to glow fiery red. The room tinted with the scarlet luminance. A glow of bright crimson undulated in the corner by the divan. Beside the brass tray table. In front of the locked door.

Near the window overlooking the garden, the ripples assumed a vaguely human shape. Lavinia rose halfway from her seat, but they dimmed and faded into nothingness. Fighting tears, she dropped back into her chair.

All at once, Mehadeh stood, her head cocked at the faint moan that broke the tense silence in the room. "Behind the screen." They leapt from their seats and, in a flurry of skirts, raced to the tall black screen that separated the sleeping area.

"Yasir," cried Lavinia. He lay sprawled, face down on the floor, unmoving. His wrist was bound to a curved metal bar, a clear tube protruding from his hand. She bent towards him, but drew back as a dark shape flickered between them. *Is this evil magic from Mehadeh?*

Lavinia turned towards the door. Shuffling? Footsteps in the hall? She locked eyes with Mehadeh. Already?

A pasty, slim hand appeared, clutching the bar attached to Yasir's wrist. As though a veil slowly lifted, the arm was revealed, then the whole figure of a woman in a long white coat and men's gray trousers sprawled face down on the floor. She let go of the bar and squinted up at them, a lavender splotch tinting the lump on her forehead.

"Who are you?" The apparition spoke with a cool, clipped accent similar to the woman's in the silver palace, but her voice shook.

A ghost . . . Lavinia stepped around her and knelt beside the djinni. "Yasir." Her hand flitted over him, touching his back, his head. "He's breathing, thank God." She looked up at Mehadeh. "Help me turn him onto his back."

Mehadeh squatted beside Lavinia and they positioned their hands to lift him just enough to—

"My p-patient." The pale woman pushed up from the floor, her eyes dazed as she turned her head towards Yasir, the lump on her forehead now the size of a walnut and deep purple. She sat back and stared at them, her eyes so wide the whites surrounded her hazel pupils.

"My patient . . . do not touch my patient." She put her hand to her forehead and murmured a litany under her breath, "My God, my patient. He's special. Special. Keep him drugged or he'll . . . The blood tests. I . . ." She squeezed her eyes shut, opened them and blinked rapidly.

Keeping the woman in her sight, Mehadeh braced her hands against Yasir's back. "Move him towards me," she said to Lavinia, and lowered Yasir onto his back as Lavinia positioned him.

He moaned.

"Oh, Yasir." Lavinia clamped her hand over her mouth as Mehadeh gave her a nasty glance. But Yasir couldn't have heard the panic in her voice. He was barely conscious, his face the color of cold ashes.

The woman in the white coat shook her hands as though they were wet, and blew air through her pursed lips in a protracted hiss. She approached Yasir, her eyes timid like a doe's one moment, full of fierce determination the next. "My patient—"

"You are taking care of him?" Mehadeh looked sharply at the woman. "You put this needle in his hand?"

"I am Dr. Kushner—"

"You keep the djinni for Rakhshan, eh? You practice your potions to keep him prisoner." Mehadeh spat at her.

"M-Mr. Rakhshan? Is . . . is this *his* residence?"

"Hmph." Mehadeh sniffed. "Residence?" She laughed. "Yes, *Mister* Rakhshan lives here."

The woman slipped her shoes on, staggered to her feet, wobbled and held onto the nearest chair. Her face blanched whiter, green tints at the edges, and she rested her head on the carved border of the chair's tall back.

Lavinia studied her. Brown hair wound into a prim knot. A thin clock strapped onto her wrist, one of the hands moving in tight little jerks. Her long stiff white coat with her name embroidered in blue above her heart. Not a ghost, but perhaps she would vanish in the same way she had appeared. She clearly wanted to interfere with Yasir and—

Dr. Kushner raised her head, her face blotchy red, and Lavinia gasped as she looked directly into her eyes, full of deception and determination.

"I am a doctor. Mr. Rakhshan hired me to—" she nodded at Yasir. "He is under my care." She reached into the pocket of her white coat and pulled out a clear cylinder with a silver needle at the end. She held it up, hands trembling.

"He needs this now." Her voice dripped with authority. Unsteady at first, she walked to Yasir, her black high heels clicking on the tiles. She knelt beside him, removed the cover from the cylinder and straightened his arm, aiming the needle.

Reaching across Yasir, Lavinia grabbed the doctor's wrist. "You'll not use that on him."

The woman tugged, but Lavinia held on.

"You can't tell me what to do." Dr. Kushner scowled and yanked her wrist away. Lavinia tottered, but she felt Mehadeh's sturdy hands on her waist, steadying her.

"You are Rakhshan's torturer." Mehadeh fixed the woman with her eyes.

Dr. Kushner looked Mehadeh up and down. Lavinia could see her eyes grow contemptuous as she glared at Mehadeh's dark skin, her elaborate garments, her hair like twisted serpents.

"I beg your pardon. I am his physician." The doctor tapped the cylinder. A drop of clear liquid glistened at the tip of the needle. "Perhaps you are unfamiliar with my," she looked around at the room, her mouth pursed in disdain, "sophisticated methods."

Mehadeh raised her hand slowly. "I am more concerned with your abuse of your trade."

Dr. Kushner sneered.

"Leave her to Rakhshan." Yasir's voice was weak, but laced with venom.

As one, they looked at the djinni, who raised himself on his elbows. He grimaced and lay back on the floor. Mehadeh passed her hand over Yasir's chest, her magic causing his odd blue tunic to rip open, baring his wound.

Lavinia hovered over him. "It's worse." She glared at Dr. Kushner. "Oh, Yasir, what has she done to you?"

"She . . . kept me drugged and . . ." His breath came hard and he closed his eyes.

"I'll give him this injection. Then we will call for Mr. Rakhshan. He will see to us." Dr. Kushner took Yasir's arm.

"You will use the needle another way." Mehadeh skimmed her fingers across the woman's forehead, leaving a line of pale blue powder next to the walnut-sized lump.

"Don't you dare touch me again or I'll—" Dr. Kushner's eyes grew huge in her wan face. With stiff mechanical movements, she took the syringe and plunged it into her own arm. She blinked and drew a breath, staring at the needle in her flesh.

"What have you made me do?" The doctor jerked the syringe from her arm, her face contorted in horror. "This is formulated specifically for my patient. We don't know what it will do to a normal hu—" Her eyes went blank, rolled up into her head and she collapsed into a heap.

"I give the doctor her own medicine." Mehadeh let out a quick, disgusted snort but stopped at a sound in the hall. "We must hurry." She drew a silver flask from her skirts, uncapped it with a quick snap of her wrist and poured thick yellow liquid onto Yasir's wound. The smell of almonds permeated the air. She manipulated her hand above Yasir's chest, spreading the mixture without touching it, smoothing the viscous yellow substance over the bullet hole.

"A potion just for the djinni." Mehadeh answered Lavinia's inquiring look.

Mehadeh hadn't touched the potion. *Poison, what if it were poison? But if it were truly a potion to help him . . . ?* Lavinia stifled the urge to wipe the yellow concoction away with her skirts. *After all, what did she have to save Yasir, except for her prayers.*

The djinni's chest heaved, his breathing loud and uneven. Lavinia's mind screamed, *Poison. It was poison.* And she had done nothing. She looked up at Mehadeh, surely she was a witch, and hovered over Yasir as if she could protect him.

"It is taking effect." Mehadeh reassured her, her dark eyes flat, giving nothing but a gleam of light here and there.

Lavinia touched Yasir's forehead. Cold. He lay still, his breathing slow.

"*Maham, maham, sato, sato, maham. Maham, maham, sato, sato, maham . . .*" Mehadeh's chant rumbled its way into Lavinia's very bones. She tried to block the tones, the cadence, as she watched the yellow liquid absorb into Yasir's skin. The bullet wound stayed unhealed.

Lavinia placed her hand on Yasir's cheek. Her heart shrank at the iciness of his skin. A soft flutter in her belly didn't warn her sufficiently for the surge of energy that rushed like warm oil into her chest, down her arm and through her hand, transferring into Yasir. Then it was finished. An offering from the child to his father.

She jerked her hand away from Yasir at the sound of voices in the hall. She looked at the door, then at Mehadeh. *Lord in heaven,* the soldiers. She latched on to Mehadeh's arm. "They're coming, what—"

"Command Yasir to take us far away." Mehadeh fixed Lavinia in her panicked stare.

Lavinia shook the djinni, harder than she meant. "Yasir. Take us to a safe place." Her words fell over one another, squeaking like mice abandoning a ship. *Please be strong enough to work your magic and save our child.* The baby stirred in her womb.

Footsteps rang in the hall. Mehadeh waved her hand and her magic snuffed out the lamps. The moonlight shone in the window, shadowing the room with its brightness.

Yasir opened his eyes. He raised his arm, a wooden movement, and motioned Lavinia closer with stiff fingers. His presence pulled her towards him, though it was much diluted. He must be growing stronger. He must.

The djinni moved his lips, a faint whisper. Lavinia bent closer. "Have Mehadeh place her ruby on my chest." *He knew about the ruby.*

Mehadeh knelt beside him, as calm now as if she were secure in her own home, and held the glistening ruby over the bullet hole. The stone's surface rippled red, scarlet and vermillion, shooting thin rays of light into Yasir's chest. He grasped the ruby. His hand trembled as he set it on his skin, the stone riding the rise and fall of his chest like a seabird on an ocean wave.

Lavinia turned her head at the fumble of a key in the lock. A subdued click. The door creaked. She could tell by the whispers of noises, the change in the air, that it was open. Shivering, she imagined the guards peering through the moonlight for her, more sinister than if they had forced their way in, shouting her name.

Lavinia reached for Yasir, but Mehadeh shook her head.

The shuffling of sandals. The squeak of leather armor. The ring of a spear on stone. *Angels help us*, Rakhshan's guards were in the room and . . . Lavinia looked to Yasir. His eyes were still closed. He hadn't done anything, he—

The screen swayed.

Mehadeh slipped the great ruby into her skirts and took Yasir by the arm. Lavinia clasped his hand. He lay still as if he had drifted to sleep. There were no signs of his magic. But Mehadeh's magic . . . the doctor's form slumped on the floor. Had Mehadeh rendered Yasir powerless for Rakhshan?

Ya'Qub and five guards jostled around the screen, knocking it down with a resounding crash. Lavinia drew her shoulders towards her chest and bowed her head, protecting their child, praying that Yasir, at least, would escape. Large calloused hands seized her and lifted her to her feet, pulling her away from Yasir.

*That brute Ya'Qub.*

She couldn't see past the three soldiers surrounding her and she daren't call Yasir's name. She wouldn't give him away. Perhaps Rakhshan didn't know he was here. Mehadeh was nowhere to be seen either. If she was truly magic she might have vanished. Or she might be taking Yasir to Rakhshan at this moment.

The guard with the gruesome scar on his face, grasped her arm, forcing her towards the door. Straining to find Yasir or Mehadeh, she looked back, but Ya'Qub brought up the rear, his huge shape blocking everything behind him. The guard lifted her off her feet for a moment to hurry her along, but set her down with a fierce scowl.

She felt it in her midsection first. A slight vibration that she thought was the baby, but the vibration moved outside of her. A soft sound, like a moan, coursed from the shadows of the room. They stopped as one, several guards bumping into their colleagues, armor and swords clattering. Even Ya'Qub craned his head to find the source.

*"Bechstah! Bechstah!"* Her guard let go of her, the fear in his voice unnerving.

Lavinia stepped behind him only to be seized by another soldier. The sound shrilled. She thought she felt a tremble in the stones of the floor, but no, it was her body quivering.

Ya'Qub slid his sword from his scabbard. The scrape of other swords being unsheathed was all but drowned out by the keening in the dark corners. With a heave, the floor undulated, slanting the room at impossible angles.

*"Moktabk."* Her guard yanked her closer as he gaped at the walls. The furniture and floor shifted, melded into the darkness. The room groaned and creaked like a ship in a gale. The guard's hand slackened and the raw fear in his shriek near petrified her. The room heaved upwards as if a great whirlpool sucked it towards the sky.

Lavinia wrenched loose from the guard just as he was sucked into the swirling mass. A force swelled over her head. She staggered to the floor, hugging a massive trunk to keep from being swept away.

"Yasir!" she screamed, but she couldn't hear her voice in the dissonance. She buried her head between her arms and held tight to the trunk. Her hands slid across the smooth brass lid as she was dragged away.

"Yasir," she screeched, clawing at the trunk. Where was he? *Angels in heaven,* where was he? The roar of the force deepened, howling and booming like a tempest as she was swept into the chaos.

# 11

$\mathcal{L}$avinia sat up, the covers sliding down to her waist. Her hands pushed against the mattress. She pressed into it with her fingers, tilted her head. Her mattress here at Rakhshan's wasn't so soft. They must have switched it. Yawning, she adjusted her shift, running her hand over the fine linen. Shapes of furniture rose from the darkness like people indistinct in a crowd. A soft scent tinted the air, familiar. A flower. Rose? Jasmine or—

To her left something moved. She stayed still, peering from the corner of her eye. A pitch-black silhouette, barely visible. *My God,* someone was there.

The figure didn't move. A guard? Inside her room?

Lavinia pulled the blanket around her, the drowsiness clearing as she snapped awake. She must be imprisoned in some secure part of the palace those men in the hall had mentioned. And Yasir? Her heart sank. She had brought him straight to Rakhshan. The magician would be gloating at how easily she had been manipulated to offer up the djinni. She should have smashed Mehadeh's gaudy ruby into a million pieces and sent her scurrying away.

The silhouette moved. A crisp scrape, then the bright flare of a match. She raised her hand to her eyes as the wick in the lamp caught, the reflector illuminating the room in a diffused glow.

Lavinia gaped at the figure. The blanket slid down her body.

"P-Peter?"

Peter sat in a chair beside the bed. Her bed. In Bramley House. The same rose-colored curtains, her brightly flowered embroidery chair at the same angle by the window, her basket of threads and hoops overflowing onto the carpet. He poured tea from a yellow-flowered china pot.

"After all this time you must be thirsty." He passed her the teacup. The thin porcelain cup and saucer rattled in her trembling hands. She caught the bitter aroma of steeped herbs.

"Dr. Thornhill said you might revive any moment. Fleming kept replacing the tea so it would be ready." He reached out, as if he might embrace her.

Lavinia pushed the cup and saucer into his hands.

"But you must drink. Dr. Thornhill said this would restore you." He set the saucer down and held the cup out. "My dear . . ."

She swiveled her legs off the bed and planted her feet on the floor. "W-what happened?" Her voice sputtered.

"They found us in the garden, unconscious." Peter reached for her. She turned away. The heat of his hand on the small of her back radiated through her nightdress. She took a breath, stilling the panic brought by his touch.

"I had not a scratch on me. But, Lavinia, you were splattered with blood—"

She let out a piteous cry.

"B-but darling, you were not hurt. The doctor found no wounds. There was a gun, a rare pistol from my collection—"

Lavinia looked up at him, wild-eyed.

"When?" She grasped the bed covers, squeezing tighter and tighter. The thick satin crested from her fingers like the wake of a boat. "When was this?"

"Yesterday. No one could wake you, not even with smelling salts. Lavy, I-ah-I, you were unconscious all day and night." Peter moved nearer, his eyes shining. "We—I was so worried."

Lavinia rose to her feet. The room tilted, the floor slanting like the deck of a ship. Peter jumped up, his arms around her. His smell, tobacco and horse, the warmth of him. She flailed her arms, but he held her tighter.

"Breathe, Lavinia. In. Out." Peter's breath was moist on her hair. Strands blew in her face. His body warm against her back. He calmed his horses in much the same way. The room quit spinning, the floor solid beneath her feet.

A panel of her wardrobe had been left ajar, her satin and silk dresses half-lit inside like voyeurs spying from the dim recesses. Through the door to her dressing room, her dressing table stood cluttered with perfumes, powders, paints, creams and—she gasped—the urn, sitting amongst the jars and bottles, shining eerily in the shadows.

She swayed. Peter pulled her closer and pressed his lips to her hair. The possessiveness of his touch made her heart ache—for Yasir, for when she first loved Peter, for the impossibility of what had happened. It was almost unthinkable to believe Yasir existed. She turned and peered into her dressing room. The urn was there in plain sight. Real.

"I have you. I'll keep you safe." Peter turned her towards him and kissed her cheek. She looked at him fully for the first time since she'd been back.

He gazed at her, his pale blue eyes shining. A slight smile curved his lips, the strong boldness of his jaw now relaxed, no longer clenched in rage as it had been when he shot Yasir. She inhaled quietly, her eyes fast upon him, watching for any sudden movement. But Peter didn't remember, did he?

He had said nothing about Yasir.

Not yet.

He could be waiting for her to let down her guard, to let something slip. And then he would accuse her of being unfaithful—

"Lavinia." Peter held her by her shoulders.

She braced herself for the words, the blame. For that horrible change from tenderness to wrath. She was alone with him, weak, still in shock. He could do anything he wanted.

"When the doctor examined you . . ." Peter caressed her cheek, his eyes moving over her, glistening with warmth.

Lavinia didn't dare to breathe.

"Lavinia, at last, you're going to have my baby."

# 12

In the garden of Bramley House, the warm sun beamed down, making Lavinia increasingly lightheaded. She willed herself to rise from the bench and walk the short distance to the shaded wisteria arbor, but a smothering lethargy kept her prisoner.

Her mind spun round and round, but she could make no sense of it. She had been gone from Bramley House two or three days, but then . . . She stared at the hedge, the borders of dainty pink Dianthus. The garden looked the same as ever. In all the confusion she couldn't be sure how long she'd been away. Yet according to Peter, she had been here the whole time. And for most of that time she was unconscious. He said the shooting in the garden happened the day before yesterday.

Lavinia put her hand to her head and closed her eyes. She should have worn a bonnet, brought her parasol. The heat from her hair warmed her palm and the sun's rays started work on the back of her hand. Peter knew she couldn't fire a pistol. Why, the recoil would probably break her arm, but he had asked her if she had shot someone. Surely there must have been gunpowder on his hand from when he shot Yasir. How odd that neither he nor Dobson noticed.

He had asked her whose blood was on her dress. She stared at him, her mind working—the blood and monkey's spit stiffening her clothes had vanished when she was in the urn's great hall. She must have looked confused, because he had Fleming bring in the unwashed dress. The blue and white stripes had ugly streaks of dried blood, but there was none of the monkey's putrid green saliva.

*Saints and angels,* she couldn't have dreamed it all.

Obviously the blood wasn't Peter's. Or hers. She had gotten hysterical. Dr. Thornhill, when he arrived, had calmed her, ordering

Chamomile tea, afraid to give her anything stronger because of the baby.

She had finally squeaked it out between sobs in front of them both. "I-I don't remember anything Peter, s-same as you."

Peter had given her that perplexed stare, and Dr. Thornhill had taken him by the arm. Outside in the hall, his calm tones overrode Peter's stern rejoinders until Peter entered by himself, apologized and kissed her goodnight, resigned to the mystery, thank God.

She stared at the wisteria blooms. "Could I have hallucinated Yasir, the silver palace, Rakhshan—all of it—when I was unconscious? Surely not." She put her hand to her mouth. No servants should catch her muttering to herself. They would tell Peter. And Peter was already eyeing her with suspicion.

Yasir and Mehadeh weren't just people in her dreams. They couldn't be. They were real. Real. They must have escaped. Or they were prisoners. Lavinia placed her hand in her lap, covering it from a beam of sunlight with a fold of her skirt. Last night she had tossed and turned, worried about Yasir. What if he had gone back to the urn and needed help? Not trusting her ring, she had gone to her dressing room and opened the urn. Nothing happened. Nothing. Not even a puff of mist. She wrung her hands together.

Where was Yasir? Was he off in a healing place? A prisoner of Rakhshan? Or . . . She couldn't bear to think that. Thinking it could make it so.

Gathering her skirts, she rose from the bench. The day had started drowsy, cloudy and cool, but the sun had burst through before she ventured out. The flowers shone vivid in the sunlight, but not as unearthly brilliant as in Rakhshan's garden. She wobbled on her feet and grasped desperately for a handhold, as the ground seemed to lurch beneath her. Clutching a leafy branch, she steadied herself, reeling from the parade of images in her head: the dark encounter with Mehadeh, the baby's blazing magic, Yasir and the pale, frigid Dr. Kushner.

She placed her hand on the hard curve of her stomach hidden by the folds in her gown. At least she hadn't imagined this. This was tangible, but the baby had been still since she awakened in her room with Peter watching over her. Peter's zeal now was frightening and she didn't know what—

"Pardon, madam."

A muffled cry escaped her lips and she turned as if struck.

A tall, broad man loomed from the shadows on the gravel path.

"I apologize if I frightened you." He turned his head for a second at a noisy rustling in the yew bushes, his hook nose like the beak of a predator. The scream of a hawk shrilled the air and birdsong silenced for a tense moment.

"Lady Bramley, I presume?" He bowed. "Hafique Al Saddani. Your servant, madam."

Something about his accent made her spine tingle. His bulk blocked the path. The sun shone on his black hair, glossy in a pompadour, drawing the scent of his toilette into the air—spicy and foreign.

"I met with your husband the other day and, unfortunately, left something of mine behind. I fear Lord Bramley did not receive my note about my visit today. The butler suggested I wait, and I retired here to your wonderful garden as, I am sure you will agree, it is such a beautiful day."

"Yes. It is a wonderful day. Please enjoy . . ." Lavinia lost her words and stared. A vision of Yasir rose in her mind. Mr. Saddani studied her curiously.

His disquieting eyes appeared to see inside her head and lock on the picture of Yasir. She willed the image away. Yasir's countenance faded slowly into the chaos of her brain. Too slowly, she guessed by the look on the man's face. She blinked. *Her imagination. Again.* Yet there was something peculiar about this Mr. Saddani, his expression a bit too calculating, his guise a bit too perfect, his eyes shifty, cunning.

She wasn't ready for company. She could barely contain herself, let alone keep up a conversation with anyone, not to mention a complete stranger. Especially *this* stranger.

"E-enjoy your perambulation. I fear I must return for an appointment." She didn't have to converse with this, this interloper. She turned and walked towards the house. Where were the gardeners, the prying servants, when she needed them to escort her to safety, to put this man in his place?

She heard the crunch of gravel behind her. My God, he was following her. She picked up her skirts, meaning to hurry to the house and set Dobson or a footman on Mr. Saddani, but a sudden sinking spell sapped her strength. His breathing rasped behind her, steady, not winded like hers. The baby kicked, and kicked again. She stopped, clutching her belly at the cramp radiating into her legs.

"May I be of assistance, Lady Bramley?" Mr. Saddani took her arm and helped her to a bench surrounded by a massive hydrangea bush, the stems grown into woody branches, the huge blossoms like pink and blue fantasy flowers.

"There." Mr. Saddani stood beside her, his black suit, swarthy complexion and dark hair as though he were rendered with broad, harsh strokes in India ink and set into the soft pastel of a spring garden.

She eyed him suspiciously.

"I will go to the house for help. It will only be a moment." He started up the walk. She worked her leg as the cramp lessened, readying herself to hurry away by another path when he was out of sight. But he turned back, a smile pasted upon his face. She rose, stiff, and grimaced as the spasm took hold again.

"On second thought, it would be neglectful to leave you here alone. Permit me to carry you to the house." In one quick motion he had her in his arms.

"No. Put me down this minute." She hit his chest, but he held her fast as if she were but a light parcel.

"Lord Bramley would never forgive me if I left his wife in need and unattended." He carried her down the path.

"But the house is the other way. Put me down. I'm feeling better."

"Lady Bramley, you are not better."

She stared at him. His pleasant expression belied his changed voice—deep and sinister. Her heart pounded. Why hadn't she noticed this before? Her throat went dry. This was the man who wheeled Yasir away in the silver palace. She had seen him only briefly, and the odd carriage was moving and she was semi-hysterical over leaving Yasir. But she was sure. His bulk, the way he moved, his distinctive hooked nose.

"Put me down or I will scream." Lavinia kicked at him.

"You will not scream, or I will drop you." Mr. Saddani's voice became menacing. "On the hard ground. The baby wouldn't like that. In fact, it might end your pregnancy."

"H-how could you." Lavinia tried to push herself upright in his arms, but fell back. How could he know about her baby? She didn't show. The man had met with Peter before even Peter knew about her pregnancy. She studied his face. There was no compassion there. Cold radiated from him and her insides seized up as if her blood were congealing.

His mouth turned up at the corners into a hard smile. Saddani walked fast, faster than a normal human. In the silver palace, she had seen him change from Ir-A into this, this brute. So he must be magic. But if this Saddani was magic, it was magic from Rakhshan. And if so, she had been caught again. That would mean what happened was real. She hadn't imagined Yasir and his world. Rakhshan had her followed here, putting her household in danger. So Saddani should know what happened to Yasir.

She narrowed her eyes at the man.

"Where is Yasir?" she blurted. Saddani's mouth twitched. And for a split second a corner of his lip rose in a sadistic sneer.

"Your husband, Lord Bramley, might like to know about your question. I could show him a thing or two. I hear he has a rather nasty temper."

"There's nothing to show." Lavinia said.

He jostled her in his arms and raised his eyebrows. She clutched at him, afraid for a moment that he might toss her to the ground, but his huge hands clutched her in a firm grasp.

Even if Saddani told Peter. What exactly would he say? Your wife's having an affair with a djinni? Peter would laugh him out of his study. Or would Saddani use his magic to somehow show her with Yasir? Nevertheless, dealing with Peter would be easier than being imprisoned by Saddani in some god-forsaken place where no one could find her.

Besides, she had gotten away from Rakhshan's palace—through Yasir's powers? If she had escaped, perhaps he and Mehadeh had also. And if Yasir were stronger, perhaps she could summon him for help. The image of the urn sitting on her dressing table loomed in her mind. She concentrated on it, focusing on Yasir. Envisioning reaching for the urn, opening it. She tried to stanch her thoughts, but the awful question surfaced again: what if nothing happened?

Saddani picked up his pace. She might not have much time. Her ring hadn't worked at Rakhshan's. Was that temporary? She stroked the ruby three times and paused, feeling as though she had taken a step over the edge of a precipice. Saddani's footsteps crunched the gravel path in a persistent rhythm, birds twittered in the shrubs, and nothing else happened. Where was Yasir? She blinked and ran her finger thrice across the ruby again. Nothing, not even—

"That ring is only as good as the giver." Saddani's breath was damp on her hair. "Go ahead, try again. You will see I am correct. After all, the—"

"I'll do what I want with it. It is none of your business. Now put me down." What was he hinting at? Did he mean Yasir was again a prisoner, or worse? Or had Saddani incapacitated the ring? Lavinia turned, trying to look him in the eye, but he was gazing ahead, a hint of anticipation in his posture.

He glanced at her, his eyes dark and hooded. "I will keep my appointment with your husband, and retrieve my rather expensive purchase of a few days ago. Perhaps you recall seeing it? A quite unique pistol." Saddani watched her closely.

A tingling rose in her chest, dizzying her head. Did he say pistol?

"A work of art. Engraved, inset, and lethal from my master's spell."

Her stomach clenched. She bent forward, feeling as though he had punched her. Peter had shot Yasir, but Saddani, Saddani made it all go wrong. Yasir suspected something, but he didn't know Rakhshan had found him at Bramley House. She put her hand to her mouth, trying to quell the sick rising into her throat.

"Ah, what a shame I have not had a chance to shoot the pistol. I hope your husband has kept it safe and sound for me."

She heard the lilt in his voice. Her checks burned with anger. He got the reaction he wanted. He had cruelly cursed Yasir. What would he do to her, to her baby?

They were nearing one of the sheds and she looked for a gardener, or one of the maids who came to cut flowers for the house. Perhaps they were behind the shed. She opened her mouth to scream, but thought of her baby. Saddani *would* drop her. He would watch eagerly to see if she writhed in agony, moaning as the baby—she clamped her mouth shut, and breathed slow and long. The pungent scent of his spicy perfume nauseated her.

Through the foliage on the left side of the path, she glimpsed a fancy carriage, brass fittings gleaming on black metal. As they rounded a bend, a coachman and three footmen in ochre and black livery jumped to attention. *Thank God,* help finally. She would wait until they were close, so they could catch her if Saddani tried to drop her.

One of the footmen opened the door and pulled the footstep down. The huge black horses stamped their feet, their lustrous tails shimmering. Saddani carried her closer. Just a few more paces and she would be able to make her plea. Then she would be rid of this brute. She envisioned Peter shooting Saddani with the same pistol. Saddani screeching in—

"Mahaf, in the carriage," Saddani barked. The footman climbed in, leaving the door open wide. She stiffened. Saddani's carriage. His servants. If Saddani stole her away Peter would never find her.

"Take me to my husband. He will pay handsomely to have me back. I assure you, he will—"

"Madame Bramley, I could buy your husband and his fortune with the pittance in my pocket." Saddani set her on the gravel by the carriage.

The thug. She held her stomach and feigned being unsteady on her feet. When she saw him take his eyes off her, she whirled around, kicked him in the shin and ran. She heard his footsteps thudding after her. His meaty hands closed on her arms and she shut her eyes, breathing hard, as he marched her back and forced her through the doorway into the footman's hands.

"Hold her, do not let her out. And keep her from screaming, but do it delicately. For now." Saddani's voice was low and fierce. The footman took her in hand, set her down inside the carriage and closed the door.

As he sat down, Lavinia jumped up. He moved to grab her, but she stuck her finger in his eye. She lunged for the door, opened it and screamed, "Help! Help!" She stepped onto the footstep. She could run for it— The footman let off a savage oath as he jerked her back into the carriage.

"Damned bitch." He slapped her. She stood stunned, the sting on her cheek biting into her skin, roaring into a fierce hurt. She swayed. Stars blinked in the patches of black that blotted out part of the footman's angry visage.

Muttering curses, eye watering, he forced a silken scarf into her mouth. She tried to bite him, but he pulled the scarf at both ends leaving her gasping for breath. He tied the cloth tight at the back of her head, the knot painfully snagging her hair.

"You fine ladies are like cats in a bath. Worse 'n whores. Rather tangle w' a man any day." The scarf pressed against her bruised cheek. Tears wet her face. Devil take her if she would let him see. She turned her head away as he bound her wrists in front of her with silk sashes.

Lavinia worked her tongue around the tight silk scarf cutting into her mouth and swallowed, her throat almost cramping with the effort. If only she could have Yasir deal with that cretin. She grimaced at the pain in her cheek as she turned away from the footman and peered out of the quarter light window next to her.

Saddani stood outside, a look of satisfaction on his face. The same aspect Lavinia had seen when he wheeled Yasir away in the silver palace. A blur of motion beside him. Sunlight glinted off a flash of metal. A hand fringed in bracelets thrust a curved knife between Saddani's ribs.

Saddani's haughty expression altered to one of wide-eyed surprise.

Lavinia wriggled closer to the window, a clumsy maneuver with her wrists tied in front, and sat up straight to block the footman's view. Through the thin window glass she heard Saddani grunt at the fierce man who stared him in the face.

"Roma King. You mistake who I am. Are you not a friend to the dark arts?" Saddani's voice sounded strong and haughty in spite of the knife in his ribs.

"No friend of yours." The gypsy snarled. He pulled the dagger from Saddani's side and pressed the point a few inches above the wound, drawing more blood.

Saddani gritted his teeth. "Gypsy gutter magic." He stayed still, his chest heaving. Saddani glanced at the top of the carriage to the box where his driver sat, then towards the back footboard where the rest of his footmen should be. His expression remained impassive, but by the slight slump of his body she could tell something unfavorable had transpired with his men.

The carriage door nearest her flew open. Startled, Lavinia sucked in her breath, hindered by the gag, almost choking herself. In a rustle of glittering beads and charms, a gypsy in an orange headscarf bounded over the threshold, just missing her legs. She shrank into the corner. He struck the footman, but the man rallied and punched him in the face. Staggering towards Lavinia, the gypsy caught himself on the doorframe.

"Blasted *pikey.*" The footman lumbered towards the gypsy. Lavinia stuck her foot into the aisle. He tripped, careened off the Roma who seized the opportunity to pull his knife and drive it into the man's chest. He heaved the footman up, kicked the opposite door open, and pushed him out. Leaning over her, the gypsy yanked her door shut with a bang. He sat on the opposite seat, grinning as he wiped his knife on a bloody cloth. His deep-set eyes, set off by squint lines, never once moved from her. A fresh "c"-shaped scar lined in blood blossomed from a purple bruise on his cheekbone.

Was she next? The knife blade glinted. My God, he could slit her throat and she couldn't even cry out. What would she—

The deep fierce voice startled her. She twisted towards the window. "—as you did before. Take your carriage and leave this place, or I will slip my dagger between two more ribs, and then two more. Nice and slow for you to enjoy the sensation." The gypsy king curled his lip, a look of contempt so fierce that Lavinia huddled into the coach seat.

Saddani turned away and Lavinia saw his scowl of fury, but he composed his expression and faced his enemy. "You fight a losing battle. You know not whom you challenge."

The Roma king tossed his head, his deep blue skullcap, festooned with embroidery and amulets, holding his dark wavy hair out of his eyes. The fringe on his russet cape swayed. "I know well who is your master."

"Then you are foolish." With a gesture from Saddani, the dagger fell from the gypsy's hand. The Roma grasped for it, but was thrown hard to the ground as if by an invisible assailant. The knife plunged straight for the gypsy's throat.

Lavinia screeched through her gag. Her guard leapt to the window, but before he could open the door, the Roma's knife hovered above his chest, stayed by an unseen hand. The blade flashed in the sunlight, arcing in a wobble, and stabbed into the gypsy's arm.

"Roma magic is weak." Saddani looked disdainfully at the king sprawled before him, then jumped upwards towards the coachman, his body extended like a leaping tiger.

The gypsy king pulled his own knife from his arm. He sprang to his feet and looked up towards the front of the carriage. The assemblage rocked in uneven lurches. *A yell from above. A dull thud somewhere on the far side.*

"*Del dinilo dook,*" shouted the Roma king.

The horses whinnied. The carriage moved forward, bumped backwards. Lavinia's head banged against the window and she cried out through her gag, the pain radiating into the bones of her skull. With her wrists bound, she flailed her arms to right herself as she slid to the floor.

The gypsy guard pulled her across the aisle towards him, enveloping her with his smell of sour sweat and scented oil. Would he kill her now? She struggled, looking to see if he wielded his knife. But his knife stayed in its leather scabbard and he set her straight in the seat as if she were a doll.

Outside, she heard the uneven thud of hooves. The carriage rocked to stillness and the gypsy next to her murmured, "Fine, we've took the horses then." She arched away from him towards the window, straining to see.

A large object fell past the glass. Lavinia twitched in surprise, then peered out. The Roma king landed on his feet, sheathed his knife and smirked up at the front of the carriage. So he must have won. What would that mean for her? Would he—

Saddani appeared behind the gypsy and seized him in a strangle-hold. "Ah, not bad for a fortune-teller." Saddani twisted the gypsy's head as if he might pull it off.

With a sharp gutter of the Roma tongue, Saddani's bulky body stiffened. The gypsy king broke free. "Your misconception. I am *Chovihano.*" In a blur, the Roma pulled his knife and slit Saddani's throat with a graceful arc of his hand.

Lavinia lurched backwards in horror as blood sprayed in a gush of crimson, spattering the window with a series of small plops. Saddani crumpled, shriveling like a punctured balloon, and vanished in seconds. The Chovihano wiped his knife on the manicured grass and replaced it in his ornate scabbard.

"We have not seen the last of him."

# 13

*T*he carriage door burst open. Lavinia pushed into the seat, holding her breath, her arms pressed tight against her chest. The Roma king stood before her, eyes lit with a burning fierceness. He held out his bloodstained hand. She cowered away until the gypsy guard forced her to the edge of the seat, so close to the king she could smell the coppery odor of blood on his fingers. Praying for strength, she inhaled. Would this be her last breath? If he wanted to kill her, she wouldn't go like a lamb to the slaughter. She looked him full in the face, head held high, and caught a flicker in his eyes that muted his intense expression for a moment.

He glanced down at his leather vest, embroidered in swirls of color heightened with splotches of blood, his full-sleeved white shirt spotted in scarlet. As he raised his head, she saw with surprise that his brow was furrowed over eyes full of concern, Saddani's blood on his face still bright red.

"I beg pardon, Lady Lavinia. I am Chovihano Besnik. I owe you every consideration." He bowed stiffly and, as he straightened, he directed his focus to her ruby ring.

She sat still, trying to ignore that he had picked out the one thing that was Yasir's, but the gypsy's eyes were different from any she had ever seen: one a deep red-brown like the rich chestnut coat of a fine stallion, the other, aqua ringed in cold gray-blue. In the middle of his forehead, a tattoo of three wavy green lines made each eye stand out separately. She looked at one, then the other, unable to take in both simultaneously, making it harder to read his expression, determine his intentions.

He grasped her by the wrists—his warm grip sending a frisson of fear, or was it magic?—and helped her from the carriage, slipping his hands around hers and holding them far longer than he should, had they been in polite company. His finger pressed against her ruby ring. Startled, she looked up and inhaled sharply at his grim expression of resolve.

He *knew!* He knew about her ring. She felt as though she were suffocating. The air around them glowed golden, turning into a mist obliterating the carriage, the garden, his gypsy troop. She stood alone with the Roma king. The murmur of the men, the sound of them cleaning their weapons, the birds' twittering, all replaced by an eerie silence. The blood marring the Chovihano's face vanished as he fixed her with his odd-colored eyes. She couldn't move.

A bright light glinted off the talismans, beads and coins on his cap, leaving his features in deep shade. She half-closed her lids from the sharp glare, then opened them as a faint glow diminished the shadows. Golden eyes gleamed from the Chovihano's dark sockets.

"Yasir?" The name escaped her lips before she knew what she'd said. She had somehow spoken plainly through her gag.

The Roma king opened his mouth. A strange dialect, softer than the guttural Roma, flowed out. The indecipherable words appeared in the air as he spoke, the calligraphy mesmerizing in its yellow loops and curls. Her skin tingled with each new stroke. The Chovihano's voice changed timbre. She tilted her head. Her heart raced. Yasir's voice, washing over her in a gnawing sense of loss. She reached out, but her bound wrists made it an awkward lurch.

The air rippled. The glowing nimbus surrounding them faded. A bird called out an answer to a chorus of questions. The breeze sang through the trees. A cow lowed from far away. She stood in her own garden as before, bound and gagged. The Chovihano narrowed his mismatched eyes at her, the blood spatters on his face turning dark as they dried. She had heard Yasir's voice issue from the mouth of the gypsy. What had Yasir said? *Lord in heaven,* she couldn't remember. But it was *his* voice.

She eyed the Chovihano. Had she imagined this? Had the gypsy hexed her?

Sunlight flashed off the ornaments on his cap. She squinted. Eyes watering from the sun and a mounting feeling of dread, she raised her bound hands, blotting her eyes with her bindings. Preparing to face the Chovihano, she lowered her arms.

She looked wildly about. No. This couldn't be. Soft velvet cushioned her. She sat in the carriage next to the window, facing the bloodstained Chovihano through the open door. The carriage and the Chovihano faded. A loud buzzing blotted out the birdsong. She reached for the arm of the seat to keep from falling, but her bound wrists made her movements clumsy—

The Chovihano reached in and righted her, nodding at the gypsy guard who hauled her upright. The cool breeze from the open door wafted over her. She gulped the fresh air and focused on the Chovihano.

He smiled as if they shared a secret, bowed the same as before, a little stiff at the waist, and, his voice, tinged with the slightest sarcasm, repeated, "I beg pardon, Lady Lavinia. I am Chovihano Besnik. I owe you every consideration." As though she were a marionette worked by his will, she went through the same movements as earlier, angling towards him, staring at his eyes. He grasped her bound wrists in an identical movement. As he helped her from the carriage, she felt the same frisson, but this time she knew it was magic.

Lavinia stepped onto the ground. He waited until she was steady, then with a knowing look, let go of her wrists. She was reminded of an actor ending his performance with a sign of recognition and appreciation. The earth under her feet swayed and she glanced nervously about, recoiling at the red stains on the grass and gravel.

"Saddani is gone, and none too soon, no?" The Chovihano put his fingers to his lips and emitted a piercing whistle. Lavinia flinched, then turned towards the musical sound of tinkling chimes, nearly losing her balance.

In a jangle of bells, a magnificent white horse trotted from a path overarched by pink-blooming crepe myrtles. Dense leg feathers fanned below his knees to his hooves as though he had sunk into a bank of billowy clouds. His lustrous mane rose and fell with the rhythm of his gait. Lavinia squeezed her eyes shut. Surely this creature was a figment of her overwrought mind.

The hoofbeats continued. When she looked again, the horse was closer. Peter's stable housed thoroughbreds, but nothing like this amazing creature. The beast's tail cascaded in a foamy waterfall of silky strands onto traces that hitched him to a brightly painted gypsy wagon resembling an over-decorated house on wheels.

The horse slowed, pulling the conveyance to a halt next to the Chovihano. His men gathered beside him: sturdy, swarthy gypsies, eyes like eagles'—cold and rapacious. What did they want with her? *My God,* where was Peter?

"If you please." The Chovihano clasped her bound wrists, and drew her in front of him, prodding the small of her back, inching her up the three steps of the caravan. On the small, railed porch, he pulled open the carved wooden door, gaudy in gold and green. He gave her a gentle shove and shut the door with a bang.

She squinted in the dim light. Through the door behind her she heard him treading down the steps, issuing commands, then a flurry of action and the sound of horses nickering and hooves thudding on the ground. The wagon moved. She clutched the post by the door, but the wagon jolted to a stop, and she fell forward with a muffled cry.

She collided with a warm body. A shove and she was upright, staring into the intense eyes of a self-possessed young gypsy. The girl's raven hair flowed past her waist, partially obscuring her yellow-and-green-striped blouse and spilling onto her voluminous orange skirt. She swiveled to Lavinia's side, arm around her waist.

"Shh. Shhh." The girl walked her towards the back of the wagon, eyeing Lavinia with pity. "Shh. Shhh." Why would the girl keep shushing her? A continuous low whine wove through the wagon. Why, it was her own voice. The girl's arm felt warm, but Lavinia couldn't stop shivering. She was locked in a gypsy wagon, soon to leave her home. If she didn't escape now, she wouldn't know how to return.

The gypsy girl pulled aside long yellow drapes and sat Lavinia down on a slim berth. She turned away, then faced her. The poniard in the girl's hand glinted with the light from the windows.

Lavinia hit at the gypsy with her bound hands. "No! No!" she cried, but the gag made her voice into a horrible inhuman sound.

"I am Simza. Please. I will not harm you." The girl set the knife down and took Lavinia's wrists in her hands. "Let me cut your bindings." Her voice lilted soft and melodic, even with the burr of her accent. From the cut of her figure, rounding softly into just-blossoming womanhood, she looked to be around thirteen years.

Lavinia held out her arms, the yellow silk bindings bloodstained from when the Chovihano touched them. Good riddance to the bindings, to Saddani's brute of a footman. With her hands free, she could remove her gag and slip out when this gypsy child wasn't looking. They were still in the garden. The garden of Bramley House. She said it in her mind because she could have been in a foreign land for all that had happened. Why, she was only a stone's throw from her house, from Peter.

The girl inserted the knife between her wrists and sawed up and down until the taut silk fell away. Finally. Lavinia stretched her arms, working out the cramped muscles. She rubbed the red marks on her wrists, it felt so good to—

Lavinia froze as the girl held up her knife.

Simza smiled and touched her on the arm. "Please, turn your head. I will have to pull the scarf tighter to sever it. If the knife slips, it could cut your face, so I will cut it at the back of your head. I will be quick."

Lavinia winced as the gag cinched her mouth. When it fell away, she sagged with relief and spit out the sodden cloth. "Water." Her voice creaked like an old woman's.

The gypsy walked a few paces to a small counter with latched cabinets above and below, removed a covered pitcher and poured water into a thick pottery mug. As she put the mug in Lavinia's hands, her hair fell over her shoulder in a whiff of exotic perfume. She tucked a pillow behind Lavinia's back and looked up, her eyes shining with a wildness that belied the gentle nature she had shown before.

"Don't speak until I've given you something for your throat." Simza stood above her, unsmiling, just staring with those dark eyes. Lavinia dropped her gaze and took a drink. She clamped her hand to her throat, almost spilling the water. *Dear Lord.* It felt as if there were a razor slicing its way down, making way for the trickle of liquid.

Simza reached out and righted the cup. "Sip the water slowly."

Lavinia sank back onto the pillow and watched the girl walk to the minuscule kitchen. Gypsies. Travelers. Nomads who roamed the English countryside. Rumors she'd heard: that they stole children, kidnapped men and women for ransom, for unspeakable things. Tales of blood sacrifices, mysterious rites to enhance gypsy magic. She had escaped Saddani only to become prisoner of these gypsies—from the pan into the fire, as her nanny used to say.

So far, though, aside from a brief scare, this Simza seemed unthreatening. Perhaps the gypsy was mollifying her, so she could work her evil deeds when she least expected.

Lavinia sat up. Simza was preoccupied in the kitchen. They were still in the garden at Bramley House. She would only have to walk to the manor. Lavinia slipped from her berth, opened the door and stepped onto the porch. The same gypsy that had been in the carriage grinned at her. Below his orange headscarf, his deep-set eyes leered. On his cheek, the bruise from Saddani's footman bloomed purple blotched with blue, his fresh scar a crevice of vermillion.

"We leave soon. I will be here to keep you both safe." He touched the curved knife at his side and opened the door, indicating with a nod that she should go before him.

Lavinia walked back into the small house on wheels. The man nodded at Simza before closing the door. She flashed a quick smile at him. "He will make sure none of your enemies can find you. But you had best sit down now," the girl said.

The wagon lurched and started moving, swaying the window curtains like a soft breeze. How far away would they be when the wagon stopped? And how could she know which direction to take to get back? She shrank into the pillow, her plan of sneaking from Simza's lair crushed with each roll of the wagon wheels.

When she had tried to escape Saddani in the garden, she was hindered by a terrible cramp. Lavinia ran her hand down her belly. She would not risk her baby. With her palm pressed firmly on her womb, she tried to recall the last time she felt the baby move: her son had been quiet since the bout of indisposition in the garden with that blackguard, Saddani. Why the display of magic only with Mehadeh? Why had the baby done nothing when Saddani abducted her, when the gypsies took her?

She would keep track of the days, that way she could get an idea of how far they were from Bramley House. Perhaps during one of their rest stops after she relieved herself in the woods, she could venture onto a road, catch a ride in a cart, and escape.

She watched Simza light a fire in the small iron stove resting in a wooden partition, fill a metal teapot with water, and set it on the flat stovetop. From a green tin, the girl sprinkled tea into the water, and the smell of peppery spices filled the air. As she sliced dark bread, the gypsy looked over at her. "You need to eat."

At Bramley House right about this time, Lavinia's maid, Fleming, would be setting a steaming cup of Earl Gray in front of her with crisp biscuits fanned in a half circle on a china plate, and fresh milk to swirl into the dark brown tea. Bramley House. By her reckoning, she had returned there for two or three days. But by Peter's reckoning she had never left.

She closed her eyes. And Peter. Happy to have her back. He was busy with the estate, but at some point the servants would let him know they couldn't find her. Could he overtake the gypsies? How soon? And Yasir . . . She sighed, then grimaced, her hand to her throat. It felt as if a bird's nest of tiny brittle twigs had lodged there.

"This is ready to drink." Simza handed her a mug filled with liquid as murky as stagnant water. Lavinia inhaled the warm steam and drew back from the pungent smell, burning as it permeated her nostrils. "W–what is this?" Her voice creaked.

"Ginger, roasted barley, garlic, rose hips and Malabar pepper." Simza sat beside her on the bed. "Good for your throat." She indicated Lavinia's midsection with her eyes.

"And the baby."

How did Simza know? Lavinia touched her stomach, hard and round. At around four months, she showed only a little through her clothes. But did they know about *this* baby?

"We recognize your child is of the djinni Yasir who resides in the urn," said Simza as though Lavinia had spoken her thoughts aloud.

Lavinia met Simza's shadowy eyes. *My God,* like Yasir, this young girl could read her thoughts. A true gypsy fortune-teller?

"Please drink, it will revive you." Simza looked at the mug of tea in Lavinia's hand. "The Chovihano Besnik sent you to me for a reason."

Lavinia curled her lips in distaste but, desperate to feel stronger, she took a small sip. She raised her eyebrows in surprise. The tea had a strong, but not unpleasant, spicy taste and went down smoothly, soothing her throat and warming her insides.

"And what reason was that?" Lavinia asked, as she took another sip.

"I am young, but do not be fooled. I am the seventh daughter, the *lace romni.*"

Lavinia furrowed her brow. *"La-laceee romnee?*

"I am a sister of the hidden spell," said Simza.

Lavinia caught a glimpse in the gypsy girl's eyes of a great power or a bit of madness. She slurped a small mouthful of the tea.

"The Chovihano Besnik?" Lavinia shut her eyes and saw the Chovihano's brown eye and blue eye glinting in the sun. *Chovihano* — his Christian name or a title?

"A powerful Chovihano." Simza's tone changed from confidence to quiet reverence.

"Chovihano?" The word rolled off Lavinia's tongue. Her voice sounded a bit stronger.

"Our shaman. He speaks with spirits and the dreamer's soul. He travels to places we cannot imagine."

The girl's eyes sparkled eerily and Lavinia felt her stomach clench in alarm.

"It is time for you to have nourishment, but keep drinking your tea." Simza went to the small kitchen and busied herself with removing a plate from the cabinet and food from what Lavinia supposed was the larder. In no time, the girl stood before her and placed a tray on Lavinia's lap containing a plate with chunks of cold roasted chicken, tomatoes and rough brown bread spread with pale butter. "Please, drink all the tea. And eat. You have had a hard day." With her innocent heart-shaped face, the girl bore such a serious expression coupled with her ridiculous understatement that Lavinia burst out laughing.

The gypsy straightened, inhaling as her nostrils flared. "It was hard, no?" Simza said, her voice measured.

Lavinia sat very still, her laughter dying. Had she insulted this *lace romni*? Did the gypsy believe she ridiculed her sincere hospitality? Lavinia tried take a breath to calm herself, but the earlier part of the day stood bright in her mind: Saddani imprisoning her in his arms, the footman slapping her, gagging her, the blood. Her hands shook. She should say something. Make amends. Someone should be on her side.

"*H-hard* makes it sound easy." That was a start. Her voice had wobbled just a little. She took another breath. "Forgive me. I wasn't laughing at you. I think I may be a little hysterical. It was a horrendous day. I-I was kidnapped twice in less than two hours." Lavinia slopped the tea on her dress. She set the cup on the tray. If she were reasonable and continued the conversation in a pleasant way, perhaps the girl would not be affronted.

Simza shrugged, her eyes opaque pools reflecting nothing.

"I thought I-I might . . . be killed." A shudder quaked up Lavinia's arms into her chest. She bit into the dark bread, her body's need for food overriding the need for quiet recovery.

"He was a bad man."

Simza had summed up Saddani in one plain word. But what did she know about him?

"Yes, he was." *Was.* The word in Lavinia's mouth was as nourishing as the food.

*Was.*

The Chovihano had said, *We have not seen the last of him.* But Simza had said "was." The gypsy girl believed Saddani was dead. Lavinia could only hope the little *lace romni,* sister of the hidden spell, had more insight than her revered Chovihano.

# 14

*T*hat night Lavinia lay in the slim berth with the yellow drapes. The wagon's lurching and rolling had stopped around dusk when the gypsies made camp. It must be hours from sunset now. She couldn't sleep. The baby felt heavier, pressing on her insides no matter what position she tried. Each escape plan she laid out in her head unraveled at the end because of her pregnancy. She couldn't just simply run away in her condition.

But they hadn't covered much distance today, thank God. She would be able to walk at a slow pace to the road, which was close by. Then at dawn, she could catch a ride in one of the delivery wagons on the way to Bramley House. Earlier, Simza had told her to hold on, the ride would be rough until they stopped to make camp. Lavinia started counting right then—she got up to 100. Not so far, really.

She raised her head from the pillow, surprised at the effort it took. Inside the wagon she stared into the deep black of night, broken in fits and starts by the faint orange light of the campfire flickering through the curtains. Her limbs heavy with exhaustion, she listened to the soft whisper of Simza breathing.

If she reached the road and it was still dark, she could wait for a wagon to come by. Better than hurrying. Now would be the time to go. Lavinia pulled her dress over her shift, slipped on her shoes and wrapped the blanket around her shoulders. With each move she felt stronger and her eyes adjusted to the darkness inside the wagon. She stopped, listening hard. Simza kept the same rhythmic breathing. Lavinia steadied herself with her hand on the wall. Cringing at squeaks from the wooden planks, she made it to the door. Would the guard be there? She would make the excuse that she needed to relieve herself, that the chamber pot was full.

She pushed the latch down, locked, of course, but trying never hurt. Earlier this afternoon, she had pretended to be asleep when Simza locked it and placed the key somewhere nearby. The dim light from the window made it easier to make out the objects on the wall beside the door: a small woodcarving of a fox, a tin icon with a candle, a metal trivet with hooks on it.

She ran her fingers along the smooth wood of the carving, examined the metal trivet and the icon. The fat candle in front of the icon's saint toppled. With a swift motion, she caught it before it hit the floor and clutched it to her chest, slumping against the doorframe. *Angels in heaven,* that would surely have woken Simza. She held the candle over the shallow holder, and almost set it in place when she spotted an irregular shape at the base. So that's why the candle was so wobbly— the key made for an unstable foundation.

The lock opened with barely a click. She pocketed the key and stepped onto the tiny porch. By some miracle the guard wasn't there. The campfire burned bright in the dark, outlining the nearest trees in glowing amber. High-pitched squeals punctured the night at eerie intervals, and an owl's haunting cry came from behind the wagon.

Lavinia crept down the three steps and looked in both directions. No guard. The mud sucked at her shoes. She almost lost one, but pulled it from the gunk with effort, stumbling along. The dew-strewn grass wet her slippers, spreading its sweet smell as she hurried away from the light of the fire.

Behind the wagon she would find the road. As she walked farther from the fire, a cold dim glow kept the wagon ruts from vanishing into the darkness. She glanced at the sky. The full moon, a bright galleon sailing the heavens, just cleared the thick clouds racing alongside it. Counting slowly, she took her time and picked her way with care, stopping to rest whenever her heart beat too fast, which was probably more from fear than being winded.

Shadows from the tall trees plunged her into inky darkness and she took the uneven path one step at a time. Her foot caught on something hard. Lurching forward, hands fumbling for a hold, she cried out as a stiff grip on her arm pulled her upright.

She stared, trying to see if she recognized the man, but couldn't make out any features in the deep shadow that was his face. He neither moved nor spoke. She stood still in his grasp. The sound of her heartbeat pounded in her ears, louder and louder. Alone. No weapon. He pulled her closer. Did he have a knife? What would—

Cinnamon? Myrrh? Her skin tingled at his scent. She sank with relief. He had come for her at last. "Yasir?" She reached out, feeling for his face. His soft skin, his firm jaw. Her hand brushed his earring, his hair curling over his shoulder. "You are healed?"

"Do not leave here." Yasir's voice, hushed in the darkness.

Lavinia kept her hand on his cheek. "What do you mean? Your voice sounds strong. You must be well." He just looked at her. She took her hand away. "Please answer. You're scaring me. Yasir?" Her voice rose. "Why did you send me to Peter? Please talk to me. If you are well, why didn't you come for me sooner?" She buried her face in his chest. "Take me from here. Hurry. Before they find me."

He broke their embrace and held her further from him.

"What are you doing?" She stopped and stared, angling to the side. His eyes glowed golden in the cold moonlight, obscuring the rest of his face in darkness. She tried to focus, to see clearer, but his features blurred.

Yasir shook her. She blinked. The moonlight brightened and she stared at lusterless eyes, a wavy tattoo of three lines above them.

"Chovih—?" Her voice strangled his name.

Sitting huddled on her berth in the gypsy wagon, Lavinia tried to reason it out. She had no memory of coming back here. She shivered. The darkness in the shadow of the woods, absolute, like a darkness of the soul. The dull eyes, the wavy tattoo. Her feeling of panic grew and she pulled her nightdress down to her ankles in spite of the drops of sweat sliding onto her forehead. She blotted her face with her sleeve.

Was it a dream? She could almost feel the muddy ground under her feet, smell the dewy grass, see Yasir's golden eyes glowing like moons.

She pressed her foot against the floor, something solid. She needed that.

The grip of the Chovihano, his magic muddling her mind. Why hadn't she recognized him? She absently moved her foot, inching her toes across the floorboards. Why this confusing him with Yasir? Her foot found one of her shoes.

And the voice. Yasir's mellifluous voice at first. She was sure of it. She wriggled her toes into the slipper. It all felt so real. The dank smell of mud, the penetrating damp. The forlorn cry of the owl. Yasir's voice.

Could the Chovihano be doing Yasir's bidding? Was she supposed to be here, a prisoner with the gypsies? Or was the shaman manipulating her with his magic, using Yasir's image to sway her, to convince her the djinni was his ally?

The things she had said to the Chovihano. But it was no secret she didn't want to be here. She had given nothing away. Or had she? But the shaman hadn't heard her, unless he could inhabit her dreams. A sudden chill prickled up her spine, sending trails of burning cold shivering into her neck. Shifting her foot, she sat stock still, her body rigid.

Tingling sensations rose up her leg. She drew her brows together. The slipper felt wet.

She shook her foot, but couldn't loosen the shoe. In a frantic movement, she bent and yanked it off, holding it up to the glow from the window. The soaked leather glistened with dirt and bits of grass. A pebble stuck in the thick mud on the sole.

Lavinia squeezed her eyes closed at the bright light of late morning and let out a low moan. She squinted up at the girl who hovered nearby, arms crossed.

"Who are you?" Lavinia's voice grated so scratchy and hoarse she could barely make out what she said. The girl spoke. Her name? She stood in front of her but remained unreachable, existing in another dimension. She stared beyond the girl. The smell of pungent spices and an unidentifiable rich, earthy fragrance gave the brightly colored room an exotic feel at first glance, but the low ceiling and close walls revealed it to be small and cluttered. Lavinia stretched her arms, trying to loosen them. So stiff, one would've thought she'd been bound—

She sat up straight. A cry escaped her lips. She held her wrists in front of her, no bindings, no marks. She had been freed. It was her first morning in the gypsy camp. Spreading her fingers, she frowned. Her mouth moved silently as she stared at her bare finger.

"My ruby ring!" Lavinia couldn't swallow. "My ring." She jerked her head towards the gypsy girl, eyes flaring. Her name, her name—Simza, yes.

The girl turned away.

"Where is my ring?" Lavinia's voice shook. "Look at me, child."

Simza turned towards her, lips pressed tight.

Lavinia swung her legs over the edge of the bed. "It wouldn't just fall off." She jumped up and seized the girl's arm. "What have you and your—your—" *The man from . . . yesterday? . . . his knowing expression, his finger touching her ring . . . I am Chovihano—*"Ch–Chovihano done?"

Simza let out a squeal as Lavinia's nails pinched into her flesh.

"What have you done with it? Give it to me!"

Simza's voice sounded small, wounded. "No. No. I have not taken your ring, missy." She looked up at Lavinia, biting her lip, her dark eyes huge. "I did not take your ring." Her dusky skin reddened like a bronze sunset.

Lavinia pulled Simza close. "I had it when the Chovihano helped me from the carriage. He stared at it. He held my hands, pressed the ruby with his finger. And now it's gone." She put her face to the girl's and said in a low, deliberate tone. "You *know* something . . ." Her eyes narrowed.

Simza pulled away. "You—you cannot call the djinni," she blurted. "The Chovihano . . ."

Lavinia raised her eyebrows.

"The Chovihano says . . . absolutely not." Simza blinked and ducked her head as if avoiding a blow.

"W–why?" Lavinia gripped Simza's arm tighter. Perhaps her ring had become stronger since she escaped Rakhshan's palace. The Chovihano must have sensed that. She studied Simza's eyes, the gypsy girl's expression changing with each of Lavinia's thoughts. At the last one, Simza turned away.

Lavinia shook her. "What? What don't you want me to know?" Her hold slackened and she clapped her hand to her mouth. "God in heaven. Is Yasir . . . dying? D-dead?" She stood straight, resigned to the worst. "Tell me."

Simza pressed her lips together for a moment. "I do not question the Chovihano. What you have seen of the Chovihano, what you have seen of his powers, is like glimpsing only the tail of one of our horses as it vanishes into the forest."

She bit her lip, her face shadowed. "You do not want to chase the stallion into the dark forest."

# 15

*L*avinia had tried to mark her days in the quaint little house on wheels, even though they were as hard to sort as the shadows dappling the roads they traveled. The moon had gone from a thin curl of fingernail to less than half full, and she had counted ten days. They were a good distance from Bramley House.

The wagon jerked to a stop, almost toppling Lavinia, her center of balance skewed by her growing belly. She must be around four and a half months along. Last night Simza had told her the big camp was nearby. Now they were there, wherever that was.

So far the gypsies had taken passable care of her, but now that she had arrived, she worried their true colors might show.

She twisted a strand of her hair as fragments of the events in her own garden played in her mind, always ending with golden eyes staring from the Chovihano's shadowed sockets taking the place of the gypsy king's one blue and one brown eye. What did he know of Yasir? Was he friend or enemy? She looked at the patterned carpet. Friend or enemy? The words haunted her. It was harder to tell than she would have ever imagined. The answer was a matter of life and death.

Lavinia scowled, murmuring under her breath. "My ring. Yasir's ring. You conniving thieves." Each time she was alone in the wagon, she searched, hoping that the occasional guilty droop in Simza's demeanor meant it had been hidden there.

"Brigands. You stole me. You stole my ring," she mumbled, glancing at Simza who was busy fitting a top on her sewing basket. She marveled at how the girl stuck by her side almost every waking moment. She hadn't been aware of how carefully she was watched until she started her quest for the ring. But when night had fallen, after a day of tromping to the woods on the many stops they made for her to relieve herself—in consideration of her pregnancy—nothing mattered save tumbling into her berth, ring forgotten, anxious for the cool of the pillow, the numbing refuge of sleep.

"*Rawnee*, we are there. Come." Simza smiled broadly and caught her by the hand, tugging her towards the door of the gypsy wagon. Lavinia had said she may call her by her Christian name, but Simza insisted on addressing her as *Rawnee*, that *Rawnee* meant great lady.

Lavinia dragged behind, resisting the girl's enthusiasm. She hadn't dared peek out the window. What was waiting there? A field of pocked mud littered with dirty, sagging tents? Fires with cooking pots, black smoke and ashes tainting the air? Half-naked children playing in trash?

Simza opened the door. "*Rawnee*, please to step outside."

Lavinia let Simza pull her out onto the small ornamental porch. She held onto the railing and gawked at the scene before her.

Blue, yellow and orange domed tents, like fanciful mushrooms, sat scattered in a small sunlit meadow lush with green. Enormous trees surrounded the clearing, their chartreuse leaves rustling in a breeze fragrant with sweet spring grasses. Near a tent with yellow canvas rolled up to its domed top, a boy, hair braided down his back, combed the long mane of the white horse that had pulled the wagon. The fairy-tale creature stamped its hooves, leg feathers like dandelion fluff, and nickered to the black horse tethered nearby like a shadow.

Simza waved to a group of women sorting through a mound of herbs, their tresses long and dark as a starless night. She turned to Lavinia. "Welcome to our home."

*Home.* The word struck her like a slap.

Where was her real home? She had come from Rakhshan's—somehow. She was only at Bramley House for one day, two days? And Bramley House wasn't safe. And the urn—Yasir's prison, but somehow his refuge as well.

Lavinia glanced at her gold wedding band. They hadn't stolen *it*, she fumed, only the djinni's ring. She ran her finger over each stone inset in precise order: diamond, emerald, amethyst, ruby, epidote, sapphire and turquoise, the first letter of the name of each stone spelling *dearest*.

Dear Peter. He had been so happy to have an heir on the way. Lavinia exhaled a sniff, the harrumph of a smothered laugh. Funny if it weren't so, so poignant. An heir that was a djinni's spawn.

She managed a weak smile and gazed out at the gypsy camp. Like a May Fair, her favorite festival when she was a child. How could such a place hold evil? But the figure of the Chovihano Besnik loomed in her mind, his enigmatic eyes, his hidden magic.

The moon in the dark sky had been full twice. Two months with the gypsies and not a word from Yasir, or Peter. Lavinia's stomach had grown and she figured she was nearing seven months. She had eavesdropped on conversations, on gossip, and searched for her ring anytime she wasn't watched, but had found neither clues nor the ring. Her escape plans had dwindled as her belly grew. She placed her hand there. Easier to find now. Would she have the baby with no one she loved by her side?

The morning started sunny and cool. Lavinia paused at her embroidery, rearranged her legs on the folded blanket, and gazed at the sky, the trees, the gypsy camp. A normal day. She received no portents, neither good nor evil, as she sat by the fire with Simza, shaded by the gypsy girl's orange tent.

During the first weeks she had lived with the gypsies, Lavinia had watched them construct a domed tent like Simza's near the edge of the camp. Men cut long flexible willow branches, bent them into a "u" shape and stuck them into the ground. They wove smaller limbs around the main branches forming a strong dome higher than a grown man. The next day, after the sun dried the heavy dew, they spread a huge canvas on the ground and pulled it over the frame, weighting it on the bottom with stones and stout logs. Such an odd abode, but livable. She might even call it, on occasion, cozy, especially with Simza at her beck and call.

In the branches of the nearest oak tree, a flock of goldfinches twittered teLLIT-teLLIT-teLLIT, their faces a mask of blood red. A day that any other time would be filled with happiness, free from worries and fears, but now . . . Lavinia tried to exist only minute to minute.

She thrust her needle into the front of the yellow blouse Simza had given her to embroider, pulled the blue thread through and created the first of a series of detached chain stitches that would become a cluster of bluebells. Now seemed the right time to ask.

Before, each time she had started to put the question, something happened to stop her: Simza had spilled hot tea. A gypsy came from nowhere to call Simza to an urgent task. The Chovihano arrived with a request. It was clear they didn't want her to ask. Didn't want to answer.

Lavinia took a breath. "What . . . how . . . do you know about him? The djinni."

Simza continued searching through the basket of beads on her lap, head down, the tiny glass spheres clicking together, snick, snick, as she moved her fingers through them. Lavinia watched her for awhile, listening to the soft ticks, the rhythm like a clock gone awry.

Ignoring her unanswered question, Lavinia said, "Simza, what do you think of my stitches? Are they as good as your example?" She held up the blouse. The girl raised her head, face somber with her expression for assessing work. She took the blouse and studied the embroidery.

Lavinia pointed to the end of her last stitch. "Oh, and . . ."

Simza glanced up from the stitches and waited. Lavinia took Simza's hand in hers. "What do you know about the djinni?" Simza narrowed her eyes, as if Lavinia had caught her doing something wrong. The girl looked away.

"Simza, please . . . tell me something." The gypsy adjusted her cape, the garish orange calico lining clashing with the bright green of the outer wool. Lavinia glanced at her own rough linen skirt, so different from the fine gowns of silk and satin in fashionable hues that filled her wardrobe at Bramley House.

She squeezed the girl's limp hand in hers. "You know I carry the djinni's child. You must know so much more. Please . . ." She pulled Simza's hand to her rounded stomach. "Please, for the sake of the child, to set his mother at ease, tell me what you know."

Simza stared at the string of yellow beads on her lap. "The Chovihano came to me and bid me prepare for a guest." She pulled her hand away, picked up the beads and ran them through her fingers like a rosary. "The night before, he sent a messenger who led me to one of our fire gatherings." She looked up and met Lavinia's eyes. "In the fire I saw you, *Rawnee*. I saw the djinni who lives in the urn, and a dark woman shining blue. You looked frightened. The Chovihano let me hear only some of the djinni's message. These words. 'Life or death' and 'child.' "

Lavinia breathed, deep and slow. A vision. Yasir. Mehadeh. Were they alive?

Visions. Visions of angels. Visions of the departed. Her face tightened. Perhaps Yasir was speaking from the hereafter. That might be the only way to reach him now. The gypsy camp, the green meadow, the bright tents fuzzed in the haze of her tears.

*Life or death? Child?* She could cobble them into a semblance of sense, but she wanted more than four words. "But why? Did Yasir say why I'm here?"

Simza shrugged her shoulders, her eyebrows arching in tandem. "To keep you safe? I only heard the words that I told you." She arranged the yellow necklace in a basket that fit into her palm, a nest of tiny winking eggs, and pressed the lid on top.

"Is the djinni . . .?" Lavinia's voice caught. "Is he . . ." She burst into tears.

Simza patted her hand. "He fares fair."

"Oh. Oh." This pregnancy had made her into a weakling who cowered in fear, who cried at any sad thought. Lavinia crumpled the blouse in her lap and sat for a moment, struggling to control herself. "I thought . . . I feared."

"Yes, yes, my *Rawnee*. I know, I know."

Lavinia touched the blouse to her face, blotting her tears. She stopped and clapped her hand over her mouth. Why did it take her so long to put things together?

"*Rawnee*. Are you sick in your stomach?" Simza touched Lavinia's shoulder.

Lavinia shook her head. No. Yes. No.

"What? What do you need?" Simza pulled her closer.

"He's not healed is he?" Lavinia sat up. The blouse slid onto the dirt. " 'Fares fair' isn't healed. That wound is a curse from Rakh—" Lavinia peered around the camp. "A curse."

"My *Rawnee*, he is in good hands."

Lavinia cupped her elbows, hugging her arms close to her chest. They always said, *in good hands*. They said it when they were unsure what would happen. They said it to reassure themselves as well as the loved ones. So Yasir was not yet healed. His power not fully restored. He couldn't rescue her if he were still suffering from Rakhshan's wound. And Peter—he wouldn't be able to follow the trail made by the wagon if it had been obliterated by the Chovihano.

She glanced round the camp, the gaudy tents serene under the great trees. The deep forest in its magnificence almost nullifying the strangeness of these people and their arcane ways, just as a sunny day and bright blue sky could make a person forget, for a moment, about the tragedy their life had become. The tents, the gypsies, the horses, the whole of this place could be cloaked by magic, unseen by those passing by. A pall of cold enveloped her. She might be with the gypsies for a long, long time.

Simza picked up a stick and fiddled with the fire. Lavinia caught her staring, her gaze shrewd. Simza looked away.

"What else do you know?" Lavinia focused her gaze on the girl. "Why did they bring me here?"

"The large man with the hooked nose—"

"Mr. S—" Lavinia stopped. Saying his name could bring the one he worked for.

"Saddani. It is not his real name. So we can speak it." The girl slanted towards her, her voice hushed. "He is of the Dark Magician, the one whose name you must not say."

Lavinia felt the blood drain from her face. "That Dark Magician's henchman. He died in front of me."

Simza's eyes widened.

"I was bound in a carriage when the Chovihano cut Saddani's throat." Lavinia bent her head to her lap and fiddled with the folds of her skirt, trying to stop the repeating image of Saddani's blood spurting on the window, the plop, plop, plop sound as innocent as raindrops.

"Oh, *Rawnee,* and you carrying a little one." Simza placed her hand on Lavinia's arm as if she could remove the image from Lavinia's brain.

"Saddani put a curse on the pistol. My husband shot Yasir with it. Somehow Saddani found a way to meet with Peter. But I'm sure . . ." Drawing her brows together, Lavinia hesitated, "I-I don't think Peter had any idea about Saddani being connected to Rakhshan. My husband knows nothing of the djinni or any of this. He doesn't even know where I-I am." She dug her nails into her palms, trying to keep her frustration at the gypsies, at her situation, from consuming her.

A high-pitched screech rent the air and Lavinia jerked in that direction. A little girl ran from behind the tent, hands in the air, followed by a pack of children running pell mell after her, dust trailing behind. "*Rawnee,* do not be alarmed. They are just playing." Simza bent to the ground, her hair a length of shiny silk serpentine on the packed earth. From the basket beside her, she lifted a strand of blue beads.

Lavinia straightened the blouse in her lap and removed the needle, tucking it into the cloth for another stitch on her bluebells. "I don't understand why Peter gave Saddani permission to meet with him. He only sees people that are recommended by his associates."

"Oh, this Saddani was well-disguised." Simza coiled the beads in her hands. "No ordinary human knew him as anything but a respectable foreigner. A rich foreigner. But *we* knew of him, this tall, dark evil-doer." The unease in Simza's eyes glistened like a rippling current through a placid stream, mirroring Lavinia's own alarm.

"The Dark Magician believes the djinni is dying." Simza sat back. Lavinia clutched the gypsy girl's arm.

"He fares well though—the djinni? Is he better? Is he worse? I need to know."

"I cannot tell you more. If the Dark One or anyone who is his henchman finds you here, he will see into you. He must see the turmoil, the doubt, the fear that the djinni is dying."

Lavinia let go Simza's arm. She shut her eyes. At least Yasir was alive, for now. Or was Simza toying with her?

"My *Rawnee*, my *Rawnee*." The girl's voice sounded peculiar, tinged with—some urgent need? Lavinia opened her eyes. Simza held out the strand of blue beads that had been curled in her palm. "The Chovihano wants you to wear these. Do not ever take them off."

"But—"

Simza held up her other hand, her dark eyes grim. "You must let me finish. I do the Chovihano's work now." She paused, mumbling in her language. "My *Rawnee*, you must bow your head." Lavinia obeyed. She didn't want anything from the Chovihano, especially something she had to wear all the time, but this was also from Simza. The cool glass of the beads ringed the back of her neck, sending a frisson of dizziness through her head. She stared at her lap. A blue light played over her hands while Simza chanted murky words in her serious voice. Was this a spell? She closed her eyes, asking Yasir to protect her.

"My *Rawnee*, this should keep you safe."

The blue light vanished along with her dizziness. Lavinia looked up. Simza's eyes sparkled. Little dots of sweat clustered on her forehead. Had the gypsy been afraid to do this, or had casting the spell been hard work? At least, if she were careful, she could remove the necklace when she slept.

Simza looked expectantly at her. Did she want a compliment?

Lavinia ran her fingers over the beads, following the strand to the middle of her chest. She paused at the smooth silver cylinder, took a breath and clasped it. A jitter flashed through her fingers. She hadn't known this was there. She'd never seen one on any of the countless necklaces Simza had made in front of her.

"You made this?"

"I strung the beads." Simza indicated the cylinder. "The Chovihano crafted the silver talisman. Strong magic inside." Lavinia let it drop from her fingers and fall to her chest.

Simza looked at the necklace with an air of satisfaction. "I also contributed, for my meager magic and work will protect you as well."

So that was their explanation. But was it true? If it was to protect her, how could she take it off at night? *Protect.* The word could be deceiving. It could mean preventing her escape from the gypsies' clutches, or keeping her from the Dark Magician, or even Yasir. Lavinia clasped her hands tight in her lap as her thoughts tangled in a flurry of confusion. She would play along. For now. "Thank—"

Simza held up her hand. *"Rawnee.* It is to shield you from the Dark Magic. No thanking for this. Just wear it as I said. We shall not speak of it again." She spread her fingers wide and rolled her shoulders as though an exaggerated shrug could rid her of any associations with the evil she just mentioned.

"I must attend to another task for the Chovihano. To be completed before night falls." Simza pulled a cloth bag from the basket and emptied it onto her lap. Coal-black beads rolled out. It looked as though the gypsy's orange skirt had been pocked with holes.

Simza inserted black thread through the eye of a needle, the sharp point shining in a ray of sunlight, and scooped up one of the beads. She pushed the needle through the small hole drilled into the bead. "The Chovihano wanted me to warn you." She pulled the black thread through. "Do not try to contact your husband, for that is how the Dark Magician last found you." Simza looked up. "Do you trust him?"

Lavinia straightened from retrieving the blouse she had dropped. "The Dark Magician? You must be—"

"Your husband." Simza leveled her gaze straight at her.

Lavinia drew back as if struck. "P-Peter? You think he . . . he betrayed me?" She tried to rise from the blanket but her legs were as limp as the thread in Simza's needle. "To the Dark One? Why that is mad."

Simza looked her in the eye. "It is something you should think hard about. Consider the possibilities."

Lavinia drew away and shook her head, running Peter's exploits through her mind: his odd behavior when he returned from Egypt, his gift of the urn, his beating her almost to death—all because he'd opened the urn in Egypt, had been Yasir's master. But Yasir had seen Peter's portrait of her, his Thalia, and spell-cast Peter to give her the urn and forget he was master first. And Yasir's spells had further deleterious effects on Peter.

Now Peter knew she was expecting. Thought the child was his. Was thrilled to have an heir. He had been so tender.

But he had met with Saddani. At least that's what Saddani told her. And if Peter knew Saddani, was he fooled by his charming persona or had he been ensorcelled to do Saddani's bidding? Was he aware Saddani was working for Rakhshan? If that, then did Peter know Yasir was a djinni? When she last saw him, had Peter feigned forgetting he found her and Yasir in the garden? Had he feigned forgetting he shot Yasir? Her husband wanted the baby, but if he knew the child was Yasir's . . . Her breath came hard with the awful possibility. Could Peter and Saddani have planned her kidnapping?

When Peter confronted her with Yasir in the garden so long ago, he thought Yasir was a filthy gypsy. Her husband could have gone through that charade to throw them off, but wouldn't she have somehow known he was on to them?

She put her hand to her head. Saddani could have been lying about meeting with her husband. Most likely wasn't lying. He said he put a curse on the pistol. And Peter . . . She exhaled long and slow. Peter had shot Yasir, and the bullet was killing the djinni.

Simza sputtered. "I am sorry, but you must understand." The girl stretched one leg in front of her, her hands quavering, but she managed to pick up her work and pass the needle through another bead. "If the Dark Magician finds you again, here in our camp—"

Simza winced and pulled the needle out of her finger. A droplet of blood welled on her fingertip. She stuck it in her mouth, her expression somber.

"Now that the Dark One believes the djinni is no threat, he wants only your baby. Not you. You see?"

# 16

"My baby?" Lavinia slanted away from Simza and stared at the crackling fire, the folded blanket under her settling as her weight shifted. She hadn't put the events, the snippets of warnings, together in that way. They were oblique and vague, arcane puzzles making her mind whirl. Where was Yasir? Mehadeh? What did Peter know? These and a hundred other questions kept her awake at night, staring at the ceiling, searching the shadows for answers.

But to hear Simza say the words. Say that Rakhshan was after her baby only. She felt as though she were sinking. Sinking. Neither Peter nor Yasir could save her. She was alone, and the Dark Magician was after the one thing, the most precious thing, she had left from Yasir.

She heard her voice as if it were someone else's, high-pitched in disbelief. "But the Chovihano can keep the Dark Magician away? Keep him from stealing Yasir's baby?"

"My *Rawnee*." Simza reached out and pulled Lavinia's blue beads towards her, careful not to touch the charm. "This," she looked at the talisman, "is our promise to you."

A promise. Lavinia had heard promises, from Peter, from Yasir. Perhaps the gypsies were sealing an agreement with the Dark Magician at this very moment. He would pay well, and from what she had heard about gypsies . . .

She turned away from Simza's dark eyes, raising her gaze to the sky. She would look upon the tranquil blue heavens, the puffy white clouds. The same as she saw from Bramley House when she was safe, before Peter had returned from Egypt with the urn. Before she unleashed all of this when she opened the vessel.

But the day had turned cloudy.

A gust of wind whorled Lavinia's hair in front of her like black flames. The wind stoked the smoldering campfire, the embers winking eyes of Lilliputian creatures. Clouds of dust foamed from the narrow road leading to the camp as giant raindrops splashed onto the domed tents and splattered the ground with dull thuds.

Squinting from the dust, Lavinia snatched up the embroidery, the blanket, and helped Simza gather her baskets of beads and sewing supplies. Together they dashed for the tent, looking behind to find the source of the eerie hum that seemed to emanate from both ground and sky. The raindrops fell faster and closer together. Inside the tent, Lavinia gripped the canvas flap to keep it from shaking in the wind, and peered from the doorway at the blue-black clouds that churned in the darkening heavens.

She sniffed the fresh scent of rain, crisp in the heavy air, and stood behind the flap, brushing her arms as a sharp tingle vibrated over her skin. Capillaries of white lightning sparked through the towering black clouds, crackling like kindling in a fire. A bright flash. Lavinia glanced up just as the top of a tall pine tree exploded with a deafening blast. She jumped backwards into Simza.

Lavinia squinted into the blinding light. Branches fragmented into pieces, trailing fiery trajectories. Flames blazed scarlet and tangerine. With the thrumming drone of a thousand cicadas, water poured from the sky, and the orange flames vanished into the gray curtain of rain. Blasts of thunder boomed from all directions.

Simza secured the tent flap. The raindrops and wind drummed on the canvas as fierce as the onslaught of a battle. Unrelenting. Terrifying.

"Do not touch the cloth of the tent while it rains," Simza yelled over the force of the storm, pointing at the canvas vibrating from the assault. "It will leak." A portion of the tent wall bunched outwards then fell back in a billow of wind. The gypsy lit an oil lamp in the gloom, set it on a wooden table and, muttering in her language, retreated to her bed where she pulled the covers up to her chin. The sour smell of wet earth and leaves permeated the cool damp that rose from carpets covering the dirt floor.

Under her blankets, Simza slept soundly as if the day were sunny and calm. What could be wrong with her? This wasn't like the energetic girl Lavinia had come to know. If Simza couldn't stay awake, then she would. *Someone* had to keep watch. She pulled her shawl tight around her shoulders, sat on the thick rug and rested against the wooden chest that held her clothes. Simza had made a fuss over obtaining Lavinia her own trunk, but Lavinia had seen the attention the girl spent on keeping her gypsy possessions separate. *Gadjes* and gypsies rarely mixed.

The rain hammered down, a monosyllabic symphony punctuated with the roar of thunder. Each rush of wind died in eerie whistles, only to come alive again. At a loud thud, Lavinia glanced up to see one of the supports vibrate. Would the tent collapse, leaving them to the elements?

How long would Simza sleep? It had been awhile. A lonely while. The noise and bustle of the gypsy camp served as company, distancing her worries, but the storm kept everyone huddled in their tents. Kept them isolated. A little while longer and she would check on Simza. Perhaps wake her for a nice hot cup of tea.

Lavinia drew her arms tighter around her legs, slipped her shawl over her head and pressed her back against the solid trunk. Warmth wrapped her like a cocoon, muffling the chaos outside into one continuous drone. Her fears dulled and streamed away, dissolving in the storm, her eyelids heavy with their release.

The abrupt thought that she could escape right now made her sit up straight. No one would be outside to see her slip from the tent. But she didn't know where to go, and she had no idea how far it was to the main road from the camp. It wasn't for lack of trying: every time she walked outside the camp's perimeter, eyeing those who left, Simza or another of the gypsies would find her and lead her back. Besides, she would be soaked in this downpour. If she weren't around five months along she wouldn't hesitate, but if she got a chill, the baby might suffer. She wouldn't risk Yasir's child.

An earsplitting crash of thunder rattled the tent. It grew darker. The oil lamp flickered on the table, yet the air inside hung still and heavy. She cocked her head, listening to the din of rain and wind, and looked for a draft. There, at the front, by the tightly closed flap, something moving in the shadows.

She opened her mouth to call Simza, but froze as the form expanded, taller and broader. She tried to scream, but her voice curled deep inside, as if it were afraid as well. The blurred form detached from the shadows and glided towards her, contours defining as it came closer. In the space of a breath, the shape brightened in a sparkling golden haze, diminishing the amber flame of the oil lamp. She held her breath, a light mist flowed around the figure, so like the mist from the urn.

Lavinia stood on her knees. The rain slowed. A lambent silence followed, a suspension of time, like the seconds after a glass vase slips from one's hands, before it shatters on the marble floor.

"Yasir." Her voice was a whisper as she rose from the carpet.

He stood in front of her, healthy and whole, golden eyes shining with tenderness. The drifting haze set off the radiant glow that surrounded him. He had appeared just after she received her necklace from Simza. A good omen.

"Lavinia, come to me." Yasir's voice sounded strong. He held out his hand.

"Take me away from here." She made to clasp his hand, but her fingers passed through his flesh as though nothing were there. "Yasir, don't go. Save your child." His figure became solid. She fell into his warm embrace. "Take us away now." She looked up.

His face darkened, his features obscured. The golden mist vanished into dark shadows. An amorphous shape loomed in front of her, transforming before her eyes. "Yasir, stop this nonsense. Take me away." She felt the hair lift on her neck, stand straight on her arms. *Angels in heaven*—this was happening again. Just as it had the night when she escaped Simza's wagon. How could she be fooled once more by an illusion of Yasir? Hope was truly her nemesis.

She stood stuck in place, yet she knew the eyes that would stare at her next would be one blue and one brown with a wavy green tattoo centered above, same as before. She crossed her arms over her chest, irritated with herself. What did the Chovihano want this time?

A draft guttered the oil lamp, throwing light on the figure. Lavinia unfolded her arms and moved back. "No." Her voice compressed into a thick whisper of dread.

Saddani stood before her, looking the same as he had in her garden. A gust of rain pummeled the tent. She kept her focus on the nightmarish figure. In a movement so sudden as to be barely detectable, Saddani seized her by the arms. She screamed. He clamped his hand over her mouth. She struggled and sank her teeth into his flesh, gagging at the slimy mush. Saddani's hold loosened, the now pulpy mess of his figure dissolving into wisps of fog. She spat and scrambled backwards, watching his body fade into the shadows, vanishing into nothingness.

"Simza!" Lavinia shrieked. She ran to the gypsy's bed, ripping the covers away.

Empty.

"No." Why would the girl leave her? "Simza." Had Saddani done something to the gypsy? Fingering her blue beads—*a talisman of protection*—Lavinia stretched them in front of her as she frantically searched the strand. Her thoughts scrambled, her body rigid. *Lord in heaven,* the silver talisman was gone.

She stood there holding her beads, the relentless rain beating on the deserted tent. How could her talisman just vanish? Right after Saddani? In spite of her panic, her mind worked: the way Saddani's eyes met hers just before the shadows took him. He had held out his palm—a gleam of silver. Reaching for her? No. *Showing her.*

A brush of air at her back. Her muscles stiffened, but she forced herself to turn. Nothing there, thank God. The rain shrank to a patter and the tent darkened as the wind picked up again. A crash of thunder made her jump. She would leave, find shelter with the nearest neighbor. Almost to the tent flap, she stopped, her feet rooted to the carpet. Between her and the door, swift shadows gathered, a darker area billowed outward, its features growing more distinct by the second. A light shape stood out. A saffron turban with a glittering emerald aigrette, a tall broad figure. One more powerful than Saddani. The one who had imprisoned her.

*No. Not here.*

He couldn't have come for her. She held the hard curve of her belly and backed away. Her breath came shallow. She fingered her beads, again searching for her talisman. But Saddani had flaunted his prize, showing her that he had stolen her one defense against his master.

The tent flap burst open.

*"Gadje Gadjensa, Rom Romensa,"* bellowed a deep voice. In a whoosh of driven rain, the Chovihano Besnik strode in, his eyes ferocious. *"Gadje Gadjensa, Rom Romensa, Gadje Gadjensa, Rom Romensa."* The shaman's chant filled the tent. His spell spun into her, each syllable expanding as if her insides were a vast cavern. She longed to go to him, but Rakhshan stood between them, his glimmering eyes focused on her. He opened his mouth and countered the gypsy shaman with his own words.

Like a parasite, Rakhshan's incantation wove into the Chovihano's chant, dimming the radiance inside her. She put her hand to her chest, guarding the magic of the gypsy's spell, and cried out as the shaman staggered, slurring his words. He reeled backwards.

Lavinia bent at the waist, stunned, as the Chovihano's power drained from her. *My God,* would Rakhshan win? A peal of thunder drowned out what was left of the gypsy's chant.

The Dark Magician rushed at the shaman, unfastened his purple cloak and unfurled it over the gypsy. The Chovihano fought for escape.

The heavy silk heaved and bucked with his rapid parries. Straining to see the glimmer of the gypsy's talismans and charms, to see his eyes, Lavinia saw only the sheen of purple.

*No! Not the Chovihano.*

In a blur, a hand escaped from a gap in a fold of the cloak, and a spray of white grains rained on Rakhshan, sprinkling the carpets with the spatter of fine sand. *Salt. Salt to restrain the devil. Salt to repel evil.*

With a keening shriek, Rakhshan waved his arm. The silk of his cloak rippled, stiffening and shrinking around the gypsy shaman, keeping him prisoner as effectively as iron bars. If Rakhshan weren't between her and the tent flap, she could slip out into the storm, get help somehow. The Dark Magician stared at her. He knew what she was thinking.

A roar of thunder shook the very ground. Rakhshan took a step in her direction. With every footfall he grew taller and broader. She tried to rip her gaze from his, but her foot lifted and set down in front of her. Her other foot followed.

Head held high in a victory stance, Rakhshan opened his arms to welcome her.

*Angels in heaven,* she would walk right into his embrace. Lavinia clasped her hands into fists, determined to back away, but shifted forward instead.

A flash off to her side. Lightning? With the distraction, she managed to halt, but couldn't release her eyes from the magician's intense stare. The wind howled outside, an eerie chorus of moans.

"*Gadje Gadjensa, Rom Romensa.*" A thin, high voice full of determination. Simza rushed in, looking from side to side. As she chanted, she came up behind Lavinia. The purple cloak covering the Chovihano twitched, seeming to soften. Lavinia's gaze unlocked from the magician's. She found her voice—"*Gadje Gadjensa, Rom Romensa*"—and chanted with Simza. Perhaps together they could save the shaman.

Of a sudden, the Chovihano's deep bass joined their chant. With a grunt, he threw off the cape, wadded it into a ball and flung it on the floor. Lavinia clasped Simza's hand as they backed away from Rakhshan. The Chovihano's chant expanded and they followed suit, their voices growing stronger with the increasing effect.

The tent lit up inside, then fell into shadow. A crack of thunder shook the structure and, in the accompanying lightning flash, Rakhshan made straight for Lavinia. She braced to face him, keeping Simza's hand in hers. He would not have Yasir's child. The Chovihano slipped in front of them and flung a handful of salt at the Dark Magician.

Did Rakhshan's hold on her lessen? Another spray of salt and the shaman herded him towards the door. Rakhshan's face fragmented at the edges. He turned to her, his lips ragged bits of flesh and shadow. He opened his mouth.

"I will have the child." His voice, commanding, mesmerizing, pulled her to him, as it had at his palace. Her feet inched forward, but with effort she managed to stand her ground, holding her hands over her belly, protecting Yasir's child. The Chovihano threw more salt. Rakhshan's face crumpled. His mouth, a tattered, bloody hole, stretched into a banshee wail.

Lavinia gaped in horror as the barbarous sound passed through her, a power unmistakable, a power that if not lessened by the Chovihano could have borne her away. Or worse. Even now as the yowl bore into her, she feared that the sound might harm her child.

A vehement Roma curse made Rakhshan pull his gaze away. Lavinia clasped her arms at her waist as the Chovihano forced the ruined phantom from the tent. The downpour abated. Water dripped and pulsed, soft on the canvas. The sweet smell of freshly washed leaves and grass wafted through the opened tent flap. Simza put her arms around Lavinia.

"*Rawnee*, come with me." The girl held her hands inches away and ran them above Lavinia's body as though she were scrubbing her clean. The numbing chill left her. Faint booms of thunder sounded in the distance.

"Yasir. H–he was here. Then the Dark One . . ." Lavinia swayed on her feet.

Simza placed her finger over Lavinia's lips. "Shhhh. We know. We know. Do not speak his name." She edged closer. "The lightning striking the tree by our tent. The Chovihano said that was the Dark One making his path to us."

Lavinia stared and shook her head, until she finally said, "And S-Saddani?"

Simza took her by the shoulders. *"Rawnee,* he is gone, for now. The best anyone could do." Lavinia nodded, but the girl's words just circled inside her head.

Lavinia eyed Simza. "Where were you? Saddani stole my talisman. Why didn't the talisman keep him away?" Lavinia heard her voice shrill. "Will nothing stop—"

"—My *Rawnee,* I was protecting you by fetching the Chovihano." Simza put her hands on her hips. "He readied himself for the fight. I stayed behind to finish his warding spell, one that kept Saddani from returning and weakened the Dark One. Then I came here."

The baby kicked. Lavinia sank onto her bed, her limbs hollow.

"Not here." Simza pulled Lavinia to her feet, eyeing the purple silk cloak puddled on the carpet. "We will not stay here until the Chovihano says it is safe."

# 17

Simza slipped into the Chovihano's tent and sat in front of the shaman. Hands trembling, she placed the basket before him and smoothed her skirts. The moon had waxed and waned once since the Dark Magician appeared. Rawnee was still in danger and bigger with child. Just today she mentioned she was eight months along.

Simza looked up at the Chovihano. He stepped back a few paces, his eyes locking with hers. At the slight agitation inside her head, she sat straight, opening her mind.

He nodded. They had been preparing. It was time.

Simza rose to her knees and whisked the lid from the basket. The contents shimmered in the sunlight, undulating like flowing water, the nebulous form solidifying into a triangular head followed by a thick, sinuous body. Flicking its red forked tongue, the adder emerged from the basket.

She took a breath. They had practiced these moves, but Naga was a moody creature. Just yesterday he had struck at her. Simza held the basket lid in front of her body like a shield, rippling her other arm above it, mimicking the serpent's sinuous movements. As in a dance, the snake followed her moves, withdrawing into the basket as she lowered her arm, the rich brown markings on his ochre scales patterned like the zigzagged straw weave. Simza fitted the lid shut.

She pulled a glass vial from her skirt pocket and laid it beside the basket. Inside, the venom shone clear like water. The shaman scooped up the vial in a blue handkerchief.

"Naga is well."

Simza nodded.

"You will let him rest?" The Chovihano eyed the basket.

"Naga will be fed, then sleep for some days. It is his way," said Simza.

"This." He indicated the glass vial. "This will enable what the djinni wants." The shaman fingered the silver spiral talisman at his neck. "Venom from Naga. At midnight by light of the awakening moon."

Simza glanced at the basket and nodded. She gazed at the ground. "This . . . This is very strong. It c-can," she raised her head, "kill." Simza's voice caught. "I like her. *Rawnee* is so sad, so alone—"

"Better than dead." The Chovihano secured the vial in a pouch by his waist.

Simza clasped her hands in her lap, staring up at him. "It will work as the djinni wishes?" Would she enter her tent in a few days and find *Rawnee* in bed, her pale skin gray, her lips blue, her soul gone to the place only the Chovihano had glimpsed?

"Three drops and a spell and your *Rawnee* will be safe." He stared down at her, his mismatched blue eye and brown eye shining. "But can you do this? It will be hard on you. This will be your first time and it will come so soon."

Simza swallowed and held her chin high. "I am ready."

The baby kicked. Was he afraid she might forget his presence? Lavinia laughed to herself as she ran her hand over the bulge of her stomach. As she told Simza today, she was near to eight months. The beginning of her pregnancy had been obscured, but, even though this was her first, she now had a feel for its progress. Her mind spun from all that had happened in the intervening time.

Simza told her never to think of what had occurred in the tent on that stormy day—that her thoughts could bring the unspeakable presence back—and saw that Lavinia took potions to keep her mind clear and strengthen her for the baby. A few days later, Simza gave her a pouch of orange and green paisley Calicut cloth. She couldn't hide her smile. "Open it, *Rawnee*."

Lavinia opened it, reached in and drew out a necklace. "But Simza, I already have blue beads." She fingered the strand she always wore.

"The Chovihano says those must be burned now. Bend your head, I will remove them." Simza threw the old necklace to the floor and hung the new one around Lavinia's neck. "There, *Rawnee*, perfect."

Lavinia held them in front of her. She gasped at the talisman's sparkle of silver. Images from the day of the storm went through her mind: Saddani's cruel eyes on her. The flash of silver in his palm. Her talisman gone when she needed it most.

Simza wrinkled her forehead. *"Rawnee*, you do not like them?"

"I-I . . ." Lavinia closed her eyes. She felt Simza's warm hand on her forehead.

"Do not think of the day of the storm. This new talisman will help with that. The Chovihano made it stronger." She removed her hand. "Go ahead, hold the charm. The talisman needs to have your touch, your smile."

Lavinia held the beads out. The silver cylinder had been engraved with flowers and leaves. "It's beautiful, Simza."

Simza beamed. "More special than the last. More powerful. It has to be." She patted Lavinia's shoulder. "Guard it with care. We will not speak of it again." Simza held out a piece of cloth, scooped up Lavinia's old beads and hurried from the tent.

When she returned, she slung a leather pouch over her shoulder and picked up a basket. As she hurried to the tent flap, it slipped from her hands and the lid came loose, spilling green glass beads on the carpet. She chased after them, muttering, *"Dinili.* Silly," her mouth as pouty as a small child's. The beads scattered like privy bugs, gathering in low spots, resembling emerald puddles on the carpet's arabesque designs. Simza made a face. She plopped the last of the beads into the basket, pressed the lid on tight and looked across the tent at Lavinia. "I will be back soon. If you go out, take care." Simza opened the tent flap and peeked back inside. "Rawnee, you remember . . . What we talked about."

Lavinia waved in acknowledgement of their serious discussion about Rakhshan, the djinni and the Chovihano's rules. The girl's long hair swung onto her loden green skirt as she left. At times she reminded Lavinia of the gypsy horses tossing their wondrous manes.

"To keep you safe," Simza kept repeating as she had laid out what the Chovihano said. Lavinia put her hand to her cheek and looked up at the ceiling. She made a face—so many rules. The shadows in the corner darkened as the sun went behind clouds outside.

Her breath caught in her throat. *The storm a little over a month ago, the shadows gathering darker and deeper until they transformed into Saddani, then into Rakhshan.* But today held sunshine and these shadows were normal. Besides, the Chovihano had worked many spells here, burning sage and performing secret rituals while she and Simza lodged with neighbors. Were all those admonitions and dire warnings just to keep her here in the gypsy camp? If she could simply go to Yasir in the urn, she would be safe, safer than at Simza's.

Lavinia waited a few minutes, then hurried to the back of the tent. Behind Simza's bed, blue floor-length curtains hung from a rope stretched across the tent supports, creating a separate partition. Late at night, Lavinia would hear Simza rummaging through things behind the curtains.

When she was left alone, Lavinia had managed to search there for her ring, but Simza usually darted back, grabbing an item, saying, "I would loose my fingers, were they not tight to my hand." Lavinia suspected the girl hadn't forgotten anything, but was merely checking on her. And Simza took care to never stay gone too long, not long enough for Lavinia to adequately explore, or go any distance from the tent or do anything significant in the way of escaping.

The Chovihano could have given Yasir's ring to Simza for safe-keeping. It would be illogical for the gypsy girl to keep something from Lavinia in the very tent where she stayed, but it made a perverse kind of sense. Lavinia peeked through a gap between the curtains. This area always surprised her by being a larger space than one would think, with several wooden trunks at the back against the tent canvas. Above them, dried yellow gourds with openings near the top hung from ropes. Woven shelves of cord, attached to the tent's arced supports, held the baskets that weren't stacked on the floor in towering columns.

She checked behind her. Still alone. The baby would come in almost a month, and then it would be even more difficult to make her way to Bramley House or the urn. She needed her ring. Steadying her nerves, Lavinia smoothed the soft cotton of her new dress, which accommodated her growing shape by being voluminous enough to hide it. She slipped through the opening between the curtain panels, reached up and shook one of the gourds. The same rattle like dried seeds inside. Peering into the wide hole, she tilted the gourd. Orange clay beads spilled into her palm. A clever way to store them. She always rechecked these, for Simza could easily slip a ring in with the beads.

She knelt by one of the trunks that she hadn't searched. Locked. Closing her eyes, she tried to use what little intuition she had inherited from grandmother Spencer who could heal with her hands and words, who could find lost objects. She felt nothing.

Pushing up from the trunk, she stood and ran her hand down the suspended baskets to her right. The lid of the cream-colored one proved easy to lift.

She pulled out a knitted cap that fit into her palm, a doll-sized dress made of the Calicut lining from Simza's cape, and tiny leather shoes with woven orange laces. Baby clothes. How strange that Simza hid these. She pictured the girl, smile stretched across her face, proudly displaying her latest embroidery, jewelry or piece of clothing for Lavinia's praise. Lavinia fingered the metal charms on the cap. Were these a surprise for her baby?

After looking through the fifth basket, Lavinia again chastised herself for disregarding Simza's privacy when she brushed against a large gold-colored basket with bold brown zigzags spiraling from bottom to top—one she hadn't seen before. She touched the lid. The baby kicked, startling her. She exhaled, long and slow with a deep-seated relief that came as a surprise. He had been still for a few days. Now she knew she had blocked the worry from her mind.

Perhaps this basket held what she was looking for. She set it on the floor and attempted to pull the lid off, but it was a snug fit. With her fingernails under the rim she pried upwards, and almost fell over when it came loose. Outside voices from far away filtered through the canvas walls. She heard Simza return a greeting. A bead of sweat rolled down her forehead. She must hurry.

Even if she squinted, she couldn't see into the basket. The tight weave of the thick straw kept out the light. She slanted closer, clutching the lid in her hand. A faint amber glow tinted the interior. She blinked, trying to make out shapes emerging from the gloom. Her mind slowed, mesmerized, as it failed to assemble the pieces. Golden. Almond-shaped. A vertical black line. Familiar in an unsettling way. What—

With a horrified gasp, she scrambled backwards just as a loud hiss resonated throughout the room. A triangular head rose almost imperceptibly from thick coils, the scales moving over each other in a *shurush, shurush* that sounded louder than the footsteps outside.

The creature struck at her, expanding like a whip, the burst of its scales on her arm dry and cool. Her hands and feet slipped on the worn rug and she sprawled, helpless. *My God!* Where was the snake? Was it slithering towards her?

She lurched up and was on her feet as light and speedy as if her belly were flat and empty. She eyed the basket, the lid had somehow fallen in place on top of it. The lid bumped upwards and she stifled a scream. She rammed her fist on the top before she knew what she was doing. Stepping back, she heard the *shurush, shurush* inside.

The blue curtains tangled in her hands, covered her face. She thought she might smother as she fought to find the opening. Lavinia sank onto her bed and checked her arm. The snake hadn't bitten her, but she still felt the rasp of its body across her flesh.

Catching her breath, she sat up, pulled out her embroidery and was making motions with her needle on the sleeve of the blouse when Simza burst in.

# 18

The next day, Lavinia sat in front of Simza's tent on a chair the girl had scrounged "just for *Rawnee*." She smoothed the blouse in her lap and drew her needle through the cotton cloth, finishing the petal of an orange flower. What a conundrum the gypsy girl presented. Simza still hadn't come out to join her and hadn't checked on her in a while. Was she busy with her snake?

Lavinia emitted a soft moan as a quiver of revulsion ran through her. Just yesterday, she had looked into the serpent's glassy eyes, black slits in amber staring from the shadows of the basket. She had slept fitfully last night, waking to every sound. Hearing the *shurush, shurush* of the reptile's scales as she saw it in her dreams, slithering over the carpets, tongue flicking, searching her out.

Why in the name of heaven would Simza keep a snake in the tent where they lived? Lavinia startled at a slight sound and looked around, her hands bunched in fists—only the wind in the trees. Perhaps Simza would let the snake loose to poison her, a quick way to be rid of someone. How could the gypsies be blamed for an accident of nature?

She caressed her ring finger, bare now. A longing for Yasir filled her, yet left her feeling hollow. She pressed her hand over her eyes, shutting out the gypsy camp. In her mind she saw her ring, the ruby shining in a red glow. A pull of magic made her heart surge with joy. Yasir?

She looked around, eager. Her chest tightened when she saw the Chovihano striding through the center of camp. He must have passed by when she was lost in her daydream. When would she learn?

She should do something before the snake got loose. Or was set loose. If she had her ring and if it worked, she could call Yasir, escape.

Where would the Chovihano hide it? Was he powerful enough to make her ring vanish into a different realm, a forbidden place like the urn?

Simza might come out any minute. Lavinia moved from her chair and set her embroidery in the seat. The girl would think she had gone to relieve herself. When enough time passed, Simza would look for her. By then it would be too late.

With shaking hands, Lavinia picked up her skirts and followed the Chovihano, careful to keep as much distance between them as possible. He walked at a good clip, a man with a purpose, and headed in the direction of a nondescript tent near a clump of spreading oaks on the edge of camp. Among the yellow, orange and other colorful tents, she had never noticed it.

Hiding in the dense grove, she peered from the deep shade, studying the Chovihano's every move, wary of his tricks. He stopped in front of the tent. The drab shelter blended with the light and shade and colors of the surroundings. When she blinked, the tent was as hard to find as grazing deer camouflaged in a dappled glade. She fixed the tent in its place, blocking out the moving shadows, and saw it clearly, sitting there as solid as Simza's bright orange one.

The Chovihano undid the tent flap and a white cat skittered out between his legs. Turning, he laughed as the animal made a beeline for the trees, for her. Lavinia ducked behind a massive oak, watching the cat run past to disappear in a clump of tall, thick weeds.

She moved farther around the tree, away from the tent, and pressed against the trunk, trying to feel the Chovihano's presence. But she felt only the rough bark biting into her back. Could the tree block the shaman's power? She peered out. He must have gone into the tent while she hid.

Oak leaves rustled in the breeze, a soothing song. Shadows and light played around her, changing shapes, and the odd feeling that she had been there far longer than she perceived gripped her.

The tent flap opened and the Chovihano emerged, a russet cape trailing behind him like exotic plumage. His round velvet hat glimmered with charms reflecting shimmering stars of light onto the ground. He strode past, holding a scepter of silver crowned with a clear faceted stone. Lavinia pressed flat against the thick trunk. She inched around to the side facing his tent. Had he seen her, or was she as insignificant as a bird or squirrel to him? If he knew she lurked there, he hadn't tried to stop her.

She moved from tree to tree until she came close to the tent. Was someone else inside? A wife, children? She stayed still and listened, but heard only the leaves whispering through the wind amid the birdsong. A few steps from outside to inside, swift movements like a fish darting from rock to rock, and Lavinia entered the Chovihano's lair.

She was inside the Roma shaman's tent. How had she dared to do such a thing? Would he curse her with a spell if he found her here? She stood still, taking it all in, as she wondered if she should turn around and leave. A bed in the back, the blue curtain divider like Simza's, a small stove and stovepipe at the center. It was like any other gypsy tent she'd visited, but less elaborate.

She stepped deeper inside and halted, immobilized by a sharp pain shooting through her head. Clutching her temple, she groped for support, finally slumping against an ancient weathered chest. Perhaps she had pushed too hard keeping up with the Chovihano, but the pain vanished before she finished her thought, and she straightened and looked around.

*Where was she?* This wasn't Simza's tent. She took in the drab brown canvas surrounding her, the humble trunks and worn baskets. How had she come here? Lavinia glanced from side to side, trying to recognize something, anything.

She absently touched her empty ring finger. The Chovihano's tent. *She was in the Chovihano's tent to steal her ring back.* She squeezed her eyes shut, attempting to get her wits about her. She had forgotten for a moment where she was, what she was doing. Like the rumblings and chittering of hidden creatures in the woods, magic lurked around her. Magic to harm her?

She'd best be quick about this.

The dilapidated trunk she had rested on swam into her vision until it was all she could see. She pulled on the heavy brass padlock forged in the shape of a crude dragon, its jaws clamped on the pocked metal hasp. The beast's mouth parted and the shackle slid open, silent and sure. Lavinia stared at the lock in her hands. This proved too easy. Perhaps it was an auspicious sign. Or a warning.

The lid creaked as she raised it, the hideous yowl of cats fighting in the night. With a strangled inhale she dropped it, the lid hitting the rear of the trunk with a bang. Flinching from the loud noise, she stepped back, wary of what might lurk there, but the huge trunk was packed to the brim with a hodgepodge of bric-a-brac. She moved closer in wonder at the cotton and silk brocade pouches, inlaid and patterned paper mache boxes, metal figurines of animals and people, glittering scarves, tooled leather belts, and—she leaned forward in disbelief—"Dolly?"

Her whisper expanded through the silent tent, overarching the rustling leaves of the oaks outside. Her childhood doll lay crossways over the cotton and silk brocade pouches and compact wooden boxes, arms and legs askew in her embroidered pinafore. Eyes closed.

*Here? Dolly was here? In a gypsy shaman's trunk?* Lavinia put her hands to her forehead, pressing hard. *How? How?* The words shrilled inside her head. She slid her fingers into her hair as her mind turned and twisted, but no matter the scenario, it didn't make sense.

Lavinia picked up her doll. The padded body still soft, still faintly scented with the lavender perfume her old nanny wore. Dolly's black spiky lashes fluttered. Lavinia had been so proud to have a doll whose eyes opened and closed when she handled her. At her birthday party all her friends were—

Lavinia caught her breath. Dolly's ice blue eyes, always shiny, had come alive. The doll stared as if she recognized her, as if she might speak any moment. Lavinia held her away, then dropped her inside the trunk. Dolly's delicate porcelain hand spilled from a Brussels's lace cuff, her pale index finger pointing to a crude pouch of dingy white. Lavinia could make out faded brown and blue stripes running through the rough cloth. Tied with a frayed brown string, the bag was marred by dark mildew splotches.

Careful not to touch Dolly—those eyes, so eerie, best they stay closed—Lavinia extracted the pouch. She sank to the floor, set the bag in her lap and picked the knot with her nails. So tight. *Stars in heaven,* she would be here all day. She glanced at the entrance, which ruffled in the breeze. Would she be able to hear the Chovihano's footsteps, or would he tread like a ghost and seize her?

At last, the string came loose and Lavinia opened the bunched fabric. Her ring lay there, the ruby shining bright against the faded material. She beamed even as shivers cascaded down her neck. Again, too easy. She clenched the ring in her fist, her face hot with anger. The nerve of him. The Roma king had stolen it even as he reassured her that he owed her every consideration.

She slipped the ring onto her finger. The room blurred with vestiges of Yasir's golden eyes, his gleaming jewels, the subtle feel of his impossible magic. Taking a deep breath, she pulled the ring off and placed it in the hidden pocket sewn into her skirt. She couldn't wear it. They would see. They would steal it once more.

She cocked her head. Was that the crunch of gravel and fallen leaves outside? In haste, she bunched the cloth together like before, but without the ring. The footsteps passed by. The rough fabric felt warm as if it had been too long in the hot sun. She studied the splotches. They weren't mildew. Rust-colored, uneven, like drops of . . .

*My God.*

Blood. She ran her hand over the bumpy fabric. In Peter's tragic tale of how he came by the urn: *Ne'bi the peddler unrolled a dingy white cloth shot through with faded brown and blue stripes—revealing the unusual brass vessel . . . The hook-nosed Bedouin knifed Ne'bi . . . Ne'bi thrust the bundle, stained with his own blood, into Peter's arms.*

This was a piece of the cloth.

She knew it in her bones. The same jittery feeling as when she touched the urn had been pricking her nerves since she handled the pouch. She tied the string around the cloth in the exact spot as before and replaced it next to Dolly, then let down the trunk's lid until it settled quietly into place. With a snap, the dragon's jaws clamped on the metal hasp. Why was this so effortless?

She fingered her pocket, the ring safe inside, and rushed towards the entrance. How long had she been here? The Chovihano could return any minute. She brushed against a stack of baskets. They wobbled, threatening to collapse. If the lids fell off she would have to put them together again—*and all the king's horses and all the king's men couldn't* . . . Holding her hands to either side of the baskets she steadied the column, gradually bringing them into alignment until the stack was stable.

She turned and avoided tripping on a light yellow basket with bold brown triangle designs that wound from bottom to top. She had seen a similar one before, but where? Had Dolly led her to this, like she pointed to the ring? The ring hadn't worked without help at Rakhshan's. It might not work here. She dare not try to call Yasir in the Chovihano's tent. Perhaps there was something in the basket that would aid her, if needed, when she found a safe place to use the ring.

She knelt, reached for the basket's lid but hesitated, her hand to her side. Where *had* she seen it? Flashes of textures and patterns sped through her brain, too fast to comprehend. She couldn't place the basket. A vague apprehension coursed through her. Being here in the Chovihano's tent scattered her thoughts, played with her memory, disturbed her already overwrought imagination. Yet she could remember when she came to the gypsy camp, could remember Yasir, could remember the Dark Magician appearing in Simza's tent. She thought through the preceding days, this morning. A blank. Tamping down the panic that rose inside her, she reassured herself that when she left this place her memory of more recent events would return.

She pulled the lid off. The dark interior obscured the contents. As she stared, she caught a glint near the bottom. Ignoring her tightening chest, her shallow breathing, she angled the basket to the light, feeling the weight of it, and squinted inside. Shadows swallowed the dim illumination, making it hard to see anything but more of the triangle designs. Her heart pounded. She reached for the inside, but paused at the basket rim.

She already had the ring. She should leave. But there was a reason she opened this basket. It was another portent. She couldn't stop now, in spite of this unfounded apprehension.

She moved her hand to the rim, but paused before she touched it.

She reached inside. The object felt cool to the touch. Smooth. She gripped the long slender shape and pulled out . . .

A pistol.

She held it in front of her until her brain registered what her eyes already recognized.

*Impossible.*

This was the gun that shot Yasir.

The same ornate scrolls at the edge of the butt, and that metal sphere in the middle like a jewel. The engraved silver inlay of the ducal crest with the letter "Y" and the curious inscription—*metamorphose.* It couldn't be anyone else's. Peter's gun.

Did Peter hire the Chovihano to kidnap her? Peter had never been comfortable with her small bit of clairvoyance. And he had been suspicious of her ever since she opened the urn. No, she was sure Yasir's spell worked, that Peter hadn't a clue he was master first. But the spell could have worn off at some point. Peter could've remembered.

She stiffened. Had she heard a footstep? Her hand curled tight around the pistol. The blue curtains swayed. She rose to her feet, peering around the tent, the metal of the gun cold in her palm.

*Foolish, foolish.* If not for Peter's gun she would have left. It always came down to Peter didn't it? Peter neglecting her. Peter clueless about the djinni. Peter unaware she was kidnapped in his own garden. A wave of heat flushed through her. *Damn Peter to hell.*

"Beware the jinx." A high-pitched sing-song voice, heavily accented, right behind her. She whirled around, only to face the column of baskets.

"I am the djinni Yasir." It couldn't be anyone else, she would never mistake his lyric baritone.

"Yasir!" She turned towards the direction of the voice. Nothing. Then checked the tent. No one was there.

"You're my wife and when I want you, I'll have you." Peter's demanding tone cut through her, the inflection, the insinuation. Her cheeks burned.

Alice's bird-like falsetto tittered through the tent. "An urn?" Her voice tinged with concern. In succession, the familiar voices spoke the very words that haunted her:

"Beware the jinx."

"I am the djinni Yasir."

"You're my wife and when I want you . . ."

*Was she living her life in reverse?*

"An urn?"

*How did the Chovihano know?*

"Beware the—"

"You're my wife and when I . . ."

"Stop!" Lavinia screeched. She dropped Peter's gun, a dull thump on the rug, and clapped her hands over her ears, but still heard the voices, the pointed phrases. Still felt the flood of emotions they evoked.

*Oh, Yasir make the voices go away. Make them stop.*

The yammering through her muffled ears died. She took her hands away. She picked up Peter's gun and shut it inside the basket. The Chovihano should find no concrete evidence that she had been here. She ran to the entrance, keeping her eyes straight ahead.

Lavinia fumbled with the tent flap. With a surge of strength, she opened it and staggered out, managing to secure the flap as she had found it in spite of her trembling hands. She put one foot in front of the other, making her way as normally as she could towards Simza's tent. Just through the trees, she saw the Chovihano walking in her direction, his russet cape over his shoulders.

Her body stiffened, but she made herself move as if she were on a leisurely stroll. She couldn't avoid him. Soon, the stink of his scented oil surrounded her. The shaman stood inches away. She kept her gaze to the ground, refusing to meet his eyes.

"You look unwell." He sounded concerned.

She forced herself to raise her head.

"I–I . . ." She couldn't say anything. She kept her mind blank and met his eyes. After all, he had saved her from Rakhshan. "I walked a bit too far, and am feeling weary."

"You should not be alone. Surely Simza discussed the danger you are in. No?"

Lavinia nodded. "It was just a simple stroll." She surprised herself when her voice wobbled, and made her hands into fists, concentrating on tightening her muscles to stay calm.

He cocked his head at her. Did he know where she'd been? She placed her hand on her stomach, bent her head and pretended she was in pain. She might fool the Chovihano, then she wouldn't have to speak with him. A soft breeze lifted her hair.

His hand on her arm, the shaman drew her close. "We are not the enemy. These things you try—you jeopardize your child. You put us all in danger. Must we imprison you?"

Lavinia trembled from the anger in his voice. He brushed her forehead with his hand. But her thoughts were focused on him and his threat. She was sure he didn't get anything. Lavinia watched him walk away. After this, the Chovihano would have Simza dog her every minute of every day.

She made her way, slow and unsteady, to Simza's.

In the shaman's tent, did Yasir banish the horrible voices? And had her very presence caused the appearance of Dolly, the cloth that had wrapped the urn, Peter's pistol, and the harrowing voices? That the tent held magic wasn't surprising, but that it contained objects from her own life discombobulated her. If the Chovihano could do that, wouldn't he know about the ring? Or did her asking Yasir for help make the ring fully hers again so that no one would know, no one could interfere?

She was still master to the djinni. She could command. "Yasir, make the ring only mine. No one can know I have it. No one else can possess it." She mumbled it to herself in the lowest voice, just enough to be heard. Would that it would reach—

"Rawnee!"

Lavinia stopped, rigid as a spike. Simza stood in front of her, a worried expression darkening her face.

"You are crying, *Rawnee*. Are you hurt?"

Lavinia wiped her eyes. She *was* crying. Crying for Yasir.

Simza took her by the hand. "Come."

In Simza's tent, the yellow drapes by Lavinia's bed had been tucked to the sides. Simza helped her onto the mattress and fluffed a pillow behind her back. With a sigh, Lavinia sagged into the softness, the baby, quiet, weighing heavy on her insides. The baby had been silent through all this. No warning as she encountered Dolly, found her ring, and confronted the Chovihano. She caught Simza's quick glance at her midsection. Was she worried about the baby as well?

Simza took her hand. "My *Rawnee*, you must rest. Take refreshment. Please, not to worry." She knelt and looked up from under her brows, wrinkling her forehead.

Lavinia studied the gypsy girl. She squinted, then opened her eyes wide, viewing Simza from different angles. With each intermittent glimpse, the girl's features became clearer—her penetrating expression, her straight nose, her full lips. How could Lavinia not have seen it?

Simza, the seventh daughter—the *lace romni*, who drew her power from the spirits. She was the Chovihano's daughter.

# 19

*L*avinia held out her hand, the ruby in her ring scintillating, its fiery red brilliance hypnotizing in the afternoon light filtering through the orange tent. Only one day since she possessed the ring again and she hadn't had the courage to try and summon Yasir. Now she was alone, Simza having scurried out just minutes before with a basket of her necklaces, saying she had to barter for some food.

Lavinia set her embroidery to the side. With a deep breath, she stroked the ring once. She had never dared go this far since that afternoon in the garden when Saddani carried her away from Bramley House. Desperate then, she had stroked the ring thrice and nothing happened. Saddani had said, *The ring is only as good as the giver.*

In spite of her promising herself she would not put credence in that blackguard's mutterings, her mind had pondered the phrase, twisting and turning the words to extract their hidden meanings. Did he mean Yasir was dead, or suffering horribly at the hands of Rakhshan, or was it merely some slur against the race of the Djinn?

The baby kicked. He was eager to have his father with them. She stroked the ring a second time.

Then a third.

Opening her eyes wide, she scanned the tent, alert to any change in the quiet atmosphere. She could feel her heart beat, hear her shallow breaths. A bird trilled outside.

The sun angled now on the west side of the tent, more birds had joined the lonely one's song. She inhaled long and deep, moving her muscles, stiff from holding still. Had it been minutes, half an hour, or more? She stood, jostling her embroidery off the edge of the chair. Yasir wasn't coming.

She sat. The ring glinted. She slid it up over her knuckle, then back as she checked the inside of the tent once more. Not a wrinkle in the air, not even a wisp of smoke. She laughed to herself. Of course, how could the ring work in Simza's tent? The Chovihano, both of them, had made it impossible for her to summon the djinni here. She would have to find a place where their gypsy magic would be dispersed. Then she could call Yasir and leave this place forever.

It would need to be soon. Before her baby was born. She couldn't have her son here. She wouldn't have him here.

She sat straight at the sound of footsteps, at the scrabbling of the tent flap. Lavinia pulled the ring from her finger and slipped it into the secret pocket in her skirt. Only after it was off did she notice the loss, a hint of the feeling she had when Yasir was nearby: a euphoric lift, the joy of knowing that something you wish for is possible.

But it was only a spark of what she would feel when the gypsy magic was lessened or alleviated. Now, so soon after removing her ring, she yearned even more for the djinni, something only the ring could give. She restrained from fingering the stone in her pocket, fearful her expression might reveal more to Simza than she intended.

It was nearing eventide and she hurried to her bed, pulled the covers up to her chest and mussed her hair. Simza was becoming more and more like a guard with her questions and suspicious looks, but she always liked it when Lavinia slept. Said it was good for the baby, especially with Lavinia so near her time. And if Simza thought Lavinia had napped while she was gone, the girl wouldn't pester her with questions about what she had done in her absence.

She heard Simza open the flap and walk inside. Lavinia closed her eyes. A few thumps and some rustling—Simza putting the food away. Then every movement became muffled. The girl must have seen her sleeping and made to be quiet so she wouldn't disturb her.

Lavinia sat up in bed, stretched and faked a yawn.

Simza stood, holding a basket lid. "Oh. Did I disturb you? I'm sorry, I—"

"No, I was just waking." Lavinia closed her eyes again, like she did when she first awakened in the morning. She had to be careful around this gypsy girl who held her secrets close. Simza had never told her she was the shaman's daughter. What else was she hiding? Everything the girl said about Yasir, had it all been a lie?

She looked up to see Simza standing over her, twisting a yellow scarf in her hand, winding and unwinding the lustrous silk. Lavinia regarded the cloth with a growing sense of unease. *Stars in heaven*, it was the gag that Saddani's footman had forced into her mouth. How many months ago? Simza must have hemmed the severed ends, but why?

"You recognize it, no? I mended it. See." Simza shook the scarf, letting it fall its full length. "The cloth had been fowled by the Dark Magician's minion, but to destroy it might have given a sign you were with us. The Chovihano cleansed it and bade me use the fabric. Even though the Dark One knows you are here, I will still keep it. "

Simza held out the strip of silk. "Look at my blind stitches. Everyone says they are the best they have ever seen."

Lavinia feigned interest, took the scarf and angled the silk in three different directions before she saw evidence of the tiniest of stitches. The girl's handiwork rivaled any Lavinia had come across. "Simza, this is perfect craftsmanship. You must show me."

"Only if you accompany me tonight."

"You know I'm most fatigued at the end of the day." Lavinia gestured towards the chair by her bed. "I have my nightdress out." With Simza gone this evening, she could find a place where the ring might work and be rid of this camp forever. Lavinia didn't bother to banish these thoughts. Simza didn't yet have the Chovihano's eerie gift of reading minds, at least not all the time. Even when she did, the readings weren't always accurate, and Lavinia could often dispel Simza's obvious conclusions by her attitude or a casual comment.

"But you napped." Simza attempted a smile, but only looked desperate, clearly upset that Lavinia balked. With a haughty expression, she tossed her head. "I am best at the blind stitch."

Lavinia sighed, ruing her lie about the nap. She held the scarf close, studying a place where Simza must've joined the pieces. Could the girl have used magic? She said she would teach her. It would keep her busy, keep her mind off of the ring and Yasir. Yet it didn't matter, now that she had the ring and was leaving soon.

"My nap was fitful. I had a nightmare about the horrible things that have happened here, so I'm still tired." There, that should make Simza feel for her and let her forego the event.

Again that flash of disquiet in the girl's eyes. Simza reached for the scarf and Lavinia dropped it into her hands. The girl rolled the fabric between her fingers with a faint *shurush, shurush,* the sound of her snake's scales as it slithered.

"We sit at the fire tonight." Simza looped the scarf around her neck. "We should go now." She put her hand on Lavinia's arm.

From months before, Simza's voice played in Lavinia's head, *in the fire I saw you and the djinni who lives in the urn.*

"I should stay here. It would be best," said Lavinia. She reclined, resting her head on the pillow. What did the Chovihano have planned for her at the fire? Did he know she had the ring?

"You should not be alone here at night. The Chovihano would be angry. Remember the storm, the darkness? Please *Rawnee,* I do not want to miss the festivities at the fire."

Lavinia sat up and crossed her arms on her lap. "Have someone stay with me if you are so afraid."

"And if that someone with no powers should encounter the Dark One's magic, then what? We will all be at the fire. Anyone could come and take you." Simza twisted the yellow scarf.

"It shouldn't be a problem. You can just put a spell on the tent. There's probably one here already to keep us safe. Even that should work." Hah, she had the girl now.

"You remember that it was this very tent where both the Dark One and his minion appeared and almost snatched you from us." Simza sat beside her. "*Rawnee*, it is just one night. There will be good food." She eyed Lavinia's belly. "I have no supper planned, and you need to eat for the baby. There will be music and dancing. All happy sounds and laughter. Good for the baby. And you."

She took Lavinia's hand. "I fear that the Chovihano himself will come fetch you if I do not succeed in bringing you. He will not have another incident like what happened during the storm." Simza stood and shook back her hair.

"All you need is something to ward off the night chill and you will be ready." The girl strolled behind the blue curtain by her bed. In a moment she returned, draping an azure and yellow shawl over Lavinia's shoulders. The soft wool enveloped her in a cloud of warmth.

"There. It goes perfectly with the deep blue of your dress. You look nice, *Rawnee*. And it will do you good to be with us and the music and laughter."

Envisioning the dark form of Rakhshan reaching for her during the storm, Lavinia nodded. If she failed to find a place where the ring worked tonight and Rakhshan found her, she would be taken. Then she would have her baby at Rakhshan's, if they survived that long.

Simza latched onto her arm, bringing her to standing. "Do not be afraid. I will be by your side."

Outside the tent, Lavinia drew her shawl tight against the twilight chill, the soft wool warm over her linen dress, but an underlying restiveness in the camp made it hard to feel comfortable. When they reached the gathering, people were already seated in an ever-growing circle around a stack of wood the height of those that tended it. Simza stood patiently at the crowd's edge, greeting the many who passed by.

"Aha, got you." Simza snatched up the little girl who pulled on her skirts and swung her around, the child's ruffled petticoats swirling like a carousel. "Magda, who told you to surprise us?" Simza set the little girl down as Magda pointed her chubby finger somewhere in the crowd.

Simza whispered in the child's ear. With an eager grin, Magda wound her way to the firewood in the center of the crowd. After a flurry of exaggerated gestures, pointing and head turning, she led a man, three women and a string of children from their places at the front. They inclined their heads at Lavinia as they trouped past. In their dark eyes—suspicion, awe, fear? Lavinia tried to sort out the evening's atmosphere, but only succeeded in heightening her sense of apprehension.

Magda took her hand and pulled. "Come Rawnee, I will show the way." Her voice rose, squeaky and brimming with enthusiasm. They wound through the seated crowd to a space at the very front. Tittering with excitement, Magda brushed off the thick rug and helped Lavinia sit next to Simza. The child squatted beside her and placed her pudgy hand on Lavinia's stomach. "Will the gadje baby move for me?"

Lavinia suppressed a laugh. She had grown used to the women touching her, asking what would be considered crude, rude questions at Bramley House, but Magda's curiosity was innocent, the same as every child's.

"Let's see." Lavinia laid her hand on her belly next to Magda's. The silence of expectation cocooned them and the commotion of the crowd faded. Lavinia felt her heart beat, slow and steady. She imagined Yasir's hand beside hers, waiting for the slight movement of their child.

"Is he sleeping?" Magda scrunched her fingers into Lavinia's hard belly, furrowing her brow as she tried to feel the baby inside.

"Yes, I suppose so." Lavinia ran her hand over Magda's hair and followed the thick braid that fell down her back. "Let's not wake him. He needs to be strong for when he's born."

Magda rubbed her cheek, eyes bright and patted Lavinia's belly a little too hard. "Will it be tonight?"

Lavinia flinched, sucking in her breath. "Not if you wake him."

"Oh!" Magda yanked her hand away. She raised her head, finger on her dimpled chin. "Maybe we should sing him a sleepy song."

"What song would you like to sing?" They both looked up. The noisy banter of the crowd had died, as though a pall had fallen on the chattering gypsies. Lavinia and Magda followed the group's eager gaze to the brilliant violet flame bobbing high in the air, coming closer.

Everyone clambered to their feet and parted for the Chovihano and his blazing torch. The charms on his cap glittered in the firelight, taking Lavinia back to when she slipped into the Chovihano's tent. She fought to banish the sudden haunting voices of Yasir and Peter and Alice that crescendoed in her mind.

The shaman's russet cape flowed behind him in spite of there being no breeze. He stared straight ahead, oblivious, his mismatched eyes on something far in the distance. Gasps and expressions of wonder came from the crowd as they saw that he held not a torch, but his scepter—the fist-sized crystal on top emitting the flame, flaring an otherworldly violet, magenta and deep purple.

When he walked past, so close Lavinia could have touched him, a wave of glamour poured into her as surely as if he had cast a spell. Her fingers went numb. Her shawl slid to the ground. With a sharp intake of breath, she stood straight just as Magda let out a tiny squeal of wonder.

She was tired of the Chovihano's strange magic, the gypsies' odd rituals and customs. The urge to run far away came so strong her legs trembled. But where would she run? Lavinia glanced at the gypsies surrounding her, thronging around the shaman. Why hadn't Yasir or Peter found her?

Would she stay here forever?

The shaman stood before the stack of wood, his chant rumbling to life. He touched his scepter to the edge. A flash of bright purple streaked from the crystal with a thunderous bang and branched through the pyre in a tangle of glowing veins. The crowd jumped back as one, their faces lit lavender. A fierce blaze roared into the darkening sky with the intensity of a gale, shooting tongues of crimson and orange and an odd yellow-green like the epidote in her wedding ring, like the feline eyes of Rakhshan's familiar.

After a short time, the fire settled into a steady slow burn, crackling and popping in the growing silence of the evening. The gypsies had settled as well, seated facing the fire. An owl's forlorn *whooo, whooo, whooo* pierced the quiet. Magda grabbed Lavinia's hand and looked to the dark forest, then whipped her head around at the high notes of a flute rising from somewhere to their right. The gypsies' voices started slow, a few here and there, then more, until they welled into a haunting song, the rich syllables of their polyglot tongue interweaving in the melody. She could hear Magda's high voice piping a little off-key, as she tried to keep up.

Simza had insisted that Lavinia attend tonight, but why make such a production of it? Lavinia looked away from the gypsy girl and found the Chovihano—a serene silhouette before the flames. Had he discovered that she stole into his tent, that she took her ring? Would he publicly shame her? She glanced at the indigo sky, shadowing as the light faded. On the far horizon, the last rays of the sinking sun glowed a deep otherworldly gold, broken by a band of aquamarine, orange and magenta, a vivid bruise above silhouettes of the trees.

She turned her attention from the sunset and sought the Chovihano, but he wasn't there. Why, she had only looked away for seconds. She inspected the crowd. The gypsies stared into the fire, their song drowning out the crackling of the bright flames. Magda, still singing, but in a soft voice, had let go of her hand and snuggled her small warm body against Lavinia. Was the Chovihano somewhere nearby, waiting to . . . what? Why would he even give a thought to the djinni's *gadje* that they kidnapped? Yet each time she sat quietly, the same premonition floated into her consciousness, a voice hinting that the Chovihano had something planned for her tonight, something she wouldn't like.

Two burly men sauntered to the center near the fire. They shook their long dark hair, rattling amulets and beads, and set diminutive squat violins on their shoulders, the deep red wood the hue of fine aged wine. The singing stopped, and the crowd held their breath in anticipation. The musicians grinned, teeth glinting in the firelight. They raised their bows. Their eyes flashed. In an instant, they skidded the toy-like bows across the strings, tearing off a lively melody. Magda laughed. She jumped up and started clapping, her colored bangles jingling. Couples rose and danced, then more and more until the most of the crowd whirled to the spirited music.

Without a break, the musicians went from one tune to another, moving in rhythm with the music cajoled from the *lautaris,* their bright beads and woven sashes swaying like ribbons festooning a maypole. Magda insisted Lavinia stand and clap her hands. A few people stopped to catch their breath, then more and more sat, fanning themselves, exclaiming about the dancing, the music.

Three boys brought mugs of beer and roasted chicken for the musicians as they set their bows and *lautaris* against a tree stump. More boys and girls served the crowd. Magda and a friend brought plates heaped with oily chicken and bread and went back for mugs of beer. Lavinia looked again for the Chovihano until Simza tapped her shoulder.

"*Rawnee,* who are you looking for? We are all here." Simza indicated their little group. "Are not you liking the music?" She grabbed a mug and thrust it at Lavinia, placing it in her hands. "Here, you must drink. This is good for the baby." She pushed a tin plate over. "Eat too."

More and more it seemed Simza wanted her here so the girl could enjoy the festivities, and wouldn't be stuck in the tent guarding her. Lavinia sipped the beer and tried to calm down, but the baby weighed heavy and she couldn't banish that feeling of a great fate about to befall her. She swallowed more beer, the yeasty flavor bold and filling. Perhaps she should just relax and enjoy this bit of fun.

Magda put a piece of chicken to Lavinia's mouth. "The baby told me he's hungry." And it was good and greasy, roasted with oil and garlic and herbs.

"Mmm. The baby wants more." Lavinia reached for her plate.

"No, the baby wants me to do it." Magda held out a chicken leg and Lavinia took a big bite. The baby kicked. "I saw it. I saw your stomach move. The baby likes the food." Magda smiled and gleefully shoved more into Lavinia's mouth.

She would enjoy the evening, worry be hanged. "Magda, the baby says he wants to sleep now. I think he's full." Magda squinted at Lavinia's stomach—hoping for a kick to disprove Lavinia's statement?—then put the bit of chicken in her own mouth.

"I hope the baby got enough." Magda licked her fingers and pointed at the musicians reaching for their bows and taking up their lautaris. The random noise of the crowd broke into an excited murmuring. Clapping her hands, Magda turned towards the fire. The music started at a slow pace this time, the musicians moving their bows like lovers, drawing out the chords, gentling the tones into plaintive strains. Lavinia clasped her hands over her belly. The sounds reached deep inside, pulling at her heart.

Voices of the gypsies rose as one, their words weaving with the melancholy music. Night crept from deep shadows in the woods, bringing the bittersweet smell of loamy soil and decaying leaves. A thin crescent moon scarred the lapis lazuli sky. The stars blinked smaller and farther away than Lavinia had ever seen them. In this isolated place, with these extraordinary people, loneliness and fear lurked like wolves beyond the fireside.

Lavinia yearned for something familiar. For home. For Yasir.

It was full dark now, the flames pouring yellow-orange into the inky black sky, tingeing the faces in the crowd a dull rust. She snuck her hand into her hidden pocket, and fingered her ring.

The acrid smell of wood smoke wafted through the cold air, mixing with the music and voices. Would the ring work here? They were at the edge of the camp near the forest. Perhaps in this location, any spells that kept the ring from functioning would be weaker. She didn't see the Chovihano, it was as if he had faded away as the fire blazed brighter and higher.

If Yasir appeared right here in front of her and Simza and Magda, the gypsies should welcome him. After all, Simza and the Chovihano had emphasized over and over that they were collaborating with the djinni, that they were his allies.

She would command Yasir to take her to the urn. In the seconds that he obeyed, they would be safe inside the magic vessel before anyone could take action. The gypsies would be glad to be rid of the djinni's gadje, and the threats from Rakhshan and his minions. They might even have another gathering celebrating her departure.

Lavinia slipped the ring onto her finger. No one could see. It was dark and they were all absorbed in the amazing music. Half-obscured in the folds of her skirt, the ruby glowed in the firelight. She closed her eyes. The stone throbbed against her skin, warming her flesh like Yasir's formidable presence.

She stroked the gem and breathed deep, reveling in the slight touch of the djinni's power. In her mind, the figure of Yasir burst forth as though he had opened a door and stepped through.

Lavinia pressed hard on the stone. If she moved her finger across, this would be the second stroke.

If she tried three times and Yasir didn't appear, would that mean he was truly gone? That she would live with the gypsies forever, raise her son in this God-forsaken camp? But if Yasir answered her—

"No!" screamed Simza. She grabbed Lavinia's ring hand. A few people stopped singing. Lavinia shrieked and tried to pull away from the *lace romni*.

Simza put her face to Lavinia's and hissed. "It is not safe to go to the djinni." She glanced at the forest, eyes wide. Lavinia searched the ragged silhouette of the woods, dreading to see a blurry shape manifesting under the trees, a figure dark and evil. The forest loomed, black limbs snaking among shadows in the rustling leaves, odd cries shrilling through the blue mist, but nothing emerged from its depths.

She turned and stared at Simza. The girl lied. Lavinia jerked her hand away and, looking the gypsy in the eye, put her finger on the stone. And dragged it across.

The second stroke.

One more.

Simza wrenched the ring from Lavinia's finger, her eyes darkening. "NO! You must not call him here." Simza's "no" boomed in Lavinia's head, as loud as the resounding peal of a bell.

Lavinia clenched her teeth, hands shaking. She lunged at Simza. "Give it back!" Lavinia caught Simza's hand and pried open the gypsy's fist.

"It is dangerous!" Simza plucked her hand away.

"Dangerous to whom? Not to me. The djinni wouldn't hurt our child. Does it thwart your plans?"

"You have seen the Dark Magician inside your tent. Who rescued you?" Simza lowered her voice, a cajoling tone. "If you use the ring, the Dark One could follow that magic directly to you. We would not know until it was too late. He wants you. He wants your baby."

"That's a lie. You—you lied to me all along. I'll have it back now." Lavinia charged at Simza. Hands grabbed her. The women held her tight, fingers pressed into her skin, bangles clanking as they pushed Lavinia's arms to her side. She gasped for air, inhaling their acrid oils and perfumes. They crowded closer, shushing her and clucking their disapproval, their thick hair falling around her like a prison. She couldn't move.

When she got her breath, she fought the urge to screech, to keep struggling and pull her hands free. Hanging her head, she relinquished herself to her captors. She let her hands go limp in theirs, still aware enough to fight the hysteria building in place of her initial shock.

The maudlin gypsy music had ratcheted her soul into a loneliness she had never felt before. She wanted Yasir. She wanted to be safe. Her hand had been hidden by her skirt. How did Simza know she had the ring? Know that she stroked the ruby? She glowered at the gypsy girl—always spoiling her plans.

The knot of women fell back. Simza and an ancient lady with gaps in her teeth and white hair cascading in frizzy waves, sat on either side of her, each holding her hand. Magda knelt behind Simza, peeking over her shoulder, hiding when she thought Lavinia glanced in her direction.

Simza squeezed her hand. "You know this. Say you understand. Say you will not go to the djinni." She looked long and hard at Lavinia.

"No. No." Lavinia resisted the urge to attack Simza once more, to snatch the ring from her closed fist. "I'll do it." She tried to curb the panic in her voice. "I mean. I–I won't do it."

"I won't call Yas—the djinni. I promise. I just . . . I need the ring." Her voice thinned, her control over her actions all but gone. "It's all I have of him. All I have." Lavinia's voice trailed off and she sobbed, her chest heaving. Simza angled nearer until they touched shoulders, and patted her back as she would soothe a small child.

Lavinia dabbed her tears with her shawl. Tears that came easily whenever she thought of Yasir, so sick and so far away. But alive, please God, alive. She took Simza's arm and, with all her will power, kept from fixating on the gypsy's hand curled into a fist around the ring.

"Please, Simza. My ring. He gave it to me. I have nothing. Nothing else of him."

"Nothing else?" Simza eyed Lavinia's swollen belly and raised her eyebrows. "The djinni entrusted you to us. You must not call him here." She stared at her. "You have *seen* why."

Lavinia faced the *lace romni*. "I promise. I won't call him. I just need the ring. It makes me feel whole. It—I need it. Please." She swallowed and gulped a breath.

Simza's expression softened. She took Lavinia's hand, her eyes narrowing. "Remember. The djinni himself asked us not to contact him. He is concerned for our protection. We should take the same care with him."

Lavinia focused on her lap. Was this a lie, a conspiracy between Simza and the Chovihano? She glanced up as Simza slipped the ring into her vest, but looked down before the girl saw her.

The old woman draped the shawl around Lavinia's shoulders. The women settled into their places around her. They sat close beside her, her keepers, her warders. Had it come to this?

The music picked up tempo and Lavinia watched the musicians' eyes glaze as their bows glided across the violins. The rich melodies enfolded those around her, and they turned away from the hysterical *gadje* with the ring. More of the crowd joined in the singing. The chords of the *lautari* intermingled, a mesmerizing high-pitched harmony that swirled through the gypsy camp, growing in tone and cadence, taking over the sounds of the forest, new verses supplanting preceding ones, spinning away into the night.

Lavinia gazed at the sky, seeing not the placid heavens that gave her such peace, but an oppressive, impenetrable black canopy weighing upon them. Clusters of stars wheeled overhead, pinpricks in a thick velvet cloth, leaking stingy specks of light. As the strains of the *lautaris* grew stronger, a star shot across the heavens. The music swelled further in intensity, vibrating inside her, the odd harmony rife with chords and voices that made her body tingle. Her hand went to her chest. The desolate hollowness there, the same as when the chaos at Rakhshan's swept her away from Yasir.

She hunched her shoulders and prayed this part of the music would pass. She sat up straight, cocking her head. Was that Yasir's golden baritone? Mehadeh's deep contralto? The stern bass of the Chovihano? Lavinia shut her eyes, listening with her whole body until their voices were the only ones she could hear. Simza's wavering soprano rose out of the gypsies' melody, separating and flowing into the familiar voices to join their private chorus.

The four were speaking to one another with their peculiar magic. Talking around her, thinking she didn't suspect, that she wouldn't recognize them and their scheming. Simza, her profile dark against the firelight, sat next to her lost in concentration, still clutching Lavinia's hand.

Lavinia moved closer to her warder and asked permission to speak with Simza for a moment. The old woman, still singing with the crowd, frowned but nodded and let go of her hand. She kept her eyes on Lavinia, the crease on her forehead deepening.

Lavinia took a breath, her heart thumping. If she broke Simza's trance . . . If they caught her this time, it would be worse, much worse. She turned toward Simza and pretended to whisper in her ear as she let her shawl fall over her arm and slipped her free hand into the gypsy's vest, gliding the ring out. She began to slip it onto her finger.

But no, too dangerous. She pocketed it, careful that no one saw, not even bright-eyed little Magda.

# 20

*E*arly the next day, Simza looked up at the Chovihano, wrinkling her forehead. "Can you not see where it is?"

"This Lavinia, she has a quality, perhaps from the djinni, perhaps inherent. You have experienced this as well. I am unable to see into her mind as I can in others. My access is sporadic, unpredictable." The Chovihano paced, a frown compressing the three wavy lines tattooed on his forehead. He stopped and sat down beside Simza on the rug. "Last night you took the ring from the *gadje* and placed it securely in your vest. What did you do next?"

Simza exhaled, and after a sidelong glance at her father, spoke. "The voices . . . came through the songs, through the music. The voice of the one who sits beside me, the Chovihano." She turned to him, averted her eyes. "Then the voices of the djinni and the woman who shines blue. I heard . . . heard what I must do. How . . ." She pressed her hand on her stomach and stared ahead, silent. The Chovihano's magic had been different this time, perhaps because it had been combined with the djinni's. She felt her father's gaze.

"I obeyed. I feel like the worst kind of thief." This morning she had hurried from her tent at the Chovihano's summons, leaving Fifika and Aishe guarding Lavinia, who lay oblivious in a potion-induced sleep.

"She does not know what I did." Simza turned to him, her voice rising. "How can she survive this? How—?"

The Chovihano gripped her shoulders and shook her gently. "*Chav,* you completed your task perfectly. Flawlessly." He caressed her forehead. "Your sacrifice is for the djinni and his lady. You have saved them. They will be safe now." His eyes darkened, his expression grave. "But you must never tell her what you did."

She would be the liar that *Rawnee* had always thought her. A tear coursed down Simza's cheek. "*Rawnee* will be so sad. It is all she has of him."

"You are forgetting one other thing. Where is it?" The Chovihano tilted his head as he studied her. "Try to remember your actions."

"I put the spell on *Rawnee*, put the drops of venom in her beer." Simza met his eyes. "The correct number of drops. You carried her to my tent." Her voice faded. "Then the . . ." She put her head in her hands.

"Continue. You did nothing wrong." He stroked her hair.

"But it feels so . . ." Simza blinked back tears. "You said the conjuration for me. Then the spell took hold." She clutched her stomach and bowed her head.

The Chovihano stood and she heard him chanting in a low voice, felt his hands hovering above her. Simza straightened and tried to smile. "I know you speak true. Perhaps it is only this . . . this condition working its way into me." She stared at her lap, her hair a curtain around her.

"As for the ring, it must have somehow slipped from my vest." She raised her head and looked around the Chovihano's tent as if the ruby ring might appear from one of the stacked baskets or jump out of the ancient trunk at the far side. "I have everyone searching for the ring. They wouldn't dare steal it. They know it is the djinni's. The fear of his power shows in their eyes."

Drowsy and hollow as though she'd slept for days, Lavinia watched the morning sunlight on the orange canvas. Dazed, she took in her surroundings. This wasn't the urn. Or Rakhshan's palace. Or Bramley House.

A heart-shaped face filled her vision, the onyx eyes regarding her in a way that made her instinctively withdraw. A dusky girl, garish clothes, gaudy beads and earrings. Lavinia attempted to place the face, the eccentric clothing. She struggled upright.

"Simza?" Lavinia blinked. Last night: the Chovihano lit the bonfire, musicians played, everyone danced, and she heard Yasir's voice. She had stolen her ring back from Simza. Then . . . What else?

Simza reached for her hand. Her eyes shone bright. "Please do not be sad. It might be for the best. You are safe and unharmed." Simza squeezed Lavinia's fingers. "But, my *Rawnee*, you lost the baby."

Lavinia stared into the gypsy's eyes, falling into that black abyss, dropping like an anvil, plummeting through the air with nothing to stop her. She tried to remove her hand, but Simza tightened her grip.

What did the gypsy say?

Impossible words. Lavinia curved her hand protectively over her stomach, a hard bulge under her nightdress. The same as yesterday. *Please little one, kick now. Kick—*

"Yes, you are almost as large as you were, but your womb will soon shrink." Simza touched Lavinia's cheek, her eyes drooping in sorrow. "My *Rawnee*, nothing was damaged. You can still have other children."

The weight on Lavinia's chest made it difficult to breathe. Her heart pulsed in her temple, pounded in her ears. Hard to think.

It couldn't be true.

Not Yasir's baby.

Simza moved her mouth, but her words vanished into the roaring *swish, swish, swish* of Lavinia's heart—beating in tandem with her child's. Yes, she was sure the tiny pulse throbbed along with her own.

"N-no." Her chin trembled. Tears pressed at her eyes. Her baby, gone? But . . . but . . . the baby was still safe inside her. She crossed her arms over her stomach and stared at Simza.

The girl lied.

An older woman appeared at Simza's side with a round tray that held a terra cotta cup. Simza offered the cup to Lavinia. "*Rawnee* drink, it will help you feel better."

The woman, her set-smile suspicious, stood waiting with Simza. Lavinia had been friends with this woman, but couldn't remember her name. Fifika? Aishe? No. Violca? Names swirled in her head, filling her arms and legs and chest until her body became so heavy she collapsed into the bed pillows. *Gypsy names. Not Anne or Mary or Elizabeth. Pagan names.*

*The gypsies. They plotted this. They stole her baby.* She curled her fist. The heat of a flush flamed on her skin. *She would make them pay. She would call Yasir. Command him to*—but her fist uncurled, soft as a wilted lily, while the strength ebbed from her body.

Her voice, flat, vaguely confused, came from far away. "But I don't hurt. I didn't cramp. I don't remember s-something g-going wrong."

Vivid orange. Yellow. Flames crackling. She had sat amongst them. The Fifika's, the Aishe's, the Violca's. Her friends.

Her betrayers.

*The singing, hypnotic. Bows on violins coaxing an eerie summons to the wild. Her ruby ring on her finger, shining for a brief moment.* But not here. She would never show it here again.

"You had pain, but we gave you potions." Simza placed her hand on Lavinia's arm. "We made you comfortable. We made you sleep afterwards. That is why you do not remember."

Out of the corner of her eye Lavinia caught a glimpse of dark blue—the dress she had worn last night at the fire. Someone had carelessly draped it over the chair next to her bed. Had they found her ring? Taken it? Without looking, she inched the garment towards her as if it were an afterthought, and hugged it to her chest, sneezing at the smoky odor. Her hand found the hidden pocket and she slipped the ring onto her finger. She turned the stone to the inside, careful to keep her other hand in plain sight resting on her simple muslin nightdress. She let the tears slide down her face, forcing them out and snuffling when she would have preferred to grab Simza by the throat.

The vein in her neck twitched like a heart pulsing out of control. *Nothing had happened. They were lying. Lying, thieving gypsies. She still had her baby. Why would they want to upset her so? To what end?*

She flung her arms as she stood. The cup and tray went flying, thudding against her bed and onto the carpets. Lavinia shoved past the stunned Simza. She shoved the older gypsy out of her way. The woman fell to the floor, knocking her head against a wooden trunk. She groaned.

Simza lurched at her. *"Rawnee!"*

Lavinia ran to the kitchen. Simza had hidden the knives. She fumbled inside the gypsy's bag. She knew the girl had a small folding knife. Ah. She pulled it out and opened it just as Simza took hold of her shoulders and spun her around.

*"Rawnee, I—"*

Lavinia thrust the knife at the girl's throat and held it there. Simza gave her a horrified look. Lavinia forced her back. "Sit in the chair or I swear I'll kill you."

Simza fumbled, clutched the chair seat and lowered herself into it. *"Rawnee.* If you hurt me, you ruin everything. All the djinni's plans. Your plans. The baby—"

"You lie. Don't try to cajole me with some fancy story."

"But it is true, I did not want to do it. But I did it for you. For you, *Rawnee.* A great sacrifice." Something flickered in Simza's eyes, a look that made Lavinia pause. An expression of intense sorrow, changing into wide-eyed terror.

"If you cry out." Lavinia brandished the knife and pressed Simza further into the chair. My God, Simza had said *sacrifice.* A pagan ceremony like the fire gathering, only . . . only a *gadje* baby, just born. Killed. Sacrificed. Blood and fire. The squealing violins smothering his desperate shrieks as they sent her baby to a gypsy hell. They had drugged her so she wouldn't hear. What mother is deaf to her baby's cries?

She wrapped her hand tight around the knife's handle. Is a blade like this what her baby felt instead of a mother's warm embrace? The cold blade of a knife against his soft neck? She would kill this gypsy bitch, this blood-crazed heathen. She would cut her throat, see the blood spurt out like her baby's.

She pulled the yellow scarf from Simza's neck and raked the knife over her throat just as the girl tilted her head away. Simza screeched. Lavinia jerked back, her hand shaking. *Lord in heaven*. A thin line like a cat scratch oozed blood on the girl's neck. Lavinia's stomach sat hard inside her, then caved in as if a solid creature inside had scrambled off. She had meant to kill the girl, to slit her throat deep and wide, but she didn't—couldn't—press hard, and then Simza pulled back. If that hadn't happened simultaneously, would Simza be bleeding to death in front of her? How could she—

"Do not do this! You kill me, you kill all your hope and the djinni's." Simza's dark eyes flashed. In a blur, she grabbed Lavinia's hand, twisting her wrist until the knife dropped with a clatter. The girl lunged for the weapon.

Lavinia caught her by the hair, bringing Simza to her knees, and managed to kick the knife out of reach.

"Sit." She jerked the girl's tresses, and forced the gypsy onto the chair.

She kept Simza's hair taut in her hands, making the girl cant her head at an awkward angle. Lavinia dropped to the floor and picked up the scarf. "Wrap this around one wrist, put your hands behind your back."

Simza just looked at her. Lavinia yanked her hair.

"Ow." Simza obeyed. Lavinia let go and bound the gypsy's hands, tying the scarf with a jerk of the knot. She crawled to fetch the knife, then sawed off the long remainder of the scarf.

"An eye for an eye," Lavinia mumbled to herself as she held the knife in front of her. But she couldn't do it. Couldn't kill this girl. May God forgive her. She knew Yasir wouldn't.

Simza pulled at her bonds. "*Rawnee*, you must stay here. You do not understand. If only I could tell you. Oh, this is wrong. All wrong.

Surely the djinni made you *see*, showed you in some way. Please, let me try to—"

Lavinia forced the scarf between the girl's lips just as Saddani's footman had done to her. Oh, she knew how to gag someone. She knotted the cloth tight, not caring if it hurt.

She refused to look at Simza again. Those eyes. The eyes of a betrayer. A thief. Lavinia ripped open the flap of the tent. She stumbled into the chill of the morning, catching her breath, her strength waning now that she had taken care of Simza.

Free?

Free to grieve her baby. Free to face Yasir with her failure to avenge their son's death. Free to have him devastate these pagans. She would—together she and Yasir would—seek their vengeance. And have it. A surge of energy burst through her. She fled past the fires, the simmering pots. Past the grazing fairytale horses. Past the tents, mute in the cool pale sunlight.

The forest grew thick with undergrowth amid huge ancient trees, their roots heaving from the earth like massive twisting serpents. Lavinia ran, then walked, floundering some, but drinking the air as if it were a magic elixir. She turned onto a worn path that narrowed until it became lost in the leaves and dirt under the towering trees.

Her stomach cramped. Liquid flowed down her thighs. She stopped to catch her breath and ran her finger under her nightdress. Pale pink. Blood and fluid. She gasped. Her baby.

*Please. No. Simza was lying. Lying!* They hadn't sacrificed her baby. They hadn't done anything. She still had her son, safe in her womb. Lavinia took a step, her hands fluttering as though they might take wing. She pulled her arms close to her chest but the tremors spread from her hands, racking her body.

*You lost the baby.* Simza's voice came from the broad oak looming in front of her. Lavinia turned and staggered towards a small clearing. *You lost the baby.* Mushrooms sprouting on a decaying log reproached her, their voices growing into a loud taunt. *You lost the baby. You lost the baby.*

Lavinia pressed her hands tight over her ears, but she still heard the beastly voices. *You lost the baby.* She stifled a sob as she picked her way through the bushes and trees. There must be another trail. She tripped, her hands stripping the leaves from branches too small to support her as she fell, tearing into the soil, crying the hurt out.

The smells of earth and old leaves and fresh green shoots rose from the cool loam dampening with her tears. Her hands pressed into the soil as she pushed onto her knees, shaking the dirt and leaves from her hair. She spit grit from her mouth and looked to heaven. Would she make a prayer for her child? Could she?

But she saw no blue sky, no soaring birds, only drooping swags of gray moss hanging from heavy branches high above her. Ragged funeral shrouds dulling the light as it strained through the hoary clumps and reached the long way down to the littered forest floor.

Shouts growing louder, moving closer. Her breath came in short noisy gasps, breaking the silence of the forest. They would find her. They would use their evil magic to do it.

She struggled to her feet, grabbing for handholds. The sweat beading her arms and face turned chill. Gold glinted on her finger. She turned the band so the ruby faced outward and steeled herself to face whatever consequences would come when she stroked it thrice.

Voices. The burr of the Roma tongue. The crack of branches underfoot. The rustle of bodies crashing through the undergrowth. They were coming for her. Already. The Chovihano wouldn't be so lenient this time. Her body tensed, craving to flee, but she forced herself to stay still. Any noise and they would be on to her sooner.

She drew her finger across the ruby, fast sure strokes. By the third one she was shaking so hard she thought the ring might fly off. She couldn't find her voice for the command. Tears streamed down her cheeks as she mouthed the words, then her voice spilled out in a raspy whisper. "Take me to Yasir."

# 21

*L*ighter than air was all Lavinia could think to describe her body when the forest dissolved around her like a gossamer tissue in water. Snatches of the gypsy's voices pierced the brilliant glow that enveloped her. She floated—different from when she had said, *take me with you*, after Peter shot Yasir. That time it was a squeezing darkness, a terrifying journey, but her choice. She would have had no one to blame but herself if she perished, but now . . . now she went to the djinni in a blissful luminescence, saved from the savage gypsies.

The floor against her feet, solid and hard, her flesh protesting all the while at being poured into a substantive form. Light surrounded her, in her eyes, over-bright, illuminating glittering gilded furniture, silvered mirrors, inlaid wood, bejeweled mosaics. Scents of myrrh, sandalwood and spikenard curling from bundled sticks in cloisonné vases. The alien melody of the djinni's music that always set her on edge: a sly flute, odd thrums of a stringed instrument like muted foot-steps, chimes of zhong bells building one upon another.

She backed up against the cold marble plinth of the winged lion sculpture behind her. She was in . . . Yasir's room? She blinked the dizziness away. Yes. That was her command. But where was he? The bed in front of her lay empty. His bed. Their bed when she was here. She frowned. The covers were bunched in disarray. She half closed her eyes and studied it. A diaphanous shape . . .? No . . . Yes. He wouldn't keep his human form when she was not there.

Her eyes darted to the door ajar onto the hall, the passageway dark and eerie. Had she seen something, someone, move? She bent over the bed and whispered, her voice dreamy and soft like wind in the grass, but nevertheless startling her. "Show yourself to me."

Light shimmered on the lemon silk of the sheets. Wisps of smoke floated above the brocade bedclothes, gathering like puffs of cotton. She held her breath as the nebulous form coalesced into a human shape.

Yasir, her djinni, her beloved, asleep in his bed. Even with his mesmerizing eyes closed he looked otherworldly. His straight nose, his full sensual lips, his dusky skin combined into a rare beauty. Lavinia smiled at his earrings, golden spirals glimmering with diamonds, twisting and turning like the workings of the mind. He wouldn't be parted from at least some of his jewels, even in his sleep. His kurta was unbuttoned and she slipped the cloth away from his chest to see if the bullet had left a scar.

She stifled a gasp and pulled her hand from the weeping, inflamed wound. He was not healed. She had removed the bullet, and Ganesha had taken care it wouldn't hurt Yasir anymore. With the djinni's powers, with the urn's powers . . . How could it be he still suffered?

She stroked his soft black curls. His breath came slow and peaceful in his sound slumber. Like an infant. Her stomach clenched and she gulped a sob. She tried to stop, but the tears came harder, her blubbering noisy and sloppy.

Yasir stirred, turning towards her. Clamping her hands over her mouth, Lavinia muted her sobs. He opened his eyes. Those amazing eyes. Golden. His pupils round and black, shrinking into pointed slits. He blinked, his long dark lashes shadowing his sleep-clouded gaze.

"My *del ara* . . . Forgive me." He looked through half-closed eyes. "I have forsaken you. I . . . ." His lids fluttered as he woke.

Their baby lost. He didn't know. She couldn't hold her tears. He stared and something formed in his expression. An emotion she couldn't read.

"I-I . . . It was the only way. I . . . ." Yasir squeezed his lids shut and opened them, the pupils rounding until they filled his eyes, the gold a bright halo around the black circles. He jerked to sitting.

"Lavinia!" His eyes focused. "*Mastara?*"

She moved nearer. "Yasir. Oh, Yasir." How could she tell him? The anguish wrenched her insides. He jumped up. Startled, she took a step back. Yasir seemed strong and vigorous. Perhaps the wound was in the last stages of healing. Perhaps it was mostly healed.

The djinni stared down at her. "Lavinia. You are here?" He glanced around the room, then rested his gaze on her again. "How?" He took a deep breath and shuddered as if he were striving to break free from his human form. His stern gaze cut through her sorrow.

She shrank away.

"After my instructions, why did you use the ring?" His voice sounded flat and cold. His eyes looked through her, sparks flashing through the gold.

Lavinia's mouth fell open. Did she hear correctly?

"D-dare you rebuke me?" Her mouth opened and closed, silent words she couldn't speak. "After what I have been through. Each. Single. Thing. Because. Of. You." Her arms spread wide, her hands pressing against the air. If only she could push him back into his form-lessness where he couldn't insult her.

"Spirited away by Rah—that dark magician, while you, you— And Saddani— I could have been maimed. Killed. I was alone with the gypsies. I lived in a tent, with no servants, threatened at every move. And, and . . ." She gulped air. Her face burned.

He stood firm, his body more solid than before, looming above her. "Neither the Dark Magician nor Saddani hurt you. And the gypsies took care of you. Nothing happened to you."

"Nothing happened? You—you—" her mouth worked. "You bastard!" She whirled around and picked up a tall rock crystal vase. "I-I could have died from sheer fright. How can you be so callous?" She hurled the vase. It stopped in front of him, dipping in obeisance. Yasir plucked it from the air and flung it over his shoulder, his mouth set tight.

At the noisy crash, Lavinia flinched.

"You don't even care about . . . about our child." Her breath came hard and quick. "You and y-your precious gypsies. God in heaven!" She burst into tears. "I l-lost our baby. I lost him!" Lavinia collapsed into a sobbing heap on the carpet.

"What do you mean?" Yasir's voice wobbled for a moment. For a split second she thought he looked sheepish.

Lavinia beat her fists on the carpet, crying harder. "You great. Stupid. Oaf. God in heaven." She sat up, pulling her nightdress tight against her stomach. "They said you could tell. Rak—the Dark Magician said you could *see*."

Yasir stared at her midsection. "He is gone." His voice sounded hollow.

Lavinia flattened her hand on her stomach. "Simza said I miscarried. But I had been fine, healthy. Then . . . that night. The Chovihano. The fire. The chants. *Your* voice too." She bowed her head, letting the sudden dizziness settle at what she had blurted. Something had just surfaced, something buried deep in her mind. Then she was sure. Sure that laced in the voices that night, she had heard Yasir—talking through the songs with the Chovihano, Simza and Mehadeh.

She swallowed hard and stared at him. Did he have a hand in this? Did he know exactly what happened? He had said no one hurt her, that the gypsies took care of her. He seemed angry that she was here. But it was his son. His son. Not even Yasir would conspire against his own blood.

Yasir pulled her to her feet, sat her in a cushioned chair and gestured for her to continue.

"I woke up the next day." Lavinia set her arms on the arms of the chair, clutching the curved ends with her hands. "The day after? The baby was g-gone." She strangled a sob. "They deceived you, Yasir. They stole my baby." Her hand fluttered to her chest. "Our baby."

He stood there, glassy-eyed. Did she see parts of the room through his body? Lavinia studied him closely. He dare not leave his human form, leave her. The expression in his eyes changed like clouds drifting through the sky. She glimpsed sadness shining there, tears that he didn't know what to do with. Disbelief. A hard, fierce acceptance. A flash of triumph.

Triumph?

He clenched his fists.

"Lavinia . . ." His voice was gentle.

She tilted her head in surprise. Why wasn't he raging against the despicable gypsies?

"Simza and the Chovihano would not harm our baby. They are more trustworthy than you know. Try to believe that." Yasir knelt and took her hands.

"I am sorry we lost our son." Tears shone in his eyes and he drew her against him.

She hammered her fists on his chest and pushed away. Lurched to a gilded chair in the corner and clutched the back, steadying herself. She stared at the floor. Why wouldn't he believe her? She had no reason to deceive him.

Something in the tone of his voice, the cast of his eye. Yasir's reaction was somehow stilted, rehearsed. What hadn't he told her? But she was so weary, and, in spite of her confident tone, unsure of what had happened.

From the back of her mind floated Simza's words . . . *I didn't want to do it. But I did it for you. For you, Rawnee. A great sacrifice.* And she had seen something flicker in Simza's eyes, a look that made her pause.

And now Yasir, a similar look. She recalled a few moments ago, his first words when he was still bleary: *My del ara, forgive me . . . I have forsaken you.* Then something like, *It was the only way.*

*Saints and angels!* What had he done? What had *they* done? She sank onto the chair and studied this creature. He stood in the same place, his eyes locked on her as though he wasn't sure what to do with her. Now that she didn't carry his child anymore. Now that she was no use to him.

"Our baby, Yasir. Our baby. Gone." Her voice was clear and strong. She wanted to be sure he heard. Be sure he understood.

"I can give you anything you desire, you only have to ask." Yasir took a step towards her, cajoling in a soft voice as if she were a toddler to be mollified with a sweet.

Lavinia rose, shaky on her feet. "Can you destroy Rakhshan?" she shrilled, purposely stating the Dark One's name aloud as if to defy fate. "Can you bring back my baby?"

"And you—" She pushed the chair to the floor. Gold shattered from the frame. "Y-you don't even care about our child." She let out a strangled cry and ran from the room.

Yasir clenched his jaw. Lavinia was wrong about his feelings. How he had grieved when he first heard about their baby, lamented for Lavinia, for her predicament. But he could do nothing, not now.

He sat on his bed. He needed strength. Mehadeh, in spite of putting great effort to heal him with her potions, had not met with success. His vigor stayed as ephemeral as raindrops in the desert. This wound from Rakhshan festered, healed over, ruptured and rankled again and again, eating away at him. He laughed at the awful ingenuity of it— the perfect torture, inflicted once, but persisting in spite of everything.

He waved his hand in the direction where Lavinia disappeared. She would come back to him. She was his now and, with the baby gone, out of harm's way. Safe at last. His plan was still in play, but she did not know, could not know—or understand. If there was a complication, it was that Lavinia had cleared the path for Rakhshan by using her ruby.

He had been prepared for that risk. He trusted that he had destroyed the path in time.

# 22

From his bed in the urn, Yasir watched Mehadeh swivel the cloisonné hourglass upside down on its axis, the minuscule silver grains swirling and flashing as they marked the time. She turned away from the shining pyramid settling at the bottom and stared straight in his direction, no recognition on her face. With his magic he looked through her eyes. Even this powerful sorceress saw only curls of wispy smoke growing longer and thicker, then coalescing into a shape more easily seen.

He sank into his human form, grimacing as the pain of his flesh and blood body greeted him. It had been a relief to be in the ethereal, although he couldn't sustain it as long as he liked.

"Ah, you are finally returned." Mehadeh examined the wound on his bare shoulder. She placed her hands on his chest. Her dark eyes drooped. "You took non-human forms and then substances of the ether as planned?"

He nodded.

"There is no change." The dull flatness of her voice shriveled the burgeoning hope that had buoyed him throughout this ordeal. Mehadeh sat heavily in the chair, red skirts bunching around her hips. Palms together, she opened and closed her hands, her long dark fingers mirrored, bending in tandem like a spider on a looking glass.

"The manticore seemed promising, but . . ." She reached into her skirts, pulled out a clear, round crystal and held it to the light. "Hmm . . . flesh and bone . . . air and ether." The sorceress gazed into the radiant stone. Yasir watched each configuration that he had assumed parade through the crystal: griffin, sphinx, dragon, mist, cloud, smoke, rainbow . . .

Yasir pushed to sitting, slipping two silken pillows behind his back, propping himself against the golden headboard. He closed his eyes for a moment.

"No matter the form I have assumed, substance or ethereal, the curse finds me there." Yasir took a deep breath and winced at the pain lancing through his shoulder. "Alice was correct in this."

He had wooed his Lady Lavinia in the wrong way. Too late, he heeded his half-sister's warning against toying with Peter's mind, turning husband against wife. A convenient, selfish way to have Lavinia without interference. The pillows swelled around him as he slumped. His spell had begun the disastrous chain of events: Peter shooting him. The bullet cursed. If he had paid attention to his half sister, perhaps Peter would not have found him embracing Lavinia, would not have shot him.

"This Alice?" Mehadeh held the crystal to catch the light.

"She knows of the prophecy. She wants me to be free." Yasir angled his hand and watched the vibrant red, indigo and violet play on his palm. Would the crystal make him better? He felt nothing from the prism's light shining on him. So different from the light of the moon after Peter released him from the urn.

That fated Cairo evening had been alive with the noise of crowds in the streets. After so long in the urn, the aroma of baking flatbread, roasted lamb, frying onions and garlic entranced him until he lifted his eyes to the full moon. The luminous orb floated in a sky of deepest blue scattered with twinkling stars. He near swooned at the power radiating from the heavenly body. Then he had seen the portrait of Lavinia on Peter's desk. He knew she was his Thalia. Hidden from his new master, Lord Peter Bramley, for a few last moments by the thick mist from the urn, he used his fleeting freedom to contact Alice, who had by then insinuated herself into Lavinia's family, gaining their trust until he could be free of Peter.

Yasir moved his hand out of the light from Mehadeh's crystal, letting the rainbow slant bright across his wound. With an almost inaudible sigh, the sorceress let the crystal fall from her fingers. It vanished in a flare of purple. She turned to a small chest on the bronze and silver table next to his bed and removed five pear-shaped bottles. Glancing at him, she set them in a row. "She will never forgive you."

"Why? I heeded Alice's advice. Eventually." Yasir moved the pillows to the side and lay flat on the bed. "She would have no reason—"

"Not Alice." Mehadeh stared into the room. She faced him. "Lavinia. Lavinia will not forgive you."

Yasir pushed himself up, trying to ignore the ache in his wounded shoulder. How could Mehadeh say such a thing? She knew what had been at stake. "I would have lost them both otherwise."

"Perhaps you have lost her even now." The sorceress gave him a grave look and motioned him to lie down. She placed the first bottle, half filled with rust-colored liquid, inches from his wound.

"I have not lost her." Chin to his chest, he strained to see. As she moved the bottle nearer the inflamed bullet hole, the liquid sparkled. How long to heal? Not for the first time, Yasir wondered if the dark sorceress had a pact with Rakhshan to keep him weak.

"Your magic is not the same. You do not know what she is thinking." Mehadeh removed the bottle. She shook the second one and set it in the same place on his chest. The blue potion churned, sending a stream of pale bubbles to the surface in a frothy mass that collapsed and dissolved. He startled when the clear liquid in the third bottle stained red as blood.

"This one. It will hurt." Mehadeh glared at him. "You weakened when you used your powers to assist the Chovihano and his daughter to banish the one who cursed you to the urn." Her eyes sparked with hatred. Were these her true feelings towards Rakhshan? Yasir studied the sorceress. She mumbled to herself. Incantations? Curses?

He struggled to a seated position. Mehadeh's curses, even when directed at someone far away, could have unintended consequences to those physically in her presence. The sorceress thrust both hands out, palms up, blocking his escape. "Lavinia cannot fathom how much it cost you. *All of it.* Just for her." She motioned him down again with a flick of her palm.

Stifling a surge of anger, he lay on his back and nodded his permission. She pulled the cork from the bottle. The stench of stagnant pond water made him draw his muscles tight. With a steady hand, she poured the red liquid onto his wound. He clamped his jaw at the numbing pain, his body, beyond his control, bowing upwards in agony. *By the Djinn.* He attempted to escape into the ether, leaving this human flesh and blood, this suffering, but the pain kept him imprisoned, fettering his magic.

Mehadeh watched, her eyes glazed over, as if she were stirring a pot on her witchy fires. Did she enjoy hurting him? Did she think he deserved it?

She waggled her head. "Lavinia will not know how much you love her. You cannot say what you did." The sorceress pulled a reed-thin glass vial as long as her little finger from a hidden pocket in her skirt, white pellets inside lined up like peas in a pod. She snapped off the end. "Open your mouth." Mehadeh poured the contents onto Yasir's tongue. His mouth watered at the sharp tang.

"Let them dissolve. They will return the strength you lost shape-changing." She crossed her arms, studying him as a surge of magic shot through his body. He raised his hand. The vial floated to him in a show of his power, but his arm trembled and dropped onto the rumpled bedclothes, his magic vanished.

Mehadeh touched his forehead, her dark eyes full of concern. "I will bring food. Stay here. Use no magic. Your body, your essence, be it flesh or ether, can lose nothing else."

Did her touch weaken him more? No, she was trying to heal him. How could he doubt her when they had taken a blood oath?

Lavinia paced down the hall, her mind teeming.

*Why was Yasir so unfeeling when she told him about their baby? She knew he wanted the child as much as she did. Why it was as if . . .* She halted in mid-step. *As if he were pretending to be shocked.*

He should have been horrified about losing the child, yet there was something stilted in his actions. Something false. Yasir was canny and shrewd in ways a human couldn't fathom. If what the gypsies said were true—that he was working with them to keep her safe—Yasir would know what had happened. What was his game?

She set her hand on her stomach. The aching pain in her womb was now from her grief. Her child gone. The gypsies's betrayal. Yasir's strange reactions.

Lost in thought, she looked up just as she veered into the wall, catching herself with her hand smacked flat against the marble. Her fingers sank into the clammy surface. Repulsed, she attempted to pull away, but her hand stuck fast. Several doors glided past, then a dark corridor. Was the urn moving? Or was she? *Stars in heaven*, she couldn't tell.

She tugged at her hand and pulled back, exerting more force, but her hand stayed fixed to the wall. The urn moved by faster and faster in a blur of color and gilt, making her so dizzy she closed her eyes.

Without warning, her vertigo ceased. The wall was hard now, cool under her palm like marble should feel. She opened her eyes. The urn was still and solid, nothing speeding by. She made sure she stood steady on her feet, then jerked her hand away and hurried into the hall's center, as far from the wall as she could go.

A gilded door stood ajar in front of her. Yasir's door. The only gilded door she had seen in the urn. All were ornate with reliefs, embedded with jewels, but not gilded. Could Yasir have brought her back to him in this strange way? She felt her heart leap. He would beg for forgiveness. Enfold her in his arms.

In the hall leading up to the door, there were no familiar land-marks, but then the urn kept changing. She shrugged and gave the door a little shove. It swung open. Heart thudding in her chest, she gripped the doorframe.

No. This was wrong. Wrong.

In front of her, where Yasir's chamber should be, was *her* room at Bramley House, every item in its place: gossamer lace curtains filtering light from the casement window, her embroidery hoop tucked neatly into the sewing basket, her blue satin wrapper draped over the chair, angled away from her writing table, just as she had left it.

Lavinia walked out, pulled the door shut, and pressed hard against it, staring at the diamonds glinting in the hall ceiling. What sorcery was this? What went on in the djinni's devious mind? Where was he?

She would burst in, command him to leave her alone, to quit this bedevilment. Lavinia depressed the handle, hesitated for a moment, then with a slow, deliberate motion opened the door.

"Lord in heaven." She breathed the words out in a shaky whisper. Still *her* room. Just as she had left it when she went to the garden to summon Yasir. Just before Peter shot him. She stared at the curtains gently swaying in the breeze, the fresh scent of new-mown hay wafting through the stuffy air.

If only she could change things. She would have called Yasir to her room, safe behind a locked door so they wouldn't be discovered. She would have considered the risk he took to appear in the very house where Peter was truly master. She would have taken care not to lead him to peril.

She lifted her foot over the threshold. Dare she put it down? Would she be transported back with Peter? She fingered her ring, her link to Yasir.

Home. It had been so long. Before she realized it, she stood on the carpet inside her room, where all this had started months and months ago. In her memory, events compressed as if chunks of time had been sliced away. She had left for a walk in the garden. A simple walk in the garden. Then . . . then things she could never have imagined. And now she stood in her room at Bramley House. An illusion?

She looked down at her feet, her silken slippers from the urn dotted in brilliant jewels, glittering with gold against her familiar wooden floor. The fantastic and the ordinary. She put her hand to her chest. *Lord in heaven*, she could barely breathe. She sank into her chair by the window and flicked away a line of red thread from the upholstery, a stray from the poppies she had embroidered on a handkerchief for Alice. Was Alice trying to find her? Was Peter?

If she looked outside would she see into a room in the urn? Would she see Yasir laughing at her? She cringed, and faced the open window. Distant trees, clouds floating across a blue-gray sky, cows lowing in the meadow. Real. Just what she always saw out this window.

A gust of wind billowed the curtains. The dressing room door opened just a crack, then groaned and swung wide. She gripped the chair arms. She should leave. This wasn't really her room, was it? She was in the urn, in the place where Yasir's chamber should be.

But there was something . . . something she had to see.

Lavinia rose from the chair and crept towards her dressing room. What if her maid Fleming breezed in? Or Peter? She looked back at the door to her room, imagining running to Peter's study. But the door led to the urn. And if she saw Peter what would he do? Would he welcome her or condemn her? A chill enveloped her. She folded her arms over her stomach.

She walked into her dressing room. The chest of drawers and looking glass shone without a speck of dust and smelled of beeswax polish. Neatly arranged on her dressing table, her crystal bottles and porcelain jars of powders, creams and scents sat just as she had left them, a trace of her lavender perfume in the air. She picked up the brooch of a calla lily that Peter had given her, the silver smooth and cold. Lavinia averted her eyes, loathe to view her reflection in the mirror. She drew in her breath.

The brass of the urn glistened amongst the crowded assortment on the dressing table. She reached for it, but stopped, her hand hovering above the lid, her mouth so dry she couldn't swallow.

Lavinia pulled her hand away and looked around, her eyes unfocused. She was *INSIDE* the urn. But the vessel was here, in front of her. She bit her lip. How could she be IN the urn and IN her room at Bramley House? The room contained the urn, the urn contained the room, and she was in both of them. Nausea flickered through her stomach as she lurched through the door.

She stumbled past her bed. The bedclothes, heaped over a solid form, rustled. Lavinia froze, her mind racing. How could she not have noticed that someone was in her bed? But when she had entered the room, the silk coverlet had been spread flat and smooth, the embroidered pillows fluffed and arranged the same as every day. She hunched forward and slunk towards the door when an arm flung out from under the covers, a slim hand hanging over the side.

A glimmer of red. *Her* ring. *Her* hand.

She stared in horror. *Upon her soul. She* was *in* her bed, sleeping.

Her legs wouldn't move.

A murmur came from the figure, unintelligible, then, "Peter? Yasir?" The covers rustled, the person sat up. Lavinia turned towards the door. A scream cut through the room.

Lavinia staggered, picked up her skirts and fled through the door.

In the urn's hall she stood, hands in tight fists, breathing hard. She looked again to make sure. The door she had slammed shut was gilded—Yasir's door—the only gilded one in the urn as far as she knew. Would the person in the bed awaken fully, open the door? Lavinia turned away and looked down the hall.

Did Yasir create this Bramley House scene to throw her off? If so, she was suitably shaken. She started to lean against the wall, but viewed it with suspicion and moved away, holding her arms to her side. Her child, lost. Her home, far away. She narrowed her eyes . . . and Yasir, lying and scheming like the gypsies.

She marched up to the gilded door. Gripped the handle. If she had to face herself, by God she would. She pulled it open.

Of its own accord, her hand clamped onto the doorframe, somehow keeping her upright, when she would have slid to the floor in astonishment. Her room at Bramley House had vanished. In its place was Yasir's chamber, opulent as a paradise, the djinni nowhere in sight.

Had she imagined the disturbing scene at Bramley House? She splayed her hand on her chest, her fingers brushing a hard, cold object on her dress. *Angels in heaven!* What thing—? Slapping at it in fear, she looked down. The silver brooch. From Peter. She must have absently pinned it to her gown after she took it from her dressing table.

She slumped against the door, averting her eyes. If she could make her legs work she would run from this room, but she wasn't sure they would hold her up much longer. She fumbled for the door handle. Surely she—

"Lavinia?"

She raised her head. Yasir sat in the gilded chair, the gold showing no sign of the damage she had caused yesterday. Did everything automatically heal here? Everything but Yasir? But he looked hale and healthy now. He had kept his human form, his usually inscrutable face showing surprise.

Oh, he was surprised. Surprised she wasn't cowering in that magicked room, slinking away from the urn, from herself in her own bed. Surprised she hadn't fallen for his trick.

Lavinia strode towards Yasir.

"Bring my baby to me." She kept enough distance between them so he couldn't put her more under his sway. He drew up his chest, watched her for a moment. She had startled him. Perhaps he didn't know about her room at Bramley House appearing in place of his. Perhaps someone or something else caused these disturbing occurrences.

"You are in the urn now, Lavinia." She stiffened at his harsh tone.

"It is different here." His eyes shone hard. She attempted to hold her hand up against the dazzle, but her body wouldn't obey. "Outside you are my master. I am your slave." Yasir didn't blink. Did she catch the flash of a grin? But his expression was somber now.

"In here . . ." He swept his hand over the room, the air shimmering in its wake. "I have power, even over *you*, my *mastara*." Yasir twisted the word into almost a curse.

"How . . . how can you say that in such a manner?" Lavinia started towards him, but halted. How dare he talk to her that way. She clenched her fists. "What game are you playing with me? You wanted this baby as much as I. I can't understand—"

"It is no game." His voice had a tone she had heard before, when he had spoken of his capture and torture by Rakhshan. She looked up at him, unsure of what she would see. His face distorted with anguish as if he again felt the lash searing into his bleeding back, the ropes eating into his raw wrists and ankles.

"Whatever has been done, has been done for you." His eyes drunk her in with an intensity that reached deep inside her, drawing her to him. She recoiled even as her breath came hard and fast, her legs unsteady with the thought of seeking his embrace.

"But your wish will be fulfilled . . . In time. I see your doubt, so I will grant a portion now." He ran his finger over the cobalt blue beads of her necklace and stopped at the talisman. Yasir gave her a peculiar look. "The Chovihano made you a strong charm. He would not do that for just anyone." He gently lifted the necklace and rolled one of the beads in his fingers. The strand felt warm on her skin. He drew his hand away. A bead rested in his palm, growing before her eyes.

"Hold out your hand, *mastara*." Yasir placed the warm bead, now as large as an apple, in her palm. It was all she could do to curve her fingers around it to keep it from rolling off. The heat radiated down her arm, into her chest, growing hotter, almost too hot.

"Yasir?"

He took her arm.

"Do not fear—"

"Oh." Lavinia doubled over, clutching her stomach. She looked up at Yasir, her face twisted in pain. What was he doing? Why? She had only been kind to him and—

Her body came to attention as the oddest sensation spread through her. She rose slowly, feeling each motion as she stood. Different. She felt different, as though she had become accustomed to a heavy load strapped to her back and, in an instant, had been relieved of it.

Where was the bead from her necklace? She looked on the floor. Absently felt for the necklace. It lay around her neck, the talisman in place, no beads missing.

"The necklace is important. The Chovihano's talisman will work no matter where you are." Yasir indicated her midsection. "You are healed. But the rest must happen in its own time."

She studied him, this djinni, standing in front of her speaking in riddles. "Will your magic bring my baby to me?"

"He is my child as well." His eyes focused in the distance as if he were in communion with someone far away. "Like your seasons, there is a time for certain magic. You must be patient."

More riddles. She could question him on and on, but each time she had, he implored her to be patient. His words settled into her, gentle words, said with tenderness. He looked at the floor. His shoulders slumped. Why, he was sad. And he attempted to hide it. She tried to see his eyes, then she could tell if he were truly sad, or just—

He raised his head and met her gaze. Everything around him clouded, blurred until there were just those golden eyes.

In one motion, swift as thought, he swept her into his arms, his desperation all but making her cry out. He kissed her cheek, her eyes. Small caresses. His lips touched her brow, her mouth, soft and slow. She had let him come too close, his power surrounding her, seeping into her pores. She pushed against him.

"No. How can you think I want to be with you? I just gave birth—" She backed away, holding her hands out. "Don't come near me." She stopped and rounded on him. "I'm tired of your riddles. You profess to know the gypsies, that they wouldn't harm us. You're hiding something. Do they have my child?"

He stood before her and dropped his arms to his side, head bowed. "Our son is dead." She put her hand to her mouth. "Through no fault of the gypsies. You miscarried. The child came into the world too early. He couldn't survive."

She sat heavily in some chair nearby. So Simza hadn't lied. If the girl were here she would wrap a blanket around Lavinia's shoulders and bring herbal tea, saying in her soft accent: Rawnee, *drink this and I will rub your feet and sing to you*. Yasir had healed her womb, but she needed comforting now. She put her head in her hands and wept fully for their infant son.

Heaving a sigh, she blotted her tears with her nightdress. The same nightdress she wore when she ran from the gypsies, what seemed weeks ago, but was surely less than a day. How long had she sat there, her grief all-consuming? She peered around the urn, the beautiful furnishings glittering gold and silver, the jewels' rainbow colors cold and hard. Where was Yasir? She had expected him to at least offer sympathy. The ingrate. She burst out, "How could he leave me so distraught? Is he completely devoid of feeling?"

She tilted her head. When she was crying, she looked up to catch her breath, tears streaming down her face. He had turned away, but not before she glimpsed his face—ashen, his golden eyes wide and staring. She had felt him grip the chair back, then cup her shoulders, as if he would scoop her into his strong arms and comfort her. Then he was gone. Only now did she shiver at his unusually cold hands.

She huddled in the chair. How she yearned for some solace: a warm touch, a gentle voice. With a start, she sat up straight. Yasir's expression—

Fear.

Yasir had left because he was afraid.

She stood up. Near the freshly spread bed, an elegant table had been laid with one place setting. The ornate china dishes were empty and no serving pieces were in sight. She could almost taste steaming soup, hot bread with butter and—

A bowl of soup appeared on her plate, a loaf of hot bread wrapped in cloth of gold and, beside it, a silver plate with yellow butter molded in the shape of a rose. The robust taste of wine passed through her mind and a graceful stem of fine crystal appeared, filled with deep red liquid. No, white would be better.

The wine changed color. She sat and took a sip. Dry, yet sweet. The soup proved hot and filled with vegetables and white bits of chicken. Perfect.

Was she to be alone the whole night? She had escaped to the urn, coming to Yasir for . . . Well, not for this. She had expected his open arms, his outrage at the gypsies, his gallant rescue of their child. She should be holding her baby now. But he . . . He—

"Yes, not what you wanted. Not what you hoped for."

She swiveled to her side. Yasir stood there, looking down at her.

"Not what I hoped for." In spite of all, she smiled at him. A weary smile, one of sad acceptance. A turmoil of protest churned inside her, but she stemmed it. Not now. No, she'd had enough. He sat across from her, his hands clasped on the table, averting his gaze when she directed her eyes at his. No doubt about it—guilt. Guilt and fear. She couldn't unravel it, didn't care to try. Not tonight.

"Yasir, please—"

"I am sorry. Sorry for what happened to our son, for us in this predicament. Until I am fully healed, my magic is not always there when needed. Even human's gods fail them, yet many keep faith. Lavinia, this curse will be countered, and we can have our wishes."

She took his hands in hers. He gazed into her eyes. Acceptance and compassion imbued his sadness. He conjured a crystal carafe and poured two long-stemmed glasses full of what looked like dark red wine. He placed one in her hand.

"This will help us both. It is wine, but more. You do not know it in your time." He sipped and his eyes sparkled. She drank from hers, the crystal so light she feared the touch of her lips might crack the fine glass. The wine tasted sweet and, as it went down, imparted a strength or a kind of fortitude as if one prepared for battle.

"I know there is something you're not telling me, something important . . ." She fiddled with the heavy silver soup spoon and laid it on her plate. "But I can wait for when you're ready." She drank more of her wine. Truly, it made her stronger. That, together with Yasir's healing, and it was as if nothing untoward had happened to her physically.

She took his hand, warm now. A surge of—want, longing?— rushed through her. She needed him, needed to have hope. A new life for them.

He looked deep into her eyes. "It has been so long." His voice trembled.

He slipped his palm from hers, walked around the table and stood before her, taking both her hands in his. So close to him. His desire pulsed in his wrists, in his very form, yet he held it in check, counter to his way of understanding the world. Waiting for her.

She walked into his arms.

"Just be still with me," he murmured. They sank onto his bed. From deep inside her a small spark of rage flared, but she staunched it, relieved that the crushing weight of grievances had disappeared with Yasir's healing.

His warmth. The way he shut his eyes when he pressed his body against hers. The moan that escaped him. She buried herself in his enfolding arms, his almost intangible scent. Yasir's eyes sparkled, dust of gold scattered in moonlight, absorbing her. His lips curved at the ends, a burgeoning smile, an angel's beseeching, his breath redolent of cinnamon and cloves.

She pressed her lips against his. The potency of his touch, the power of his presence. Her mind swirled, bright flashes amongst visions of Yasir kissing her, holding her, claiming her. She clutched his back, reeling.

Suddenly he was inside her, surrounding her like the endless night firmament, silent stars with shimmering coronas skimming by, receding into depths unknown. His body heavy against hers, the scent of myrrh and musk. He moaned, "Lav—"

She opened her eyes. Yasir arched above her in the throes of passion, glowing golden. Touching her cheek, he faded away in a dusting of glimmering light. Yet he hadn't moved—the full length of him still weighed on her body, the tingle of his magic rippling through her. She lay there, absorbing his warmth, fully sated, floating as if she had joined him in the effulgent glow surrounding her.

The light sparkled, ice crystals warming to sun rays, bringing her to a joyous ecstasy as his shape emerged: a being of enchantment, a flesh and blood man.

Yasir rested his head on her chest and she closed her eyes, the rise and fall of his breath slowing to a steady rhythm. He was part of her, more now than before. She was his Thalia, he was her djinni. She ruffled his dark curls and he met her eyes, his face flushed. He had given her what she asked and it was enough. But doubts fermented underneath her satiety: what had Yasir done that made him afraid, that made him bow his head and avert his gaze in guilt?

# 23

*W*ithout a sound, Peter leapt from the bushes and seized her arm. Lavinia grimaced at the pain, wrenched away and took off down the garden path, splashing into a puddle. She landed hard in mud up to her ankles. As she pulled one foot from the muck, Peter caught up with her, his face stony with determination.

"No, Peter." She stepped wide to the opposite edge of the puddle.

"You're mine. Mine!" Peter lunged and caught Lavinia's hand. He pulled her through the puddle towards him. The water eddied higher. Skirts bowing, she sank, fighting the current as it sucked her down, down into a whirlpool bobbing with leaves, twigs, the Chovihano's glowing scepter, Lavinia's beads and talisman, the ruby ring. Peter lost his hold. She sank for a moment, then surfaced, the water lapping at her chin.

"Yasir!" Lavinia's scream died abruptly. Water flowed down her throat, muddy and gritty. She gulped and choked—

Lavinia bolted upright, clutching the covers. Her throat hurt. Had she screamed out loud? In the dim light, the opulence of the urn glittered gold and silver around her. She pulled the covers up and sat staring into the room. A dream. Only a dream. Next to her, Yasir stirred, then fell back into a restless slumber.

Last night, Yasir's magic, his body on her bare skin. How she had missed his touch, his presence. She placed her hand on her chest, reassured that her nightdress—Simza's handiwork—was still gone. Yasir had vanished it without a thought. The garment had been one of the last reminders of the gypsy girl, gone, *thank the angels*. And good riddance.

Almost afraid to look, she raised her hand in front of her. The ruby ring, still there. She clutched at her neck, fingers searching the beads until she found the silver talisman. She was under Yasir's protection now. She didn't need it. Didn't need the Chovihano's and Simza's help anymore, if that's what it was. She lifted the beads halfway off, but stopped, the touch of the glass calling up the day of the storm in Simza's tent: *shadows gathering in the corner, cruel eyes capturing her gaze, a palm flashing a glint of silver.* Lavinia held the talisman at her throat. She would keep it.

She slipped from the bed. Cold water. She would splash cold water on her face, bathe the filth of the puddle from her skin. But it was a dream, only a dream. She rubbed where Peter had seized her, and gasped at the sharp pain. Furrowing her brow, she held out her arm and stared, disbelieving, at a dark blue bruise.

When she returned to their bedchamber, the vestiges of her dream flooding her with a wary uneasiness, she found Mehadeh bending over Yasir. Lavinia pulled her silk wrapper tight and glowered at the sorceress.

"Why are you here?" She should have known—the bottles, the potions in Yasir's room—of course they were Mehadeh's witchery. How dare she interrupt them after they had been apart for so long.

Mehadeh looked up, an inhuman move so sudden and swift, Lavinia almost cried out. Only a thin edge of white surrounded the huge dark irises of the sorceress's eyes, thin crescent moons in the darkest sky. Lavinia inhaled sharply and stepped back, almost tripping on the lengths of her wrapper.

"Lavinia." Mehadeh beckoned with a roll of her head. "Here. Press this cloth on him and don't move, even if it burns you." Mehadeh guided Lavinia's hands onto the poultice covering Yasir's wound.

"Hold it like this. There." Mehadeh ran from the room, her red skirts flying.

Lavinia stared at Yasir. "Lord in heaven," she murmured. His eyes were closed, his complexion drained of healthy color. Dull yellow stained the flesh surrounding his eyes and mouth. He had been in fine fettle last night, flinching now and then with pain from the wound when he moved his shoulder the wrong way, but downplaying it when she noticed. During the night he tossed and turned on occasion, but nothing unusual. Before she went to her toilette, she hadn't detected anything untoward, but she had barely looked at him in the dim light. Her hands occupied with the poultice, Lavinia placed her cheek on his forehead. She jerked back at the searing fever.

Had she enhanced the curse when she used her ring and fled the gypsies? Simza and the Chovihano begged her not to go to Yasir, but she didn't believe them. Yasir had barely touched her—until last night. Was it her touch that made him worse?

"Yasir?" He didn't respond. She started to shake him, but if she pressed hard on the poultice it might cause him pain. Eyes watering, she turned away from the burning menthol of the *kafur*, camphor, rising from the pouch. "Yasir," she cried out as she pushed against the bed with her legs, jiggling the mattress, trying to rouse him. She needed to hear from the djinni what to do. Not Mehadeh. Not the witch who found her at Rakhshan's.

As if the thought of the woman conjured her, Mehadeh rushed into the room leading a tall, gaunt man, a purple-striped turban wrapped around his head. "Is doctor," she said breathlessly. The doctor's white baggy trousers and knee-length shirt shone in the dim light, seeming to advance in front of his tea-colored flesh. In his left hand he lugged a bag whose weight pitched his right shoulder upward.

"Poultice must come off now." Mehadeh maneuvered Lavinia out of the way and took the gauze pouch off the wound. From the other side of the bed, the doctor examined Yasir, the top of his turban swirling the stripes into a pointed ellipse: an amethyst eye boring into her, tightening her chest with fear. Another sorcerer? He lowered his bag on a table that appeared just as he set the bag down. Moving like a snail, he took out three ornate gold instruments and applied each one to Yasir's wound.

After a long while, he shook his head. "This spell . . ." he moved a glittering instrument from Yasir's chest, "grows stronger even as I stand here. There is nothing I can do." He clamped his bag shut, the pop like the snap of jaws in the grim silence.

It couldn't be true. This was a magic doctor. Surely he knew of an alternative. The doctor blinked in rapid fluttering movements. He unfurled his handkerchief and dabbed at his eyes while he picked up his bag. Mehadeh took his arm.

"What of the child?" The doctor whispered, too loud. Mehadeh shook her head, and indicated Lavinia with a tilt in her direction. At the door, he glanced back, his eyes moist with pity.

Lavinia sank into the chair by Yasir's bed, her heart struggling with the doctor's grim prognosis. Anguish for Yasir compounded her mourning for their baby. She took his hand. Still burning with fever. Yasir opened his eyes—lustrous as pearls. His body flickered with light, solid flesh diffusing to translucence. His hand, substantial in hers, faded, until her fingers grasped at nothing. Lavinia could see the shimmering silk of the bedclothes through his body. Putting her hands to her mouth, she staggered up from her chair as if in a dream. Yellow sparks streaked through the darkness growing at the corners of her vision. She groped for support.

Mehadeh appeared by her side and helped her to sit again. She clutched the solid arms of the chair while the sorceress raised Yasir's head and shoulders and propped him against the pillows. Her dark hands showed through his chest.

Yasir turned slowly towards her. "You?" He squinted at her, his voice weak. "You look . . . so different."

*Dear God*, he wasn't sure who she was.

"Yasir, I haven't changed." She tried to control the wobble in her voice. "S-something is wrong. What is it?" She reached for him, but pulled back. If she touched him would her hand go through his body? Would she hurt him?

He watched her. She could feel him yearning for her touch. He reached out and clasped her hands, his flesh ebbing and flowing. An unbearable dread shot through her, bringing the same penetrating

chill of terror as when Rakhshan appeared in the gloomy shadows of
Simza's tent. Her skin prickled.

"No. No." She struggled and searched the shadows in the room.
"Yasir, let me go. Let me go. He . . . I feel him here. He could hurt you.
We will call another doctor. Save you."

Yasir released her and looked to the ceiling. "Rakhshan, you may
have me once again." His voice was flat. "But do not touch her." He sat
up in bed, his flesh solid now. Light from his eyes glimmered over her
and she breathed in his glorious magic.

"I will protect you." Yasir reached for her. "Always." He took her
hand again. The air grew heavy as the shadows crept outwards. Did
she see a mist rising, seeping around them? Yasir said something in
that tongue he used for spells, and released her hand.

"Yasir? The mist—"

"What have you done?" Mehadeh grasped her firmly, fingers
pinching her arms.

"I-I . . . ah." Lavinia glanced at the sorceress.

"He has done this for you." Mehadeh gave her a shove, thrusting
her forward in her chair. "And your son."

Lavinia whirled around, the gray mist thinning from her sudden
motion. "What do you know about my son?"

Mehadeh's eyes flashed. She pressed her lips together. "That you
lost him." The sorceress put her hands on her hips, looked Lavinia up
and down. She focused over Lavinia's shoulder. Her mouth opened in
surprise.

Lavinia turned towards Yasir. In the few seconds of their exchange,
he had slumped onto the pillows, his skin tinted pale blue. His body
shimmered: solid, translucent, transparent, and back again. He
motioned for Lavinia.

"I am going," his voice a whisper like his body.

She clutched what there was of him and shivered from the cold
creeping into his flesh.

He gazed up at her, her djinni. "Go and live with Peter. You will be safe, *mastara*." Yasir faded before her eyes. "Never mention the Djinn."

If she held on, surely she could keep him from whatever was destroying his human form. She would have his other shapes, the smoke, the—

"If the gypsies come, follow their bidding." Yasir's eyes glistened, effulgent, brilliant as a beacon. She pressed closer.

"*Zeeba delara*, beautiful beloved. My heart to yours." His voice cracked, wavered like his body. The light in his eyes shone. For her? Then dulled.

"My heart." Lavinia whispered, placing her right hand over his heart, his over hers. The beat of their hearts filled her palm, her ears. Hers fast and strong, supplementing his slow fading pulse. She laid her cheek upon his. The trill of birdsong. The rustle of wind in the leaves. The warmth of his lips pressing against hers. Sweet nectar. Balmy sunshine. His body firm against her softness. The beat of their hearts, so different, synchronizing until they pulsed as one.

Gasping for breath, she felt stillness under her hand. Lavinia raised her head. She touched his lips with her fingers. Kissed his mouth, his eyes, his cheeks. "Oh, Yasir." Her tears dropped on his face and still he didn't move.

"Yasir." She shook him gently. "Yasir."

He lay quiet.

She shook him. "Yasir. Yasir." She touched his neck, his wrist. Cooler now. "No."

"Mehadeh!" she screamed. "Mehadeh. No, Mehadeh."

A strong hand grasped her shoulder and gently pulled her away. Mehadeh touched the top of his head, the center of his forehead, his throat, his heart center. She looked up at Lavinia. Mehadeh's great dark eyes glistened, a deep pool filled with pain.

"He is gone, little one." A heaving sob tore from Mehadeh's throat. "And I could not save him." The sorceress wailed through her tears.

Her keening vibrated Lavinia's very bones while Mehadeh hugged her so tight she could barely breathe.

*I hope she squeezes the life from me.* Lavinia envisioned her own body, arms limp, eyes vacant, falling on the bed to join Yasir.

"A black sorceress should have beaten the Dark Magician," Mehadeh whispered. Her hot tears ran down Lavinia's neck. Lavinia willed her breath to leave her lungs, willed herself to go to the place where Yasir had gone.

"There was something else. There must have been something else." Mehadeh let go of Lavinia and stared at Yasir's body. She wrung her dress with her hands, twisting it until it writhed in her grip like a thrashing serpent. "The Dark One alone could not have become that strong. Did he have Yasir now, forever, with no peace for the djinni's soul?"

# 24

*M*ehadeh stared at Yasir's lifeless body. No matter what magic she had employed, nothing worked. In the intervals when his powers had been stronger, he would take another form, but each one bore Rakhshan's curse. A glint of gold flickered from his bed and she stepped forward, hoping for a miracle, but saw only the glitter of his earring in his dark hair.

She closed her palm, feeling an earring from long ago inside, the gold hard and unyielding. Soft magic, like the nibble of a minnows, engulfed her. So long ago, yet not so long, as the time spun in the world of the Djinn. Her chest tightened. The faces of her clan washed into her memory, etched with hard, accusing stares when they saw how she had failed to keep the spell she worked at her first initiation. The scowls said plainly that a five-year-old sorceress shouldn't let something startle her from conjuring—even if it was a young djinni tumbling from a tree branch into the *umhlaba nezulu* circle where she plied her magic.

They had surrounded Mehadeh and hustled her inside the sacred cave, but the shaman cast her out, saying she had the hex of the Djinn. Spoiled. She was not even as good as the slave from the Jahabi Clan that only had one shaman, and a bad one at that.

Her family made her sleep in the goat hut with a guard outside. When old Namtu fell asleep, she crept from the hut, tripping on the surly nanny goat, its startled bleat lost in the jungle sounds of the night. Stars dusted the dark hollow of the sky and a harpy screeched in the mountains. She clutched the earring tighter, feeling the magic grow. When the earring wriggled in her hand like a *kumna* bug, she knew where they held the djinni.

He was slumped in the corner on a pallet. Asleep? His curly hair shone in the moonlight, his rings gleaming like rainbows on his fingers. She steadied herself on the rickety basket she had pulled up to the slave shed, and wrapped her hands around the window bars, drinking in the djinni's magic. Strong. Almost strong enough to break their shaman's spell. She shrank back. Soon this djinni would be free.

But she had her task. Could she do it? Her face burned. He had ruined her life. Of course she could do it, but—

She let out a cry as golden eyes stared into hers. Without her sensing any movement, he stood in front of her. The djinni reached through the bars and took her hand. Her legs wobbled. Would he cast a spell? Turn her into a *gava gava* or a shrieking *treney*?

He opened her fist. "You brought my earring." He smiled and with a wave of his hand it glistened in his ear like a wink.

"Why did you curse me with a djinni spell?" Mehadeh glared at him, surely her fierce stare would make up for the quaver in her voice.

He laughed a soft laugh. "I merely frightened you. That is what stopped you working your magic." He squeezed her hand. "I was exploring your world and felt the pull of your power. As I sat in the tree your spell startled me, making me fall." He laughed again. "Felled by a child. You were only just beginning your task. If I had fallen later, you would not even have noticed."

Mehadeh cocked her head. A warm glow spread from her heart, rising to her checks then her ears. Did he mean it about her power? Or was he flattering her so she would help him escape? She knew next to nothing about djinnis, but when people whispered—*djinni, Djinn*—the word *halystana*—trickster, always followed.

"Remove your hex." She pulled her hand from his. She shouldn't have let him take the earring from her. She had planned to bribe him with it so he would give back her magic. Now she had nothing to bargain with. In her mind she heard her mother's voice: *You can tame your enemy if you have something he wants.*

"There is no hex, no spell. You are just as you were." The djinni spoke softly through the bars.

She gripped the window bars and peered at him. "Not to them. They think I am hexed. That I am ruined and cannot do magic."

"See that papaya hanging on the tree." He pointed over her shoulder. "The one nearest the stone path."

She turned her head, searching, then nodded.

"Bring it over here."

She wobbled as she turned to climb down from the basket.

"No. Use your magic." He put both hands on the bars, his rings glowing as if they were lit from within.

"The magic *you* took." Mehadeh crossed her arms and scowled.

"Just try."

She faced the tree, said her spell with care, enunciating each word as she had been taught, trying to forget about the djinni and his laughing eyes behind her. The papaya stayed still, mocking her in the cold moonlight. She whirled around, her fists clenched. The trickster.

The djinni held the big orange fruit in his hands. "See." He grinned, his eyes flashing.

She looked at the tree. The papaya was gone. "You did not do that?"

"It was all you. You may show your people you do not have a djinni hex." He let go of the fruit and it floated behind him like an ungainly bird. "But first free me. Your shaman's anger has made a strong spell, so I need a little of his own tribe's magic to overcome it. You are talented. You can do that. It will be like a little push."

Mehadeh looked up at him. A light shimmered around his body like puffs of dust dancing in the breeze. He put his hands through the bars. "Place your hands on mine with your fingers on the stones of my rings."

The stones were warm as if they had sat in the sun. They tingled her fingers. A faint sound like bells or a tinkling stream emanated around her. The djinni's golden eyes looked huge and she realized his pupils had shrunk to the tiny vertical slits of a serpent's.

"Listen to the gems." He tilted his head, a faraway look in his eyes. "Now say the spell with me."

Her head spun as she repeated the words, words that tangled her tongue, words of a Djinn spell. The stars whirled above her head, the blackness enveloping her, the sounds of the spell spinning into her very being. She felt his warmth beside her as he lifted her off the basket. The bars were still blocking the window. She opened her mouth to ask—

"A quick conjuration, thanks to your help." He set her on the ground and stood beside her. If her family knew what she had done . . . She hadn't thought what the djinni might do when she freed him. She hadn't thought further than giving him his earring and asking for her magic back in exchange. But had she gotten her magic back?

"Now you know you can be the sorceress your people need, little one." His voice sounded gentle.

"Mehadeh, my name is Mehadeh." She gulped and clapped her hands to her mouth. Why did she say her name? He could use it against her. Had he already started another spell?

"I am Yasir. And we owe each other nothing now, little Mehadeh. Let us be brother and sister in magic. Here."

He waved a curved dagger.

She pulled back, almost falling, but before she could bolt, a streak of blood glistened on her palm. He swiped the dagger over his palm and held it out, an identical line of blood beading onto his flesh. He held up his hand.

"Raise your palm."

She wanted to wipe the blood on her clothes and go back to her mother, her father, but his palm glowed, lit all around with golden light, the rainbows of his rings displaying their vivid colors in the dark night. Magic. Magic that he would return to her in his blood.

The djinni pressed his hand against hers. As their skin touched, he glowed brighter. Yasir moved closer. "We will each be the stronger for this. And no one will know."

Mehadeh startled at the last shrill of a harpy from the low valley. The night sounds of the jungle grew dim, and Yasir's voice faded with his glow. Time danced, wavering and bobbing like the trickster it was and she left her childhood behind. She looked around, taking in the richness of Yasir's urn.

Mehadeh raised her palm, the faint scar, old now, like another life-line only white. With a rush of agony, she viewed Yasir's body. So still. His earrings dull, almost hidden in his dark curls. She closed her eyes.

After all these centuries, she still could feel his power from that long-ago night pouring into her, and something leaving her as well, a feeling like warm tears streaming down her face.

Now, in spite of the powerful magic of the djinni's urn, she had failed him, just as she had failed her initiation.

Her family had not believed her. Her father spoke for them. "Your conjuration is adequate, but how do we know it is not the djinni's curse giving you this little magic?" Inside she had trembled with fear. Perhaps they were right. She knew what she had done. Her finger felt a sting as it traced the long rust-colored scab in her palm.

The next day they sent her to Idris. No one embraced her. Her mother, her father, her sisters and brothers stood with their arms stiff by their sides as if they too had been Djinn-hexed.

"There is no Djinn hex on you, child." Idris put her hand to her chin, squinting her tea-colored eyes as if she could see inside Mehadeh. "But there is something different in your magic. It's no wonder they sent you." With a clatter, she laid out her divining jewels. They sparkled on the white marble table as they slid into lines and angles. Keeping her hands in her lap, Mehadeh slanted forward, the bright rows of stones shifting, longer, shorter. At last, they took shape. A perfect star. Her scar throbbed on her palm.

At Idris' gasp, Mehadeh looked up from the jewels. The witch stared at the star shape, mouth open, but reassembled her expression as she saw Mehadeh eyeing her. She scattered the stones, destroying the star shape.

"No. I want to see it longer." The brilliant colors of the jewels had started to light up the lines and angles, casting colored shadows, creating another star alongside this one. Mehadeh tilted her head, watching Idris, but the witch busied herself putting away the jewels. Mehadeh jerked at the blunt force that pushed into her. She turned. No one stood there. She looked up at Idris, at the sorceress's faint smile, and knew where the force came from. Idris had tried to make her forget what she had seen.

Afterwards, the witch kept her close, even moving Mehadeh's bedding into her own room. Idris took her to the palace, where they stayed together in a room of silk carpets and wall coverings. Mehadeh acted as Idris's maid when the witch conjured for the courtiers, when she conjured for the master magician, Rakhshan. Idris hadn't known he favored her maid with trinkets of his affection, with private audiences.

Stirring from her memories, Mehadeh blinked, becoming aware again of her surroundings. She was still in the urn, her hands stiff from clutching the doorframe. Her feet straddled the threshold, bad luck surely. For a moment, she became puzzled at the aching emptiness that filled her body. A short time ago, the sounds of her wailing had filled this room, the anguish building in her like a storm.

She looked up. Yasir, his body tranquil in death, lay on the bed, Lavinia weeping by his side.

"We will each be the stronger for this. And no one will know." Mehadeh said the words, but heard Yasir as he had spoken them so long ago. She answered in a halting whisper, "But Yasir, neither of us was strong enough."

How gullible she had been. But she had been young, tossed from her family of sorcerers for failing her magic initiation. How glorious she felt when Rakhshan gave her runic sticks for conjuring, golden and jeweled charms against counter spells, and praise for her magic. She would've done anything for him. Could that powerful magician have seen fully what Idris could not? Could Rakhshan have seen that she was linked forever to Yasir?

# 25

They sat in a stupor, numb in the silence of the urn. Lavinia placed her hand on her chest, the rise and fall of her breath laborious. Sluggish. Diminishing. She closed her eyes. She breathed in, a fraction of a breath, so slight she thought she might suffocate, but she didn't care—she willed it so. Her breath could gradually cease until, with the wisp of an exhale, she would keel over, her spirit floating to join Yasir.

A stifled sob. Not hers. She raised her head. Mehadeh beside her, face wet with tears, brushed Lavinia's arm with the hand that had held the djinni's—a hand cold with the chill of death. Lavinia shrank from the finality of a rigid corpse and clasped her hands in her lap.

"It–it's just his body, gone. He can take many shapes. Won't he come back to us in another form if I wish it?" Lavinia straightened as a terrible weight dropped away. He would shape another body. Yasir would come back to her.

Mehadeh clucked her tongue and shook her head. "Little One, the djinni spent long hours assuming flesh and ether. But each and every form he took bore a corresponding flaw. The manticore, which looked so healthy, acquired an abscess on his chest within minutes of Yasir taking its shape, and proceeded to die in agony. That—that almost stopped us. But in the end . . ." Mehadeh directed her gaze to the floor. "It became clear that the curse was bound to the djinni, no matter what."

Lavinia rose to her feet. "How can you say that? How can you destroy my hope?"

Mehadeh seized her. "Shhh, little one, you must not disturb him. The djinni has much to decide."

"But. But, you said he was . . . You had tried everything. That he is g-gone." Lavinia squirmed from the sorceress's hold.

Mehadeh clasped her hand, a firm gentle grasp. "It is all true, but djinnis have to pass through many, ah . . ." the sorceress searched the ceiling with her eyes, "heavens after they leave the realm of the living. We must leave him in silence."

Lavinia gazed at Yasir. So still.

"We must go now. Together."

Lavinia pulled her hand away. "No."

"It is part of the ceremony. I promised him." Mehadeh glanced at Yasir's body. "He will rest peacefully until we return."

Lavinia moved closer to Yasir. "I will stay here with him."

She would send him thoughts of encouragement for whatever he had to do to take the correct path. He might hear her. Come back to her. He was magic. He could do it. She sat down in the chair next to his bed and reached out for his hand. It would be cold. But soon he would be warm, welcoming. When he came back to her. She clasped her hands in her lap, ignoring the sudden chill in the room.

"You must come with me." Mehadeh touched her shoulder. Lavinia kept her gaze on Yasir. Even this close she felt nothing from him. She would be truly alone here when Mehadeh left the room. Would Mehadeh return? A shock of fear tinged through her, prickling her skin. She wouldn't be able to leave the urn without the sorceress. She didn't know how to leave. Yasir had never told her how. Gasping, she clapped her hand to her chest.

Mehadeh wrapped her fingers around Lavinia's neck. Cold, like death. Then, in a rush of warmth Lavinia inhaled, almost strangling as the air rushed into her. The sorceress produced a vial from the folds of her skirt, pulled off the cap and held it under Lavinia's nose. She took a long slow breath filled with the fragrance of lavender and something sharp and stinging. A steady calm enveloped her.

Mehadeh took her hand and helped her from the chair. "Do not worry little one. The djinni has entrusted you to me." Lavinia let the sorceress lead her away. It didn't matter where she was going. Her wish was to join Yasir. *Her wish.* She scoffed at the irony. *Her wish*—a wish that could never be granted.

Mehadeh didn't say Yasir's name. She had warned Lavinia as they walked down the hall. Speaking aloud the name of souls recently departed would cause them to lose their way. They would want to come back to you, become confused and wander. Yasir had said nothing like that about their baby, their son. What if she had chosen a name for him, had been calling to him? She could have unknowingly damned the baby. If the gypsies didn't have him, if she had truly miscarried. A spark of anger pricked at the numbness of her grief.

Near the door to the great room stood a woman, the same color from head to toe, gray eyes, gray hair flowing onto a long gray robe enveloping her small stature. Mehadeh indicated the woman with a sweep of her hand. "This is Tsura. She will follow us back to the djinni's room and prepare him."

Tsura wavered behind Mehadeh, a hoary specter. The sconces flickered as they passed through the long hallway, transforming their shadows into ghoulish distortions. Did she actually see Tsura walking between them, her shape vacillating in the light, or did she imagine it? Had she imagined what happened to Yasir? Had she caused his horrible death?

The gypsies had warned her not to use the ring, had said the djinni forbade it. But they were thieves and liars. Yasir had accepted her when she appeared in the urn. "All in my head. All in my head," she whispered to herself over and over. He had not died. It was all in her head. The djinni would greet them at his gilded door, radiant with health.

They paused at the entrance to Yasir's bedchamber and visibly braced themselves. The light played on Tsura, making her a dim shadow one moment, a solid being the next.

Mehadeh opened the door.

The room felt vacant. Lavinia looked for Yasir, healthy, waiting for them, but saw only a shape on the bed. She stifled the impulse to run, yet she longed to be anywhere else. Anywhere she wouldn't have to face Yasir, still and cold.

A hard lump rose in her throat. She couldn't swallow. Her tears blurred the room, fuzzed the dim light, burned her face. They flooded down her cheeks. She walked towards his bed, too frightened to look, to see Yasir there with no life in him.

Mehadeh and Tsura halted in front of her. Lavinia raised her eyes. She blinked the stinging tears back and stared through a smudged haze at the bed.

Empty.

# 26

*L*avinia hesitated under the portico of Bramley House. She hadn't remembered how grand it was, how intimidating, with its many soaring Doric columns. The massive doors loomed before her. She glimpsed her dark reflection in the highly polished wood, a disembodied spirit unable to break through to her previous existence.

She reached out, as if touching the door would make things different. Should she ring the bell? Open the door and walk in? After all, it was her house, but it had been . . . . How long *had* it been? She had no idea, and until this moment she never bothered about what day it might be.

Her heart fluttering, she pressed down on the handle.

Locked.

Of course, she had no key. She possessed nothing but her rings from Peter and Yasir, her necklace with the talisman, and the green silk gown she slipped on in the urn when she awoke that morning. The morning her life turned on her.

She stepped back. The marble floor of the portico had been swept clean as usual. The sidelights of beveled glass dusted free of cobwebs. The bronze doorplates freshly buffed—she caught a whiff of vinegar. She looked through the copper-leaded panes to the grand entrance hall. Inside, a silhouette blurred into the hidden passage to the scullery.

Should she be here? She turned around. It would be easy to walk to the road. To disappear. Lavinia twisted a lock of hair around her forefinger. She looked at her slippers. Not a speck of dust marred the green velvet. She didn't remember walking up the road. She didn't recall a carriage ride. She had just appeared here. Appeared on the front portico, straight from the urn. Lavinia reached for her reticule, but her arm had nothing hanging from it and her fingers slipped down her gown. She had left empty-handed and was returning the same. She absently cupped her still-rounded belly.

Well, almost the same.

Her finger hovered over the doorbell. Why was she here? This was madness.

"Go and live with Peter. You will be safe, *mastara*." Yasir's voice, weak with his last words, surrounded her. She turned, then sagged with disappointment. Of course he wasn't here. He would never be here for her again.

Lavinia grasped the doorbell knob, pulled it out and pushed it in. Chimes pealed through the hall, trailed by delicate tinkling bells. Sounds she had heard a hundred times before. Louder than she imagined, from where she stood.

She hugged herself, her arms secure across her midsection. What would Peter do when he saw her? He had caught her in the garden embracing Yasir, yet when she had seen Peter last, he behaved as though the incident never happened.

But Peter was devious.

She forced her arms to her side, to rest there, relaxed, poised. There was a possibility he would turn her away.

A gentle breeze ruffled her hair. Sunshine brightened the smooth green lawn. Distant laughter and voices of servants loading supplies in the storerooms near the stables wafted in the air amid the occasional bang of pans from the scullery. A goldfinch's silvery twitter trilled over the grounds, sending shivers down her spine, taking her back to the gypsy camp just before the storm that brought Rakhshan to Simza's tent.

The door opened slowly.

Dobson's congenial visitor face went blank. His mouth gaped in surprise. It took him a moment to reassemble his face into a proper English butler's. He spoke hastily, in a rather strangled tone. "Lady Lavinia, we were so worried."

Struggling to keep his composure, he opened the door wide. "Please . . . do come in. May I get you anything, milady?" Dobson's hand trembled as he closed the door, his eyes asking all the questions he wasn't permitted.

Lavinia attempted an answer, but couldn't speak. Instead, she strode down the grand entrance hall, her gait faltering here and there at the faint odor of beeswax polish, the sweet fragrance of fresh flowers in vases. Smells of home. At the door to Peter's study she hesitated. Would it be locked? Would she have to knock, wait? Wait for him to confront her and slam the door in her face?

She took a breath, pressed the handle. The door swung wide and she stepped inside, steeling herself to face Peter who would look up from behind his desk.

Empty. She checked again, walking farther into the room, trying not to tremble at the spicy smell of his tobacco, the faint odor of horse from the stables, the sharp burnt smell of India ink. She walked towards the screen hiding Peter's reclining couch. He could be there, a glass of brandy in his hand, studying his ledgers as he rested on—

"Milady, milord is at the stables."

Relief found her words. "Please have his Lordship come at once." Her voice rang through the study, high and wavering. Someone else's voice.

"I'll have him up promptly, milady." Dobson turned from her with a bow, and, from the look on his face, Lavinia pictured him sprinting to the barn calling out, *she has returned, milady has returned.*

She stood in the middle of Peter's study, feeling grossly out of place, even while noting that the room looked the same as always. The stuffy air weighed on her and she turned towards a window with the thought to open it, but just then a puff of breeze stirred the curtains. For a moment she questioned again if she still belonged here, but with Yasir gone . . . Lavinia had promised herself not to think of him today, if only to keep her sanity. She fanned her face with her hand. The room had become stifling once more. From Peter's desk she snatched a thin bound ledger, which afforded a fair breeze. As she fanned herself, she glanced at an unfolded letter under the faceted crystal paperweight and read her name penned in a competent hand:

. . . *herewith Lady Lavinia Bramley, in a delicate Condition (expecting the Heir to Bramley House), whereabouts unknown for these Six Months, cannot be accounted for. The Circumstances surrounding Lady Bramley's Disappearance being such that Foul Play is suspected. We have interviewed over fifty Personages in and around the said Area and have concluded that it is Unknown what role the Victim played in the Proceedings. It is unlikely that—*

The fast clip of a galloping horse. She looked up. *My God,* he was riding straight from the stables. A jitter in her stomach translated to her muscles. In a short jerky motion, Lavinia set the ledger on Peter's desk. No. It should sit on top of the letter, almost covering the writing. As she picked it up again, she could barely feel the book in her hand. The ledger's lower corner hit the paperweight, skittering it across the desk. Reaching for the crystal, she scattered a bundle of letters. A last minute grab. She fumbled, the side of her hand propelling the paperweight toward the desk's edge. Her sharp inhale broke the silence of the room before it was filled with the shattering glass.

"Angels in heaven." She breathed out the words in a hushed voice. Glittering fragments scattered on the oak floor. With the edge of her gown shielding her hand, she swept the pieces under the rug, grimacing when a shard pierced her palm.

The creak of the double front doors opening. Dobson's muffled voice. She jumped to her feet.

*Peter!*

She straightened and brushed her hands together, smearing the drop of blood from the small cut. The hard leather soles of his riding boots echoed through the grand entry hall. She looked about, hands fluttering and sought someplace to hide. But Dobson had told Peter she was waiting. She closed her eyes, praying she could get through this, and gripped the back of the closest chair as the door opened.

Peter halted inside the threshold, leather riding crop stiff in his hand. His queue had come loose and his blonde hair flowed about his shoulders. He stood stock-still, eyes fixed on her. Lavinia had forgotten how blue they were, how pale, like the sky in early morning. Black-eyed gypsies. Golden-eyed djinnis.

Blue eyes. She didn't know what to do with blue eyes.

Her knuckles whitened, bleached bones on the curved chair back. The muscles in her legs stiffened, readying to flee at a moment's notice.

She kept her eyes on Peter, unsure of what he might do. In her mind the memory of a shadowy image became distinct: a hand, Peter's hand, raising a sturdy cane, his face distorted with anger. The crash of the blow against her skull, the searing pain, the numbness of the black void enclosing her. She had awakened, healed by Yasir's magic, but Yasir couldn't save her now. Her heart thumped in her chest, pounded in her ears.

"Lavinia." Peter stepped forward. The shine of his knee-length boots reflected the daylight from the windows. The flush on his face heightened. Clouds of anger gathered in his eyes. He walked towards her, a puzzled expression settling on his features.

"God in heaven, Lavinia." He picked up his pace, hurrying to catch her as she crumpled to the floor in a dead faint.

# 27

"Yasir!" Lavinia screamed. "Yasir!" Her throat burned.

She stared at the bed. Empty.

She ran through the hall, passing rooms with doors ajar, the shadowy insides gleaming with lavish furnishing, but no Yasir. A cloud of steam poured from an archway in front of her.

"Yasir?" She waved the mist away enough to see, and hurried through. A woman, her back to Lavinia, stirred bubbling liquid in a huge kettle.

"Mehadeh? Is that you?" Lavinia's voice sounded muffled. "Where is Yasir?"

The woman continued stirring, concentrating on the contents of the cauldron. Had she heard? The woman turned towards her, a deep black shadow where her face should have been. The steam swirled and hid her in great clouds of pungent mist.

Lavinia tried to run, but her body twirled helplessly into the eddy of steam.

"Lavinia. Lavinia!" A deep voice buried in the mist grew louder and louder. "Lavinia."

She opened her eyes.

"There you are." Peter smiled and took her hand. He sat in a chair next to the bed where she lay almost smothered under the covers. She squeezed her eyes closed, and opened them once more. This was her room in Bramley House. Light shone outside the windows. Daytime, and—

"Lavinia dear, you had a nightmare or should I say a daymare." Peter crossed his arms, never taking his eyes off her. Fighting the covers, she sat up, and with an exhale of exasperation, shoved them away. She was fully dressed—her green gown. Her room looked the same as always. As if she had never left, as if Peter had never shot Yasir, as if she hadn't just been in the urn. She pressed her hand against her stomach. As if she'd never carried a child. Her eyes stung with tears.

She put her hand to her throat. "Peter, where is my necklace?"

"Those gypsy beads? Strewn over the floor. Slipped on the damn things. Had Fleming clean them up." He brushed at his sleeves as if stepping on the beads had somehow tainted him.

A knock at the door. She startled and clutched for the covers. A footman entered, holding a tray with a china tea set. He moved a walnut tea table beside her bed and laid out cups and saucers and savories. The silence in the room weighed upon her, a living thing sucking the air from her lungs. She had never felt awkward in front of the servants, but now she didn't know where to look.

"That will be all." Peter nodded. The footman closed the door behind him, leaving her alone with her husband. Lavinia stepped onto the floor. She would follow the footman out. Leave this place. Find Yasir.

Peter took her hand. She flinched. Turned her head and met his pale blue eyes, soft and welcoming, then narrowing into a hard stare. He smiled, but his eyes did not. He slipped his hand from hers and leaned close. Lavinia stiffened.

"My dear, you fainted." He poured tea, added a bit of milk and put the delicate china cup in her hands. "This should make you feel better."

She pulled her legs back on the bed and put the cup to her lips, the milk purling in a vortex, the hot liquid soothing her raw throat. Why was he looking at her that way? She took another sip. The tea's earthy smell and the solid cup in her hand further awakened her. Inside her head she saw herself standing, hesitant, on the Bramley House porch. Dobson's shocked expression, the tap of Peter's boots on the hard marble floor of the hall. Her hand trembled as the memories came flooding back. She was again in Peter's study reading the letter about her disappearance. Was it only a few hours ago?

She studied Peter, sitting calmly in the chair beside her bed. Did he suspect that somehow she had a role in her own kidnapping? Had his solicitors subtly implied as much? Or was he remembering how he had found her in Yasir's arms, the shot of his pistol as it recoiled in his hands? He hadn't taken his eyes off her since she awoke from that terrible dream. She took another sip of tea, the panic from her nightmare threatening to engulf her.

Peter set his teacup and saucer on the table with a loud clatter. He gazed steadily at her.

"Lavinia, who is Yasir?"

She choked on her tea. Her fingers slipped from the handle and the cup dropped onto the covers, spilling hot liquid onto her skirt. She let out a sharp cry and leapt from the bed. Grimacing, she stumbled to the chair by the window and held onto it as she pulled off her skirt. *Lord,* her drawers were partly wet and the liquid was still hot. She slipped them off and whisked the shawl on the chair around her waist.

"That was quite an answer." Peter walked over. "Are you hurt?"

Lavinia stared at him. She coughed. Oh, how she hurt. She ached for the sight of Yasir, healthy, hiding his mischievous smile under a guise of seriousness. She smoothed the wet part of her skirt, put her hand to her chest. Her heart beat slow and steady, each pulse a reminder that Yasir wasn't here with her. She closed her eyes.

How did Peter know the djinni's name? She took a slow breath. When she awoke Peter had said something about a nightmare. A bitter cold numbed her stomach and bled into her chest. What else had she called out through the swirling mist in her eerie dream of the urn? Did she say something to remind Peter that he was master first? He didn't look angry, but his temper could turn as quick as the weather. She would have to be on her guard.

She sat down in the chair, adjusting the shawl for modesty's sake. It had been so long since she'd been around Peter, he almost felt like a stranger. She lifted the shawl and checked for burns. Peter had asked if she were hurt. She looked up at him. "A patch of skin is red and blistering. Perhaps Fleming should bring some salve." Her voice was a croak. Lavinia readjusted the shawl, careful to keep it from touching the tender spot.

"By all means." Peter tugged the pull cord in the corner. Fleming rushed in. She had been waiting outside the door, listening. Peter sent the maid for salve, pulled up a stool in front of Lavinia, and crossed his arms.

"Lavinia, you disappeared. Fleming said you acted strange that morning. She watched you stroll to the garden and went to fetch you when you didn't come in for lunch. None of the gardeners had seen you, but we found a strange carriage, what looked like bloodstains and footprints of men and horses. I helped the constable and his men track the trail, but it dwindled away. I hired professionals. They found nothing." Peter took her hand.

It was all she could do not to yank it away. When she was bound and gagged in the carriage, the Chovihano's man jumped inside, stabbed Saddani's footman and tossed the body out the opposite door. His body must have vanished like Saddani's. What would she tell Peter? Why hadn't she thought to concoct a story? Quick, quick, think . . . yet her mind moved as if it were mired in treacle. He wouldn't get the best of her this time. Peter had taken enough from her.

A sharp rap at the door. She jerked her hand from his.

"Enter." He sounded annoyed. Yet he knew perfectly well Fleming was to bring the burn salve.

Lavinia gave her a wan smile. "Thank you, Fleming, dear. Would you put the cream on my burns and then I need—"

"Fleming, my wife can manage her needs and, if not, I am able. Before you leave lay out a wrapper and towels just here." Peter indicated the arm of Lavinia's chair. The silk of the blue wrapper brushed Lavinia's arm as Fleming laid it down next to the neatly folded towels.

She gave her maid a weak smile. In a moment Fleming would be gone, and Lavinia still wouldn't have a story. The door clicked closed.

"Please, give me a moment."

"Your burns?"

"I'll dress them first, but—"

Peter opened the shawl.

"No, Peter I—" She looked down at her bare thighs. The burn had expanded—pink on the edges, tiny white blisters inside. She felt her face blush and imagined it as red as her injury. She wasn't ready—

"You're my wife, in case you forgot." Peter sounded stern. Angry? He removed the top of the jar with more force than necessary and spread the salve on the burn at the top of her thigh.

She grimaced. He pressed too hard. He pushed her legs apart and held them open with one hand while he smeared the salve on the part of the burn continuing to her thigh's inside.

"Ow."

"Am I *hurting* you?" He looked up at her and slapped more salve on. The pain brought tears to her eyes.

"Yes, you're hurting me." She thrust his hand away. "On purpose, you did that on—"

"You don't think I hurt? Did you know rumors are being spread that you may have conspired with your kidnappers? That you left me intentionally?" His voice rose. "There wasn't an hour of the day when I wasn't worried about you. Were you still alive? Were you somewhere helpless, hurt? Who took you? No one could find you. Damn it, Lavinia."

He stopped and slumped forward, his face reddening. "You . . . Lavy, I thought you were dead. For God's sake, what happened?" He sat up, started to say something. His eyes narrowed and he stared at her midsection.

"Our baby?" His voice choked.

Her baby. A wave of heat coursed through her. She hadn't thought of her baby since she arrived. Yet, she thought of her baby every minute, every second. She couldn't meet his eyes. Of course he would want to know what happened to his heir. He knew she would have delivered or be close to delivering now. *Lord in heaven,* why hadn't she thought of that?

He took her hand and held it with tenderness, his eyes soft and sad. Please, please don't let him cry. Lavinia swallowed hard. He looked at her as if he could see inside her soul. It was just the two of them, nothing else. Peter's breath, warm on her face, the loamy, earthy aroma of tea mixed with the rich tang of brandy. She could hear no noises, no servants carrying out their chores, no birds singing—only her heart beating. And Peter's pale, pale blue eyes staring into her. He squeezed her hand. Gentle. Compassionate.

She closed her eyes. Why did he do that? That one small motion. She swallowed hard as she felt the wall collapse. The wall she had built, stone by stone, to keep her safe. The wall that guarded the place in her heart where his questions could penetrate.

No. No. No. In her mind she hefted the broken stones one on top of another, frantically rebuilding the wall. Nothing must get through. Nothing.

Peter let go of her hand, gently grasped her shoulders and drew her close. "Lavinia. What happened?" His pale eyes—heavy with the pain she had put him through, burdened with the hurt from Yasir's scheming magic—seared into her.

Lavinia stood still, staring but not seeing. She was home, safe from djinnis, gypsies, magicians and sorceresses. Did those beings exist? The burn on her leg stung. Peter's hands were warm and tender on her shoulders. She looked into his eyes. The anguish there was real. These things were real.

She clasped her hands tight, then let them go. Like a dam breaking, her words poured out. "Peter, the urn you gave me. I opened it. There was a djinni. He put a spell on you."

Peter drew back.

Lavinia took a breath. Tears flowed down her cheeks.

"You saw him in the garden. Peter . . . " She sobbed, messy and noisy. "You . . . you . . . *shot* . . . him." She sniffed and wiped her tears away with a corner of her gown. "He took me to his urn and went to a place of light and a magician kidnapped me. I wasn't here with you like you thought. I came back and you found me, but I was gone to those places." Her eyes caught his.

"You *saw* me, the doctor said I was pregnant. In the garden, Mr. Saddani"—Peter scowled—"had me bound in his carriage, but the gypsies killed him. And his body, it disappeared. Then the gypsies they—" She gasped, and stammered. "T-the baby, Peter, I *lost* the baby."

Peter narrowed his eyes.

She put her head in her hands and sobbed. "I r-ran away to the urn. The djinni—the bullet was cursed. He—we—tried to save him." Her eyes darted to her embroidery chair, to her dressing room. An image of the urn rose in her mind and she started to shake. Was the urn in there on her dressing table amongst her perfumes and creams?

Peter had said Yasir's name. *She* had said Yasir's name. But Yasir was hopelessly, forever lost to her. "Yasir's dead, he's gone, like my baby, gone." She clutched Peter's hands, pulled away, then collapsed into him.

Peter put his arms around Lavinia, held her as she cried. "Lavy, Lavy. It's all right. You're home. You're home." His voice was soft, like a lover's. But there was something in his tone, the way he spoke each word that made her struggle in his arms.

Peter's shirt, wet with Lavinia's tears, stuck to his chest. With each sob, she shook in his embrace. Peter pulled her closer. If he let her go she might run through the house screaming that name. He heard it, louder and louder, as if each sob called it out. *Yasir. Yasir.*

He had his wife back, his Lavinia.

But dear God, she was mad—raving mad.

# 28

*P*eter walked the hall, striking his riding crop against his trousers. His wrist bent with purpose, sending a sharp, crisp rap that repeated faster as his agitation heightened. What on earth had happened to his child? Lavinia claimed she'd lost the baby. In the state she was in, she could have actually left it somewhere. But most probably, she meant she miscarried. How far along had she been? A grief that surprised him turned heavy in his gut.

He murmured to himself. "A genie. In the urn I gave her? Daft. Absolutely daft. Demented ravings." He stared down the hall, switching the crop impatiently. "Except that damned part about Saddani." Where in the deuce had she heard the man's name? He had never mentioned Saddani's visit, never said that his guest purchased his antiquities, purchased his Scottish dress pistol but happened to forget it. What would she care?

At the sound of horses whinnying, he strode to the door. The footman flung it open, timed perfectly for Peter to sail through without breaking stride. The carriage had arrived, finally. The horses trotted up the drive. He descended the front steps and when the carriage came to a halt, wrenched open the door.

"Peter." Alice took his hand and stepped down in a swirl of brown, her cape woven so loosely that, at first glance, it looked as though she wore feathers.

"Is she better?" Alice gave him a perfunctory hug. Peter shook his head.

She stepped back and heaved a sigh. "Well, let us hope for the best." She turned and hurried up the steps, her cape ruffling like plumage.

Peter caught up with her in the hall. He took her by arm. "Alice, please. Come into the parlor first. I must speak with you."

Alice slowed her pace and walked alongside him, noticing the changes in Peter since she had last visited—his face a bit thinner, his eyes not so bright. She sensed that missing Lavinia was less a strain on him than her return.

"She arrived almost a week ago." Peter ignored the footman and closed the parlor door with a sweep of his hand. It slammed shut with a loud bang. Alice glared at him, but he didn't seem to notice, and ushered her to a chair.

"The servants must not overhear." Peter pulled a hassock next to her and sat. "The nights have been difficult, but Fleming stays with her."

A distant screech resounded through the hall, and Alice had the impression of people scurrying inside the recesses of the great manor. Peter tilted his head towards the direction of the noise and said in a weary voice, "She cries out in her sleep."

Alice made to rise, but he grasped her hand. "Please, Alice, just hear me out." Peter slumped his shoulders as if he were caving in on himself. Surrounded by smudges of exhaustion, his pale blue eyes pleaded his case.

"Lavinia fainted when she first saw me. And then in her faint, she screamed a name." His eyes became cold, erasing the wan pall of fatigue. His lips curled. "The name, Yasir."

Alice drew her small body in, like a bird tucking its wings. She stifled the shock spreading through her so that there was no flash of recognition on her face.

Peter wrinkled his forehead. "A gypsy name, I think."

Good, he was truly befuddled. He didn't remember anything. Yasir's spell had worked in time for that, at least.

"When Lavinia regained consciousness, she launched into a story." Peter took a breath and turned his head away. He gripped the arms of the chair, then faced her, his eyes hard.

"She said the urn I gave her contained a *genie*—" His voice broke. Alice couldn't tell if it was a half-sob or a squelched peal of laughter.

"That he put a spell on me, that I shot the genie and *they*, whoever *they* are, tried to heal him. That she lost the child she was carrying. *My* child." Peter mouthed other words, but they remained unspoken. His face crumpled, his eyes glistening, but he soldiered on. "She said that the genie died." Peter frowned at Alice and, with an impatient huff, continued. "Then she became hysterical. Screaming. Wailing."

Alice found she couldn't move her hands. She should reach out to Peter, show sympathy. She was so good at these human sentiments. Yet she sat there. Just sat there.

Yasir. Dead.

It couldn't be true. She had received no message from the Great and Exalted Djinni, Zamyad. Her father. Yasir's father. Wouldn't he have felt it? How could the magic he'd spent to arrange this be swept aside by a paltry English lord?

The years she had given, ingratiating herself into this family since she was what they believed to be thirteen human years old. All for naught?

This could not have happened. The plan had been laid out long ago, years and years before Lavinia's mother and father had adopted her. One of many actions orchestrated by Zamyad's magic to prepare the way for her half brother. Since Lavinia's mother's death, Alice, always a favorite, had become a stalwart fixture in the family.

Alice closed her eyes, trying to perceive Yasir's presence anywhere, in any realm. She sensed only chaos. She could imagine how the shock showed on her face—a suitable reaction—but her response was for all the wrong reasons. Reasons Peter must not know.

What made Lavinia tell Peter the truth? Had he done something to her? She studied him.

Peter shifted in his seat. He had acquired that wary expression men get when they aren't sure whether a woman will faint or sob, and had one hand on the arm of his chair, ready to push to standing and call for help. His eyebrows creased together and she saw that he'd realized she wasn't going into immediate hysterics.

He took her hands in his. "I know, Alice. It's a shock. Our sweet Lavinia returned this way. I-I can hardly believe it."

Alice didn't know if she could actually *say* anything.

"Do you think you can help her?" Peter looked lost, like a lad who had run away and had to face the coming night alone.

Alice found her voice and sat up. "Let me see her. Now."

Alice had never entered a room that contained such maelstroms from a mind's turbulent workings. By the time she reached Lavinia's bedside, Alice was so battered by her niece's fears and insecurities she imagined that there must be bruises on her body. But psychic sensations did not leave such tangible marks.

Lavinia lay sleeping, if one could call it that. Her body moved and her face worked as though she were in the middle of a painful conversation. Then she went limp and gasped for breath, her chest heaving.

Fleming rushed into action. She lifted the cover of an engraved silver box, removed a damp cotton pad smelling of vinegar, and placed it on Lavinia's wrist near her pulse. Lavinia's body twitched alive. Her breathing evened out. She folded her arms over her chest, her face pinched, and the cycle began once more. It was possibly the most exhausting sleep Alice had ever witnessed.

"Wake her." Alice ordered Fleming. If she touched Lavinia now she would access her psyche whether she wanted to or not. Such an agitated state in a human might harm her. The maid stood still for a moment and glanced at Alice with a look that said: *Are you certain?* Alice nodded. Fleming set her muscles as if she were going to battle and rocked Lavinia gently. There was no reaction. She placed both hands on her shoulders and shook her with a bit more force. "Milady, it is time to wake."

Lavinia's eyelids fluttered softly, and Fleming's rigid expression relaxed into a faint smile. With a frightful shriek, Lavinia jerked upright. The maid backed away, hand clamped against her heavy bosom. Lavinia stared, eyes wide, the expression more disturbing than her harried sleep.

Fleming held her mistress firmly by the arms. "Milady, all is well." The maid kept her voice soft, but Alice could hear the concern underneath her forced calm. Lavinia focused on something across the room and whimpered.

Careful to close herself from any access Lavinia could have, Alice gathered her powers and sat in the bedside chair. With a quick inhale, she took her niece's hand. Alice had looked into Lavinia's mind since her niece was a child—a normal mind with everyday cares. But now she encountered turmoil. The mind's image of a white horse galloped by, long mane flying. A massive iron cauldron belched steam. Deep voices spoke in threatening, garbled phrases. Faces distorted with anger ran at her on spindly jointed insect legs. She ducked and whirled through the labyrinth, then stopped with a force that almost caused her physical body to tumble from her chair.

A black wall blocked her, in it a single closed door. She pushed against the door, and felt the strength of Lavinia's will. She forced it open. Her body tensed in surprise. She had never seen this in a human mind—simply a bare white room with doors open to white hallways. Silent. Airless.

Alice went further inside. A blur of movement, then a perfect mind-image of Yasir, all in white, hooded, gliding down an empty hall. Lavinia's idea of herself scurrying after him, white dress flowing into long silk tendrils curling into the walls, slowing her. Her niece's fear that she would never catch up with the djinni streamed into Alice, gripping her in a vise-like panic.

"Yasir. Yasir!" Lavinia called, her voice a wail echoing in the empty spaces. The djinni, far away at the end of an impossibly long corridor, turned a corner. Lavinia skittered after him, tears trailing on her cheeks, her arms reaching and reaching.

Alice let go of Lavinia's hand. "By the Djinn," she murmured, "a maze." A labyrinth of the mind, of the heart. Stupefying, bewildering. Alice looked on her niece with pity. How would she find her way in that?

Her mind-reading had taken only seconds. Lavinia sat in bed, sheets rumpled around her, staring across the room. Alice mustered her most cheerful tone. "Nia dear, it is Alice, your aunt. I am here to help you."

Lavinia turned, forehead creasing. Her eyes locked on Alice and bulged in horror. "No! A bird. No!" She thrust her hand in front of her face, fingers spread stiff. "Get her out." She leapt from the bed and beat Alice with her fists. "Get! Out!" Lavinia screamed, spittle spraying Alice's face.

Fleming hurried between them and wrestled Lavinia back into bed. Lavinia fighting with all her strength, trying to keep her eyes on Alice. Screaming, her words unintelligible now.

Alice rose from her chair and backed from the room. She shut the door with a whisper of a click. Catching her breath, she sank against it as she stared into the vacant hallway. Her niece knew who she was. When Alice happened upon her and Yasir after Lavinia had opened the urn, Alice took the form of a bird to warn the djinni onto the correct path. But that was a tale that shouldn't be told.

Alice shuddered. *Thank the Djinn* they all thought Lavinia was mad. Alice would have used her magic to calm her niece but for Fleming's presence. Then again, she dared not use magic before she had fully assessed Lavinia's condition. She could help her, but . . .

Was Yasir truly dead? Zamyad hadn't contacted her, which was out of character for him if anything was untoward. But if it were true, then Zamyad might be in almost the same state as Lavinia. If Yasir *were* dead, it could be more harmful to help Lavinia than to let her lapse into permanent madness. She wouldn't be a liability if she were deemed insane. Whatever she said would fall on deaf ears. Alice's gaze clouded. All the years and years of planning, and now this.

"Can you help her?" Peter stood to her side.

Alice whipped her head towards him, her mouth falling open. He had caught her unawares. She was still braced against the door to Lavinia's chamber as though barring it from opening.

Peter cocked his head and looked her up and down. "Alice? Is anything wrong? Lavinia . . ." He moved to grip the door handle. "Is Lavinia—?"

Alice moved from the door and touched Peter's arm. "Lavinia is resting now. Fleming is taking good care of her." Her hand shook and she forced it steady, thankful that the maid had settled Lavinia with a minimum of fuss.

"Peter, I can help her, but I need time." He must not sense her fear. Her fear for Lavinia's condition. Her fear that Yasir was truly dead. Her fear that her niece could be an adversary.

Alice gathered her senses, weak from Lavinia's onslaught, and looked inside Peter's mind. Just as she thought. He had heard Lavinia's screams. She removed his doubts, at least the ones she could banish with her magic compromised. He must have confidence that she could help his wife.

Alice summoned a convincing smile. "Our dear little one needs to rest now. And *I* need to rest. Is a room prepared?"

Peter's face sagged with disappointment. Did he think merely seeing her aunt would cure Lavinia? Alice wondered if any of Yasir's spells still enchanted Peter, but she was too addled to check him again.

"Dear Alice, forgive me. You must be tired after your journey." He visibly shook himself. "Your usual room is readied. Your luggage was taken up some time ago." Peter took her arm, a bit too forcefully. "Do you . . . Do you think she will ever recover?"

He blinked, an anxious air about him. He was truly desperate and she wondered why. At first he had seemed madly in love with her niece, but his many interests got in the way until Lavinia became another of his possessions, merely his wife, physically pleasing to him. Perhaps absence did make the heart grow fonder. And there was poor Lavinia to consider. She should be given a chance to live a good life, if that were possible under the circumstances.

"Peter. Her situation is . . . severe. It will take time." Alice squeezed his hand and turned away. It wouldn't do for Peter to see the emptiness of defeat in her eyes.

Lavinia wielded the needle, small and a bit blunted, in and out of the cloth, depositing dots and lines of color. Her hair, brushed and clean, shone. She laughed at something Fleming said.

Alice watched her niece closely—a good time for this. Alice prepared her voice.

"I see your embroidery is coming along." She settled into a chair opposite Lavinia and tried not to stare at the threads twining into a splotchy mass of chaos on the linen. Flowers, they were possibly flowers, but nothing like Alice had ever seen. Fleming curtsied and closed the door quietly behind her.

"It occupies my mind without occupying my mind." Lavinia placed her work in her lap. She smiled. Her eyes stayed frighteningly dull.

Alice took her hand. "Lavinia, I haven't asked you this before. You weren't ready." She looked deep into her niece's eyes. "Why did you tell Peter the truth?"

"Oh. That," Lavinia said in a small voice. She picked up several skeins of thread from the table, running the silky green, orange and purple filaments through her fingers like a rosary.

"It *was* the truth?" Alice tried to see Lavinia's face, but she kept her head bowed.

"Unfortunately, yes." Her niece twisted her pale fingers into the threads as if she could weave herself out of existence. "I need to rest now." She pushed up from her chair, the threads lost to the floor. Her embroidery frame dropped with a soft thump.

She grabbed her aunt, her nails cutting into Alice's forearms. "He is gone. And the baby. Dead." Her mouth flattened into a grim line, her eyes lit with a peculiar glow. "It wouldn't have happened except for Peter." Lavinia jerked the small scissors from her sewing basket. They fell open in her hand, the edges gleaming. "It's Peter that needs to be dead. They would be here if it weren't for him." She marched for the door, then stopped and turned.

She drew the scissors behind her back, hiding them from Alice. The change in her demeanor was alarming. Her face beamed, her expression calm. Her animated smile shone in her over-bright eyes.

"Alice, I would dearly love to see Peter. He hasn't received my proper attention since I returned." Her voice played soft and melodic, just like the old Lavinia. "When you go downstairs, could you tell him that I want to see him?"

Alice stared up at her niece. Her scalp prickled. She spoke in a gentle tone, pretending she was having a normal, relaxed conversation, not trying to placate a madwoman with a lie. "Nia, Peter is in London for a few days."

The scissors fell onto the carpet. Alice resisted the urge to dive for them. She tried to keep her pleasant expression as the calm in her niece's face clouded. Glazed blue eyes stared out, refusing to focus.

Alice took Lavinia by the waist and guided her to bed. She would arrange for her niece's door to be locked from the outside.

# 29

*P*eter sat across the dining table from Lavinia. She refused to look at him. The fork drooped in her hand, a bit of potato skewered on a tine about to drop into her lap. Alice had cautioned him, but today Lavinia seemed, hmm, improved. The scissor incident was a week ago, at a particularly low point, and everyday Alice had been "helping" her niece, as she put it. However, he had instructed that Lavinia's meals be prepared so she had no need of a knife. He ordered Lavinia's favorite foods, and encouraged her to partake. Some days were better than others.

"You hardly eat anymore." Peter tapped his fingers on the tablecloth. "The beef is savory with sauce, yet you've only eaten a few peas." He made a nod to her fork. "And a bit of potato." He raised his hand in the air and gestured. "I am not Hades, trying to trick you into eating so you'll be bound to stay. And you are not Persephone."

Lavinia threw him a dark glance from under her brows and took a small bite from the potato. She swallowed, set her fork down with an elaborate sigh, and pushed the plate away, glaring at Peter the whole time.

"A game. Do you think this is a game? Our family is at stake here. Our future heirs." He threw his napkin on the table.

Lavinia stared at her lap as Peter strode past, his faint scent of tobacco and horse making her queasy. Hades and Persephone indeed. She knew her classics. He didn't have to spell it out. Persephone, the name had cascaded off his tongue like verse. Such a lovely name. Per–se–pho–ne, deceived into eating a few pomegranate seeds, dooming her to return to the underworld and her kidnapper-husband, Hades.

It was much like that, Lavinia mused. Only Hades was Peter, not Yasir. With Yasir gone she was trapped between worlds, neither in

Yasir's urn, nor here, in Bramley House. Would she ever be able to leave this nebulous place filled with shadows? She raised her head, preparing to cringe as Peter stared hard at her in disgust. But then he had left, hadn't he?

Lavinia sat alone. Where would she go if Peter threw her out? To Alice's? To one of her friends? She had changed so. She was different inside. Others felt it. She had seen the looks from Peter, from Fleming, from the other servants. Sidelong glances, knowing exchanges with eyebrows raised, curious stares when they thought she wasn't aware of them gawking at her.

At times a light appeared in the dim world she inhabited, whether it was in her head or real, she didn't know. She would follow the light, propelling herself any way she could, rising upward too slowly, her want bursting like lungs deprived of air. When she surfaced she gulped in the lucidity, the clear perception, the awful pang of loss— Yasir, the baby. Her legs and arms weakened and she slipped down, down, down where breathing came with difficulty. Where everything around her was clouded and vague, where distorted voices fed her simmering hatred and hot rage.

She groped for her necklace. Fleming had thrown the beads out by the time Lavinia managed to speak to her, and her maid didn't remember a long silver piece. Lavinia searched her room and other places in the house for the talisman. Fleming could have dropped it on the way to the rubbish bin outside the scullery. Lavinia crossed her arms in frustration. It could be anywhere. Squirreled away in someone's treasure box or lying in a dusty corner, even pawned and sitting in a shop's case.

She felt as if she were falling, a leaf winding down, down into some disaster. Yasir had told her to keep the talisman. If it had not been lost, things would be different. She had made it known there was a reward for the silver bead, but no one had come forward. She had no protection.

She picked up her fork. Held it tight in her hand as if it were some magic wand that could right all the wrongs, the elaborate engraving of the curving acanthus, the lilly's graceful stamen, pressing into her skin. Her china plate sat near the middle of the table where she had pushed it. The gravy, slick with fat, had congealed. A fly circled towards it, buzzing louder and louder as he neared his feast. Lavinia dropped the fork and fled.

"Thank you, Fleming. Come to me directly with any further concerns." Peter nodded, dismissing her. "Bloody hell," he murmured as she closed the door behind her. That was the fifth  servant who had reported seeing Lavinia moping around the house and grounds cradling the urn like a baby. He slammed his ledger on the desk, his papers fluttering into disarray. He would not stand for an insane wife. Something must be done. He would think on it today while he finished his correspondence and his estate accounts—form a plan.

Peter broke the green wax wafer on the letter from his Egyptian colleague. He unfolded the paper with care, afraid that after so long a journey it might rip, rendering parts illegible.  As he read, he ran his fingers down the open brass spirals comprising the handle of his penknife, stopping at the sharp blade and retracing the handle's smooth curves. He slipped the letter under a blown glass bauble from Venice with the other listings of supplies and accounts, then balanced the ornate penknife in his hand. Heavy. The brass cool.

In India, he would place it against his forehead, close his eyes in relief from the heat. Six months after settling into the cantonment in Calcutta, after morning parade—a day already sweltering—he had doffed his shirt and become absorbed in writing up his weekly report. At a dull thud on his desk, he raised his head from his work. His Sikh sepoy grinned, teeth flashing white under his mustache, as he place his hand on a decorated paper bundle. "A sword for indoors, Risaldar-Major."

A cool English breeze billowed the curtains in his Bramley House study and Peter basked in the refreshing air, glad the scorching heat of India was just a memory. He set the penknife beside his gilded inkstand and ran his thumb along the blade just a hair's breadth from the razor-sharp edge. Had it ever spilled blood?

The door creaked. Of all the nerve, a servant forgetting to knock, probably intending to add to the tales about Lavinia. Peter folded his arms across his chest. He must talk to Dobson. Dampen this thing down. Her back to him, Lavinia closed the door partway and, hiding behind it, peered out into the hall. After a few moments she shut it with a click and turned, a dazed expression on her face, the urn clutched to her chest.

Peter shook his head. "Oh Lavy, Lavy," he said under his breath. He had seen vagrants on the street with that glassy expression, filthy and in rags. It was even more upsetting to see an impeccably groomed, beautifully gowned lady in this state.

He'd best put a stop to this. He rose from his desk chair. Lavinia stopped dead at the sight of him. With a slight gasp, her mouth flew open, and in a clumsy motion she secreted the urn behind her back.

"Lavinia." His voice cracked. "Do come in. You haven't visited me here—" Peter stopped himself as he envisioned Lavinia just arrived from her long absence, clutching the back of the bronzed and parcel-gilt Bergère chair in this very room, a wild cast to her eyes. He didn't want to bring up that miserable day—her becoming hysterical, calling out the name *Yasir*. He clenched his jaw.

*Dear God*, why couldn't Alice keep Lavinia in her room?

Forcing a smile, he stepped from behind his desk. "I say, you picked a perfect time. Today I'm wrestling with the accomptant's figures. Bit of a tangle this month. I will be delighted to take a break. Shall I send for tea?" He stood in front of her, hands at his side, deliberately unthreatening.

Lavinia backed away and bumped against a low table. "Y . . . yes," she said, breathy and hoarse. Her eyes darted back and forth across the study as if she had never seen it before, then she settled her gaze on him.

Careful not to make any sudden moves, he stepped to the corner and pulled the braided maroon cord. Dobson would serve tea directly. "Shall we make ourselves comfortable?" Peter motioned to the divan where he took a seat, and patted the plush velvet upholstery, indicating a place next to him.

Lavinia lowered herself to the couch, slow, deliberate movements, one hand behind her back clutching the urn. Odd that she tried to hide the vessel, as he had clearly seen it when she came in. It meant nothing to him. He wasn't sure why he gave it to her, an odd gesture, certainly.

Anxiety exuded from her like dampness from a bog. Peter placed his hands on the cushion to shift to the opposite side of the divan, but thought better of it. He must make her feel at ease. She sat stiff and wary as if she were a feral creature that might dash away any moment or . . . He had no reason to fear her. A trickle of sweat slid down his forehead.

"I see that you are carrying, ah . . . a vase." He leaned back, affecting relaxation, but his stomach jittered from her peculiar mannerisms. To his surprise, she produced the urn from behind her back.

"You know what this is." She kept her voice low, almost a growl. He wondered if he had imagined her speaking. Her eyes shone. She didn't blink. It made him uneasy, as though he sat next to a person holding a loaded pistol.

Peter kept his voice light. "Yes, I remember. I gave it to you when I returned from Cairo. It's very unusual, isn't it?" He laid his arm along the back of the divan like he did when he conversed with friends. Although the movement was stiff, he feigned a casual bearing.

She stared at him, her eyes hard chips of lapis lazuli.

Peter fought to stay calm. He moved closer to her on the divan. "Lavinia, would you open it?"

She drew back as if he had slapped her. "No!" Her voice was a bark with a strange edge, as though it might alter into a piercing shriek. He steeled himself to keep from showing his alarm and, in a studied motion, placed his hand on the urn and pulled it gently towards him. Lavinia held on, putting her weight into keeping it from him. He curled his other hand around the vessel, fighting the sudden impression that it was a part of her, that he had no right to it. She glared, those shining navy eyes almost making him drop his hold.

Peter moved his fingers towards the latch and unfastened it. He pulled the lid open. A poof of mist whirled out. With a gasp, Lavinia paled. She let go.

They stared at the mouth of the urn.

A jolt shot through Peter's hand, up his arm and down his body, sending a vague awareness through him that he should *know* something more about this odd vessel. He kept his voice calm. "Lavinia, it's merely a plain brass urn, probably used for storing oils." He set the vessel between them, holding it firmly upright on the soft cushion of the divan.

Lavinia sat rigid, her eyes hooded as she studied the vessel. She must be devastated to see proof of her delusion. Her shoulders slumped as he reached for her. She would need empathy, a tender touch and—

In a blur of motion, she snatched the urn from him and held it tight against her chest. Fire burned in her eyes. She jumped up. Instincts kicking in, Peter thrust forward to catch her, but only felt the brush of her skirt against his hand as she dashed away.

"What the deuce?" He was on his feet before he knew what he was doing, the sound of shattering glass ringing through his study. Lavinia stood behind his desk scattering his papers, mumbling, "You and your expeditions. Your antiquities. You think you know what is valuable. Ha, but you don't know—"

"My papers! Lavinia, what are you doing?" He rushed over, but she scrambled behind the corner screen. "Damn you, it's taken me days to turn these figures out." He grabbed for the papers teetering at the edge of the desk, catching only a few before they slid to the floor to settle on the remains of the Venetian paperweight. "Crazy woman, look at what you—"

The hair on his neck prickled. He turned, papers in hand.

Lavinia stood there, eyes glittering. Where was the urn? If it meant that much to her why would she—

She lunged for him. "I told you. He's dead." Her voice cold. Hard.

A flash of gold in her hand.

A sharp pain in his chest.

"You *shot* him. You killed him," she cried in a fury, her eyes full of hatred. She raised her arm. He seized Lavinia's wrist. The Sikh's penknife wobbled in her grip and clattered to the floor, the brass gleaming like Lavinia's eyes. Peter looked down at his chest. A scarlet gash in his white waistcoat. A rivulet of red. His arm shook.

"Damn it to hell, Lavinia." The ends of his cravat tinged pink with his blood. He held on to her wrist, keeping her from retrieving the penknife. "Look what you've done," he rasped, pain gnawing at his chest, stifling his breath.

She clasped the urn against her bosom. Her hand trembled, her knuckles blanched white as bones. He knocked the vessel from her embrace and gasped at the stitch that surged through his chest.

"No!" Lavinia screeched. She lunged for the urn. He held her fast, his muscles working through the pain, warm blood tickling his chest.

"I didn't kill anyone," Peter blurted. "There was no body . . . in the garden." He swayed, light-headed. "I never saw . . . your damned genie." Peter forced her against his chest. The thought of his blood mussing her perfect gown, besmirching her bosom where she had clutched the urn, almost made him smile. She struggled. He felt her breathing hard, her body warm against him.

"Lavy." He cried out at the sharp pain that coursed through his chest. *Damn her*, the little minx. She had pressed with all her strength against his wound. He tried to seize her hands, but—

Her nails raked across his cheek. He caught her waist and dragged her to him. The pain took his breath away. He staggered. She mustn't get loose. The damned penknife was here, somewhere . . .

Dobson appeared, an apparition holding a tea tray. Could he be imagining his own butler standing in front of him with a puzzled expression? No, he had sent for tea.

"I could use a hand," Peter heard himself say. The crash of the tray echoed inside his head. The room slanted, curtains billowing as if they were breathing with him. With each whistling breath, a stabbing pain ripped through his body. From far off, he heard a grave bass voice, a muffled shriek. Then his arms were empty.

He put his hand to his chest and sank to the floor. Hard to breathe. If she got hold of the penknife again . . .

# 30

"**I** can't say I wasn't warned." With a faint grimace, Peter dipped his pen in the inkwell and wrote a few lines at the bottom of the letter. He sanded it with a quick sprinkle and waved it dry as he looked up at Alice, who stood to the side of his desk. "Still, Lavinia seemed harmless enough, carrying that urn around as if it were a baby."

He winced, placing his pen in the gilded pyramid inkwell with cloisonné palm trees gracing the ends. "I'll have to get someone to write for me." His chest, stitched up by Dr. Thornhill yesterday, smeared with a salve of garlic and aloe, and bandaged again this morning by the good doctor, gave off the aroma of a dish in preparation. Alice squelched wrinkling her nose.

With her powers she followed the trajectory of the wound. Peter was lucky. The penknife, the Indian-made blade longer and sharper than normal, had barely nicked his lung and missed his heart. Or maybe it was Lavinia's luck, for if she had killed her husband, Alice would have had to steal her away and place her under Zamyad's care. Then what would happen to Yasir's plan?

"Are you in pain?" Alice tilted her head. She could feel her eyes soften with the sympathetic expression caring relatives give when someone close to them is hurt. She played her role well, but she did feel sorry for Peter. What a predicament. How could he have possibly competed with Yasir?

"Well, it's rather a painful thing to be stabbed by your own wife." Peter's voice reflected the severity of his frown. His face flushed. He turned his attention to his desk and slid one of his paperweights, a pyramid of lapis lazuli set on a gold base, to the center of a stack of documents. The gold glittered in the light reflected from the paper.

Alice crossed her arms. Poor Lord Bramley, his wife returned, yet the trust had been broken, the love forsaken.

He pressed his lips tight. "The wound . . . I'll heal." Peter managed an unconvincing smile. She knew he was smarting from the fact that his small, deranged wife had managed to stab him. Poor man. She imagined Lavinia, smaller, weaker, assaulting the tall muscular man sitting in front of her. Alice smothered a laugh as she loosened her shawl and settled into the chair in front of the massive desk.

"And Lavinia, Peter. How is Lavinia?"

He looked up. His hand closed over the lapis pyramid. "She barely eats." He clenched the pyramid tighter, his fist taut. "She has moments when she is unaware of what's going on. She glares at me, like she might attack again." He opened his fist and laid his hand flat on the papers.

"Please. Forgive my manners. Let's make ourselves comfortable." Peter stood and gestured for Alice to follow. He stopped, his face pale, took a breath, then led the way to the cluster of furniture at the center of his study.

Peter let himself down into the winged armchair across from Alice, gripping the arms as he settled into it. "I am at my wit's end. I am wary of her now. My own wife." His gaze unfocused. "I admit, I lock myself in my room at night."

He shook his head, an almost imperceptible back and forth. "Alice, I thought your being here would snap her out of it. But look what she has done." He held his arms out as though he were an exhibit, but all Alice could see was that he was not Yasir.

"You are her last hope." Peter took a shallow breath and shut his eyes for a moment. "Perhaps you can work your magic on her."

Alice felt her eyes go wide. But of course, the idiom was merely an expression of respect for a person's competence. She suppressed her momentary shock at the thought that Peter might know who she was, and stayed quiet for a moment. Had Lavinia let something slip in her grief-stricken ramblings? Outside the open window a gust of wind ruffled a stand of elms.

Months ago, Alice had seen Yasir present in this very house, his magnificence enhanced by the joy that he had at last found his Thalia. Now, an emptiness pervaded Bramley House. Could she change this? Or was it all lost in the discharge of a pistol?

Peter tapped his finger to his lips as Alice walked to the door. She moved as though she were more buoyant than air, as if she might suddenly float above the carpet. The tails of her shawl swirled around her, trailing light. Impossible. He blinked.

A glimmer of something formed in his mind, a hint of why he loved Egypt, of what attracted him to the ancient objects he pursued, of the reason he sought beauty. Something about his last trip to Egypt, something to do with this tragedy that had befallen him. With a jerk, he startled at the sound of the door closing. A stab of pain broke his musings.

Peter stretched one leg, then the other. The hassock was set to the side, too far to inch into position with his feet. The brandy decanter, glowing in the light from the window, mocked him from on top of the French liquor cabinet. It was too much effort to lift his body, to risk the discomfort in his chest on moving. He wouldn't be able to have brandy unless Dobson happened in. The afternoon had dragged on far too long. He yawned, weary from pain, from the laboriousness of his tasks impeded by his handicap.

Peter opened his eyes. He raised his hand as a shield against the harsh glare and grimaced from a sharp pain in his chest. "What the—?" Blinding light flooded the leaded casement windows on the west wall, illuminating the room at a low angle. "Sunset? This damned wound and I act like an old man, sleeping the day away." His mumblings rumbled through the soft silence of the study. A sparkle under the divan expanded into a glow of gold.

He stared at it until he made sense of the thing. "Bloody hell. The urn," he whispered, not quite sure he was right in his assessment, aware of his displaced state of mind on just awakening. Aware of the ridiculous thought that to speak the word aloud might make the vessel what Lavinia believed it was. The thought made him squirm. He flinched from a stab of pain. "Deuced wound."

A voice to his side blared from the quiet. "Milord, may I get you anything?"

Peter jumped.

"Damn it to hell, Dobson." He clutched at his chest. "I'm not in any shape to be surprised like that." Peter closed his eyes. Did Dobson say "Master" or had he imagined it? Had the butler's voice taken on a slight accent?

"Milord, I thought you heard me enter. You were looking at me like—"

Peter waved his hand impatiently. "Never mind. I fear I was half asleep. A brandy. For God's sake, get me a brandy."

Peter sipped his drink, a golden elixir that dulled his pain, the pain in his chest and the pain of his hurt pride. His heart being a different matter altogether.

"Another brandy soon, Dobson. In a separate glass. And another. Just line them up." A beam of light hit his eyes. With a scowl, Peter inclined his head away from the path of the glare and squinted to find the source. He turned his head, working the spasm from his neck. "Dobson will you look under that divan."

The butler cut off the light with his bulky form. "Milord, it is the urn."

"Yes, yes, I know." Peter barely glanced at the vessel. "Take it to the rubbish bin. And make sure that it's burned. I'll not have it here another second." Peter took a swig of his drink. "Before you leave, put the brandy bottle here." He indicated the table. "And place another in my bedroom." Peter shut his eyes. Would this day never end? "Send a footman in while you're gone and come back right away."

Dobson gave the urn to a young footman with instructions to bury it deep in the rubbish heap, to make sure it was destroyed on the morrow when the trash burning was scheduled. The footman tossed the urn into the middle of the pile and picked up the long pole to bury it, just as a milkmaid beckoned from the barn with an inviting smile. She rested against the doorframe, her breasts straining against her low-cut blouse, and blew him a kiss. He dropped the pole, made certain no one was looking, and followed her into the deep shadows.

The chickens scattered, fussing in clucks and squawks as one of the scullery maids trudged past the barn, a full pail of refuse from the kitchen in her hand hobbling her gait. She set the bucket beside the trash pile, stepping back so as not to get soiled from the slosh of its contents. With a shrill cackle, a black-and-white-speckled hen dashed towards the pail. The maid flapped her apron, shooing the bird away, then plopped down upon a scarred wooden bench, wrinkling her nose from the stink.

She gazed disinterestedly at the trash heap, the drone of flies making her drowsy, and spied the brass urn glinting like a jewel amidst the soiled cloths, boiled bones and moldy vegetables. The maid stretched her arms out over the rubbish, trying to reach the urn, but it lay too far in the middle. She snatched the footman's long pole and maneuvered the vessel out of the heap.

New hair ribbons and a second-hand dress—that's what she would buy with the money she got for the brass from the tinker. She hid the urn under the bench, and with renewed energy, slopped the contents of the bucket onto the smelly heap.

"But, Alice. He *killed* Yasir." Lavinia let her embroidery fall into her lap and dabbed the handkerchief at her eyes. The mention of the djinni's name still brought tears, deepening the colors of the spring flowers embroidered on the square of white linen, as though they, too, were in mourning.

Alice took Lavinia by the chin and looked into her eyes.

Lavinia shrank back. Her aunt's deep brown eyes saw things best kept hidden. She wouldn't let Alice go into her mind. Not this time. Lavinia turned away, reeling from the waves of dizziness in her head. Outside a squirrel sat on the oak branch, nibbling an acorn. For a moment their eyes met, then the squirrel shook its tail and skittered higher into the leaves. She would run from the room, run far from Alice—but she only sagged into the cushions of her chair, squeezing her eyes shut.

Her aunt was there, in her mind. Lavinia smirked. Alice would get what she deserved. Now she would experience the anguish, the horror that her own niece had endured. And after she had suffered, Alice might at last understand.

"Nia." Her aunt's voice tunneled through her brain. Lavinia sat up straight. Alice's eyes were filled with compassion. "What good would it do to kill Peter?"

Lavinia squinted hard at her aunt. How could Alice ask that question after seeing what she had gone through?

"He killed Yasir." Lavinia bent forward. The burn of anger rose in her face. "And my baby, *our* baby, lost, because of P-Peter." She pressed her handkerchief over her eyes. If she had to listen to her aunt, at least she wouldn't look at her.

Why was Alice tormenting her? "Go away. Take care of Peter if you are so fond of him." Lavinia peeked at Alice from under the edge of her handkerchief. Odd sensations of tingles and twinges—Alice working her strange magic—pricked inside her head. Bits of fear, hatred, sorrow, the detritus of her brain, gathered into a sordid pile.

"Think." Alice gave Lavinia a little shake. "Peter shot a strange man whom he caught embracing you." Alice's hold was firm and fierce. With a mewling cry, Lavinia dropped the handkerchief. Her aunt stared hard into her eyes. "And somehow, a magic bullet was in the pistol." Alice's hand felt warm on her cheek as she angled Lavinia to face her. "Nia, it was not Peter's bullet. He hasn't the knowledge or power."

"Magic bullet . . ." Lavinia heard her own voice, trance-like. She couldn't focus. "Yes." She nodded, but didn't want to speak, didn't want to tell her aunt anything, yet her voice kept on. "I took the cursed bullet far away from Yasir. I was afraid to touch it. It's imprisoned inside a jade box in the urn." She gulped a breath. Her eyes grew clearer.

"Nia, someone, even now, is out there. They are a danger to you." Alice crossed her arms over her chest while Lavinia daubed her nose with her handkerchief. "Yasir wanted you to come back here to live, to be safe with Peter, to be safe with an English lord." Alice watched for her reaction.

Lavinia couldn't stop the surprise that flashed through her eyes.

"Yes, I know what Yasir planned." Her aunt kept her voice soft. "Yasir instructed me. Mehadeh confirmed it."

Lavinia touched her aunt on the cheek. How she longed for Yasir. Alice had contact with him, with Mehadeh. How much more did her aunt know?

Alice pressed her hand on Lavinia's. "You must make up with Peter, be his adoring wife. It is important that he love and trust you once more."

"W-what?" Lavinia pulled away from her aunt. "Yasir wanted *that*?"

Like a schoolmarm finished with nonsense, Alice put her hands in her lap. "You heard what I said. Yasir contacted me." She continued as if giving a lesson. "Next, you must heal from your two losses. You may—"

"But . . ." Lavinia rose from the chair, knocking it over. "Yasir wouldn't forgive Peter. I know it. He—"

"Yasir is not as predictable as you think." Alice pushed Lavinia back into the chair, which had mysteriously righted itself, and pressed closer, swirls of gold in her dark eyes. "Of course, he would want you to grieve and keep a special place in your heart for the loved ones taken from you, but you must move on and think of the future."

Alice brushed Lavinia's fingers and held them a moment, a curious look in her eyes as though she wanted desperately to tell her something, but couldn't. "When you have done this, you will be ready. Then and only then, a gift will come to you from Yasir. A boon of great significance."

# 31

*Woodthorne Hall, Alice Smithson's home*

Alice walked up the sweep of the grand staircase, her hand trailing on the curved mahogany rail. Peter had been thrilled when she suggested Lavinia visit Woodthorne Hall to "recuperate," as Alice so delicately put it. Persuading Lavinia proved difficult. Alice received the impression her niece wanted to stay and keep an eye on Peter. From that, Alice surmised the urn disappeared in the hubbub after Lavinia stabbed him two months ago.

Where was it? Lavinia would only tell her the briefest of things and those were muddled by her mental state and her grief.

A few hours before, Lavinia returned to Woodthorne Hall from her weeklong visit at Bramley House. She stepped from the coach and, with a bitter pout, handed her aunt a letter. The thick cream-colored stock addressed to Lady Alice was sealed with gold wax and stamped with the honeybee of Peter's signet ring, emphasizing that Lavinia had not tampered with the correspondence.

"Nia, you must be tired. I'll just tuck this in my writing desk and join you in the parlor for tea." Alice waited until Lavinia followed the footman into the hall. She broke the wax wafer and unfolded the letter:

*Dearest Alice,*

*Lavinia seems to be doing well. We have resumed Our normal Affairs. She appears calmer, more placid. She didn't mention Anything out of the ordinary. When I caught Her unawares, I found Her searching for Something, possibly the Urn. Please continue what You are doing, as She is more her old Self.*

*In Gratitude,*
*Peter*

Alice stared at Peter's crabbed cursive. Did Peter have the urn? If so, he would be master. That is, if Yasir were still alive.

At tea, she put particular questions to Lavinia, but detected few signs of the disturbance that caused her to stab Peter. She sat close, even managed during conversation to caress her niece's temple, surprised at seeing glimpses of Thalia and Yasir as young lovers. Signs that Lavinia was absorbing Thalia's memories. Indication that the prophecy was beginning. Without Yasir?

An expletive slipped from her mouth in a hushed whisper, *"Baten en ghoul."* Belly of the beast. Scenes played in her head, moving always to their tragic conclusions: Yasir captured by Rakhshan. Tortured. Imprisoned in the urn to keep him from Thalia, Rakhshan's beloved daughter. Alice longed for the thousandth time to cajole her father, Yasir's father, the great djinni Zamyad al Din, into taking action against Rakhshan, but she had tried before to persuade him and he stared a stern warning: *When it is time and no sooner.*

As Alice poured tea, she slid the carnelian stone in her ring open and angled the hidden chamber over Lavinia's cup. One tap, and a pinch of white powder floated on the surface. She nudged the carnelian back into place and spooned sugar into the dark tea. With a stir, the powder vanished like mist from the urn, like Yasir's body. Fate was too cruel. Yasir near triumphed over the urn, over Rakhshan.

From the first there was a glimmer of hope. From his bejeweled kurta, Yasir had pulled a scroll filled with Thalia's dainty handwriting, ornate with small loops and curlicues, promising she would return to him through her renegade conjurers' magic—

"Alice? Your hand is shaking. You'll spill the tea."

Alice let Lavinia take the cup. Her niece tilted her head, eyes narrowed. "You were miles away."

Alice composed herself. "Dear, I'm afraid my sleep was disturbed last night when the cook's cat jumped on my bed. I have never been more startled. Perhaps you heard my shriek of surprise." She must be more careful. At this juncture, Lavinia was most receptive to her thoughts. And *these* thoughts could prove destructive. She widened her smile and poured milk in Lavinia's tea, hiding any odd taste from the potion.

"Now, would you like a biscuit? And do tell me about Peter."

Lavinia made a face, then drank a bit of tea. "When I first arrived, we dined in the garden pavilion. The one nearest the pond. The servants arranged hundreds of vases of roses. When I noticed there were no knives at the place settings, not even his, I . . ."

Lavinia's voice faded away. Alice sipped her tea . . . At last, after centuries, Yasir had appeared through the ether to Alice, ecstatic that he had seen Thalia in Lavinia. He begged Alice to insert herself into Lavinia's life—*do this for me, your half-brother*—unknowing that their father, Zamyad, years earlier, had instructed Alice to do the very same thing.

Alice didn't resemble Lavinia's dark-haired, blue-eyed family. To squelch young Lavinia's embarrassing questions, her mother had pulled her aside and explained that Alice was adopted into the family when she was thirteen, after Lettice, her mother's favorite sister, had succumbed to scarlet fever at the tender age of eleven. By the time Alice's memory spell, enhanced by the great Zamyad, had worn off, this story had become family history.

She had held her tongue when Yasir told her he invoked Thalia's spell, speeding the prophecy along. Was Lavinia truly Yasir's Thalia, come to him through the centuries? Now Alice was certain. Lavinia *was* Thalia, returned to Yasir. The plan had begun. Could all be lost so soon afterwards? How would she—

"Alice." Lavinia glared at her and crossed her arms. "You weren't even listening. I thought you would at least have a comment after you heard what Peter said when—" Lavinia opened her mouth into a yawn that rippled through her body. "Oh, never mind. I . . . I am suddenly horribly, horribly tired."

Alice reached over the tea tray and took her niece's hand. "Poor dear. You're worn out. Here, let me help you to your room." The sleeping potion should take full effect soon. But with the changes Lavinia was undergoing, it was hard to predict just how long or how soundly she would sleep.

Lavinia tugged her arm from Alice's grip. "I can go by myself."

"Of course you can. I'll just walk along beside you." She eyed Lavinia. The drowsiness was a normal reaction so far, but not this cantankerousness. Alice raised her hand to cast a spell, hesitated, and let it fall. She had avoided using spells up to now, for they could trigger more instability. It wouldn't be worth the risk. She would have to rely on the potion.

"I'm cold, and so tired." Lavinia shivered as Alice settled her in bed and slipped off her shoes.

"Nia, after your nap, we'll have a nice hot dinner." Alice spread the silk coverlet over her. Faint sun rays, lazy with dust motes, beamed from the edges of the primrose yellow curtains. Their magical glow illumined Lavinia, her chest rising and falling with the soft rhythm of sleep. Alice stood still for a moment, rapt with attention. Her niece, so beautiful, her dark hair spilling on the white silk pillow. If only her mind could be so calm. If only she would come back from that dark place.

Lavinia stirred, heaved a sigh. Her eyelids fluttered. She sat up.

Alice stepped back at the wild look in Lavinia's eyes. *By the Djinn*, had the potion failed?

Her niece sloped in her aunt's direction, narrowing her eyes. Alice put on a calm demeanor. Had she given Lavinia the wrong potion? *Inaltiare* was a white powder, but instead of causing sleep it enhanced the stronger qualities of humans. If in her haste she had confused them, then *Inaltiare* would exaggerate Lavinia's madness. In that case—

"Alice," Lavinia said in a flat monotone. She fumbled at the bedside table, picked up a brass candleholder and held it up, her arm pulled back.

Would she throw the thing? Alice stood still, afraid any movement would antagonize her niece. Lavinia forced her arm forward. Alice stepped to the side. With a crash, the candleholder hit the floor to her right. Lavinia collapsed onto her pillow, eyes tracking under her eyelids as if she were watching something, her breathing fast and hard.

*By the hand of the Djinn.* Her niece had fallen fast asleep in a few seconds. Alice watched her for a moment, wary of another episode, then found Lavinia's reticule and slipped out the keys. She would have to do this like anyone else. With Lavinia so restless and unpredictable, it was too risky to use the particular magic she needed. She hurried over to the luggage piled in the corner. Alice had instructed the maid not to unpack until she gave her permission, using the excuse that her niece must rest undisturbed.

The first trunk had been unlocked. Alice searched through the silk negligees and wrappers, careful to replace each one as she had found it. The third key on Lavinia's silver key ring, the smallest one, opened the next trunk. Just as Alice raised the lid, Lavinia moaned in her sleep.

Alice stood straight, ready to jump behind the dressing screen if necessary. Lavinia thrashed her arms. One of the pillows slipped off the bed and her niece rolled over, reaching for it. She settled for the silk coverlet bunched into a soft ball, and stilled into sleep again.

Bending to her task, Alice thrust her hands into the clouds of taffeta and damask gowns, her fingers entangling in silky ribbons and lace. She should be able to sense the urn's presence as she had before, but felt nothing. So many things had changed. It could be right here in this room without her knowing. She unlocked another trunk and plunged in, feeling for the hard curve of the brass vessel.

If Lavinia had the urn in her possession, she must have packed it in one of these trunks, but which one?

The silky velvet upholstery on the arm of the chair crushed under Alice's finger, ruby red trailing into deep maroon. Her search, so far, had proved fruitless. The urn wasn't in any of Lavinia's trunks. She could have brought it with her and hidden it somewhere in this very house. Or Peter had it.

Alice gazed out the parlor window to the rose garden profuse with scarlet blossoms. What variety? So many palaces and grand houses in her life. Hard to keep up. Yet she had been pleased at the feel of the opulent, landed estate her husband, Lord Robert Smithson, had brought to the marriage.

It had been two months since her niece had moved from Bramley House into Woodthorne Hall and, though greatly improved, Lavinia, on occasion, watched her in that menacing way when she thought Alice wasn't looking. Lavinia's eyes would narrow, her body would become rigid, and she stared, a scowl dragging down her mouth. When Alice attempted to see into her niece's mind at those times, barriers deterred her. When she could break through, she caught snatches of sinister thoughts, visions of malevolent deeds concerning Peter and, sometimes, herself.

A soft knock. Alice dragged her finger backwards over the velvet, the nap trailing from maroon to ruby red. "Enter."

The butler opened the door. "Milady—" Before he could finish, Lavinia tottered into the parlor, dropped onto a chair and sank into the chintz cushions.

"Alice . . ." At the anxious whine in her niece's voice, Alice set her hands on the arms of her chair. Did Lavinia have a weapon? She looked her niece over—both hands in sight, no mysterious bulges under her thin silk gown.

"I dreamed about Yasir and our baby." Lavinia gazed at the floor, her face as white as the handkerchief limp in her hand.

"Oh, you poor dear."

Lavinia looked up, her eyes red and puffy. Her niece had mentioned in a muddled sort of way that something happened to the baby at the gypsy camp, but remained vague about the particulars, lapsing into near hysteria whenever she tried to tell the tale. Those times Nia attempted her tragic story, Alice would *see* the gypsy camp, *see* Lavinia pregnant. Then nothing. She would feel the child's presence in Lavinia, but had no hint of the baby departing as a soul leaving a dead body. Yet gypsies were adept at hiding, even from a djinni, those things they didn't want revealed.

"This was the worst dream." Lavinia stifled a sob with her handkerchief. "I s-saw my beautiful b-baby. . . . for the first time." She bent her head, staring into her lap, her hair a curtain around her grief. Alice walked over and embraced her, using an almost undetectable amount of her power to see into Lavinia's mind and, indeed, she glimpsed a baby, an infant imbued with magic. But he faded as if he were light in a deepening shadow. That was the first time she had seen the child. If only she could find the urn, she might be able to discern what happened to the baby—and to Yasir.

Was the infant really dead? Was Yasir? She had tried to contact the djinni in other ways, but something always interfered. Could the plan have utterly failed? She patted Lavinia absently on the back. She could feel her ribs through her gown. How could it all have gone so wrong?

"Nia, I think it is time to leave the house for a while."

Lavinia raised her head, her mouth gaping. "You . . . you want me to *leave*?"

"No, no, dear." Alice brushed a few wayward strands of hair from Lavinia's face. "I think we both should set off on a little outing."

## 32

*L*avinia considered her aunt sitting opposite her, and gripped the deep blue velvet armrest of the carriage—a sleek black barouche. She averted her gaze as Alice turned from viewing the flower-strewn meadow they had passed. Did her aunt know where the urn was? Was she allied with Yasir, or Rakhshan, or merely with Peter? She felt Alice's gaze, but kept her eyes on the scenery as the barouche rolled and pitched in the grooves on the packed dirt road.

The countryside surrounding Woodthorne Hall proved more varied than that of Bramley House, with sweeping valleys, and hillocks rising gradually to rounded heights. Flowers bloomed canary yellow and melon pink. The sunshine gave a fresh appearance even to the ancient stone walls, weathered and overgrown with fuzzy green moss.

Alice had sent for a picnic to be packed and the footman delivered a wicker basket from the kitchen, the aroma of fresh-baked bread filling the air as the feast sat at their feet. As much as she resisted Alice, perhaps her aunt's idea to leave Woodthorne Hall for the day was for the best. Venturing outdoors diluted anxieties, bleeding them into the ground, the air, the flora and fauna, clearing one's head. A brook, water reflecting the sky, followed the road for a while, then veered down into a meadow in a froth of rapids.

Since Lavinia had left the urn she had been fleeing the haunting images of Peter shooting Yasir. Rakhshan looming from the shadows. Yasir's body laid out, cold and lifeless. Now, the familiar flash of rage at Peter surged through her.

Before Peter shot Yasir, Lavinia had sought out his trunks next to the grand room featuring his gun collection, and absconded with treasures that struck her fancy. That evening when she opened the door to her room, she paused on the threshold, and gaped at the momentary strangeness of saris gathered at the windows as curtains, the dressing room doorway hung with amber beads, and the rectangle of Turkish carpet at the foot of her embroidery chair. She knew this was evidence of Thalia's essence coloring her desires, of Yasir's exotic ladylove merging with her. Would it be unsettling that in time she would be unable to distinguish betwixt the two?

On her side of the barouche, a broad meadow took up the view, the delicate grasses strewn with yellow flowers as bright as egg yolks. She readjusted her feet, pushing the picnic basket to the side. A lovely day. Alice had insisted on having the hood folded back. The sky arced over them, bird's-egg blue with nary a cloud in sight.

Lavinia placed her hand over her wide yawn. Torn with finishing her poor revenge on Peter as opposed to reconciling with him as Yasir had wished, she awakened at night to screams of anguish inside her head. Thalia's screams? Her own screams? Steadying her trembling hands, she folded them in her lap.

The horses slowed through a patch of road partly overgrown with weeds swaying in the breeze, and flushed a covey of partridges in an explosion of sound. *Rick, rick, rick.* With a flurry of gray-brown feathers they rose into the air exposing their white bellies—ashes to snowflakes. The horses shied, rocking the carriage.

Alice called to the driver, just behind her on his elevated box. "Why are the horses so nervous today?"

He cocked his head towards the sky and tightened the reins. "Full moon, milady. What as always raises their blood."

Alice reached across the aisle and took Lavinia's hand. Her aunt looked worried, and with good reason. Lavinia had heard tales of werewolves, spirits flying free and people struck mad from gazing at the full moon. At least before the moonrise, the worst of it, they should be safe inside Woodthorne Hall.

"The copse of trees off to the right. A perfect place for our picnic."
Alice raised her voice to be heard by the coachman. He guided the
horses off the dirt road and the carriage plodded up the hill.

"Just here," Alice said.

The driver jumped from his high seat and helped them down.
They stood at the top of the hill. The breeze, warm, then cool, as if it
couldn't make up its mind, ruffled their skirts. Alice strolled under
two spreading oaks, looking up at the winding leafy branches and
stopped at a grassy area in deep shade. "We'll picnic here." With the
arc of her hand, she indicated a thick patch of grass where the driver
set the basket and unlatched the lid.

"See to the horses. Then make sure no undesirables are lurking
about." Alice unpacked the tablecloth as the driver strode towards the
carriage.

Resting against the smooth gray bark of the largest tree, Lavinia
stared at the sky through the fluttering leaves. "I'm glad we came."
The phrase had slipped out. She clamped her mouth shut. She must
keep up her guard around her aunt. If she let other things slip out they
would have her under lock and key again.

She glanced up as a sparrow took flight, the dull-colored bird
becoming lost in the motion of the leaves until it soared into the sky. If
only she could do that. Fly away to Yasir.

"Nia, come help with the picnic." Her aunt shook out the white
tablecloth, readying it to lay over the grass. Lavinia turned away and
glared. One minute she distrusted her aunt, the next she wanted to
confide in her . . . With a smile, Lavinia took her end of the cloth
and helped spread it. They placed the cutlery and sparkling glasses,
arranged the china plates with sliced roasted chicken and ruffled
lettuce, red tomatoes, creamy amber cheeses, olives rolled in salt, and
hearty bread.

"The footman forgot the wine." Alice sighed, waved her hand,
and a tall bottle appeared on the tablecloth next to the box of sugared
almonds. Lavinia's eyes darted from Alice to the wine and back again.

She reached for it, hesitated, then wrapped her hand around the sloping shoulder of the dark green bottle.

"It's cold." She picked it up. It sat solid in her hands, as real as anything else around her. Her lips pressed tight, she set it down. Alice was so subtle with her talents that Lavinia mostly forgot she had magic. Magic just like Yasir. Yasir and Alice, connected in some mysterious way.

She scowled at her aunt and said in a low voice. "Do you know where Yasir is?" Alice didn't move. The sun slid behind a cloud. Gold flecks in Alice's eyes darkened.

"When Peter told me what you had said. Everything. All about Yasir, the urn, that Yasir was . . . that he was . . ." Alice looked down at the tablecloth and rearranged a wineglass.

"Don't hide this from me. You knew who Yasir was when you discovered us after I first opened the urn. You called him by name. And he treated you like an old friend. Or enemy." Lavinia snatched the cheese knife. Her aunt must tell her. She must. "You know things about him." Her knuckles whitened around the handle. "You know his secrets."

"Nia." Alice raised her hand and rose to her feet, her eyes fixed on Lavinia. "I didn't control him. You well know that. He resisted even my suggestions."

Lavinia sat back, clutching the knife and glowered up at her aunt. "You're not telling me everything." The sun broke from the cloud, blindingly bright, shining through the leaves. The wind swirled Lavinia's hair around her face, interweaving the long strands like a black lace veil.

"I know only what you told me. That Yasir—" Alice swallowed. "That he . . . died. That his body disappeared from his chamber in the urn." Her voice stayed soft, each syllable careful and controlled.

To hear someone else, even Alice, say it—say Yasir was dead, made her stomach clench. She felt the hollowness in the wake of the blackness rising through her. She felt it deaden her eyes, poison her mind. Lavinia flicked her hair from her face as Alice continued in her soothing voice. That maddening soft voice. The sound that said what her aunt wouldn't say: she still thought her mad, someone who should be treated as a child who couldn't know what the adults all knew.

"Nia, you know tha—"

Lavinia dropped the knife as she lunged. She grabbed Alice by the shoulders. "Don't you dare lie to me!" she screamed. "You *know* what happened to him. Tell me!"

One of the horses whinnied and stamped his feet. Alice's solid body faded to emptiness in Lavinia's hands. Lavinia kneaded the air with her fingers, grasping for the warm flesh that was there a moment ago. "Alice?" She twisted around, searching for her aunt. How could Alice do this to her? Tricks and obfuscation.

Her aunt appeared by the horse and stroked his head, murmuring, "*Dast dim humari.*"

Lavinia started towards them, but Alice suddenly materialized in front of her, blocking the way. Lavinia let out a screech, stepped backwards and tripped on the wine bottle, tipping it over. She regained her foothold, swayed for a moment, then steadied herself, keeping a wary eye on her aunt.

A subtle golden glow wavered around Alice. "Yes, Nia, I know Yasir from long ago. I know many things. I am here to help you, but you resist." She vanished and her voice came from behind Lavinia. "Let me help you. Show me what you have seen."

Lavinia whirled around, only to find Alice gone.

"How do I know you are for Yasir?" Lavinia called out to the air. She turned to see Alice standing calmly in front of her and braced herself, legs wider apart. "Yasir didn't like you." Lavinia moved backwards, away from her aunt. "He objected to things you wanted him to do."

Alice rose into the air and floated to where she was suspended inches above the tablecloth. Lavinia dared not blink. She stared into her aunt's eyes.

"Paltry disagreements, Nia." Alice glided nearer. To Lavinia's horror she felt their noses touch. "Yasir and I are close. We grew up together." Alice's breath was warm, yet chills prickled Lavinia's neck.

Lavinia sidled towards the horses. Alice kept pace. "You cannot escape me, Nia. But you must understand I am here to help you."

Lavinia screeched. "No!" What would Alice do to her? Some spell that might—

In a panic, she shoved Alice away and ran for the carriage. She pictured her aunt speeding up behind her, heard her voice as if she were speaking into her ear: *I am only frightening Nia with my thoughtless magic when I merely wanted to please her.* In her mind she saw Alice raise her hand, the wine still spilling from the bottle onto the tablecloth behind her.

One of the horses nickered and pawed the ground. Lavinia ran faster, but stayed in the same spot as if she were in a dream. But this was real. Alice would catch her. Lavinia breathed hard, her heart pounding louder and louder.

All at once her muscles locked. She looked helplessly at her hand, frozen in the motion of sweeping up her skirts. Her body stood stiff like a statue, one leg bent forward, her other foot hard on the ground in an attempt at a sprint. She tried to turn and call to her aunt, but couldn't move.

*Lord in heaven!* What had Alice done?

# 33

"I chose this wine especially for you, Nia. I wanted this outing to . . ." Alice kept talking, going on about the picnic, the balmy weather, anything that sounded normal. Her niece had quit listening after the first sentence, but if Alice stopped, her befuddlement of Lavinia would cease as well. Alice followed the direction of her niece's gaze to the wine bottle sitting precariously between them on the tablecloth. She latched onto Lavinia's thought thread: *didn't Alice conjure the wine?* Then Alice heard her own voice inside Lavinia's head, something she had tried to erase from Lavinia's memory: *the footman forgot the wine.*

Alice kept her timbre just the right pitch, explaining how the rainy April had been wonderful for the flowers, and carried on: "the kitchen has turned out the most wonderful bread. A new recipe that . . ." Alice continued speaking. She would have to finish this minor befuddlement spell and pray it worked.

Meanwhile, she could see Lavinia's thoughts spin on: *the bottle had appeared from nowhere right here on the tablecloth, chilled as if iced. No. Alice removed it from the picnic basket a short time ago. Wasn't there a . . . a . . . fight? I asked her if she knew where Yasir was. And Alice, she lied. But it was all a daydream? Wasn't it?*

Inside Lavinia's head Alice saw a vein throb red, growing brighter as the thought that produced it flashed by: *Lord in heaven, had Alice spell-cast me?* The blood vessel pulsated and Lavinia's confusion grew. Alice slipped out of her niece's mind and continued her endless conversation as she laid out the food. " . . . so I do hope the footman didn't filch pieces of the cake. He's done it before, you know. I must talk to Mrs. Belcher about feeding the young lad more." Alice set out the wine glasses. "The bottle has stayed wondrous cool stored in the basket." She popped the cork. The tang of freshly sliced apples burst into the air as the wine splashed into the glass, the dull chartreuse tinting to pale-straw yellow in the sunlight.

Alice set the wine beside Lavinia. A line of bubbles streamed to the surface of the pastel liquid.

"Ahh, this vintage sits well on the palate." Alice lowered her glass and looked expectantly at her niece. Lavinia hesitated, then sipped. She shut her eyes. The tautness in her face relaxed.

Lavinia raised her head, eyeing her aunt as if she had put some potion in her wine. Alice exhaled in a huff. *It was wine, plain wine, excellent, but no enchanted potion. How could Lavinia think that?*

Alice smiled. "Do you like the wine, dear?" She kept her expression calm, hiding her panic at the sudden obstruction that blocked her from Lavinia's mind.

A saffron butterfly flitted between them, lit briefly on Lavinia's wine glass, then took wing and floated away on a soft breeze. Lavinia turned to her aunt. Was that a look of satisfaction, or was the darkness that had seized her niece fading?

"Alice, thank you for this picnic." Lavinia's voice had lost the sharp edge that threatened to teeter into hysteria. "A change . . . A change is good for the soul." She set her wineglass on the tablecloth, stood and walked the few steps separating them.

Alice rose to meet her. She prepared herself. Lavinia still harbored rage against Peter. Against her? But Lavinia held out her arms and embraced her.

Alice felt her niece's heartbeat align to her own slow pulse. Lavinia wasn't accomplished enough to block both her mind and body. With her most subtle power, Alice sought answers to what had happened to Yasir.

Her eyes grew wide. A matter that Lavinia hadn't mentioned, a matter of which she was most certainly unaware. A seed had been sewn and thrived.

Joy obliterated Alice's despair. The plan may not be dead. Was this a magic child of the Djinn or Peter's true heir?

"Return by way of the straw meadow road, then veer towards the old well at the stone gate," Alice said to the driver before he closed the barouche door with a gentle click. She faced Lavinia and took her hand. "There's a field of wildflowers I want you to see, and a small pond where the horses can drink."

The carriage swayed like a cradle, the hoof beats of the horses as rhythmic as a lullaby. Cool breeze flowed through the open sides of the barouche, playing with Lavinia's hair while warmth radiated from the sun shining on the black leather hood above their heads. Her eyelids closed and she slumped onto the velvet-upholstered seat in a half-sleep. In this pleasant stupor, she became aware that she was smiling and half-opened her eyes. For once, she felt unbound by the awful constraints of sorrow and grief.

They traveled on a dusty road past a tavern and a cluster of cottages fronted by gardens. She yawned as the carriage stopped at a dense stand of blooming May trees and spiky holly bushes—a riot of green and white buzzing with insects. The occasional distant voices and a horse's whinny punctuated the monotone thrumming. Lavinia's eyelids drooped. The sounds drifted away.

"I think we missed the old stone gate. We needed to turn there." Alice's voice blared like a sudden trumpet blast. Lavinia, blinking herself awake, gradually deciphered her aunt's words. Had they gotten lost while she dozed? Why on earth didn't Alice use her magic? She could do it without the driver knowing. But her aunt persisted on navigating without it, a game really. Or quite possibly she *was* bringing her powers into play, but concealing the fact.

Lavinia shifted in her seat and whispered to Alice. "I . . . After all that wine . . . I need to visit the bushes."

Alice called to the driver. "We'll stop here."

Yawning, Lavinia made her way through a gap in the dense green thicket. White flowers covered the foliage like drifts of snow. But for a voice in her head protesting that it was summer, she almost shivered in the sunshine. She took a breath to clear her fuzzed drowsiness and inhaled the lemon scent of hundreds of soft round blossoms. Careful of the thorns, she pushed aside a cascading branch and ducked under a tangled overhang. Sunlight shone through a thick weave of leaves and dappled the ground in patches of washed-out gold. The perfect spot for a necessary.

It looked as though there was room enough to stand. She straightened. In a jolt of pain, her head was pulled back. She stood still, her neck at an awkward angle. Her fingers grasped something smooth and hard. She laughed to herself, coming more awake as she found each thorn, and untangled her hair from the crooked limb.

Lavinia rose from her squatting position, dodging the thorny branches. She adjusted her drawers, let her skirts fall, and with a flick of her wrists shook them, shedding dirt, bits of dead leaves and sticky white blossoms. As she smoothed the soft linen, she squinted through the puzzle of flowers and leaves.

Blobs of yellow, blue and orange filled in large areas between the foliage. Wary of the thorns, she found a gap in the thicket and stared at the gaudy domed tents ringed around a clearing. No, this must be a nightmare. She squeezed her eyes shut. When she opened them she would see only a meadow bright with flowers. But no, the tents were still there. A door in one of them flapped open and a gypsy girl in an orange dress, blue beads around her neck, sauntered towards the woods, her gait awkward.

Lavinia clapped her hand over her mouth. *By the stars in heaven.* Simza?

The breeze plastered the gypsy's dress against her front and Lavinia gaped at the girl's round belly. She looked as if she would deliver in hours. Lavinia counted on her fingers. She had been gone from the gypsies around three months. Even if Simza weren't newly pregnant when Lavinia had first arrived at the camp, it would be impossible for her to be this big so soon.

Lavinia pressed her hands against her face. The sweet smell of flowers in the bower had become cloying, the buzz of insects droning so loud she couldn't think. The girl looked her way. Lavinia ducked behind a jumble of branches. It was definitely Simza.

How could this be possible? Unlike the English, gypsies were not priggish about those things. Simza would have spoken of it. Or maybe there was a reason not to tell a mere *gadje*. Especially a *gadje* whose baby they were planning on stealing.

A bee dipped around her head in an awkward dance. As it veered towards her face, she backed into the foliage. Thorns pulled at her clothes. She ducked as the insect buzzed around her head. Bright colored with a hidden stinger, deceitful—*like that sneak Simza*. Lavinia curled her fists, envisioning her hands around Simza's neck, forcing a confession: yes, she had stolen her baby, yes it was just inside the tent.

The bee droned in a lazy circle amongst the intertwined branches that formed the bower's ceiling, the incessant sound like a worsening headache. Lavinia lifted her skirt, pulled two layers of fancy petticoats out of the way, and tore a strip from her plain under-petticoat. She would befriend Simza as she walked to her tent. She ripped another length of linen, longer this time. When they went inside, she would gag the gypsy and bind her hands. Then, at last, she would bend over the cradle and cuddle her child in her arms.

She wouldn't panic as she had when she stumbled from the gypsy camp, still suffering from the birthing. She would be brave and forceful and retrieve what was hers. That turncoat Simza would surely burn in hellfire.

The bee landed on the ribbon that wound around Lavinia's bodice, its stripes disappearing into the yellow of the silk. Lavinia stood still. She started as the insect zoomed towards her face, but it circled and landed on a white blossom.

Gripping the strips of linen, she slipped through a large gap in the thicket and walked towards the dense woods, keeping near the undergrowth. She rushed over patches of dirt and clumps of grass. In a blur of orange, Simza emerged from the trees ahead. Lavinia slowed. When she hurried, she made a racket. She must be silent. She set her foot down and the loud snap of a twig resounded through the trees.

Simza jerked her head towards the sound, while Lavinia cowered in the shade, not moving. The gypsy stared hard into the bushes, then turned and meandered through the grass back towards camp.

Lavinia stroked the lengths of cloth. She would be so sweet to Simza, say how good it was to see her, kiss her on the cheek, then she would— Her foot caught on a stone and she grabbed at a branch, righting herself for a moment. She sank to the ground as her legs trembled. *What in heaven's name was she thinking?* She glanced at the strips of her petticoat in her hand. Simza was a *lace romni*—daughter of the Chovihano—magic.

She struggled to her feet, glancing at the trees and bushes. They all looked the same. Was she lost? She caught a glimpse of Simza and tamped down her panic. Her baby was there. She wouldn't miss this chance.

Besides, she had never really *seen* Simza do magic. Perhaps she was still being trained. And Simza wasn't expecting Lavinia to return to their camp of her own volition. Surprise would put Lavinia at an advantage, especially—

The hair on her neck prickled. She stopped. A mossy log encrusted with brown mushrooms lay next to her foot. Something or someone lurked near her. What kinds of animals were in these woods? Badgers? Polecats? If she were still and quiet, they would probably go away. Instead, the presence grew stronger. Lavinia hardly dared to breathe. Her flesh tingled with goose bumps.

She flared her nostrils at the scent of sweat and strong musky perfume. The Chovihano stood in front of her. Here. In these woods. Her mouth gaped open. She hadn't heard or seen anything odd—no mist or shimmering in the air. He simply stood in front of her. The three green lines on his forehead wrinkled into a frown and his eyes bulged in fury.

Her body felt cold. So cold. She couldn't move. No one knew she had gone farther into the woods. The Chovihano could do what he wanted to her—

"You will not make a sound, understand?"

She nodded.

"You may not speak to Simza. Or let her see you." His voice growled fierce. "The djinni suffered from your rash actions. More than suffered." He looked her up and down, sneering. "My Simza will never see you. Do you understand?"

Lavinia stood there and stared, trying to control her breathing. She crushed the strips of the petticoat in her fist. Curse him. She wouldn't cry. She wouldn't. She sniffed, angry at the tears that dripped down her cheeks, mingling with dust on her face.

With a scowl, he whipped his knife from the painted scabbard at his side.

Would he kill her this very moment? He could bury her here. She would never be found. She wasn't ready to die, not now, she had a life to fix, to live. Her fingers felt numb as if they had frozen stiff. The lengths of cloth fluttered from her hands to the ground.

He yanked her to him, turning her forearm wrist up. Before she could blink, he had drawn his knife over her flesh. A sting, burning, as blood welled in a line as long as her finger. She squirmed as the pain increased. Would he do the same to her throat when he was—

"Lick it."

She looked at him. *What did he say?*

"Lick it." He tilted his head, indicating her cut.

She bent her mouth to her arm, the coppery taste making bile rise from her stomach.

"Swallow." He watched her closely. "Now dip your finger in it and . . ." He pulled her bodice down, baring her left breast. She gasped and covered herself. He thrust her hand away, exposing her breast again.

The Chovihano held his knife at her face, the edge red with her blood. "Quiet, or I use this on your throat." He indicated her blood-soaked finger. "Paint a cross over your heart."

Her hand trembled. She dragged her finger over her breast, making a vertical mark over her heart. Then slid it over her skin in an awkward horizontal line. The Chovihano nodded as he assessed the blood cross on her flesh.

"Say this: "The *lace romni* Simza will never *see* me." He waited until she stammered out the sentence and continued.

"The *lace romni* Simza will never *hear* me." Lavinia repeated after him. An owl screeched and swooped down by the Chovihano, feathers shushing like a mother's sigh as the creature flew into the shadows of the woods. The shaman kept on, waiting for her to say each syllable as she almost choked on her fear. "I will never speak of the gypsies. I will never accuse any gypsy of stealing or harming my child with Yasir."

She swayed on her feet and he jerked her arm, steadying her. She looked at his knife, shining in the dull light. "Now say these words: *Sângele meu ma leaga în promisiunea de a Chovihano. I-mi dau viata pentru el, daca voi zdrobi încrederea.*" His voice took flight with the force of the alien phrase as if it were a religious intonation, a thrumming chant.

Was this the final vow? Would the Chovihano kill her after the words left her throat? She opened her mouth, but her voice wouldn't come. He touched her forehead. The harsh gypsy words flowed from her as if she had said them a hundred times. She flinched as the last word, *increderea,* launched from her tongue, sure that part of her insides trailed after the odd syllables.

A hint of a cruel smile played on the Chovihano's lips. "You are afraid, but you wonder what you promised me, no? Here is what you vowed upon your life: 'My blood binds me in promise to the Chovihano. I give my life to him if I break his trust.'" He turned his mouth down in disgust. A thin vertical line that she'd never noticed before creased his skin from cheekbone to jawline on both sides of his face, giving him a more sinister look.

"I did not presume gratitude from one who could not understand, but I never expected hatred for my sweet Simza." A sudden breeze swirled around them, raising the dank smell of the forest floor. "You have pledged your life if you disobey your promise. A Roma oath is binding forever. You will find only bits of bones left from those who have broken their covenant. Pray you will not be one."

He held her arm fast. A trickle of blood ran down her wrist. "There is no one now to protect you but yourself. You saw to that. If you interfere, there will never be anyone to help you."

He let her go. She stood shaking, tears drying on her face. "You say nothing about this, about meeting me here. To anyone." The Chovihano turned and vanished.

She lurched to the spot where he had stood and looked wildly around. The wind rustled the trees. Had she fallen asleep? Dreamed? She held out her arm. It still stung from the long cut on her blood-smeared wrist. She glanced down. Her breast lay exposed, a crude red cross drawn over her heart.

"*Ayevalelh!*" A quiver jittered through her stomach at hearing her voice speak the oath Yasir used. She pulled up her bodice, covering her breast, but the wound on her arm still showed. What would she tell Alice? If only her cap sleeves hid her forearms. She stood there swaying, staring at the trees, at the dirt. A fall—that would explain it. Lavinia knelt on the ground, lay face down and wriggled back and forth. With an expression of disgust, she staggered to standing, wiping her mouth. Perfect. Her skirts were hopelessly dirtied. She smeared the blood on her wrist. There, it looked like a scratch from her fall.

How she found her way back to the carriage was a mystery.

"Lavinia." Alice narrowed her eyes.

She could feel her aunt trying to see into her mind, but some way, she didn't quite know how, she kept her out. As near as she could tell, if she stayed alert and determined, she managed to keep her aunt from prying, but other times Alice just walked into her mind and there was nothing she could do to drive her off. Perhaps she would manage this trait as she better absorbed Thalia's knowledge into her own.

"I–uh." Lavinia steadied her voice. If she cried, Alice would know something terrible had happened. She forced herself to laugh, and then to stop. Hysteria wouldn't do here.

"I fell. Flat on my face. Running from a bee." She punctuated this with another few laughs. "I know, it's silly, but for some reason I'm afraid of a little insect." She made herself smile and held up her bloody arm. She was far enough from Alice, and showed her wounds quickly. If she were lucky, her aunt wouldn't fuss over her.

Alice crumpled her forehead, a look of disquiet filling her eyes.

Lavinia whisked strands of hair from her face as she strolled to the carriage, gamely trying to set her gait to normal while her legs wobbled as if she had just disembarked from a ship. She must look a disaster, which might keep Alice fretting over her instead of probing. Thank God the Chovihano didn't make her draw the cross on her forehead. She stopped her hand as it went to her chest, if she pressed there, the blood might soak through.

On the trip back, her monotone answers to Alice's comments and questions put an end to any lengthy conversation, and, free from her aunt's intrusion, she could let her mind roam. Did the Chovihano's words that spiraled from her tongue really change anything? Before this, she had spoken of the gypsies to everyone who needed to hear. Told her story to anyone who mattered. He'd merely stopped her from facing Simza. And that could have been— She sat straight and almost let out a cry.

What was in Simza's tent? Something so important that the Chovihano had to appear, terrify her and stop her from seeing? Proof. His actions were proof. She turned and spat from the side of the barouche, but the taste of her blood lingered in her mouth.

She threw a furtive glance at Alice, and looked away in relief that she hadn't met her aunt's eyes, only the back of her head as she took in the view from the opposite side of the barouche. If she said anything to Alice now, if she even mentioned the word gypsy, somehow Alice would know. Know everything. The oath. Everything. *If she didn't already.* Would that count as her telling, if Alice inferred what had happened? Lavinia stared at the passing scenery—blurs of green and brown—perhaps the last thing she might see.

The Chovihano had warned her against interfering, against contacting the gypsies. Oh yes, he warned her. Lavinia ran her finger above the crude cross on her breast, hidden, thank God. But when he said, *If you interfere there will* never *be anyone to help you,* his voice, his softened expression implied something more.

Did he mean someone might help her if she submitted to his demands and if she survived this curse?

# 34

*T*he tap of her kid slippers followed Alice as she strolled through the grand entry at Woodthorne Hall. Lavinia was not telling the truth about what happened to her, but it had been impossible to ferret out the events that transpired in the woods. There was something strange about the state of her niece, and it had to do with magic; strong powers that took Alice's own magical inquiries and ensorcelled them as if they were but a charlatan's. What could Lavinia have encountered in the woods? Certainly something more than a bee.

A ghost of a word arose as a whisper in Alice's mind, eliciting visions of glittering silver and colored glass charms, dark faces in amber firelight, the sweet musky scent of patchouli.

*Gypsies.*

If Lavinia had crossed a gypsy there was nothing to be done about it.

Alice paused by the gold leaf table, fingering a velvety pink petal in the massive bouquet of cabbage roses. She inhaled the fruity scent. Ah, the delicacy of nature, of magic. She eyed the sharp thorns on the roses' stems. The harshness as well. Things even *she* couldn't touch, or, she pursed her lips in amusement, was wise enough not to touch.

Lavinia had handled her trauma in the forest admirably. No one else would have been able to tell she was lying about her fall while fleeing from a bee. Her niece was becoming quite the accomplished actress, no doubt about it. Alice smiled to herself. Lavinia was, at last, ready to live with Peter.

❖ ❖ ❖

The footman opened the front doors and Alice stepped onto the portico. Lavinia stood silhouetted against the light pouring between the marble columns, a lone figure facing her future.

"I'm afraid." In pink silk and palest blue lace, Lavinia stood by her trunks and bags, reticule in her hand, face stony. "Are you certain he's forgiven me?" She hugged her chest and looked at the ground.

"Lavinia dear." Alice took her arm. "He has written us both saying he will have you back for good. Can you not accept that he forgives you?"

"Well . . . no. No. I cannot accept it." Lavinia dragged her shoe on the travertine floor, watching the shiny silver buckle catch the light. "Alice, I stabbed him. He bled. He suffered pain for weeks. It's Peter we're talking about."

"Precisely, it's Peter. Your *husband*. With whom Yasir said it was necessary to make a life." Alice brushed a spec of lint from Lavinia's sleeve. Her niece looked up when she heard Yasir's name, her eyes bright.

"Remember?" Alice inhaled deeply. Lavinia could try her patience like no other.

"Yes. And I have been forbearing. But when?" Lavinia's voice dissolved into a whine as Alice inched closer.

"It will come. The boon from Yasir will come in time. But you must be ready. And that means reconciling with Peter. You should be entrenched in your station as wife to Lord Bramley." She gave her niece a tender look. "This is for your own good. To keep you safe from what plagued Yasir. We will mention no names, especially today."

The day before, Alice had managed to embrace Lavinia once more and sense the child within her. Try as she might, Alice detected no magic. The child was not Yasir's. She was convinced of it, and in that surety had been distressed that night. With Yasir gone, she would have had his child to love and nurture. But this was Peter's offspring, the heir that he so desperately wanted—Lavinia's passage into Peter's heart.

"I am convinced that you still love Peter." She took her niece's hands and held them, observing her expression. "You can still love him, can't you?" It was imperative. Yasir had demanded it. The one last thing Alice could do for him, for Lavinia. "I can make it easier for you, easier for Peter." Lavinia gave her a hard look. Of late, her niece had been skittish anytime magic was hinted at.

The luggage had been loaded onto the coach. The horses stamped their feet as the driver climbed to his seat and the footmen milled behind. The atmosphere was one of leaving, sad goodbyes, and wistful hope of what was to come.

And distrust. Alice sensed it. Along with her disillusionment with magic, her niece, dear soul, deep down had never trusted Alice after she saw what she was.

"I will write." Lavinia dutifully embraced her. "Oh, Alice, how can I thank you? All you've done. What am I going to do without you?"

Alice silently added what Lavinia politely omitted . . . *but I am delighted to escape from your mind-reading, to leave your strange magic, magic like Yasir's that makes me remember and breaks my heart over and over.*

"Which reminds me." Alice searched in her pocket. "Ah." She pulled out a small silver box, ornate with scrollwork, and handed it to Lavinia.

"Open it."

Her niece lifted the lid. She looked up at Alice with a beam of delight.

"It's a tiny looking glass," Alice said, keeping her eyes on her niece's face. "Look once more." Lavinia held the mirror closer and peered into it. Her mouth dropped open.

"Nia, I would think you would be used to these things by now," Alice said matter-of-factly. "It's a magic mirror. When you look into the glass, it can answer your questions. What do you see?"

Lavinia stared. "It's not *my* reflection." She brought the glass closer, tilting her head, an eyebrow askew. "It's Peter." She enunciated his name like a curse. "In his study. Pacing. He wears an anxious look."

"Yes, dear Nia, he is waiting for you." Alice indicated the mirror. "See."

Lavinia scowled at the glass in her hand. "Peter is most certainly waiting for me, probably in a dither that I'm returning and worried that I might attempt to harm him again."

"Dear, dear. Do try." Alice caressed Lavinia's arm. "Please accept my gift. The mirror will assist you while you reacquaint yourself with your husband and life at Bramley House. This will help you feel less alone in your mourning when it overcomes you. The mirror can be unpredictable, but, like now, if you think of someone or something when you look into it, it will comply and you can see what they are doing." Of course, she had used a magic mirror and countless other objects of power to search for Yasir. To no avail. This mirror would serve no purpose in that pursuit, for the task proved too big and powerful.

Alice ran her hand over her empty pocket, and gazed at Lavinia with sympathy. "But I feel how you are hurting, and I am the only one with whom you can share this."

Lavinia bit her lip as she eyed the looking glass.

Alice continued. "When anyone else looks into it, the glass becomes an ordinary mirror. But for you and a select few, it is always magic." She embraced her niece. She had done what she could to help her, and the looking glass . . . "Dear, this is a means to keep you safe. You well know what can go wrong. I want you to be happy."

Lavinia hugged Alice. She stepped back from her aunt, bowed her head, then looked her in the eye.

"Alice . . . could you . . . Could you have saved him?" Lavinia stood rigid. Alice saw a shiver go through her niece, the looking glass almost imperceptibly shaking.

The question stung like the cut of a razor. Wanting to keep her cool demeanor and not upset Lavinia further, she turned away. Of course her niece would ask this of her. She should have been expecting it, but the finality of the word "saved" took her breath away. She had not yet come to the conclusion that Yasir was dead. And for this question to come up . . . The tightness in her throat almost choked her. She swallowed and faced her niece.

Lavinia clutched her reticule in front of her like a shield.

"I-I . . . It was hidden from me." Alice stared straight into her niece's eyes.

"You didn't know?" Lavinia pressed her hand against her chest, fingers splayed.

A silence enveloped them, a suffocating shroud. Alice shrugged and shook her head. "No," she said in a small voice.

"How could you not know? You . . . with . . . your-your magic?"

"Even I, even Father—" Alice stopped herself. "We are . . . I . . . I am not invincible." She raised her head and squeezed her hand tight in her pocket at Lavinia's astounded expression. "The spell must have been strong. There was a spell, was there not?"

"Yes. And to unspell it there was Mehadeh . . ."

Alice nodded for her to continue.

". . . two magic physicians, an elephant god, a magus and . . . and Yasir. None could break the curse on the bullet."

"*Ayevalelh.*" Alice leaned against one of the massive porch columns. "So powerful, no wonder Fath—" She spread both hands behind her, the solid stone almost as cold as the shock from hearing details of Yasir's desperate attempt to win the battle against Rakhshan.

"Do you not see?" She stared into the distance. "The deed could not be undone." That magician, that paltry human . . . how could he defeat a djinni?

The footman held out his gloved hand, waiting to assist Lavinia into the carriage, but she stood on the gravel drive, eyes unfocused.

"Milady?"

"Oh?" She stared at the servant.

The magic mirror from Alice. Yasir gone. Peter's promise to forgive her. And now she was going home. But where *was* home? The urn? The gypsy camp? Bramley House? With a sigh, she took the footman's hand and placed her right foot on the folding step.

Lavinia sat on the edge of the tufted satin seat and looked out the window at Alice standing on the porch smiling a sad smile. The carriage rolled down the drive, leaving only a faint trail of dust as a farewell to Woodthorne Hall. Lavinia clutched the silvered mirror. She looked over her shoulder, forced a smile and waved her gloved hand at Alice. When the carriage turned onto the road she would toss the mirror into the bushes, and good riddance to all the fiddle-faddle of magic. A lot of good it did her. Not pearls and flying carpets and wishes come true, but grief and sorrow and heartbreak.

The horses picked up speed. Lavinia shut her eyes and sank into the plush upholstery, the jostling of the carriage seeming to waver into nothingness, leaving her alone, only air beneath her, as if she had suddenly stepped off a precipice.

# 35

These last two months since leaving Alice and Woodthorne Hall, Lavinia had reconciled with Peter. She was again, in her mind, Lady Lavinia Bramley, wife of Lord Peter Bramley. Her husband—antiquary, aristocrat, owner of landed estates and farms, and landlord of tenants. Her lord.

Lavinia had muted the voice inside her head that tempted her to bury the carving knife deep into Peter's chest, that directed her to strangle him with his cravat after he made love to her, that suggested she drop a bit of poison in his afternoon tea. But in the wee hours of the morn, or when she was overly fatigued, or when she felt the pull of grief, she could still hear it—a faint, insistent murmur enticing her to take her revenge on Peter, to show no mercy. "No, that is not what Yasir wanted," she would whisper to herself, squeezing her eyes and fists tight.

Lavinia sighed. When? She put her elbows on the windowsill, and looked out over the grounds of Bramley House. The perfect green grass bordered by manicured hedges, the ancient spreading oaks, sentinels guarding the stately manor. She was a figure in a painting, captured smiling pleasantly, her décolleté gown of duchesse silk glowing in the light, her sapphires artfully arranged, her hair immaculately dressed. Two dimensional. Fixed in a setting.

Her life decided.

She had done what was asked of her. When would the boon from Yasir appear? She breathed on the windowpane, a faint wash of moisture that vanished almost instantly. Merely a speck in the long history of time, Lady Lavinia Bramley.

From the road behind the screen of dense trees and hedges, a cloud of fawn-colored dust dulled the bright sky. A carriage? A dray?

A tinker's cart? She tasted the fine bits of grit wafting over the sill through the partially opened sash.

What if it were a lie? A story Alice concocted to lure her back with Peter. Yasir was gone, dead. How could he send her something? Oh, she was a foolish, foolish woman, living on a promise from someone who had turned into a bird, from someone who wasn't, if truth be told, human. How could she trust Alice? Her aunt *had* taken her under her wing, pampering her at Woodthorne Hall, helping her heal, perhaps even with potions or spells. Was it all for Alice's ends? Was she Alice's pawn in some grand scheme that would play out over the centuries, long after she was dead?

What happens when hope ends? When there is nothing left? Lavinia looked around her chamber. She possessed all she ever wanted . . . *before* encountering Yasir. She was the lady of a beautiful manor house. She had married well, the man of her dreams, yet now she dreamed of Yasir.

A carriage turned off the main road and rattled up the long drive towards the manor, fading wisps of dust from the road trailing behind. A visitor. Perhaps Lucy or Sarah or Beth. Lavinia hurried to the mirror. She scowled and plucked at her gown, an afternoon dress, wavy white stripes woven into blue muslin, but not fancy enough for her set. Fleming would need to help her change.

Lavinia made for the bell pull, but stopped by her embroidery chair, finger to her lips. Her friends would have written to see if she was accepting company or in residence. And it *had* been awhile. After Yasir came into her life she most certainly had neglected them, sending only an occasional letter. She slouched towards the window and peered at the drive. "It couldn't be," she murmured.

The carriage pulled up and the footman, his blue livery grayed from dust, hurried round to open the door. A dark shoe, a brown skirt, shades of chocolate. Alice sprang from the carriage. Her aunt looked up at the windows and Lavinia stood to the side, watching from the shadows.

Alice hadn't written to say she would visit. Had she come without warning because she somehow found out what happened in the woods after their picnic? Was her aunt angry that she hadn't mentioned the incident with the Chovihano? Lavinia had put them both in danger, chasing after Simza with bad intent. Why hadn't she learned not to interfere with these shamans and *lace romnis*? And djinnis?

Lavinia peered out the window. Her aunt had gone inside. If Alice knew, then the Chovihano, with his shaman powers, would perceive it, and he would conclude that Lavinia had told, that she had broken her oath to keep silent. She had no doubt that the Chovihano would have immediately initiated the curse. In which case, she would have already been reduced to bits of bone like the others who had broken their covenant.

With a whimper, she cringed. For a moment, she could have sworn that the shaman stood before her, the heat of his breath on her face, his scent fouling the air. He had forced her to say the oath, to draw the blood cross over her heart.

Lavinia pressed her hands against the wall as her mind careened from one scenario to another. Her excuse about being chased by a bee had been terribly pathetic. It was a wonder Alice hadn't burst out laughing on the spot. But her aunt had seen her through the throes of insanity—a peculiar phobia regarding a certain insect wouldn't phase her.

Lavinia twisted her wedding ring. She was cursed by a gypsy spell. Could Alice counter it? If Lavinia could think of a clever way to imply she was in trouble, to make clear she needed her aunt's help. But that was risky. One slip and they'd both be in desperate straits. She had been sure Alice was the enemy with her tricks during the picnic, but Alice had kept saying that she was here to help her.

Lavinia swirled a lock of hair around her finger. Her aunt was her closest relative—never mind that Alice had been adopted. She had nurtured her, reassured her, magicked her back to health. Hadn't Alice proven she cared?

Lavinia propped her elbows on the window sill, the drive vacant now, the footman tending the carriage and horses in the coach house. She would not risk it. She could keep quiet. Besides, she didn't care to speak of the gypsies again, to anyone. Settled and done.

The knock at the door was soft, but Lavinia jumped. "Yes, enter."

"Milady, Lady Alice Smithson, to see you. She requests to come up." Fleming curtsied. She had been skittish and annoyingly formal since Lavinia returned from her convalescence at Woodthorne Hall.

"I will see her in the parlor. Tell her I'll be down presently." Lavinia glared at Fleming, who bowed and scuffled out the door with a, "Yes, milady." One would almost think her maid was afraid of her. The very idea. Why, she didn't stab *her*.

Lavinia fiddled with her earrings, changing to the sapphires Yasir conjured for her, then removing them in fear of dwelling upon them, and then him, and making a scene. She fumbled in her jewelry box. There, the pearls from her mother. Lavinia hooked the second earring in place and checked it in the mirror. Her father would never speak of mother. Nanny had said she perished in a fever, begging to hold two-year-old Lavinia, but was denied for fear of contagion.

She could use a mother now, someone different from Alice. Someone she could trust, without second thoughts, to have her best interests at heart. Someone who was human.

"Just like your mother." Nanny would say in a sigh whenever she tied the last ribbon in Lavinia's hair and had her stand back, all fancy dressed for dinner. But her mother's portrait showed a smiling woman, lapis lazuli eyes lit with laughter, unlike the image Lavinia saw before her in the mirror—blue eyes haunted and dull, mouth straight and stern. She fingered a smooth gray pearl, stared into space for a moment, then walked out the door.

She was alone. She would have to take care of herself.

"Dearest Nia." Alice's warm solid body held her in a cheerful embrace even before Lavinia had decided how to greet her aunt.

"Alice." Lavinia finally hugged her in return. She found herself happy to see her aunt, eager to talk, her confused musings melting away, the unhappy leavings of a sour frame of mind. Or perhaps, she was simply lonely for company.

Alice stepped back and looked Lavinia up and down. "Thank God. I see your appetite has improved. I was worried you might become as thin as Lady Bonhair's slip of a daughter." Alice laughed and Lavinia joined her. "My dear, how are you getting on with Peter?"

Lavinia grimaced, but changed her expression to one of studied pleasantness before her aunt noticed. "Alice do make yourself comfortable. I'll send for tea." She pulled the cord in the corner and settled into a chair across from her aunt.

"A happy wife is always pleased to discuss her husband." Alice broke into a smile. She slipped her reticule onto a lower shelf of the side table. "But even if you don't want to talk about Peter, are you doing what we discussed?"

Lavinia sighed. "Alice, how can we—you—be sure something is coming from Yasir. He's—" She caught herself starting to dissolve into sorrow. "He's *gone*, isn't he?"

Alice shifted her body nearer Lavinia, their knees almost touching, and settled her soft plump hand on Lavinia's. It was warm, as usual. "My dear, I know these things are difficult to believe, and all that's happened must, at times, seem . . . unreal." She looked at Lavinia with the inadequacy of her chosen adjective reflected in her brown eyes. Oblique flecks of amber decorated her iris like a lad's marble. "But don't forget, it was as real as you and me." She squeezed Lavinia's hand.

Lavinia gripped the chair arm. Had the room lurched? Tilted at a crazy angle for a moment like the images in fun mirrors at fairs? Her head filled with all the odd things that had happened when her aunt was involved.

Alice smiled conspiratorially as the footman entered with the tea tray. China plates rimmed in gold held biscuits iced in pink, and sandwiches with slices of pale green cucumbers peeking from white triangles. A crystal bowl splintered plump strawberries into facets of deep ruby red.

"Now, Nia," Alice set three sandwiches on her plate, "tell me about Peter. Is he still afraid of you?"

Lavinia choked on her biscuit, sputtering pink crumbs onto her lap. She coughed, gulped her tea and cleared her throat. "A-afraid?"

"Why, yes, dear, I seem to remember him being reticent to be around you after you stabbed him in the chest." Alice took a bite of her sandwich.

"No. Well, at first . . ." Lavinia placed her cup in the saucer with a clink. "But we . . . ah. He seems happy enough." She coughed again and dabbed her serviette to her mouth.

Alice finished her sandwich and took a sip of tea. "And you are fulfilling your wifely duties?"

Lavinia blushed. Thank heaven she had no biscuit in her mouth this time. She looked down at her plate. Alice took her hand. "Dear, I need to know. Remember, this must be genuine, to protect you."

Pursing her lips, Lavinia exhaled, prolonged and deliberate. The last two months at Bramley House. Her muddled feelings. Her confusion. Closing her eyes at Peter's warm body against hers, substituting Yasir in her mind. Careful to call out Peter's name, not Yasir's.

With a muffled exclamation she pressed her hand to her mouth. She had not asked Fleming for her special cloths. For how long? Long enough that she couldn't fix a date in her mind. She sat up straight.

"Alice." She bent forward in her chair. "I-I think I may be expecting."

Alice dropped her gaze to Lavinia's middle and stared as if she were reading an exceptional phrase in a book. Lavinia felt a vibration, a faint buzzing inside her womb. Her aunt looked up, an odd expression in her brown eyes, and a warm buttery glow like she was lit inside with a candle.

"My dear Nia." Alice beamed. "At last, Peter has an heir." She settled into the chair cushions with a distant unfocused smile, her eyes closed.

"Alice?" Lavinia stood over her. "Alice?" She touched her aunt's arm, her fingers brushing as lightly as a butterfly's wings. "Is the baby . . . is it . . . quite all right?"

Alice gave her a crisp nod. "Dear, the baby is fine. No one in heaven or earth minds if Lord Peter Bramley has a son."

That night, after dinner with Lavinia and Peter—who behaved for all the world like a normal married couple—Alice lay in her bed, her mind alive with possibilities.

She had let Lavinia discover it for herself. She was glad the seed had held firm. Alice closed her eyes and relaxed under the warm weight of the satin comforter. She had done all she could for Yasir. His requests had been satisfied.

A smile glimmered on her face. The boon would come, just as he said. It was almost time.

# 36

Alice had left days ago, and truth be told, Lavinia missed her aunt. Today she would pen a letter and cajole her to return. What would entice Alice? At the ominous peal of thunder, Lavinia turned to the window. The rain thudded so hard against the glass that she barely heard the sharp rap on her door.

Annoyed, Lavinia pressed her lips tight and opened the door. The rainy day's dampness penetrated her room regardless of the fire blazing in the hearth. With her nausea abated at last, she wanted only to huddle in bed, cozy under the covers with a novel for company. Fleming stood poised to knock again, wearing that contorted expression that meant she couldn't make heads or tails of a situation.

"What is it?" Lavinia glared at the maid.

Fleming stepped back, her face a mask of stone. Lavinia tried to soften her expression. She had snapped at her poor maid, who had been so kind—bringing chamomile tea and sweet biscuits to ease her mistress's morning sickness. Even now the thought of the steaming tea, the soothing crispness of the biscuits, brought comfort.

She moved her hand over the slight curve of her abdomen. Peter didn't know yet. He couldn't tell. No one could. It would be several months before her pregnancy would be obvious, more if she chose her clothes carefully.

Peter's child. His heart's desire. But she wouldn't, couldn't tell him yet. Accepting this baby . . . why, it would be like canceling out Yasir's child.

"Milady." Fleming curtsied and cleared her throat. "There's a . . . a . . . visitor. In the kitchen. Mr. Dobson wouldn't let her in the front hall, sent her 'round to the servant's entrance. In this weather." She made a clucking sound with her tongue.

"She's wrapped in a hooded blue cape, drippin' wet. Insists on seeing the lady of the house. Gives her name—a Miss Simza. Even swathed in that plain cape, with them dark eyes, she's got gypsy written all over her." Fleming looked expectantly at her mistress, then frowned. "Milady, is it the nausea what ails you again?" Fleming spoke softly as one would to a child. "Jesus, Joseph and Mary, you're pale as milk."

Lavinia felt her maid's sturdy arm wrap around her waist. She clutched her stomach as Fleming helped her to a chair.

*Lord in heaven.* Simza. Here. At Bramley House.

Lavinia had done what the Chovihano asked. She hadn't contacted Simza, hadn't mentioned her suspicions that the gypsies stole her baby, hadn't tried to find the gypsies. What had she done that would bring the *lace romni* to her home?

A *lace romni* to fulfill the Chovihano's curse.

Blurry specks fuzzed the edges of her vision. She put her head in her hands. The buzzing in her ears almost drowned out the sound of the rain outside.

"Breathe slowly milady. Try and quit gasping like that. Milady? Milady?"

Someone was talking. Stop. Stop. That horrible buzzing. Like bees in the bushes before she encountered the Chovihano. She moaned as Fleming pressed the wet compress on her forehead.

"No. It's too . . . too cold."

"The cold will help. I have the bowl if you feel sick. Let me settle you a bit more comfortably." Fleming bustled around, slipped a thin pillow behind Lavinia's back and pressed the cold cloth against her forehead again.

Lavinia shivered. From the chill of the compress or from Simza waiting downstairs? She placed her hand on her chest, tried to breathe—

"Milady, do you want the bowl?"

"No." Lavinia took a deep breath.

"That's it, milady, long and slow. There."

"Remove the compress." Lavinia struggled to sound calm. Her poor maid. So sweet. Was she her only friend now?

"Milady, I will tell the gyp— the visitor you're not up to seeing anyone. That she must come another day and then—"

"No!" Could she not keep from snarling? She took her maid's hand. "Dear Fleming, I am sorry. You've been so good to me, and I may never have another chance to tell you how grateful I am." If she sent Simza away she would agonize over why the gypsy had visited. She would worry the curse was upon her. This way, at least she would know, even if it meant . . . She slumped into the cushion. Fleming angled away, eyeing her quizzically.

"I will see this . . . visitor," Lavinia said. The rain thrummed harder, streaking the fogged glass like fingers prying their way inside. She got out of her chair.

"Tell her I will be a little while." She walked to the window and ran her hand over the cold glass, wiping away the film of vapor, but outside remained a gray-blue blur. On another rainy day Simza had come to her rescue. Lavinia rested her forehead against the chill glass pane. The rain increased, battering the house with a deafening noise as if they were being invaded.

She reached for the parlor door handle, but pulled back. In her mind, Simza's dark eyes bored into her. Simza, a *lace romni*, the Chovihano's seventh daughter with powers of her own. Lavinia absently ran her finger in a short vertical line on her chest, then dragged a perpendicular stroke through the middle and looked down, half expecting to see a crude cross of blood staining her dress.

A rush of wind burst against the house, which creaked like old bones in the storm's wail. Then silence, as if a great beast had blustered through and taken cover, biding its time until its next attack. Lavinia held her breath. There was no sound. No wind, no rain. She pulled her shawl close.

She pressed the door handle and a shiver, as startling as an abrupt chime of a bell, rippled through her arm. The door opened partway. She stood still, grateful that the angle kept her hidden from the gypsy. A low rumble broke the silence. Lightning flashed from the windows, spotlighting Simza in a chair, her clothes vivid orange and green, her hair a deep black swath like a gouge out of a painting.

Lavinia stopped her hand as it made its way to her stomach. Another baby grew within her now. Did Simza know? Had she come to steal this one as well?

Simza turned towards the door. Her eyes glimmered when she saw Lavinia. She grasped a large bundle and rose, coming partway across the carpet, her face sphinx-like.

Simza drew back a flap of material covering the bundle. Snippets of images, oddments of gestures, scraps of expressions crashed through Lavinia's head. She sucked in her breath. A baby's tiny face peered at her. Rosy round cheeks, rosebud lips parted in curiosity. A cherubic face framed in glossy black curls. Lavinia clutched the doorframe as her mind swirled like leaves in the wake of a storm.

*His* eyes. *His* sensual lips.

Yasir's child. His spitting image in miniature.

Her stomach balled up, cold and hard. She had been right. They *had* stolen her baby. She struggled to take in even a small breath as her feet skimmed over the thick carpet, her body as insubstantial as the rain outside. The air in the parlor hung heavy and sparse. The buzzing in her ears blended with the rain hammering down so hard she feared it might breach the roof. She stopped in front of Simza, who clutched the baby to her chest. The wind howled, thrashing the trees outside, fearsome silhouettes encroaching the parlor, the embodiment of the apparitions that assaulted her mind when she first returned to Peter.

The baby gurgled and waved his chubby fists.

How could she have been such a fool? She hadn't seen it. What was so obvious. That look of adoration, that breathy way Simza paused before she spoke of Yasir. A djinni and a gypsy. This was *their* child. Lavinia breathed in short gasps.

*Angels in heaven.* Yasir had taken Simza to his bed.

How could he? He must have visited the camp while she was there. They did this right under her nose. *She would kill the little gypsy whore.*

Lavinia stumbled to the hearth, grabbed the fire poker with the heavy brass handle. As if in a dream she stood over Simza, her fist clenching the poker. She shook her head but couldn't dispel the image of Yasir, his bare arm around the gypsy girl, their lips meeting in—

"*Rawnee?*" Simza clutched the baby and stepped back.

Lavinia raised the poker. She had a good aim. She could hit Simza and miss the baby. The infant blinked and opened his eyes wide. A fuzzy numbness spread from her fist to her elbow.

*Blue eyes?*

Lavinia swayed on her feet. Neither Simza nor Yasir had blue eyes. Their child would never have blue eyes. She squinted at the baby's pale skin, stark against Simza's dusky complexion. Lavinia sagged. The poker clanged against the marble floor. She staggered over to a chair.

*My God*, if the baby hadn't looked at her, if she hadn't seen his blue, blue eyes, Simza would be dead on the floor, her blood splashed on the marble, staining the carpet. Lavinia bent her head, her heartbeat pulsing in her eyelids.

"*Rawnee?*"

Lavinia looked up. The gypsy stood over her, the baby secure against her chest.

"No!" Lavinia raised her arm over her head. "Please don't. I've done all I said I would." *Lord in heaven, she would never leave this room. Simza would implement the curse and there was nothing anyone could do.*

"*Rawnee.* There is no blame on you, my *Rawnee.*" Simza swallowed hard.

Lavinia studied her. Why, the gypsy was as afraid as she was. Lightning flashed outside the window, transforming Simza's face into a bone-white mask, eyes hollowed deep and vacant.

Simza shifted the child and rested him on her hip. She looked straight at Lavinia. "With the Great Djinni's and Mehadeh's b-blessing." She dashed a tear from her eye and took a quick breath, her chin set in determination. "Your son. Yasir's son."

Simza set the baby in Lavinia's lap, her hand on his back. He sat, unsteady, tilted his head and reached for her with his plump little arms. Lavinia's heart caught. Yasir's mannerisms. Yasir's expression in his deep blue eyes. The baby was around four months old. The exact age her child would be.

He turned down his mouth and whimpered. Lavinia wrapped her arms around him and lifted him close. His warm stout body settled into hers. He smelled sweet, like sugar icing on a cake or a fragrant leaf of mint. The baby crinkled his face and dissolved into tears, his black curls jiggling.

Lavinia patted his back and rocked him up and down. The pulse of her heart throbbed against his soft body, her endless days of yearning laced into the rhythm. Magic emanated from the baby like his warm sugary smell. The child snuggled his soft little body into her chest, his eyelids half-closed as he stuck his thumb in his mouth, the *chk, chk, chk* of his sucking like another heartbeat. She saw Simza bend and pat his chubby thigh, and wasn't prepared for the twinge of anger that flared through her.

"You told me my baby died." Lavinia's voice was brittle and cold. She looked up at the gypsy.

"I had to." Simza sat beside her. The rain slowed. A distant rumble of thunder grew louder like the sound of an approaching train.

Lavinia clutched her baby to her chest. He closed his eyes. "You had to? I gave birth and you . . . you stole him? From a helpless woman. How could you?"

Simza put her hand on Lavinia's arm. "No, it was not—"

"Don't you dare touch me." The rain fell harder, mingling with Lavinia's words, absorbing them into the storm. She laid the baby on the couch cushion, placing pillows around him, and jerked Simza to standing.

"You had no right." Lavinia grabbed Simza by the hair and pulled her away from the baby. She drew her close. "What do you want? Money?"

She wound the tresses around her hand. Simza groaned. "Nooo. N-not money."

"Thief! I will have you and your Chovihano hanged for this." Lavinia dragged Simza over to the bell pull in the corner of the room.

The gypsy tried to catch Lavinia's wrist. "No, no. Do not call anyone! The djinni—" Like a cannon shot, a clap of thunder boomed through the parlor, rattling the windows. Two vases fell from the mantle and shattered on the hearth tiles in an explosion of crystal, the fire spluttering and popping as fragments flew in over the top of the fire screen.

Lavinia and Simza froze.

The baby shrieked, long and shrill like a whistle, then fell silent. He cried out again, faint, gaining strength, faltering, then climbing into a full-blown scream. The rain drummed as loud as the thunder, nearly drowning out the child's cries. Simza clamped her hand on Lavinia's wrist. "Please, before you call anyone—" The child screamed louder. "Let me attend to the baby."

Lavinia sneered. "You . . . you imply I'm callous? You who stole my child and lied to me?" She put her face next to Simza's. "I should strangle you here and now. No one would care. Who cares about a dead gypsy?" Lavinia rolled Simza's hair tighter around her fist.

Simza moaned. "I cared for you and—"

"Yes, you lulled me into carelessness. Then you stole my baby."

"But if you had given birth then—"

Lavinia turned her wrist, reeling in the gypsy's hair.

Simza cried out in pain. "It-it was too soon. The child would have been born dead." Simza's head angled as if her neck were broken. "I could not have stolen your baby," she rasped.

The child wailed, hiccupping in short shrill bursts as he kicked his legs and waved his arms like a bug turned on his back. Lavinia let Simza go. "Tend to him. Hurry."

The gypsy staggered, her hair spilling to her waist as she caught her breath. She rushed to the divan, took the baby in her arms and sank into the cushions.

"Nicu, Nicu." Simza held the baby against her chest, rocking him and singing. His cries died to a whimper and he plopped his thumb into his mouth—*chk, chk, chk*. The sound sent a pang of jealousy through Lavinia. She paced the floor with arms aching to hold her child, and glanced out the window—as black outside as her thoughts. Irrational is how she had acted. First thinking Simza had relations with Yasir, then threatening the girl. Why, Simza wouldn't have come to give her the child if there wasn't some, however outlandish, explanation. With a scowl, she sat beside the gypsy and folded her arms on her chest, eyeing her with displeasure.

"Simza, you will explain to me." The rain pattered softly on the window as the sky suddenly lightened, bleeding color into the room.

Simza jiggled Nicu. "*Rawnee*, I had no choice." She rubbed her hand up and down the baby's back. "The day before the fire meeting, the Chovihano Besnik pulled me aside. I could feel his magic on my skin. He spoke almost in a whisper, 'The djinni's lady. See to it she attends the gathering tonight.' When he touched the lines on his forehead, a strange sensation grew in my belly." Simza turned to Lavinia.

Lavinia averted her gaze, tightening her arms at her chest.

"I knew he had put a spell on me." Simza patted Nicu, who sprawled across her legs. "Do you remember the chanting?"

"Yes." Lavinia didn't want to remember, and focused on Nicu in Simza's lap, his breathing slow and hypnotic as he drifted to sleep.

"In the middle of the chanting, the Chovihano gave us the signal. We stood you in front of him and he stared hard into your eyes." Nicu puckered his lips, pulsing them as though he were nursing, his cherub mouth so like Yasir's.

Lavinia reached for him, but stopped. He was content in Simza's lap for now.

"The Chovihano asked me if I was prepared." Simza looked down at the baby and covered him with a fold of her skirt. She raised her eyes, deep black, impossible to read. "A fear like I had never known stole my voice, but I nodded, yes."

# 37

"The Chovihano Besnik placed the *bakterismasko* across your stomach." Simza made a motion with her hand on her midsection as she eyed Lavinia's middle. Brow furrowed in a question, Lavinia tilted her head at the gypsy.

"*Bakterismasko,* his wand, fashioned from wood of the sacred ash, imbued with spirits of earth, fire and wind." The gypsy moved her hand through the air, fingers bent, mimicking holding a wand. "I stood face to face with you and met your eyes, hoping to receive acceptance, but you were lost to the world of dreams." Simza gazed into the shadows of the parlor.

The mesmerizing hum of the gypsies' chant on that night so many months ago circled round and round in Lavinia's head. The fire leaping in scarlet tentacles haloed by golden sparks, flickering and popping on a background of impenetrable darkness. She squeezed her eyes shut, suppressing the sound, and opened them to Simza sitting next to her in the Bramley House parlor, still relating her story: " . . . and you would not answer. The Chovihano called to the spirits in the old language. I took your hands in mine. The night had been silent, but as our fingers touched, the wind roared through the trees. Stars arced trails of glowing yellow through the sky, blazing out just as the fire flared high over our heads in angry sparks. Red eyes peered from the depths of the woods. Still the Chovihano chanted."

Simza repositioned the fold of her skirt over the baby in her lap. He jerked his arm, but fell immediately back into deep sleep. "I cried out. A sharp pain cut through my belly and settled inside as if one of the animals that stared from the forest had claimed my womb for its lair. The magicked words of the Chovihano's chant sang in me and pulled out the hurt. His talismans and amulets jingled as he moved. The flames reflected in his eyes faded. His eyes . . . his eyes . . ." Simza raised her head, a glazed look clouding her face. Was it fear or awe in her expression?

Simza moved closer. "The Chovihano whispered, 'It is done.'"

A knock sounded at the parlor door. Nicu shrieked and Simza rocked him in her lap. The rain had settled into a steady rhythm, softening, as if nature, too, were now careful of the baby's slumber.

A footman opened the door and Dobson waited until Lavinia motioned him in, her finger to her lips. For a moment, a look of alarm altered his controlled expression until he followed the direction of Lavinia's gesture and saw the sleeping baby. He slipped in and set the tea tray on the table in front of them.

"That will be all Dobson, we will serve ourselves." Lavinia spoke softly. He glanced at the child in Simza's lap, avoided staring, bowed and closed the door with a muted click. Nicu muttered in his sleep and threw his chubby fist against Simza's stomach with an audible thud. She exhaled, her eyes wide, and snuggled him close.

"The Chovihano came to our door early the next morning. He spoke about the combined magic of the djinni, the sorceress and the gypsy. '*Fatally powerful.*' I remember the phrase because I stepped back from him. The way he said it. The meaning of it.

"He pulled me close and whispered. I could barely concentrate on his words for the strength of his magic, and I asked him twice to repeat what he said: 'As we agreed, you will bear the djinni's baby.'

"My hand went to my stomach. I knew . . . I *knew* what had happened. I could feel the change in my body. But when I heard him say it, I felt the baby move inside me. I staggered. He took my arm and helped me sit on the carpet.

"The Chovihano touched the marks on his forehead and placed three fingers on the top of my head. I closed my eyes, yet I stared into the heavens, yellow, blue and white stars whirling—*inside me.*" Simza raised her eyes and met Lavinia's.

The gypsy's black pupils flared to pinpoints of white and shot an arc of shimmery stars into her. With a cry, Lavinia jerked back. Her body reeled. Inside she expanded—as vast as the dark heavens, the stars twinkling in eerie silence. Her feet, firm on the parlor floor, rooted into the fiery earth's depths, the thrum of the Chovihano's chant pulsing through her like a second heartbeat.

She bit her lower lip, wary at first of the sense of calm that almost numbed her. She was a clear pool of water reflecting the sun, red and yellow leaves floating on the surface, their rose and gold shadows sheltering flitting minnows. A burgeoning awareness anchored her, a sureness of her place in the world, the same certainty as that small body of water nestled amongst trees and boulders and moss.

Simza watched her with an expression of satisfaction. In the blaring quiet between them a rivulet flowed, a newly formed spring, pure and fresh from a deep mysterious source. The Chovihano's enchantment.

Simza whispered, her voice like a soft breeze. "A powerful blessing. It is rare to receive it." She reached out. Her fingers touched Lavinia's arm and settled there. "He said I was the only one who could carry this child, if it could not be you."

Gathering the baby into her arms, Simza gazed down at him, almost a mother's gaze, but with a compassionate reticence that made Lavinia grateful. She placed him in Lavinia's lap. He yawned and waved his fists.

Simza had made a great sacrifice for her. She had endured a pregnancy, a birth. Then she had to give up her baby. Almost a mirror of what Lavinia had gone through.

"But why? Why?" Lavinia whispered, unwilling to disturb the atmosphere that transfixed them. "I suffered so. My baby gone . . ."

"Cannot you guess?" Simza cocked her head in dismay. "The Chovihano himself told me that the djinni Yasir said, 'This will secure the safety of Lavinia and my child. It will protect us, and help break the spell that obstructs my healing.' Do not you see? If the Vile Magician . . . if he thought Yasir's child was dead, if he thought the djinni was dying, then he would not harm you. You would be just another human."

Lavinia stared at Nicu. "Was that the only way? The *only* way?" She looked into Simza's eyes, into the dark world of the gypsy.

"*Rawnee.*" Simza touched Lavinia's shoulder. "There was much going on that you did not know. There was terrible danger. The Dark Magician almost took you from us in spite of all of our magic and the djinni's as well."

Lavinia stared straight ahead, her eyes glazed. "That night of the storm? The apparition?"

Simza nodded. "I wanted to make it easier for you, everyone did. But it was impossible. There was no other choice." Simza caressed the baby's glossy locks. "I dared ask the Chovihano, 'Does the djinni's lady know?' I hoped the spell imbued understanding as it was cast, dreading that the answer would be 'no.' "

"'It is not possible to tell her,' the Chovihano said. He glowered at me, his fists clenched. I moved away. He continued. 'How could we keep her safe if she knew? She might well let it slip. Perchance she would speak in her sleep. The safety of all, even herself, would be jeopardized.'

"The Chovihano pointed his finger at me, his eyes terrible." Simza put her hand over her chest as if to protect herself. He said, 'If you breathe a word of this to her, we—Yasir, Mehadeh and I—will know at once. We will be forced to take measures.'

"I never spoke to him about it again, and took solace that the Chovihano had blessed me. Though he expended great energy working the spell, I had the most difficult job." Simza bent over Nicu, her hair falling forward over the sides of her face like blinders. "I had to carry the djinni's child and keep the secret."

She took Lavinia's hand. "I could never even hint to you that your child was safe." She sighed like an old woman, then brightened and shook her wondrous tresses. "It is done, *Rawnee*. At last, I am relieved of the burden of the secret. I understand your anger, your wanting me dead. But I beg of you . . ." Simza looked into Lavinia's eyes. "Please grant me your forgiveness."

The warm weight of Nicu in her lap spread through Lavinia like a nourishing river, prying open her heart. She squeezed the gypsy girl's hand. "My dearest Simza. I forgive you. I beg you to forgive me. I had no sympathy for what you have gone through, but that has changed. Believe me when I say I understand. I am sorry you had to sacrifice for me, for Yasir. And I am indebted to you. When I think of that awful day: me holding a knife to your throat . . ." Lavinia looked down. The shame of what she had done, how she had acted. Why, she could have killed Simza, killed Yasir's child, her own child, all from her own ignorance. They tried to tell her. All of them tried.

"*Rawnee*, I know. The fierce love of a mother for her child cannot be changed with words. And empty words were all we had for you then. Please, let us walk our road from this place and take our peace deep into our souls." Simza placed her other hand on top of Lavinia's.

Lavinia cuddled Nicu on her lap. He had fallen fast asleep again, thumb in his mouth, drool dripping onto her silk dress, coloring the lavender dark purple. She beamed at him, then focused on the gypsy girl. "But Simza, why now?"

"The Chovihano told me it was time. I know not why." Simza lifted the teapot and poured a cup full of the rich steaming brew. "You must let me take Nicu if you will have tea."

"I'll wait until later. I don't want to disturb him." Lavinia glanced down at her child. His eyelids fluttered open, then closed. She fixed her gaze on Simza.

"Surely you have some idea of why the Chovihano chose this time." The window glowed pale amber as the sun wrestled with the clouds, only to fade into a gray gloom. The rain had ceased for now. A dull boom of thunder rumbled in the distance.

Simza ran her necklace through her fingers like a rosary. "No one has been seeking Yasir's offspring. Everyone has accepted that there is no baby, and since Yasir is—" She put her hand over her mouth, her black eyes wide.

"*Rawnee*, oh—" Simza flushed. "I am grieved for you, for your son. I have not spoken of it before. It was such a shock, a . . ."

Lavinia put her hand to her head, seeing Simza and Nicu spinning with the room in long slow circles. Something sinister lurked at the edge of her consciousness, but she wouldn't let it in. She tried to stop the slight tremble in her chin.

"After all this time . . . I-I shouldn't feel it so much." Her throat felt as if it were splintering. The spinning room slowed and she closed her eyes, the soft warmth of Nicu firm on her legs. She calmed with the sound of his slow breathing. In the dark of her mind she saw Rakhshan forming in the shadows of the tent in the gypsy camp, felt the cold of his presence starting to numb her. She opened her eyes, her breathing fast and shallow. She wasn't at the gypsies, she was here, safe in her own parlor, the fire blazing warm in the hearth.

Simza Looked alarmed. "*Rawnee*. What—"

"Oh, Simza, Yasir will never see his son. He'll never see his heart's desire." Yasir had sacrificed himself for her, for her son. She hadn't understood. When she fled from the gypsies to the urn, putting Yasir in further danger, and told him the gypsies stole their baby, she had been furious at his callousness. He said the gypsies weren't their enemies, but she wouldn't listen. He tried to hint at what he knew, but couldn't say it outright. Couldn't put her in danger again. The injustice she had done him.

"My son will never know his father, will never—"

"Gah!" Nicu, fist gripping Lavinia's hair, pulled hard. He brought his fist to his mouth, cooing and slobbering. Lavinia gasped. The tears she'd been so carefully holding back overflowed.

"Nicu." Simza breathed his name in a shocked whisper. She set her cup on the table, a wave of tea cascading over the side, and disentangled Lavinia's tresses from his tiny fist. He fussed until she produced a bright blue cloth horse, its mane a rainbow of knotted threads, which he grabbed and stuck into his mouth, burbling happily.

Lavinia flicked a tear from her lashes and turned away. She couldn't handle Simza's sympathetic looks. Nicu batted at the ruffles on her sleeves with fat fingers and a high-pitched giggle. *Her* baby. Her little Yasir.

She sat up straight, bracing Nicu with both hands. This child was the gift from Yasir. The boon Alice had promised. What she had been waiting for, yearning for, these interminable days, weeks and months. Simza's pale face blurred in front of her. The Chovihano knew what Yasir wanted, knew when she was reconciled with Peter, knew when the baby was ready to be received. She clutched the child in her arms.

*Now I have something of him, something to remember him by.*

Lavinia cuddled Yasir's son, her eyes drooping from the welcome serenity washing through her body. With a sharp inhale she caught her breath.

"What shall I tell my husband?" She could not lose the baby twice. She would not lose him twice.

"Why, you must tell him it is his," said Simza as if it were the most obvious thing in the world. Lavinia studied the baby. He looked like her. The resemblance to Yasir was only for those who knew him. There was a reason he didn't have his father's eyes.

"Yes, of course." Lavinia smoothed the child's curls. "But Peter . . . He's so . . . He would never believe me. He'd most likely give the baby to one of the servants." Lavinia clutched the child to her chest. He squirmed.

"You call him Nicu?" Lavinia set the baby upright and bounced him gently.

"Nicu, yes." Simza touched his cheek. "But that is his gypsy name. The djinni would want you to give him a formal name befitting an English lord. An English name. Remember, his origin should never be spoken about." She fixed Lavinia with her somber eyes. "Never."

At Simza's words a grave foreboding dampened the parlor. Lavinia shifted Nicu's weight in her lap. Now it was up to her to protect what was Yasir's.

# 38

*P*eter tapped his cane against his leg, a consistent rhythm, unlike the rain, pounding down one moment, misting in silence a short time later. Deuced weather. No morning ride and he was as jittery as an old maid. He ran his cane over the flutes of the massive column sheltering him from sideways wind gusts, the click-click-click like miniature hoofbeats. Outdoors, but indoors, the north porch had served him well through many a gloomy day.

He turned his head at a dull thud tattooing on the sodden ground. *What the devil?* On the lawn, a bright shape loomed from the curtain of rain. A magnificent white horse, a dark hooded figure huddled over the streaming mane, leg feathers like churning clouds. The creature thundered past, tail streaking behind in a waterfall's plumes. Peter stepped back, his cane steadying him on the slick floor. He squinted into the murky morning and followed the beast as it vanished into the mist.

Only then did he register that although the whole countryside was wet through and through, the animal was as dry as if it had been a crisp sunny day. The horse's amazing leg feathers should have stuck to its forelegs, the mane plastered to its neck, the tail a stringy mass of soggy hair.

Good Lord, one brandy to warm up on a damp gray morning and—

A blast of chill raindrops hit him in the face and he gasped. "Sober as a nun, by God," he murmured. "I need a game of billiards. And another brandy."

❖ ❖ ❖

She wouldn't lose her baby twice. Peter must accept Nicu without question. But this was Peter, a man made of questions and skepticism. Lavinia jiggled the baby in her lap, the shell talisman on his necklace flopping against his chest. She tucked it into his blue shirt, careful not to touch the shell, even though Simza hadn't mentioned that.

The gypsy had chanted an incantation into the shell and translated the old language for Lavinia. Something like: *Shake me and I awaken, then put my lips to your ear.* And a verse about how the shell remembers. Then a poetic phrase: *And murmurs here as the ocean murmurs there.* And the first line—the intention of the spell: about Lord Bramley receiving this child, with favor, as his own.

Simza had given her instructions. "Remove the charm from the child's neck after Peter accepts him. But even then, whenever you take him to see Peter, Nicu should wear it. After seven days, hang it on the wall of the nursery in plain sight. After twenty-one days hide it in Peter's study."

The girl set the charm in Lavinia's palm. "Best not to finger it. Just put it on Nicu."

Lavinia couldn't hide her surprise when she looked down at a cowry shell about the size of a thimble. Porcelain-smooth, the rounded top was rust-brown with thin beige lines and uneven speckles. Off-center, from end-to-end, ran a light yellow design of what looked like crude paper-doll cutouts holding hands. She picked up the silver chain that ran through a hole in the end and draped it over Nicu's head. Would a mere shell make Peter accept this child? Yet, how could she ask such a question after all that had happened?

Lavinia had summoned Fleming, given instructions to find a wet nurse, and sent a maid and footman to purchase clouts, pilchers, soothers and such. The seamstress was to arrive after noon, bringing gowns, blankets and caps, prepared to measure for more. Now all Lavinia had to do was—she closed her eyes for a moment—tell Peter.

"Out on the north porch, milady." Dobson eyed Nicu in her arms. "Shall I fetch the master?"

"No." Lavinia turned away, juggling Nicu in her arms. He would need to be fed soon. Simza had suggested bread soaked in warm milk as a temporary substitute until a wet nurse was acquired. Lavinia wandered down the halls, past the red drawing room on the left, and the tapestry room just around the corner. She stepped into the music chamber, which opened onto the north porch.

On the opposite wall, his back to her, Peter latched the French doors. He turned, unbuttoning his damp overcoat. "Lavinia?"

She wasn't sure she liked the look of surprise on his face. Nicu jerked and uttered a cry at Peter's deep voice. The baby whimpered and turned his head into Lavinia's chest as Peter stared hard at him. "For God's sake, Lavinia, where did you get *that*?"

Lavinia gaped at Peter. How could he say something so heartless? Peter eyed the child as though he were a gargoyle come to life in her arms. Outside, the rain drummed on the windows, reminding her of the stormy meeting with Simza and how hard it was to accept a baby dropped suddenly into your life. Was she taking on an impossible task? She hugged Nicu closer.

She had found Peter, but this was all wrong. Was Simza's charm just a ruse, only the hollow home of some long-dead sea creature? She could say the baby was a servant's, that she had just wanted to hold the little one. Lavinia felt a smile stretch across her face.

"He's *our* baby." Words, without her permission, had slid softly off her tongue.

Peter frowned. "What?"

She blinked. Had she really just blurted it? Without any warning? Peter wasn't good with being ambushed, but she had gone and said it, and now she must soldier on.

"He's our baby." Lavinia jiggled Nicu, who looked towards the window at the rattling glass from the wind-blown rain.

Peter stared. She had seen that look before, when she was at her worst after she left the urn. After Yasir died. She rubbed her hand along Nicu's soft back. Peter had taken Yasir from her, but he wouldn't send her baby away. She would make her voice calm, and smile gently.

"Dear Peter, he—" The door opened in a hale of giggles and a swirl of feather dusters. Two housemaids burst in, one with a stack of rags, the other holding a pail. The first one, upon seeing her lord and lady, dropped the pail with a clang, retrieved it, curtsied, and shoved the other out the door, following her in a clumsy retreat.

"Bloody hell, we'll go someplace more private." Peter guided Lavinia past the grand piano and the harp to the blue parlor. Inside, a fire burned steadily in the hearth. An open book lay on a knitted coverlet thrown across a chaise. Peter placed a tasseled bookmark in between the pages, set the book by the tea service, and motioned for her to sit.

He put his hands behind his back and stood before her. "What in the deuce did you do, Lavinia? Go out and find a baby just to prove your story?" He puffed his cheeks and exhaled, drowning out the soothing crackle of the fire. "I thought we were past all that."

Lavinia set Nicu in her lap. "How could you think such a thing? I was expecting. Dr. Thornhill confirmed it. I gave birth, but the gypsies had drugged me. When I woke the baby was gone and I ran away." She couldn't tell him gypsy magic had transferred her baby to Simza.

He paced the floor in front of her. "Yes, I *know*." He glanced at the ceiling. A muscle in his jaw twitched. "You escaped to the urn where the djinni lived." Peter curled his lip. "Lavinia, why are you doing this? Who is this child? Is some poor woman out there—" Peter gestured towards the foggy windows—"grieving for this child?"

*Lord in heaven, he's not going to accept Nicu.* Lavinia stared into the fire. The flames flickered yellow and orange, hypnotic, calming. *But Peter hasn't really looked at his son.*

"Peter, please sit down." Lavinia patted a spot beside her. She placed the baby in his lap. Without thinking, he put his hand on Nicu's back to support him.

*So he did have some inclinations toward little ones.*

"Really, Lavinia." Peter looked down at her. "You think when you place him here I'll—" Peter's mouth fell open. "Devil take it, he looks just like you." He looked from the baby to Lavinia and back. Nicu pulled on the silver chain around his neck and put it in his mouth, dragging the shell talisman from under his shirt. He burbled. Drool dripped down his chin.

Peter lifted the shell, turning it over. "What's this?"

Nicu grunted.

"A talisman to protect him. Gypsies do that." Lavinia held her breath as she watched Peter inspect the shell. She hadn't expected him to touch it. That should make the effect even more powerful.

"Hmm." Peter raised one eyebrow. He rubbed the shell between his fingers and set it back on Nicu's shirt. Nicu plopped it in his mouth.

"The gypsy girl had a dream that she would be cursed if she kept the baby from me any longer. She came to ask forgiveness." Lavinia touched Nicu on the cheek. It wouldn't hurt to change the story just a little so it would seem more ordinary.

Peter looked out the window. Rain streaked the glass. "So that was what I saw . . ." he murmured to himself.

Lavinia peered at him. "I beg your pardon?"

Peter rubbed his jaw "When I was on the porch, an amazing white horse with a rider wrapped in a cape galloped by. The rider was drenched, water flying off his cape, but the horse was dry. The animal's long feathering fluttered as if it were a sunny day. It startled me so, that for a moment I thought I had seen an apparition." Peter ran his hand down Nicu's back. "But now, it all makes sense. A Tinker horse. That was *your* gypsy?"

Lavinia nodded. When Simza traveled here, she must have strapped the baby under her cape to protect him from the rough ride and the rain. "She only wanted my forgiveness. I had been furious with her, but when I saw how afraid she was— They believe, truly believe, in curses and such like."

The skepticism in Peter's eyes faded for a moment and Lavinia took advantage. "You thought I was insane when I told you what happened. I believed I had miscarried. The gypsy told me I gave birth, but afterwards I had a fever. They found a wet nurse until I was better, but I became delirious and truly believed the gypsies had stolen my baby. I imagined other things. I escaped, thinking they would hurt me. I was wrong. They had nursed me back to health." Lavinia looked at the carpet and warmth rushed into her cheeks. She was lying, but Peter would only think she was upset. She had to make him separate the baby from what she had blurted about the urn, about Yasir, when she first arrived.

"My imagination along with my fears must have taken me on a flight of fancy." Lavinia reached for Peter, and lay her hand on his arm. "And my suspicions that the gypsies stole our baby proved correct— the *only* thing that was true from that time."

He stared at her hand. *Would he push it away?* The muscles in his jaw twitched again. "This is all so sudden, Lavinia."

She patted Nicu's leg. "He's your heir. Our fine, sturdy son." The baby's dark curls fell over his face and he snuggled against Peter, who curved his hand around the child's back.

"So you want to keep him."

Lavinia rose to her feet. "Peter! He's our child. *Ours.* I gave birth to him." She touched his arm. "He's our son. Your heir. He's home now."

Peter looked down at the baby who had stretched out on his lap. Asleep? No, a flutter of dark lashes as the rain slanted against the windowpanes in sharp plops. He should give him back to Lavinia, but the little chap seemed comfortable.

Lavinia's pleas were a bit desperate, that's all. The jerky movements, the furtive glances, and the grim turn of the mouth from her earlier bout of madness were absent. He would recognize those. Nevertheless, he drew up, muscles taut, ready to defend himself from a quick turn of the wrist, the flash of a blade.

She had switched her gaze to the baby, her eyes smiling. Different from before when she focused on him, those lapis eyes wide, anxious—just like the baby's when Peter turned and saw him in Lavinia's arms. The child shifted and Peter picked him up, afraid the baby might launch himself off his lap. The child startled, jerking his arms with a cry, then snuggled into his chest. By God, it made him drowsy, the chunky warm body, the smell of milk and something else, something sweet and soothing.

Across from him, Lavinia had stopped her impassioned entreaty and leaned back in her chair, watching intently. Had she purchased this child? From a gypsy? She had told him they kidnapped her, stole her baby, but she had been raving at the time. Yet, here he was, a little Lavinia, only a boy child. It was most probably hers. Deuced if he would dispute it. The boy was healthy and alert. Lavinia was safe from the birthing, with no sign that she would give him another any time soon.

The baby wriggled in his arms and heaved a little sigh. The sough washed over Peter. He felt his frown slacken, his mind emptied, and a thrill rushed through him. He looked down at the infant's dark curls, the porcelain skin.

His son. He needed an heir. Why the hell not?

Lavinia held her breath. Simza's magic, would it work? Did it need to?

What she had wished for—her baby, alive. Her happy family. She turned away for a moment to hide the heartache in her eyes. Peter, with Yasir's child. After all her secrecy, her care, Peter and Yasir had come face to face. She tried to keep the tinge of hate from permeating her, when inside her head the gunshot resounded, Yasir collapsing, his shoulder bloody, the garden silent as if it had entered another realm. The start of his long demise. She stifled a cry, deep from inside. Peter's fault, but he remembered none of if. She unwound her fist from her skirts.

She must make this work. She would summon the words, speak them as though they were God's truth. She took a breath.

"It's so wonderful, you and your—." She would say it again. She had to say it once more. Why, oh why, was it becoming harder? A lie was supposed to be easier the more it was perpetrated. "—*our* son."

She squeezed out a smile as Peter gave his attention back to the baby. Her smile faded. Her lips shrank into a thin line. It all was a lie. But could she overcome it for the sake of Nicu and Yasir? She softened her eyes, her throat. Nicu clutched two of Peter's fingers tightly in his tiny fist. After all of Yasir's careful plans, his mysterious powers, his magic allies, Peter had won.

As if he knew she was thinking of him, Peter looked up. "He's the image of you Lavinia, your eyes, your hair, your skin. He's beautiful." Her husband held the baby to his chest. "My dear, you gave birth and left your child. No wonder you went . . . ah . . . "

He stopped, sympathy in his pale blue eyes. "Ah . . . were disturbed." He gazed at the child. "But now that we have our son, everything will be fine." A serene expression settled on his face as he snuggled Yasir's child to him.

On his evening ride, Peter reflected upon the extraordinary day. He wouldn't have believed the story. A child was easy to find and purchase. But the baby, he was definitely Lavinia's, no question.

The sun sat low in the sky, dying they call it, going out in a blaze of glory. Odd phrases for the setting sun, these war analogies. Blue clouds limned in gold hovered above the horizon. Coral light slanted underneath, casting an unearthly glow over the countryside as if he had been transported to an enchanted place. A setting where you could suddenly have an heir. Your wish come true.

*His son.* The phrase so new. Words he had longed to speak aloud. The warmth of the baby's sturdy body weighed on his chest as if the child were in his arms again. The baby's blue eyes, Lavinia's eyes. His curly black hair, Lavinia's also. Yet there was something about the boy. Something he couldn't put his finger on. Peter wrangled with his jumbled impressions, but remained befuddled, with no conclusions. He stroked Palomar's silky mane and turned his thoughts to the present.

His body and Palomar moved as one, coursing over the tranquil landscape. The tops of the trees, blessed with the sun's last rays, glowed like embers, the remainder of the countryside peacefully surrendering to the lilac half-light of evening. Birds, in twos and threes, winged into the forest, stragglers greeted by cries of the flock already settled for the night.

The wind played in Peter's hair. They made their way home, a quiet calm over the land as if it were under a spell. He reveled in the tranquility, his mind thankfully at rest. Out of nowhere the oddest thought came to him—his brow furrowed and his hands closed tight on the reins—if there was a baby, was there also a djinni?

## 39

*M*ehadeh settled on the rug in front of the tiled hearth and crossed her legs, bunching her blue dress so it swelled around her like a toadstool. She peered out the circular window, reassured by red stone cliffs above the thick jungle of tangled orange and chartreuse. Finally, she was home, even though it had been a sad homecoming. If only she could sleep this night without those dreams of the urn—empty. She pictured Yasir strong and healthy, but the image of him weak from the bullet wound kept superimposing itself. What kind of sorceress was she that she couldn't hold a thought?

She stiffened at the cold, clammy grip on her arm. Sniffing a faintly astringent odor, earthy like a just-sliced green gourd, she relaxed, marveling that she could still be so anxious even though she hadn't seen signs of, or heard from that harpy's pox Rakhshan.

"Ha! Neszmbe, it is only you. And I had been hoping for the djinni." She ran her hand along the serpent's smoky gray scales and fanned out his velvety crest of spiky maroon and green tendrils. At her touch, they curled at the ends like fern fronds.

"It has been over a year now, since Yasir has gone." She heard the wobble in her voice. The serpent stopped winding his way up her arm, fixing the sorceress with his violet eyes, a small dot of reflection shining in each one.

"Ah yes, I too am sad. Very sad. *Ilmada murugoodo waa qalalan sida lafaha jir,* so sad my tears are dry as old bones." Mehadeh ruffled his tendrils again and the serpent opened his mouth, emitting a twitter as shrill as a todee bug's. His forked tongue flicked, the bright yellow of a flower stamen.

"Yes, it is a *musiibo,* tragedy." She put her hand on her head, bunching the stiff braids. "How could this have happened when he was under my care?" Neszmbe slithered onto Mehadeh's shoulder and coiled, a thick epaulet, gravestone cold. She felt him staring and looked up, meeting his gaze. He had suspended the front of his body so it hung stiff and straight several hand lengths out from her collarbone, his head angled, facing her.

Mehadeh crossed her arms on her chest. "You know this. But you want to hear it again?" She gave him an exasperated look. Could she bear to repeat it? Neszmbe twittered. His tongue forked out like a flash of lightning. She bowed her head, the turquoise beads braided into her dark hair clicking like the sharp beaks of tiny *reema* birds. In a monotone, she said, "*Sheegistii ma ka dhigi doonaa sidaa darted,* the telling will not make it so," and placed her hands in her lap.

She began with Lavinia summoning Yasir to save them from Rakhshan's guards. At one point, she raised her eyes to the assemblage of sorceresses painted on the fan-vaulted ceiling as if the djinni were up there with them. "The black magic ate through my potions and . . ." Even though it hurt her heart, she continued. Near the end, when she told of Yasir's death, she paused, trying to distance herself.

The serpent's tendrils drooped. He always reacted this way. What in the nature of this creature drew him to these sordid tales? At least he couldn't repeat her phrases. She shuddered, thankful her plumed *slevot*—better at mimicking than a parrot—hadn't been in hearing distance.

Mehadeh opened her mouth, then tipped her head to the side. Perhaps stop here. But she found the words to the ending, the words that gave her some hope. "His body vanished." She put her hand to her forehead, wrinkling her brow with the pressure of her fingers. For the past year she had spent days at a time searching for any trace of Yasir. "If I find his body, at least I will know he is truly dead." She looked askance at her serpent. She hadn't meant to say that out loud.

"Could I be losing my powers, Neszmbe?" Memories boiled in her mind: Lavinia beside Yasir's body, her numb countenance changed to a mask of incredulity; Mehadeh's own abrupt inhale when they found the empty bed. She couldn't keep the djinni alive. She couldn't even place his body to rest.

Neszmbe spiraled down her arm like quicksilver and glided across the floor to a shallow obsidian bowl filled with water. He sank his head over the rim, drank and rose up, waving his crest. The serpent turned to Mehadeh and caught her eye, making sure she saw him, then, as graceful as a scarf dancer, he lowered his body over the bowl and resumed drinking.

Mehadeh studied him for a moment. She uncrossed her legs and strolled over. Neszmbe skittered across the blue marble floor to meet her, piping little chirps in short bursts, violet eyes gleaming, tongue flashing bright between sharp fangs. He escorted her to the water bowl.

She sat on the floor next to it. There were times when Neszmbe had indicated objects with power that she hadn't detected. Was this another of those? The dark water stretched drum-taut from brim to brim. If she breathed on the surface it would surely overflow.

Water scrying. Her own magic sprang inherent from her people and the unusual circumstances after she encountered Yasir when she was but a child. Long ago, she had briefly studied this ancient art, but her spells and potions won her over, leaving the practice of reading water abandoned.

She peered into the water, thinking of Yasir. Her reflection stared from what could have been a solid slab of obsidian. In the black surface a shock of maroon and green appeared next to her, followed by slanted violet eyes—Neszmbe. The water stayed motionless as they breathed. A flash of bright yellow and Mehadeh saw her eyes widen, then squint in annoyance at her snake who flicked his tongue once more. He was probably a better scryer than she, with that forked tongue, double-sensing the nuance of the ether, the sensations from the water. The snake raised his head level with hers and stared at their reflections.

A blue glow emanated from the water, bringing a chill into the room as if the weather had turned. Neszmbe tittered as Mehadeh's reflection transformed: her black hair and eyebrows, almost invisible in the dark water, seemed to be suspended above the surface as they turned white, her face collapsing into hundreds of wrinkles. She moved her hands over her cheeks, her brow, her chin, but they remained smooth. Another had appeared in place of her reflection. Something was not right.

Mehadeh shrank from the face as it broke the surface. Neszmbe's cold, hard scales pressed smooth against her arm. The head emerged from the water, followed by a skeletal body in a gray robe, bones protruding so that the creature resembled a misshapen tent. Mehadeh scrambled to her feet in alarm, stepping back. How dare someone enter a sorceress's abode without permission.

They stood face to face. The creature's eyes glinted from the folds of its skin. Its mouth opened. "Salutations to the Noble Sorceress Mehadeh, of the Clan Eredo. I bring—" The figure turned around, studying the room behind it. "You have no one here?" The voice, in fits and starts, grated like an iron wheel scraping for purchase on loose gravel.

"No." Mehadeh said. She felt a twinge of fear radiate from the being. Could it be afraid of Neszmbe?

"I am the Magus, Ir-A. You yearn for the Great Djinni." The creature pursed her lips, a trail of lines radiating into the wrinkled face as if a swathe of fabric had been clutched in a fist. "I healed Yasir, but his lady, by her distrust, and the djinni's nemesis, by dark magic and trickery, brought it to naught."

So this was the Magus Ir-A. The very magus in Yasir's recount of how he had been healed. But afterwards the djinni had been trapped in a twisted place of curing by the Dark Magician's doctor. Did Ir-A know that with Mehadeh's magic Yasir had been rescued? Mehadeh thrust her shoulders back, proud for powering Lavinia's ring to work again.

Yet there was a complication in Yasir's tale: either the magus had been corrupted after she healed Yasir in the urn, or Rakhshan's minion had taken her form when they gathered at the airport. In the end, it meant Yasir had been, as the magus said, brought to ruin.

Ir-A stood there, her small eyes, like deep holes, tunneled into her face.

Mehadeh weighed her choices. Could she trust this being? Neszmbe chirped, slithered behind her, and rattled his crest, the tendrils clacking like dried seed pods. Mehadeh felt her breath quicken at the serpent's warning. She would need to take care.

"The djinni spoke highly of the Magus Ir-A." Mehadeh purposely stated the magus's name to inform Rakhshan's minion she was aware of his deceit—if it was him. "But I am not yet ready to place my search in another's hands. So, with great respect, I must ask the Magus Ir-A to leave my dwelling."

Mehadeh concealed her hand in the folds of her skirt and pulled a vial from her hidden pocket. With a flick of her finger, she removed the cork. She would be ready if Ir-A wanted to test her. An acrid smell filled the air.

The magus sniffed and held out her palm. "Hold with your potions." Ir-A closed her fist and opened it, dropping an object into the water. Slitting her eyes, she said, "When you come to your senses, this will lead you to me."

Ir-A's body collapsed into the water as if the robe had become an empty shell, her head sinking under the surface. All this in complete silence. Not a splash. Not a drop of water anywhere.

Why had this being come here, invading her home? Nothing enlightened her about this. No matter how she used magic, she saw only an impenetrable darkness. Sudden movement broke her concentration—Neszmbe coiling and uncoiling in front of the door.

"So you have changed your mind? The water did not hold the answer?" Mehadeh held her hand over the bowl, drawing it into the air, muttering nasty epithets about serpent familiars. The door swung open. The bowl floated outside. In an abrupt move, she brought her hand down. The bowl shattered on a rock, the black water disappearing into the red earth. "Nedze, monba, medze manba." She enunciated the clearing chant with care and slammed the door.

The fire in the hearth flared, sending sparks flickering like a swarm of Todee bugs, as Mehadeh settled on the carpet. Neszmbe slithered beside her and dipped his head, rubbing her arm. She ruffled his crest.

"Ah my wise serpent. Why do I let you lead me into these situations?" But she knew. She had been desperate to learn anything about Yasir.

"What's in your mouth?" She held out her hand and Neszmbe laid a smooth milky stone into her palm. "So this is what the magus left us?"

The snake chirped at the blue light glowing inside the stone, which shadowed depressions in the raised swirls of the spiral at its middle. Mehadeh fumbled, but grasped the stone before it slipped from her hand. This night had shaken her, but she could feel nothing from the magus's keepsake.

For a turn of the moon, she had kept the stone on her altar in front of the painted ebony sculpture of Neszmbe. It would be cleansed there and she could monitor it. At night she would wake to the eerie ultramarine glow, which, from all she could tell, happened at random. At least she couldn't decipher any pattern, yet Neszmbe slithered up to the altar just a few moments before the light shone, as if he were attending a performance. When she woke before the stone came alive, she would see him there in the dark, looking like a twin of his sculpture, then the light would bathe him in its blue glow.

Neszmbe's attention to the stone made her rethink her decision to stay away from Ir-A. Would the magus have lied about healing Yasir? She had admitted to being defeated by Rakhshan. What did Ir-A know about the Dark Magician? Perhaps the magus could find out if Yasir was alive or dead, and lead her to find him or his body.

One more full moon passed and she now woke in the depths of the night just before the stone started glowing. Each time Neszmbe was already in front of her altar. He sat, coiled, his head level with the stone and soon the blue light limned his crest and reflected from his slanted eyes. In her mind, Mehadeh played with different scenarios: following the stone to Ir-A's; taking Neszmbe to help her; finding something, anything about Yasir.

At dawn the next morning, Mehadeh wrapped Yasir's embroidered belt around her waist. He left it at her house long ago, and she had only just discovered it. Although it brought to mind her failure to save him, she wore it when he occupied her thoughts, for the lovely belt held some of his essence, a spark of him. When she passed by her altar, Neszmbe slithered up, taking his usual position. The stone radiated deep blue as if in greeting. The serpent's crest wavered. Intrigued, Mehadeh sat beside him, for the stone had always been dormant during daylight, glowing that odd blue solely at night.

She could only spare a moment, today being Light Solstice, when the earth's sun star came closest to her planet and mingled light with the planet's star. Their moon would wax full this very night—a most auspicious occurrence. Celebrations started early and she had been invited as one of the ritual leaders. Wearing Yasir's belt was her invitation to him, if he still existed.

The magus's stone pulsed, the color blue intensifying, lessening, then flaring brighter as though it kept time to a drum beat: boom, boom, BOOM.

Mehadeh reached for the stone. She held it in her palm. The spiral in the center darkened, growing as big as her hand, expanding, surrounding her and the serpent. Somewhere far off she heard Neszmbe's shrill tittering as the spiral started spinning inward, whirling faster and faster, dragging them into its depths.

Mehadeh shifted, but the pain in her left buttock wouldn't go away. She kept her legs crossed on the floor, lifted up and pulled something smooth out from under her. Ir-A's stone. How did it get there? She reached out to replace it on her altar and sat upright, her hand stopped in mid-motion.

The altar had vanished along with her house. They were outside, in a place she did not recognize. The air hung motionless and heavy, the moon a shiny coin racing through the darkened sky. A blue glow spread from the stone shining in her palm. At a movement in her lap, she made to sweep whatever it was away when Neszmbe's head peered up at her as he uncoiled. He turned and faced the house in front of them.

Under the otherworldly light of the moon, the shrubs and vines near the modest abode appeared like ragged sentinels grasping spears and long swords, guarding the old dwelling.

She had let this happen. This walking into fate. Or a trap. Or a gift. Any one of those. Nothing else had worked. These last few days, thoughts of Yasir had coincided with the blue glow of the stone as if he were telling her to go to the magus. She would not let the djinni down again.

"Neszmbe, we have come to Ir-A." Mehadeh uncrossed her legs and the serpent slid from her lap to the ground. She rose. For a moment a castle loomed before her, but like a flash of memory, disappeared, and she saw the same modest house surrounded by a glittering moat. Perhaps the moat had her in mind of a castle.

She brought her head up at Neszmbe's titter of alarm bouncing off the moat, while an ungainly shape limped in their direction. It stopped, then in a burst of sudden speed glided forward, appearing to be blown by a strong wind like a boat upon the water. The cold of the serpent's body passed through the cloth of her skirt, somehow reassuring.

"An auspicious day and night for your visit." Ir-A sounded close, as if she had spoken directly into Mehadeh's ear, yet the magus stood at the spiked wrought iron gate just after the bridge, some distance away. The gate opened, creaking like Ir-A's voice. Of course, the magus was referring to the Light Solstice. Mehadeh and Neszmbe had been spirited away by the stone before they could participate.

She curled her hand around the stone. It grew warm in her palm as she and the serpent made their way onto the bridge. The moon shone on the rippling water. A large shape surfaced, sinister in the silence, and a creature the size of a calf leapt into the air. The resounding splash barely missed soaking them, as they instinctively ducked and were splattered with cold drops. Mehadeh glanced at the moat and hurried through the gate, her serpent undulating fast before her.

Ignoring the water creature, the magus hobbled up the dirt path. The dark cape she wore swirling her invisible in the night, then revealing her like a misplaced magic trick. To the side, Mehadeh glimpsed fleeting shapes in the moonlight. Were they being followed, or was it just the foliage swaying in the breeze, stirring the stagnant air?

On the wide veranda a three-tiered fountain played the water like music amidst exotic plants, the blooms fragrant in the sultry night. The arched entrance stood open to a dark interior. Without ceremony, Ir-A stepped over the threshold. They followed through a hall, turned a corner and Mehadeh held her hand above her eyes at the brightness of the richly furnished room, lit by chandeliers glowing with hundreds of candles.

The magus dropped her ultramarine cape, which shrank as small as a moth and fluttered up to the candles, blundering into one and bursting into flames. Turning his head at the sparks streaming down around him, Neszmbe switched his gaze to Ir-A, transfixed by the wrinkles that lined her face melting into a smooth dewy complexion, while her wiry white hair thickened into soft blonde tresses. Her tent-like robe grew darker and transformed into a red velvet gown clinging to her now-voluptuous figure.

"You last saw the Great Djinni when?" Ir-A's voice flowed in silky tones.

"When he . . ." If she admitted this, the magus would know she had failed, but then the magus had failed as well. "When he . . . When his human body died."

"It came to that," Ir-A said, her voice soft and flat. Her gray eyes blinked, subdued in sympathy.

Mehadeh fingered the smooth stone in her pocket. The magus in this form exuded goodness, but there was something too perfect, too good about her.

"Since I came to you in water, we will keep to the element. Please, follow me." Ir-A led them through a long, high-ceilinged hall with doors opening to more halls and chambers, then a book-lined library, expansive parlors, a grand dining room. Spaces that couldn't possibly have fit inside the modest house they had entered.

In a circular room off the music chamber at the top of the stairs, a keyhole-shaped doorway led into a simple space, different from the rest of the magus's abode. Unpolished marble floors and walls unbroken by windows contained a single table with barley-twist legs of fragrant sandalwood, the top a rare purple quartzite. Mehadeh could not map the direction they had taken to arrive here through the house, through the many rooms, the smells changing as they traveled—frangipani, gardenia, salty ocean breeze . . . It seemed a long time. It seemed a short time. Was this confusion a part of her lessening powers?

The magus stood facing them behind the table. A thick-walled ruby bowl appeared in front of her, the water deepest red so that it could have been mistaken for black. Neszmbe wound around the twisted sandalwood legs and peered into the bowl. He backed away.

Ir-A gazed into Mehadeh's eyes. "Have you had visions of the Great Djinni?"

Was she questioning her prowess? Ir-A did not blink. Under her discomfiting stare, Mehadeh flinched. The magus saw it, and for a moment, Mehadeh glimpsed a malicious smile on her face. But no, Ir-A's mouth remained straight with care and concern.

"Unknown obstacles refused to let anything through to me." Mehadeh rubbed the stone in her pocket and searched the room with her powers. She found nothing amiss, but a tightening in her chest told her she could be wrong. Neszmbe stayed quiet, at attention, his slanted eyes showing nothing, but riveted on Ir-A. Uneasy as well.

Motioning for Mehadeh to come and stand by her side, the magus dropped her gaze to the water. Did Ir-A see the weakness in Mehadeh's magic? This woman was supposed to help find Yasir, not find fault with her.

Tension along the murky water's edges kept it from overflowing the smooth basin, and sent an occasional shimmer of bright red across the rigid surface as if a wound had reopened. Reflections played on the magus's smooth young face, distorting her features, and she stiffened in a way that Mehadeh could tell was meant to hide her response.

Gold and tan and black shapes wavered across the water's surface, a puzzle to piece together. Mehadeh blinked as the colors congealed into an image of Yasir under the water. His mouth moved and he gestured, looking straight into her eyes. She strained to understand him. The water rippled. His image fragmented, receding in the wave's shadows. Mehadeh reached out to him, her hand hovering over the basin. This was the first time she had seen him since his body disappeared from the urn. Was it truly Yasir or was it—

"Shhh." Breaking her gaze, Ir-A turned to Mehadeh, her finger to her mouth. She glared, her grey eyes stern. "Remember your place. I am the magus here."

Only then did Mehadeh realize she had been calling to Yasir, repeating his name over and over. Pleading with him, for Yasir had been there, in the water, speaking to her, giving her the answers she had been yearning for since he vanished. But she couldn't hear, couldn't read his lips.

She had failed him again. She slumped against the table. Neszmbe nestled against her arm. She raised up at a slight touch on her head, thinking to see her serpent and know what to do next.

"I understand your eagerness to speak with the Great Djinni, but the scrying has been broken by your . . . enthusiasm." The magus spoke kindly, her gray eyes like a tender mother's, gently scolding her wayward child.

"Drink this, a rare wine praised by the Persians. Then, refreshed, we shall start once more." Ir-A handed Mehadeh a crystal goblet studded with precious stones and filled with deep emerald liquid. She placed a similar bowl for Neszmbe on the table.

Before the magus drank, she raised her goblet. "To the Great Djinni." The serpent shook his crest and hovered about his bowl. When Mehadeh sipped, he streaked his yellow tongue across the surface of his wine, then drew back and struck her with his tail. Mehadeh set her goblet on the table.

She scrutinized Ir-A, taking in her beautiful young face, the corn-silk hair. The freshness of her youth dazzling, but underneath Mehadeh sensed a discrepancy just as when one viewed a floating log, only to discover a crocodile.

She would try a test. "What did he say?" Mehadeh asked, purposely making the question vague.

"Who?" Ir-A tilted her head and looked puzzled.

"I . . ." Mehadeh was careful to watch the magus for a reaction. She primed her magic. "I saw Yasir in the water. He spoke and gestured, telling me—" She deliberately broke off. Ir-A gazed at her, gray eyes guarded, but she tilted imperceptibly closer. Was she intrigued because she believed Mehadeh saw Yasir and understood what he was trying to say?

The magus slanted away, her gray eyes disturbed. "You are looking for him. Of course you would see him, but that does not mean he was there." She gave a warm smile, and brightened, but a brief spark in her eyes made Mehadeh think Ir-A was not so guileless as she feigned. Ah, so her little confession rankled the magus.

Ir -A kept the smile, but now it was forced. "Let us start once more. You have something of the Great Djinni's. I would hold it." The magus looked pointedly at Mehadeh's waist.

Mehadeh clutched the stone in her pocket. She should toss it away, but it would be seen as a hostile gesture. After all, it was from her hostess. She would get rid of the stone later. Should she give Ir-A Yasir's belt? The woman could use it to hex him, as well as call him. Water scrying could summon someone, could see what they were doing, where they were, but it was not meant for spell-casting. Should she dare refuse Ir-A, make some excuse—but what?

She thought back to when she worked to heal Yasir in the urn. He had told her he summoned the magus, that she healed him, then he was waylaid by Rakhshan. So he had trusted Ir-A—if this was Ir-A, and not some illusion by the Dark Magician.

Hiding her hesitation, Mehadeh untied the belt and unwound it from her waist. She had been searching for so long, and now someone was willing to help her.

"Drop it here." The magus checked the water when the belt lay on the table, the bright embroidery like a toy in a crypt.

Mehadeh couldn't read Ir-A's face, and switched her gaze to the water, dark and unmoving, reflecting only the magus's profile. Without a ripple, Ir-A's face changed, as if her silhouette had been embossed on the front of a coin and the coin flipped over, showing a harsher profile: one with a hooked nose, a strong brow, cruel eyes under heavy dark brows—a man's face. A formidable man.

Mehadeh blinked.

In an instant, the erstwhile coin flipped again, and Ir-A's comely profile appeared the same as before. Mehadeh twitched from glimpsing the man in the water. Were her suspicions getting the best of her? Misleading her? What had she done? She had let a strange enchanter lead her away from home. She had given the magus Yasir's belt, so the woman had some sway over the djinni. Had she put herself and Neszmbe and possibly Yasir, wherever he was, in great peril?

From behind her, Ir-A whispered, chill breath on Mehadeh's ear. "See to the water." The liquid, as clear as window glass a moment ago, had turned white, creased with wrinkles like skin formed on the surface of milk. Mehadeh watched the surface blacken as though someone had spilled India ink onto it. The tiny wrinkles grew into waves that eddied between the edges of the bowl, not daring to overflow.

"Do you see it?" The magus's voice, soft like the hoot of an owl deep in the forest, prickled the flesh at the back of Mehadeh's neck.

Mehadeh's breath quickened. A haze of blue rolled over the water's surface and sank, as a shape formed under the waves: sturdy and tall, dark hair, broad shoulders.

Yasir? Careful not to say the djinni's name out loud, Mehadeh bent over the water. The inky image undulated below the swells, becoming more distinct as the waves grew smaller. The cool water wet her nose. Her heart beat faster as the features took shape. Dark eyes, straight nose, cruel curled lips.

*By the wings of Huur.* Rakhshan.

Mehadeh lurched from the bowl and faced Ir-A. "What did you do?"

The magus's eyes narrowed. Her soft gray irises became as dark as the water. She stared beyond Mehadeh, her lips, thinner, tight in a hard line.

Neszmbe hissed and Mehadeh turned to where Ir-A stared. Rakhshan's figure rose from the water, dark and menacing. Mehadeh let out a cry and made to run from the room. The magus caught her by the shoulders. But it wasn't the magus anymore. The sweet young face had transformed into the man's on the flip side of the coin, a hawk-like nose and deep malicious eyes riveting her in place.

"You. You are the Dark Magician's servant." Mehadeh's voice squeezed out in a hoarse whisper, as if she were afraid her words might make this nightmare more real. She called up a spell, but it withered, a seedling sucked dry in a drought sun.

"Everyone wants to find the Great Djinni," the magus said in a harsh, deep voice. With surprising strength, she whirled Mehadeh around to face the scrying bowl and thrust her against the table. Neszmbe sprang towards Ir-A's new shape, mouth open, fangs shining, but an unseen force threw the serpent backwards.

Again Mehadeh cast a spell. As if stuck, it hung in the air. She could feel her magic surround Ir-A, feel it working.

"Your powers are less than they were. We have seen to that. Your spell is merely an annoyance." The magus held Mehadeh immobile and forced her face into the water.

Gripping Ir-A's wrists, the sorceress tried to pry them loose, but couldn't gain proper leverage from the odd angle. The magus's large hairy hands held her fast with the grip of a centurion. Mehadeh threw another spell and Ir-A pushed her deeper.

She opened her eyes under the chill water. Rakhshan stood before her, clear in the murky liquid, an odd fire in his eyes. He wasn't going to help her. After everything she had risked when she was a child guest at his palace: incantations only for him, secret conjurations of dark magic at his request. She had gambled her soul, and for what? This betrayal?

Burning for air, she sprang up and loosened the magus's grip, gulping a breath. Ir-A drove her under water with such force that she braced to hit the bottom of the bowl, but the water went down and down and down. Mehadeh purposely weakened her hold on the magus's hands. If she didn't struggle, Ir-A might think she had drowned, and let go.

A moment more. Her lungs begged for air. Just a moment more. She tensed her body, waiting for the minutest falter of muscles in those grotesque hands. Then she would take the betrayer.

Rakhshan raised his hand.

Feigning losing consciousness, Mehadeh relaxed her muscles, but the magus pressed her deeper into the water. She couldn't hold her breath any longer. *Neszmbe. Neszmbe.* In her mind she called the serpent, but heard no answer.

Blurred spots darkened the sides of her vision, expanding rapidly. She clawed at Ir-A's hands. Her body bucked and heaved against the magus's grip in a last effort for air. With a convulsive gasp Mehadeh inhaled. Cold water inundated her nose and mouth, rushing down her throat. She choked, gagging and shivering as the iciness filled her lungs. The water around her grew even darker.

Mehadeh widened her eyes, sending out what little magic she had left in a last attempt at escape. She felt her body start to go limp. From the depths, the wavering figure of Yasir rushed to her, hands out, but he faded into the sinister form of Rakhshan.

The Dark Magician's ruby aigrette glowed deep red, almost black. He glided to her, arms wide, dark sleeves trailing like Death's serpentine banners in a *Danse Macabré.*

She folded, head flopping forward, praying she would cease to exist before she could feel Rakhshan enclose her in a ceaseless embrace of horror.

# 40

*Bramley House, seven months later*

 t the midwife's command, Lavinia clasped Fleming's hand and pushed. Early this morning, cramps had radiated through her womb in a web of pain and she woke Fleming, who had taken to sleeping in a cot by Lavinia's bed waiting for her mistress's time. Four hours later the pains came closer and closer. Now, her maid blotted her forehead with a soft linen cloth. So this is what Simza, practically a child, had endured for her, for Yasir.

The midwife straightened, her hand on Lavinia's knee. "Time to push again. I know you're tired, but you're doing well. Oh?" She ducked her head between Lavinia's legs.

Lavinia squeezed her eyes shut as she bore down. Her head pounded, the pressure building, a teakettle about to rupture. Would her head burst? She had pushed for what seemed hours. She didn't know if she could—

"Jesus, Joseph and Mary." The midwife didn't pop up this time to encourage her, but stayed between her legs. Fleming rushed over and, after a flurry of movement, the midwife rose up at the same time a raucous cry broke the silence. She held up a bloody little creature. "Milady, it's a boy."

*Bramley House, three years later*

"Mine!"

"Mine!" Stuart and James stood opposite one another, curly black hair falling into their eyes, chubby fingers slipping as they pulled on the wooden dog. Lavinia hurried over with a cloth duck, James's favorite. She had to reach them before—

The dog's painted mouth opened and yipped. James let go and stood staring in sullen silence. He pointed to the dog, blinked and let out a wail, his finger wobbling. Lavinia placed the duck in James's other hand and marched Stuart into the corner.

"It's not fair to use your magic to scare James. You are his big brother, four years old, and James is only three." She squatted beside him and stroked his arm. "Remember our talk?"

Stuart looked down at his toy dog on the floor in front of him.

Lavinia gave him a little shake. "Our talk?"

He nodded and in a singsong voice said, "I shouldn't use magic on Jamie who's a little baby. And no one should see me do it." He stuck out his lower lip.

Lavinia squinted at him. Sometimes he was as stubborn as his father. She looked into his blue eyes, her eyes. They should be golden like his father's. He had inherited everything else. Why not his eyes? But that was her saving grace. If he had, then Peter would know, know he wasn't his.

"And what is the most important rule?" She crossed her arms and gave her eldest son what she hoped was a stern, commanding gaze. Something he would remember.

Looking at his scuffed shoes, Stuart exhaled and mumbled. "Not to let Dah see."

Cook took a knife, wiped it on her apron and sliced the bread. "You'll be wantin' mustard?" Lavinia nodded. "Lettuce, tomato?" Cook sliced the ham thin and held it up, light from the window shining pink through the skin. "Cured with cloves and dried orange peel." Cook tilted her head towards the cutting board. "I'm packin' some dill pickles the maids put up." Lavinia nodded again. She would put off thinking about a solution for Stuart until she left and got some distance away.

She adjusted the straps of the cloth bag on her shoulder and walked down the long drive in front of Bramley House. Did Peter have any idea of Stuart's magic? She left the shade of the massive cedar trees and met the road in front of the manor's grounds, glad to have her straw bonnet trimmed in green with a broad brim. Good for this sunny day.

A quarter kilometer or so ahead, a line of dense willows, their long pointed leaves fluttering like thin green flags, marked the path to the River Lea. A nice, long walk. The fresh scent of water carried on the light breeze. Enjoying the warm sun on her back, Lavinia plodded down the road and stopped to readjust the straps of her bag.

Everyone had been properly occupied. The boys safe with nanny. Peter busy with his papers. She deserved time away from them and the confines of Bramley House. Her mouth watered at the yeasty smell of the thick bread, the spices in the ham and the sharp dill of the pickles Cook had packed. She would sink her teeth into her sandwich, sit under one of the huge oaks and watch the river flow by. She almost felt the cool breeze off the water on her face.

Lavinia raised her hand to her eyes, gazing at a puff of dust rising down the road past the willows. The clang of metal on metal and the muffled clump of horse's hooves grew louder as a wooden cart, a bit smaller than their new coach, trundled towards her. The panels of the tinker's wagon were clamped shut, hiding the tiers on both sides that displayed his wares. He looked to be headed in the direction of the tiny village of Tynnes-on-Dale, only a small distance up the road.

When Lavinia was a little girl, she loved the tinkers. Wide-eyed at the array of choices—rag dolls with smiling faces, spinning tops whose striped colors blended into magical blurs, ribbons and hair ornaments, bracelets that caught the light like real jewels, hard candy promising bursts of sweet orange and lemon. Her nanny gave her coins. Before Lavinia bought each item she fancied, she had spread out her palm, the silver coins sparkling.

Lavinia smiled at the little leap her heart gave even now while the heavy-laden cart, swaying gently behind the plodding horse, crept towards her.

"How do, milady." As thin as his dun-colored horse, the tinker stopped his wagon, hopped off and doffed his hat. "I have me some wonderful items." He squinted in the bright sunlight, his eyes glinting in his wizened face. "Ye might be surprised."

Lavinia stood by the side of the wagon. She caught him studying her, a faint smile on his lips, a knowing look in his eyes, but she had never seen this tinker before. He opened the latches that locked down the side panel and lifted it to form an awning over the rows of shelves displaying an unexpected variety of wares for such a limited space.

His body wavered as he passed between the bright sunlight and shadows. She shut her eyes. Opened them again. No. He was just normal folk, not like the people who appeared in Yasir's urn, materializing out of thin air.

She turned her attention to the merchandise. All shapes and sizes of pots, pans, lids, metal and wooden utensils hung from hooks at the top of the shelves. Brightly colored toys of wood, tin and cloth stood neatly on the next row. Below them, arranged by kind, were displayed all manner of things for the kitchen and hearth and then some. There were glass beads and ribbons pinned to a cloth-covered board. A riot of items. Lavinia felt her face light up.

It was still magical.

She fingered the ribbons. When she was younger she had been fascinated with the flat silky bands of color. She bought every hue she could find. The beads, hanging like exotic fruits, reminded her of Simza's, but were not as beautiful. Still, they caught the sunlight, projecting colored shadows, each bead's center shining brilliant like the seed of a rainbow, shading darker at the edges.

Painted wooden soldiers, big enough for stubby little fingers to handle, were lined up on the shelf near the front of the wagon. She chose some for James and Stuart. The tinker stood next to her, holding a worn basket with a hoop handle. She startled, sure that he was on the other side of the wagon working with the panel there.

"Would milady like a basket for her purchases?" He pushed his hat from his face. She frowned. He had no wrinkles. He was much younger than she had thought.

"I have tops and dolls." The tinker held up a cloth soldier with a laughably stern expression in his painted blue eyes.

"What marvelous detail," she studied the smart red jacket, and black tricorne with a plume of white feather. "Please give me two." The boys, for all their vexing ways, were always on her mind.

"Have a few fancy stuffs." He glanced at her. The tinker bore the strangest expression, as though he wanted to tell her something. He moved closer. He stood taller than she had noticed, and up close his face was wrinkled and old. She dropped the dolls into her basket. Just a few minutes ago he had looked so young. A trick of the light? Of proximity?

The tinker gestured for her to follow as he walked to the back of the wagon. He took a key tethered on a fraying string from his pocket and unlocked a wide panel, flipped it up and latched it in place. With a gesture of his hand he indicated the contents. "Just for special persons like milady."

Lavinia smiled at him and, to be polite, walked closer to the shelves. She could feel him staring. The special section wasn't as exciting as the cheap goods. The second-hand items were worn or clumsy copies of more expensive wares, thrilling to those who longed to own a fine item mimicking the quality's belongings.

Still, she would do him the courtesy. She examined the goods. On the first shelf sat a poor reproduction of a blue and white China vase, the blue design smudged in spots. Propped in a sitting position next to it sat a doll dressed in lace with a delicately painted porcelain face, a hairline crack snaking down her jaw. A gilded mantel clock with fat black Roman numerals took up most of the rest of the shelf. Lavinia ran her fingers down the tall mother-of-pearl handle on the delicate silver bell that graced the small space beside it.

She fiddled with her basket. Her stomach rumbled. Lunch by the river called her from this dusty hot road. She scanned the second shelf and stepped back to view the third. Just a little longer to be courteous. She fidgeted and moved to the left to see the items next to a gaudy painted box secured with more wire and rope than the other items because it extended beyond the shelf.

"Lord in heaven." Lavinia dropped her basket, spilling the contents into the dust. She stood frozen to the spot, staring at the shelf.

"Milady?" The tinker hurried to her side. "May I help ye? Milady?"

Ignoring him, Lavinia stared straight ahead. Among the items artfully arranged on the humble shelves and proudly wired in place, sat the urn.

*Her* urn.

The urn that had brought her Yasir. The urn that cemented her dissatisfaction with Peter. The urn that played in her nightmares.

The tinker checked the area. "If'n it were a mouse, milady, the wee thing has been long gone by now." He knelt and retrieved her goods from the ground, wiped them with a rag, placed them into the basket and offered it to her. She took it automatically, without seeing it. Clutching the basket, her knuckles white, she leaned in close for a better look. She could feel the tinker watching her.

It was the very same urn. She reached out. Hesitated. Pulled her hand back. Why would she want such a piece of bad luck? In her mind, she heard Peter, his voice raspy with pain—*Look what you have done, Lavinia*—removing his bloody hand from his chest after she had

stabbed him, his pale blue eyes wide with shock and hurt. She saw
Yasir beating Peter until his eye caved in, then bringing down the cane
once more with a sickening thud. She staggered, almost colliding with
the tinker.

"Milady. I'll fetch a chair." He scurried away. The urn sat on the
shelf, shadowed, the brass catching the light as the wind rippled the
trees. She thought she saw it lurch towards her and jerked forward,
hands out to catch it. But the breeze died and it sat there almost hidden
in the shade. She turned her head. She should go.

"Here, milady, it would be best if ye would sit for a bit, 'til what
ails ye leaves." The tinker set an elaborately carved chair beside her,
the remaining gilt making it look shabbier. Lavinia sank into the worn
cane seat. The chair wobbled and the tinker scuffed a bit of dirt under
one of the legs. "There, now. All steady." He looked up at her, his face
smooth and innocent. Her eyes widened in surprise. Perhaps, in spite
of her bonnet, she had been too long in the sun.

The shade of the raised back panel sheltered her and she stared
down the deserted road. She would see a haze of dust if anyone came,
that is, unless they were on foot. Was there a chance Peter would venture
this way? He was buried in his study as occasioned on Wednesdays. A
creature of habit. He would be there the daylong. She breathed a sigh
of relief.

Lavinia set her basket on the chair and walked to the shelf. She
reached for the urn and ran her hand down the warm brass curves,
fingered the engraved calligraphy spiraling around the vessel. It was
*the* urn. Yet her fingers met only plain brass. No tingling in her flesh,
no visions. She turned and gasped in surprise as she stood face to face
with the tinker. His dove gray eyes were speckled with green.

He held up his palms, a spiraled silver ring around his thumb.
"Sorry milady. I didn't mean to frighten ye." Lavinia placed her hand
on her chest and shut her eyes for a moment. She should go to the
river. Now.

But she heard herself say, "May I see this?"

The tinker gave her the urn. The brass, warm like a living being. She held it, feeling awkward, for this should be a private moment. Trying to ignore the tinker, she savored the odd script winding around the body, the arabesque vine that twisted into a handle, the sensuous curves. Yet, she still felt nothing from it, not so much as a prickle. It could be a keepsake, for she had some good memories. She would hide it. No one would ever know. Not Peter. Not even Alice.

"How much?" She looked the tinker straight in the eye. He dropped his gaze to the ground and shuffled his feet. He raised his head.

"Take it." The tinker removed his hat and stood straight, blonde hair shining in the sunlight. A regal figure in the prime of life. His rough garments could have been ermine and silks, his hat a jeweled crown.

"Beg pardon?" Lavinia tried not to show her shock. These tinkers always had tricks up their sleeves.

"Make me an offer." He grinned as he replaced his tattered straw hat and became a lowly tinker once more. Lavinia clutched the urn to her chest. She stood with the tinker in the dark shade of his wagon with the bright sun all around. She felt in her pockets. *Pish tosh*, she had brought no money. And why would she, for a picnic by the river?

Her heart beat faster as she envisioned the tinker rewiring the urn into place, shutting the panel, carefully locking it, and clattering down the road with her urn. Suddenly, she wanted it more than anything in the world.

The tinker stood still, the air alive with tension. She fumbled in her bag. He thinks I have money with me. Is there anything in here that I could barter?

Under her sandwich, Lavinia fingered a small, ridged disk. She took hold. It slipped from her fingers, but she scrambled through bits of dust and crumbs and fished it out. A penny, dull silver with a portrait of George II. She turned it over in her palm. She couldn't offer this, not even to the tinker.

But he laughed and took it from her hand. "O ye *ynnep*." He held it up, making the tarnished silver coin look even more pitiful. She tilted her head, frowning at the odd phrase.

He flipped the coin and caught it. "Backslang, milady, 's penny said backwards, common in our trade." He chortled to himself and pocketed the coin.

Lavinia stared, open-mouthed. Was the tinker accepting a penny for the urn?

"Sold that brass bottle more times than I can remember. Always came back. Ye should have heard the excuses. Too heavy. My husband says we don't need it. It fell on my son's foot." He chuckled softly and eyed the urn, still in her hands. Lavinia grasped it tighter. Something leapt from the tinker to her. A sensation like she received from Alice. From Yasir. She backed away and stared.

The tinker cocked his head, eyes sparkling from under his hat. "One even complained it was hexed." He chuckled, a soft series of snorts.

Lavinia took a sharp breath. *Did he know?*

He took his hat off once more and ran his hand through his hair. He seemed to change before her eyes, taller like a statesman, a commanding presence.

"But I have a feelin' that I won't see it no more." He held his hat in front of his waist, an emissary, his mission completed.

The tinker replaced his hat, closed the panel holding the fancy items and twisted the key in the lock. He faced her, his features deep in shade from the bright sun on his hat brim.

The day had become still, the sun overhead, dark shadows under the wagon and trees, puddles of black contrasting with the bright yellow sunlight. Noon. Eerie as midnight, a time when a fissure opens to the world of hidden magic.

Lavinia stood stock-still like the shadows, transfixed by the man.

"It's yours." With his eyes, the tinker indicated the urn in her hands. "Always has been." He turned his back to her and started closing the side panels on his humble wagon.

# 41

With each step towards the river, the urn in her bag pressed against Lavinia's side. At Bramley House they were alert to the vessel and its implications (except, of course, that it had held a djinni), ever since they saw her lugging it around during her bout of madness. She would have to make sure it stayed well hidden.

The thuds and thumps of the tinker packing his cart had followed her down the road. She kept stifling the urge to turn for one last glimpse of the man. Was she afraid? Perhaps afraid of the lost opportunity. Did the tinker know if Yasir was really dead? She could hurry back and ask him, but how would she broach the subject? He had mentioned that some said the urn was hexed. The words would surely come to her as she faced him.

She looked back down the road. Deserted. She swept her head from side to side and peered at a faint haze of dust behind a copse of trees. The foliage blocked the bend in the road she had just traversed. The tinker was on the other side. She had walked farther than she thought and couldn't catch up with him now.

She pulled at the bag's strap and rolled her shoulder. After she ate, the bag would be lighter. It was just as well she hadn't gone back to the tinker. He might have changed his mind about accepting a penny for the urn.

At the bank of the river, she set her bag on the grass, pulled out the tablecloth and spread it. Glad to be off her feet, she brushed at a fly as she unstopped the flacon's cork, tipped her head, and took a sip. The wine tasted sweeter here under the trees. She looked up at the dark branches and leaves creating a verdant roof shading the bank as well as the water. With deft fingers she untied her bonnet and flung it aside, the cool breeze a relief from the warmth of the sun.

She narrowed her eyes at the tablecloth. The bag, empty but for the urn, lay on its side. She exhaled, her shoulders slumping. "The toys. I forgot the children's presents." She pictured the stiff wooden soldiers, the cloth dolls, their happy eyes staring straight ahead. This wasn't the first time the djinni had taken precedence over her family. But she would make it the last.

Her mouth watered as she bit into the thick ham sandwich. This part of the river ran deep, the current slow, dark blue swirling with emerald. Where the sun chanced upon its surface, the water turned translucent turquoise, golden beams shining straight to the bottom where dark gray shapes lurked flashing aquamarine and amber with the swish of a tail or fin.

A world partially seen, little known to those who dwelled upon solid ground. A world holding secrets, even here, upon land she owned. Much like the urn, possessed throughout the centuries by individuals who had held it in their hands and placed it under their roofs, many unaware of its secret. And when they knew its secret, how many survived with their sanity intact? How many were swept into that clandestine world, never to be heard from again? But now the urn was empty, and its former owners had merely sensed something questionable about the vessel. Had the urn been attempting to return to her?

She threw the bread crusts into the water and startled at the fierce upheavals on the surface as the pieces vanished into the mouths of hungry fish. The day had taken a turn. She had come, hoping for peace and quiet. Instead, she further complicated her life.

She pulled the broadcloth bag towards her. The urn lay silent in the interior. She placed her hand upon the vessel, closing her eyes, hearing the birds in the trees, the whispering of the leaves, the occasional lap of water on the shore. The urn felt warm, as usual, but she received no vision, no special feeling from it.

She sighed and placed the vessel in her lap. She thought of Stuart, how much he looked like his father, Yasir. What joy he brought her—Yasir's gift. She would never see her djinni again. Ever. She stroked the urn, feeling the engraving, like scars, under her fingers . . .

Yasir. Bloody djinni. He had become an invisible barrier between Peter and her. The words unspoken, the laughter withheld, the glance turned away. The love that could have grown and blossomed. Stunted. But in the years since she returned, she and Peter had at last erased the scars left by Yasir—at least most of them.

She set the urn in front of her, seeing in her mind a flash of dark hair, golden eyes, a beguiling smile. "No," she whispered and turned away from temptation. Yet her hands made their way to the brass vessel.

With a snap, she unlatched the lid. A thin stream of mist swirled in the rays of sunshine. She held her breath and rose to her feet, following with her eyes the coils of mist upwards. Was he here? Come back to her?

The haze dissipated. Had she imagined it? She searched in the shadows behind the broad trunk of the oak. A spider, dull black, skittered down the bark towards her. Heart racing, she checked in the dense grove of willows. Not there.

Lavinia returned to the remains of her picnic at the river's edge and sat in the shade, wiping the sweat from her face with her skirt. The urn, lid open, lay overturned on the tablecloth where she had left it.

She slouched against the tree trunk behind her in disappointment. If he were here . . . She closed her eyes, feeling his lips on hers, his magic embrace. Oh, if he were here. She placed her palm on the sturdy trunk, the bark rough and craggy, not smooth as it looked when she first glanced at the stand of trees. It was never smooth, never easy with Yasir. The strange places. The magician and his minions who wanted her dead, wanted her baby dead. Little Nicu/Stuart, her first child, whose first year was lost to her forever. The gypsies and their mysteries. As she totted up the hurts and fears, the threats and horrors, her yearning dropped away to a rising anger.

"By the heavens, Yasir. I must be out of my mind to want you back." She picked up the urn and walked to the river. The water flowed by, dappled in sunlight, on occasion reflecting a blinding flare of white as if the liquid had transformed to fire.

Lavinia held the vessel, warm against her chest. Then she flung it far out into the water, holding her breath until the splash made her exhale, the water spraying up like diamonds dazzling in the sunshine. A flash of gold split the indigo surface, bubbles of amber and green and white foamed around the urn, cushioning its ride into the depths. The vessel floated downward, like a spiraling leaf caught in the current. A gleam of amber swirling through emerald and peridot, falling into sapphire and lapis lazuli, at last disappearing. Lavinia stared at the surface, the breeze dividing it into scales like a great fish swimming endlessly by.

It was finished.

A chill rose up her legs and she dug her shoes into the muddy river bed, steadying herself against the force of the current. She blinked against the glare of the sun on the water, picked up her skirts and waded as fast as she could to the place where the urn had gone in. If she hurried—

The water exploded near where the urn had sunk. She squealed in surprise. The huge splash fountained upwards like a geyser, drenching her. She held her arms out, staring at the rivulets flowing from her hair down her dress. Waves crested towards her, lapping at her body, plastering her skirts against her legs.

"Now it's mine!"

She jerked towards the sound.

At a flash of gold in the water, a small skinny figure emerged from the river.

"It's heavy, like to have drown'ded me." A boy dragged the urn in both hands and slopped towards the shore, breathing hard and splashing as he made an unsuccessful effort to lift his feet. He flopped onto the grass, his body tanned from the sun, his ragged pants secured at his waist by an old leather belt cut to fit, and set the urn beside him with a dull thud.

Why, he must be only twelve years old, if that. He stood and shook the water off like a dog. Droplets sprayed from his hair, and he moved away from the puddle he made. He stared at Lavinia, leaned his head over his left shoulder and shook it hard. "Water in me ear." He leaned the other way and banged on the side of his head with his hand. Lavinia waded towards him, walking up the small incline onto the shore, her wet skirts a hobble around her legs.

"You couldna got it." The boy looked at her critically, his hands on his slim hips. "Can't swim, aye?" He scowled and dropped onto the grass, pulling the urn closer.

She looked at him and smiled. "You're right. I can't."

The boy cocked his head and thumped the heel of his hand near his ear. He straightened and squinted at her, drops of water competing with the freckles sprinkled on his nose. "What're doing throwin' bottles in the water—then looking horrified?"

"I changed my mind." She wrung out the front of her skirt.

"Ya couldna swim in that." He looked contemptuously at the fabric clinging to her legs.

"I know," Lavinia said softly. She sat beside him in the warm sun and reached for the urn.

The boy grabbed it and pulled it out of her reach. "It's mine now."

Her face grew hot. Curse the little urchin. He could not have her urn. She stared at the vessel. "I will have it back."

He scooted away and held it to his side, away from her. "Wot's tossed away's fair game." He grinned, smug.

Lavinia held his gaze and stood slowly, shaking out her skirts. "You wouldn't steal from a lady."

The boy guffawed and rose to his feet, tottering from the weight of the urn. He looked her up and down and backed away. Lavinia followed, gaining on him. He turned, feet planted in the mud to take a running start.

"Stop, you little thief." Desperate, she leapt at him, bringing him to the soggy ground as she landed on top. For a moment, she lay stunned. What had she done? Had she hurt the child?

"Criminy! S'blood!" The boy struggled on his stomach, his leg somehow kicking her in the thigh.

"Ow!" Lavinia rolled off of him into the mud.

"Damn it to hell." He flopped upright and grabbed for the urn, clamped his hand on the base and dragged it to him. Lavinia crawled towards the vessel as he endeavored to pick it up. She threw herself on the urn, grunting as she landed half on the boy. He wriggled, trying to break free.

She clutched the urn in both hands, rolled away and staggered upright. The boy sat up, latched onto her skirt and pulled hard, ripping the cloth. With a cry, Lavinia stepped forward to regain her balance, her foot landing hard on his shin. He jerked his leg away, causing her to stumble and she pitched backwards onto her bottom, still clutching the urn.

"Cor blimey. Have mercy." He grabbed his leg and crawled a few feet, mud covering his trousers.

They both scrambled up, bits of dirt and grass flying, and faced each other. The lad's hazel eyes peered from his muddy face, shining with anger and greed. "I can get a bob, least, from the tinker fer it." He scowled.

"Ha! More like sixpence." Lavinia swayed, breathing hard. She wiped mud out of her eye and smeared it on her skirt.

"A bob." The lad held out his grimy hand and planted his bare feet in the mire.

"I don't have it here." Lavinia huffed. What a conniving little bastard—why, he had stayed around to bargain.

"Ain't no deal." The lad advanced towards her.

"No." Lavinia screamed and stepped back. "Don't you dare touch me!" She held the urn over her head. He stopped at the look on her face and glanced warily around.

"You good fer it? A shilling?"

Lavinia sniffed. "Of course." She brought the urn down slowly and held it in front of her like a shield. "You know the big house up the road?"

He nodded, watching her closely.

"Follow me there and you'll get your reward."

He dropped his hands to his side and jerked his head up. "You from there?" The boy eyed her and smirked. "Yer that crazy lady." Then a flash of fear lit his eyes and he held up his hand, forefinger and little finger in the sign to counter the evil eye. "...'wot makes spells!"

# 42

"*S*top. It hurts." Lavinia squeezed the thick muddy tangle where the comb stuck.

"It's no good, milady. I think a bath is in order." Fleming wiped her hands on her apron, leaving muddy smears, and pulled the braided cord in the corner. "I'll get the maids started heating the water." She put the dirty comb in her pocket.

"Milady." She hesitated. "You haven't said a word 'bout how you got . . ." She wrung her hands on her apron. "got this way. If master hears 'bout the boy down in the kitchen, 'bout you all soggy—if he presses me?"

"Fleming, I'm tired." Try as she might, Lavinia could think of no good excuse. Her mind felt as sodden as her hair and clothes when she had slunk into the servant's entrance, the boy tagging along with a hungry look in his eyes. Fleming stood stiffly next to the dresser and shifted her eyes to the floor, a crease between her brows.

"All right." Lavinia crossed her arms over her chest, holding them tight to her body. "Here's what happened. I fell into the river and the boy fished me out. I dropped from exhaustion onto the muddy bank. Then he helped me back to the house."

"Milady!" Fleming's mouth dropped open. "And you, not knowing how to swim." She stepped towards Lavinia. "Here, I'll unpack your bag and—"

"No!" Lavinia drew the bulky bag onto her lap, arms draped about it protectively. Her maid halted, mouth open, drawing up as though she were a leaf of the Shy Plant that closed at a finger's touch.

"I will unpack it myself." She glared at Fleming. "You may go now."

Lavinia set her bag on the carpet and locked the door. She shed her wrapper. From the bottom drawer of her dresser she pulled out a Calico print housedress and slipped it on, feeling naked without her chemise, stays, petticoat and hose underneath. From the same drawer she removed a matching blue scarf. She tied it around her head and tucked her damp hair into it. In the mirror she looked like a different person. She leaned close to the looking glass and rubbed a bit of dirt from her chin.

Clutching a shilling wrapped in a handkerchief, she crept down the hall and opened the door to the servant's stairs. *Angels in heaven,* if she ran into one of them . . . But the back stairs were usually empty this time of day, as the maids had finished their chores and tea was being served. She snuck through the hall leading to the kitchen and opened the pantry door where she had left the boy. Empty. She leaned against the doorframe. What if the rapscallion was with Peter, upping the bribe?

She peered into the kitchen. Cook, her back to Lavinia, hustled back and forth between the stove and long tables, supervising the maids preparing supper. From the scullery came the clanging of pots and pans amid occasional giggles. In a dim recess to the right of the door, the boy hunched over a table, stuffing his pockets with bread and sausage, a crumb-covered plate before him.

"Boy." She whispered. He didn't hear. If she snuck into the kitchen, surely someone would see her. She couldn't risk it. Lavinia took a long stirring stick from the table to the left of the door and reached into the room, nudging the lad on the shoulder. He whirled around, eyes big, then shot from the chair into the hall. She pulled him into the pantry.

"Here," she whispered, putting the handkerchief into his hand. She'd best get this over with and the lad out the door, out of her life.

He shook the shilling out and bit it. "'Bout time." He tossed the silver coin into the air.

"Hide it," Lavinia hissed. "Now."

He looked at her and half-closed one eye. "Yer cook," he motioned with a jerk of his head towards the kitchen, "says I deserve it."

Lavinia gasped. She took his arm and pulled him towards her. "What did you tell her?"

"That you had the bottle back. And you hadn't hexed me yet." His eyes widened. "Least not that I kin tell."

Lavinia leaned close to him. "What did you tell her about the bottle?"

"It's special's wot I know." He squinted at her and his voice took on a sinister intonation. "And the master of the house—" He looked her in the eye. "He ain't heard."

She squeezed his arm hard. "You don't know even the least of what I can do. But if you say anything else about my possessions, you'll wish you had never met me." If the lad believed she could hex him, she would use it to her advantage.

He pulled away, eyes round. "Won't say another word."

She saw him hook the two middle fingers of his left hand into a circle meeting his thumb, holding his index and little finger straight like horns.

"Now go, you've got your shilling. Don't come around anymore. If you do, there's no telling what I might do." She widened her eyes and glared as he scrambled out the kitchen door.

Through the open door to her adjoining sitting room, Lavinia glimpsed the maids filling the copper tub. When they finished dumping their pails of hot water, they stood for a moment, breathless and blotchy, only to head downstairs to do it over again. All the hustle and bustle just to get one bathed. Why, it was easier to jump into the river. The irony hit home as she scratched her head, then her arm, her leg. The river mud and grit had dried into a flaky, itchy layer.

Fleming bustled in, holding a brass tray containing a cake of white soap, a vial of soft scented soap, a wash cloth, a metal pitcher and a silver bell—much like the bell on the tinker's shelves. Lavinia dragged off her scarf, her muddy, damp tresses tumbling onto her shoulders, giving her a chill. Ignoring Fleming's dismay at her having donned the housedress herself, and in the process muddying it, she turned for her maid to help her slip it over her head.

"Jesus, Joseph and Mary. Bare as God made you underneath. Well, I never." Fleming tucked a towel around her. "Whatever else you were up to, I'm sure you won't tell me." Her maid looked at her with an expectant expression, then turned her mouth down. "That boy in the kitchen, he's been asking 'bout the master."

"Did he see Peter?" The boy should be long gone by now, his shilling safe in his pocket.

"Don't know. Cook says he was a persistent little bugger. Them's her words, not mine. You know I wouldn't speak crude to milady." Fleming plunked her wrist into the bathwater. "It's a bit too hot as yet. I'll put some cool water." She turned for the bucket.

Lavinia stuck her hand in. "No, leave it. I want it this way."

Steam rose from the bathwater's surface like mist on a lake. Lavinia held onto the tub's edge and put her toes in. She sank her foot, flinched, then with Fleming's help, lowered herself into the water.

Ah. The heat sucked the cold of the river from her bones. She leaned her head onto the curved edge of the tub. The tinker, the urn, the boy. She was rid of all but one. Out of nowhere, a stab of fear pierced her, chill in the heat of the bath, as she saw a vision of the urn swirling from sight, gone forever in the mysterious blue depths of the river. She shivered at what she had done, at how it had been undone, and at the boy's taunting words of blackmail. Would the little brat somehow get to Peter?

"Fleming, tell me at once if you hear anything about my husband finding out about . . . This. This river incident . . . the boy." Lavinia sat up. "I'm ready for you to wash my hair." She bent forward and caught her breath as Fleming poured warm water over her head. Brown rivulets flowed into the bath. Her maid massaged the creamy soap into her hair. Scents of mint and lavender mixed with steam off the water's surface and she frowned at the pull of her maid's fingers through the tangles.

If Peter discovered she had found the urn, would the love they had nurtured between them be lost? She didn't know how much he believed from what she first blurted about Yasir. When she convinced her husband Stuart was his, she had emphasized that those first ramblings resulted from the shock of losing her child to the gypsies— that the only truth was that the baby had been lost.

Her husband loved Stuart as his own now. They were a family. She exhaled as Fleming massaged the soap into her hair, then stiffened at a terrible thought. Could the urchin boy have told Peter she fought him for the urn? That would fuel Peter's feelings of betrayal and anger. She would have to convince her husband that the urn was only a token to her now: a symbol of her returning to him, of their love overcoming obstacles. How she took umbrage with the boy trying to steal from her.

Fleming's fingers worked down her mistress's neck and shoulders, kneading out the tension of the day, but bits and pieces of Lavinia's worries reassembled, swarming back at her, as persistent and indestructible as a ghost of gnats. Would her excuses work? Perhaps the boy hadn't spoken to Peter. But if he had, she'd have to convince her husband that she truly loved him.

She kept her eyes shut when Fleming doused her head again, rinsing the soap away. Bits of frothy foam floated in the tub. The boy had called her "that crazy lady." It never crossed her mind that *she* would be the subject of gossip. Of course, rumors had spread from the servants, but she assumed the talk had been of Peter's antiquities from tombs, antiquities with curses from the dead.

Lavinia sank further into the bath, and shut her eyes. She had given the servants fodder—with her disappearance, her stabbing Peter, her carrying the urn like a baby around the manor. Why wouldn't they talk about her? A crazy lady *and* a witch. Why, the boy believed she could actually hex him. She crossed her arms over her breasts. She had heard what they did to witches. But surely, being a noblewoman, she was safe. Besides, how on earth could they prove the witch part?

She tried not to think about spells and hexes or Peter and the urn while her maid washed her back. The bath felt cooler now and she braced to stand for the final rinse, relieved to find Fleming had saved some buckets of warm water.

Dripping wet, she stepped from the tub. Fleming wrapped her in towels and settled her at her dressing table. With a wide-toothed comb and rose-scented cream, she gently teased out any left-over tangles from her mistress's hair.

"Would milady like to dress for dinner?"

"Oh, I'm too tired. Bring a tray." She didn't think she could face Peter and his questions. He was bound to have heard at least some of what transpired today at the river. And if the boy had gotten to him . . . But if she didn't go to dinner, if Peter had heard anything, he would be even more curious, and if the boy visited him her staying away might corroborate the boy's story.

"Wait, Fleming. I'll go to dinner. I'll wear the deep blue dress and the sapphires from Peter."

Her maid turned, her eyebrows raised. "Why milady, the gown is in the laundry. I'll make sure it's properly ironed. But first I need to start you drying out properly."

Fleming removed the sodden towels, then wrapped her in fresh ones. Lavinia settled in her embroidery chair, her muscles as limp as the soft towels, and watched her maid line up her creams and powder and hair pins.

"Just relax milady, I'll be back soon." Fleming hustled out the door, closing it gently.

Lavinia stared out the window at the waning rays of sun slanting on the trees. Hazy blue swirled around the green leaves, dappled with orange and gold as she sank into a cold dark tunnel, bubbles of turquoise and emerald pressing against her, forcing her down, down. She raised her head, the towels snug against her hair and skin, and shivered. The incident this afternoon . . . she could have drowned if the boy hadn't inadvertently stopped her from retrieving the urn. So she shouldn't be angry with him . . .

"Hah. Shouldn't be angry with him . . ." She jerked at the sound of her voice. Raised her head. Through the window, the darkening sky streaked with orange and lavender. The lamp in the room glowed. She must have been dreaming. She looked at the clock—half past five. Fleming hadn't been gone long at all. Dinner was at seven, but she needed to start toweling her hair dry. With a yawn, she rose and headed to her dressing table, stumbling as her foot hit something hard. She looked down, her bag—she would speak to Fleming. No, she had forbidden her maid to touch the bag.

She knelt beside it and lifted the urn out, the brass warm in her hands. Lavinia studied it, then shut her eyes, envisioning *him*. She pulled the urn close. Her heart beat faster. Holding her breath, she released the latch. Put her hand on the lid. Then pushed the urn away. She would hide it. Yasir's face, his eyes . . . the image flooded her mind. Her finger slid across the metal vine, following the curves as it curled into a knob. She grasped the knob and pulled the lid open—

"My wife is in her rooms?"

Yes, milord, but . . ." Fleming sounded breathless, as if she had been running.

*My God, Peter!* Had the boy managed to see him, tell him about the urn? Is that why Fleming tried to stop him?

Lavinia picked up the vessel and looked about the room. Where could she hide it? Where? She hurried to her sewing basket, tossed out bits of fabric and skeins of threads, heaping them on the floor. She crammed the urn in. Stuffed the fabric and threads around it, smashed the lid on top, forced it down and snapped the latch closed.

The thud of his hard boots grew louder as he approached. "Leave, she can wait for her dinner gown. I will see her. Now."

She jumped up, rearranging her face and body to a normal calm, just as her towel came untucked and slid to the floor.

Peter burst through the door and halted, a startled look on his face.

"Well, it seems I came at an opportune time." His eyes raked down her body. He grinned, removed his jacket and threw it on a chair, untying his cravat as he strode towards her. "Uncover your hair, Lavy."

She raised her arms to her head. They felt boneless, and she wondered that they didn't just droop to her sides and stay there. Her fingers, working in spite of her, unwrapped the towel. Her hair tumbled onto her shoulders and down her back. She shut her eyes. The heat of a blush ran through her body.

Peter drew her close and kissed her, running his hand down her back, cupping her bare bottom. The softness of his velvet jacket, the hard leather of his boots against her bare legs, the urgency of his embrace made her tingle with anticipation. She could barely take a breath.

Even so, restless fragments flitted through her mind. Had the lid of her sewing basket come undone? She had latched it hastily. And Peter with his sharp sense of observation, even distracted as he was, might glance over, see the glint of brass . . . He removed his shirt, dropped it to the floor and led her to bed, laying her down gently, the pale blue of his eyes holding her gaze. Sitting beside her, he pulled off his boots.

He dropped his second boot on the floor, fumbled with the buttons on his trousers and tugged them off. Lavinia held out her arms to embrace him. Behind Peter, the room seemed misty, probably just the stray tendrils of steam from her bath in the sitting room. Peter's bare chest pressed against her breasts. So warm, his flesh on hers. How could she possibly entertain the idea of the djinni now? Tomorrow she would return to the river. Throw the urn in. For good this time. She had a life with Peter and the boys. A good life, free of gypsies, magicians, sorceresses. And djinnis. Alice didn't count in that respect.

Thrilling from the chills Peter created as he trailed his tongue down her neck, Lavinia wrapped her arms around his back and stared at the mist filling the room. *My God, when she stuffed the urn into her sewing basket, she had left the lid open.* Would she undo all she and Peter had with one harebrained fancy? She squirmed under him.

"Oh Lavy." Peter brought his lips to hers and continued with his pleasures.

She closed her eyes, attempting to lose herself in his kisses again. He wound his tongue deep into her mouth. She moaned, the building sensations lessening her worries about the urn stuffed into her sewing basket—surely it was empty. After all this time. The dead stay dead, even djinnis.

Her husband parted her thighs and slid inside her. "Peter." Lavinia breathed his name. He was everything to her now. Everything. He lifted his chest from hers, pushing into her. A cool draft wafted between them. She opened her eyes.

He was standing there, golden eyes glowing in the candlelight. Yasir.

Watching.

Lavinia shrieked and dug her fingernails into Peter's shoulders, raking his skin as they tore down his back.

"Ah, Lavy." He arched and moaned, pressing hard. She shut her eyes tight and heard a loud groan issue from her mouth. Peter uttered a long, low cry as if someone had stabbed him, and collapsed on top of her.

She looked over Peter's shoulder. No one was there. In spite of the heat of Peter's flesh on hers, a chill scraped up her spine.

Madness. Was it engulfing her once more?

Peter rolled to the side. He kissed her and dropped his head beside hers on the pillow. She lay there with her eyes closed, afraid to move for fear of disturbing him. Afraid to look for fear of what she might see.

The air of the chamber flowed over her. Her muscles locked, senses alert. The air was too defined, too much like . . . like magic. She swallowed hard.

Lavinia could feel her chest rising and falling as her breath came faster. She dared open her eyes a slit. Full evening, the room dim in the glow of the lamp. A trickle of sweat ran down her neck. The lamp flickered. The room looked empty. She exhaled and relaxed, opening her eyes fully.

Straight into his golden ones.

She stared in disbelief. She felt as though she were sinking, as if she had jumped into the river and plunged through the teal and emerald water—down, down, down into the frigid depths like the urn. The swish of a pectoral fin against her flesh, the prick of a sharp tail caudal, the slimy embrace of ribbons of eelgrass winding around her legs, entangling, grasping as they pulled her onto the river bottom.

She stared in disbelief, forgetting to breathe. His eyes shone, radiant as the sun. The vivid jewels of his headband sparked, blindingly bright.

"Yasir," Lavinia's voice strangled, a wisp of a sound. She tried to inhale. Her hand fluttered to her throat. Sitting up, she clasped the bedclothes, bunching the soft sheets around her breasts. She dropped her hand beside her and felt Peter's chest moving up and down—asleep. His slow rhythmic breathing made a cocoon around them.

Yasir's eyes shimmered, pupils vertical, narrow doors of darkness to a world of nightmare. An apparition. She was going mad.

Lavinia shivered and extended her arms to push the ghost away. The phantom image would distort like a reflection in water.

Her fingers touched warm flesh.

"No." She trembled.

Yasir moved closer, his palms out as if to placate her.

Lavinia opened her mouth but no sound emerged. She could feel cold air clutching her throat in place of her voice.

"You're dead." Lavinia scrambled off the bed and bolted towards the door, brushing past the apparition.

Peter sat up, blinking. "Lavinia?"

Yasir glanced at him, an annoyed look crossing his face as he waved his hand. Peter fell back onto the bed. The soft thud of his head hitting the pillow made Lavinia wish she were snug under the covers with him instead of awake in a nightmare. She reached for the door handle. Yasir materialized in front of her, blocking her escape. The desperate hope that she would come to her senses rushed through her brain.

"Lavinia, please. Do not be afraid." It sounded like Yasir. He sounded gentle. But he was dead. Dead!

"I saw you die." She backed away. "I-I tried to do what you said. Why do you haunt me?"

"Lavinia, I am not dead. You touched me. I am in my human body." He came nearer.

She put her hands out to stop him. "No. No! Stay away. Don't hurt me. I did what you said—I—"

"I will not harm you. Please . . ." Those eyes, pupils round now, dark black in front of gold flames. Coming closer. His hand snaked towards her. She couldn't move.

She could feel his breath on her face. He said he wouldn't hurt her, but . . . Numbness crept into her hands, slithered up her arms until her body filled with the vast blackness of the night heavens, stars wheeling from the void, their trails of light diminishing into the emptiness that consumed her.

# 43

*L*avinia secured the top clasp on her wrapper and shifted her position on the carpet, sliding closer to Yasir who sat with his back against the door of her room. Sitting on the floor while Peter—sound asleep—occupied the bed didn't seem to bother him. He acted as if he owned the manor, as if Peter were the interloper.

Fleming wouldn't dare bother her about dressing for dinner while Peter was in the room. After all, dinner was with Peter. She rested her head against the djinni's chest, reassured that he was truly alive by the rhythm of his heartbeat. Different from any other human even though in a human body, an elaborate throb in a hypnotic cadence. Her mind wandered, a balloon on a string, a horse on a tether, bound to Yasir.

"Where did you go, Yasir?" She held his hand to reassure herself that his flesh stayed solid. "What happened to your body after you . . ." She shut her eyes. She didn't want to say the word. She looked at him and continued. " . . . After you d-died?"

"Lavinia, I would not have left you willingly."

She sat up and let go of his hand. "You abandoned me to Peter and Saddani and the gypsies. Why?"

"These things are not spoken about in the human realm." He looked away. "I am sworn. I may tell you only what I am allowed."

She barely followed the thread of his brief story, distracted by his mellifluous voice, the timbre of his silky tones possessing her in a way different from his physicality. In every cell of her body, she felt him, a giddy presence entrancing like the view from a great mountain, the sheer height overwhelming, the sight awe-inspiring—to see the immensity of the world from such a place.

Yasir spoke of an overpowering weakness, then a vast darkness. "I was saved by—" He broke off and stared at Lavinia, his pupils contracting from round orbs to thin slits as if to lock away secrets. "—by a being strong in magic. I am pledged to silence."

"Lord in heaven, Yasir." She drew away from him. "I believed you were dead. For years I grieved for you. How I longed for a message, any trace of a sign . . . Yasir, how could you?"

"There is a measure of time for djinnis. By a hair's breadth, I was snatched from what you call death." He took her hand, his eyes intent.

"My *delara*, I have fought with all my strength to come back to you. I have traversed unimaginable realms."

She considered this revelation. That horrible moment when she saw him die would be forever etched in her memory. Lavinia slumped against the door, reliving for a moment the fear that led her to try and escape from Yasir. The fear that he was a phantom come for her. She exhaled in the renewed relief that he had returned healthy and whole, and glanced across her chamber at Peter, sprawled in bed, still sleeping. She had some time, then.

"It has been three years, nine months and seven days." When she said the words, the burden of every minute of those long years pressed upon her. "I grieved sorely for you, Yasir." She gained the courage to look him in the eye. "I lost my mind. I *stabbed* Peter."

He paled. His eyes glowed as if he were trying to hex her from saying those things.

"You could have helped me. You could have come to me sooner, let me know you were alive." She hated the peevishness in her voice.

Yasir reached for her, but she folded her arms over her chest.

"It was not my doing," he said, his voice fraught with pain. "My *delara*, I was not allowed to let anyone know I lived. They took care that the Dark Magician believe, beyond a doubt, that I was dead. Your safety and the safety of our child could not be risked."

Or your precious *prophecy*, she thought to herself. She felt a flush of anger creep up her neck. Yasir had kept silent while she dealt with the terror of being alone in Rakhshan's palace. He let her believe she had been abandoned at the gypsies. He allowed her to sink into the horror of losing her baby. If Yasir had come to her just once, held her in his arms . . .

He put his hand over hers, the gems in his rings vivid like flowers, his touch making her breath come shallow and fast. Still, the arcane circumstances made sense. But when he returned, he had crept up on her in what resembled a child's prank, scaring her out of her wits.

And now he had the audacity to give her excuses showing how concerned he was about her, about their child, when all his diabolical scheming revolved around the prophecy, around defeating Rakhshan. Why should she suffer this? "I am surprised you didn't see to it that I was sent to Bedlam. That would've tidied up everything for your *precious* prophecy." She huffed in a pique of resentment and slipped her hand out from under his.

His eyes flickered. Was he angry? Well, that would make two of them.

"You know that we are threatened. How could you not?" Yasir studied her. Assessed her with that scrutinizing gaze.

Lavinia veiled her thoughts. She had practiced on Alice, and judging from her aunt's flitting eyes and conversational lags—why Alice fairly squawked in frustration—she had at least succeeded in thwarting her aunt from accessing much of her mind. Surely she could block Yasir's attempts as well.

He pulled his hand from hers and curled it into a fist. "You were a prisoner of the Dark Magician. He meant to kill you, to kill our son."

She glanced at Peter, still asleep across the room. "I well know that. I experienced it without you. Alone. And I survived. How do you think—"

"Lavinia, I did not forsake you." Yasir grasped her shoulders and held her before him. "I must see that you understand." He met her eyes.

She blinked and focused on the carpet. He wouldn't use his djinni wiles to persuade her. He could go back to the urn. She would lock the vessel in a trunk, have the servants store it in the attic. Then she would forget about him and his precious prophecy. She was safe now, here with Peter and the boys with no ghouls hunting her.

"There is a foretelling." He paused. She dared not look at him, for he was waiting for her to gaze into his eyes, to see his sincerity, to be drawn into his world. "A foretelling about our child. It predicts he will defeat the magician. The Dark One knows."

So now he used the prophecy to lure her.

"Don't you dare bring Stuart into this." Lavinia sat straight. "I remember Rakhshan's exact words." She noticed with satisfaction that Yasir grimaced when she said the magician's name. She pretended she didn't see. "Rakhshan said, 'It is prophesied that the child will bring disaster to our family, to your family. To keep you safe, you need to be here.' He never said Stuart would defeat him. That he was in danger from our child."

Perhaps there existed a grain of truth to both their versions of the prophecy. How could she trust what Rakhshan said when he clearly meant to harm her? But Yasir, too, had an agenda. And it had left her at Rakhshan's mercy, then Peter's, Saddani's and the gypsies'.

Yasir reached for her, but she refused him. "Lavinia, I could never tell you true about the prophecy. If you had known . . . When he captured you, the Dark Magician would have seen into your mind that our son would defeat him. Straightaway, he would have killed you both."

Crossing her legs, she rearranged her wrapper. She had told Rakhshan that the baby was Peter's, but the Dark Magician hadn't believed her. If she had known about the prophecy . . . *Angels in heaven,* would Rakhshan have seen into her mind? She put her hand to her throat, forcing away the muddled confusion she experienced when she faced Rakhshan alone in his palace, the emerald aigrette adorning his white turban boring into her like a malevolent third eye.

When she had first returned to Bramley House, straight from the urn, grieving for Yasir and her baby, the pain was hers alone to bear. Now she saw the whole picture. Yasir colluding with the gypsies to save her and the child from Rakhshan in spite of her attempts to sabotage them. Yasir trying to lighten her grief, but unable to remove it.

She looked up at Yasir. The back of her neck prickled as he raised his brow and stared past her, golden eyes glassy, his round pupils closing into a vertical slit. She turned.

Peter, still in the fog of sleep, had sat up. He stared at her, a frown clouding his face. She grasped Yasir's arm, and he gestured with a dismissive sweep of his hand in Peter's direction. Like a mechanical apparatus, Peter closed his eyes and lay back on the bed.

"Could he see us?" Lavinia whispered.

"No. He knows and sees nothing. He is in the world of sleep." Yasir ran his hand along her cheek. "You must not give it another thought."

# 44

$\mathcal{Y}$asir couldn't dispel Lavinia's disquiet. It mocked him in the bearing of her body, in her expressions of distrust and apprehension. He closed his eyes and rested against the door of her room. All he had experienced when he died: his human body failing him, his struggle to discorporate too late. Then the plunge into a void so deep and limitless—unfathomable, even with all his powers had shown him. Was that what awaited when his time came? Djinnis in their natural state were not immortal. Yet, just before he had been snatched from the depths of darkness, an infinitesimal speck of light pierced the black oblivion.

"Why now, Yasir?" Lavinia's plaintive tone tore at his heart. "Why now to return? I was . . . I was almost normal once more, the grief not gone, but buried deep enough."

Was it his lot to cause pain? He placed his hand on the small of her back, a gentle caress, but also a gesture of possession. "I was released. It is safe for us to be together now. To be together with our son." He felt her heart pulse faster. Her silence weighed upon him as he struggled not to plead with her to let him see the child. To hold him in his arms.

Finally, his son.

"I would see him." He could not hide the anticipation in his voice.

Lavinia hadn't expected such a request. Of course, a father would ask to see his son. But having Yasir around was too dangerous for Stuart, too dangerous for all of them.

She must seem accepting. "Oh, Yasir. I didn't think. He's asleep now, if I disturb him, he'll start crying. But see him, at least." Would

Yasir spoil it all again? She and Peter had been doing well these last three, no almost four years, growing closer, reveling with joy in their darling sons. She should send Yasir to the urn. She should . . . But first he could see his son. Then she would command him back for good, and settle into life with Peter and the boys. A safe, secure existence.

"Come Yasir." She held out her hand. He took it and stood beside her. A frisson of something old and familiar, but yet *unnamable*, shot through her.

"Lavinia." He grasped her by the shoulders, face to face, his golden eyes so full of acceptance. "You cannot know how much this means to me. That we are together, that—"

Peter murmured in his sleep, tossing and turning under the covers.

"—Don't—don't speak, Yasir." Lavinia exaggerated her gestures as she glanced sidelong at Peter who had settled down. She couldn't bear to hear Yasir's love words, not now. With a decisive push on the handle, she opened the door and they slipped through. Her heart twisted with guilt. How Yasir would hate being confined to the urn, knowing she was free. Knowing she was happy with Peter and they were raising his own son without him. Could she be that cruel? To keep Yasir from his own flesh and blood?

Just after she had returned to Bramley House, after Yasir's body vanished from the urn, she had stabbed Peter, blaming him for Yasir's death. After all, Peter had shot the djinni with the cursed bullet. She had held the penknife in her hand, felt the vehemence of her hatred when she forced it into his chest. She flinched from the hostility in the words she had said to her husband so long ago: "You shot him. You killed him."

Would she be doing the same to Yasir when she banished him to the urn, hid the vessel in a trunk in the attic, never again to open it; when she placed her ruby ring inside and locked the trunk, effectively banning magic creatures from her life?

She glanced back at Yasir as he followed her through the hallway lit by dim moonlight. He was here. Healed. Her wish come true. But the wish was from long ago. A time of danger and intrigue. Even now, when she recollected what had happened, she would feel a wrenching in her midsection like a knife twisting, and wonder that she survived. Her life had become more tranquil since, Beethoven's Moonlight Sonata instead of a tragic opera. For the sake of her family, she had to maintain that serenity.

The door handle clicked, seeming as loud as a pistol shot in the quiet of the nursery, but the children didn't stir. Lavinia led Yasir inside, and they stood together by Stuart's bed. Holding his hands over his son, the djinni uttered words in a language different from ones she had heard him speak before. His fingers emitted a soft light on Stuart's cherubic face.

"He is beautiful." Yasir lowered his brows, his expression grave as he took in his son's full lips, his dark hair falling in ringlets, his small fingers unfurling on the covers. Something shifted inside Lavinia, but she refused it, smothered it. To have Yasir beside her, to look upon their child together. How she had pined for this very thing. But that was long ago. It was too late for her to be happy with the djinni.

Yasir put his arm around her. A slight tremble shivered through him. He stood still for a long while. "He resembles my family, but has your fair skin." His voice sounded hoarse.

She nodded. "His name is Stuart." She paused to check the djinni's reaction. "Simza said you wanted him to have an English name, one befitting an English lord. He looks just like you when he's awake. He has your expressions, but my blue eyes." She smiled in spite of herself, thinking of when she had most missed Yasir, and how her son's resemblance to the djinni had filled that empty space inside her. If she sent him to the urn soon, he would never see Stuart's blue eyes. A wave of nausea roiled her insides when she thought of her approaching betrayal. She put her hand on her stomach.

"An English name will help keep him safe. You did well." Something in Yasir's manner, the hollow tone of his voice, made her think he would have wished his son to have a different name.

"Mehadeh and I had to effect a plan to save you." Yasir's voice wavered. "To save our baby." He kept his eyes on his son. "The Dark Magician pursued you with a vengeance and found you at the gypsies. The Chovihano rescued you."

"That time in Simza's tent." She turned to him and blocked the vision in her mind of Rakhshan in the shadows. "If the Chovihano hadn't interrupted, then Rak—, he would have taken me?"

"Taken you might have been the best consequence." Yasir didn't meet her eyes. Lavinia stepped away.

*The djinni had put her in mortal danger.*

"We conferred. The Chovihano said Simza was willing to carry your baby, that she had love for you." Yasir brushed a strand of hair out of Lavinia's face, his fingers warm and gentle. She shut her eyes.

*Don't touch me. Your touch can kill.*

He tilted her chin towards him. "I am—I regret you had to experience the pain of believing you lost our son. The gypsies let you go, but watched your every move to keep you from danger. To have you act so spontaneously made the Dark One believe the baby was truly deceased."

Yasir put his arm around her once more. She shuddered, and knew he felt it. The gypsies, Mehadeh and Yasir had concocted a diabolical plan with her in the middle. With her the one that suffered. Oh, she could see the greater good in it. Anyone examining the overall strategy like a military commander would see the goal wasn't evil. Anyone who wasn't the pawn. If she had been killed, he would still have had his son to fulfill the prophecy. She would have done her job.

She kept her eyes on Stuart, who made a sucking motion with his lips, a left-over from when he first came to her at four months. Now he was almost four years old. How he had grown. She longed to stroke his soft cheek, but didn't want to chance waking him.

Yasir pulled her close. "My son has been safe here with you, growing up as an English lord. The Dark Magician does not know."

The djinni viewed the other bed, his hand to his chin, contemplative. "I see our son has a brother."

Lavinia felt her stomach drop. "Yes. James, Peter's son." Their youngest, so sweet and cuddly, bore an uncanny likeness to Stuart, as both boys resembled her. She did not want to discuss James with Yasir.

"Of course." Yasir squeezed her shoulder in a gentle caress. "Lavinia, it is good for Stuart to have brothers who are human. It is safer for all of us that way."

A pensive expression dulled Yasir's radiance, then a flash of anguish rent his eyes, such agony that Lavinia winced. With his arm wrapped around her, the warmth so familiar, it would be easy to find solace in him, but she had learned her lesson. She watched him force the pain away, and only then did he gaze upon his son once more.

She stroked the rumpled covers of Stuart's bed, trying not to feel comfort in Yasir's embrace. Sealing the djinni in the urn for her lifetime would be pitiless. For centuries, he had endured such heartbreak. She never dreamed she would be the one to betray him when he had almost reached his goal to be free.

"The Dark Magician thinks me dead from the cursed bullet, thinks the infant dead in the womb. So we are secure, but we must take care to keep it so." Yasir studied his son, his face softening. "I would like him to know me as his father." He spoke in a tone that wrenched her heart. "Someday. But that must wait." His voice changed. She could feel him squeezing the emotion from it.

He tore his eyes away from Stuart and placed his hand on the small of her back, a gesture of such intimacy that she gulped a quick breath. "One of our children will be the child of the prophecy. It has been centuries. Centuries yearning for you, searching for you, my Thalia."

She had heard the djinni's words. He said he yearned for her, searched for her. But his suffering at Rakhshan's hands, his imprisonment in the urn, had changed the motive of his quest. Yasir found her in order to defeat Rakhshan. He had searched for his Lavinia, his Thalia in order to free himself.

Deep in slumber, Stuart jerked his arm to the side, throwing the blanket off his chest. Even with the remnants of his baby fat, he had a strong sturdy body, her little child of the prophecy. Her son.

Child of the prophecy. The full import of the heroic phrase suddenly struck her. Fear sucked the strength from her legs—Stuart fighting Rakhshan as a young man, a young djinni with powers like Yasir. But Yasir's powers hadn't saved him from the Dark Magician's merciless torture, hadn't saved him from being imprisoned in the urn.

*Angels in heaven.* Yasir would unknowingly have her sacrifice her own son to save himself. She glanced at Yasir, standing there oblivious to the possible consequences of the prophecy. The soothsayers might say that Stuart would stop Rakhshan, but they didn't mention at what cost. They never stated if her son would even survive the experience.

Too much was at stake now. She moved away from the djinni and looked him in the eye. She would do it. For Stuart's sake. It had to be quick.

"Yasir, I command you to—

The door creaked. A shaft of light pierced the room like the grope of an extended eye. Lavinia rushed over and held the door—still partly open—as she peered out. The nanny's gasp of surprise filled the silence. Lavinia forced calm into her voice when she wanted to scream 'go away': "I don't need you now. I will let you know when I'm finished." Lavinia closed the door, taking care to be quiet. The faint sounds of the boys' steady breaths should have soothed her.

She looked around. Where was Yasir? Had he discovered her treachery before she could send him to the urn?

A warm grasp on her waist. She cried out. Yasir stood next to her, the heat of his body radiating scents of myrrh and sandalwood, eyes glowing golden in the pale light of the nursery. In a sudden motion, he took her in his arms.

She felt his heart slow, the dull beats spaced far apart. She looked up at him. At one time she had risked everything for this creature.

His eyes shone. "My *delara*, I have been tormented and abused by fate all these centuries. I do not desire that for you and our child. I would not want our son, Stuart—" His eyes softened when the name passed his lips. "—to suffer for me. This prophecy. I will . . ." He turned away, swallowed hard, then faced her.

" . . . I will break the bonds. I have studied this since we had our son. While you were alone." He grasped her tighter. "While you were here with your husband . . ." His voice broke. "I cannot bear it again. To be separate, apart from you. To have our son face a battle with—" He set his jaw. Gazed over her head as if he had donned his gorget, breastplate and gauntlets. "—a battle I should fight. No father should endure that. I refuse to." He pressed her close. His heartbeat strong and steady.

She closed her eyes to the pandemonium inside her—the crash of waves against a granite edifice. She couldn't bear to look at him.

She would say the words. Now.

She opened her mouth. "Yasir, I command you to . . ."

He tilted his head, pupils closing into sharp slits, the golden irises effulgent as the sun bursting above the horizon. For a moment she couldn't breathe, wasn't sure she would ever need to again. Then she exhaled long and slow.

"—to . . . be true to your word."

She stepped back, gaping at him. The words that had spilled from her lips were her words. The djinni had nothing to do with her command. She had no spell on her.

This was her heart speaking. Her betrayal would ultimately hurt her and her sons, for how could she live with herself after committing such a reprehensible act?

Perhaps Yasir could break the very bonds of fate, for Stuart's sake. She had to let him try. And if not, his tutelage might be Stuart's best hope of surviving. Surely this was the right course. Being true to herself and her sons. True to her love.

The djinni raised his brows, pressing his palm to his heart. "Ah, my *delara*, I pledge it so."

Yasir held her close as they watched Stuart sleep. How many times throughout the years had she viewed Stuart, and tamped down the yearning for Yasir to appear beside her and see their beautiful son? A sense of contentment she had never before experienced enveloped her. Yasir's magic was elusive as the air she breathed, but as tangible. She could feel his power at this very moment, pulsing around her, as real as the blood coursing through her veins. His glamour, changing the shape of things. Changing her world.

She laced her arm behind his back, letting his enchantment permeate her body. Once, she was afraid of his power and its effect. Now she felt strong and secure. He possessed magic, but she could wield this power.

After all, she was master.

END

Also by Claudia Herring

OBSESSIONS OF A DJINNI
(Book One of the Djinn Chronicles)

# Acknowledgements

The author's grateful thanks to:

Barry Smith, my go-to reader. Chris Rogers, my editor.

My writer's groups: the inimitable Roger Paulding, Bobbi Andrews, Robin Beckwith, Manal Broeckelmann, Luke Chauvin, Scott Darley, Bob Gregory, Jolene Hueber, Jay James, Joe Lanza, Kelly Urban, Shavonne Smith, Anna Fay Williams, Tina Winograd, and Darla Vasquez.

My beta readers: Pia Byrd, Kimmie Curtain, Kim Kapelos, Mary Pauline McElroy, Tabitha Monet, Marsha Wildman, Debbie Padon, Diane Pittman, Cheryl Portscheller and Mary Schulz.

For her opinions on writing and law, Kate Alsina.

For all you wonderful readers who have taken the time to read my novels, thank you. Please know that writers thrive on reviews.

Coming Soon

The next installment of *The Djinn Chronicles*.
Find out more at <u>claudiaherring.com</u>

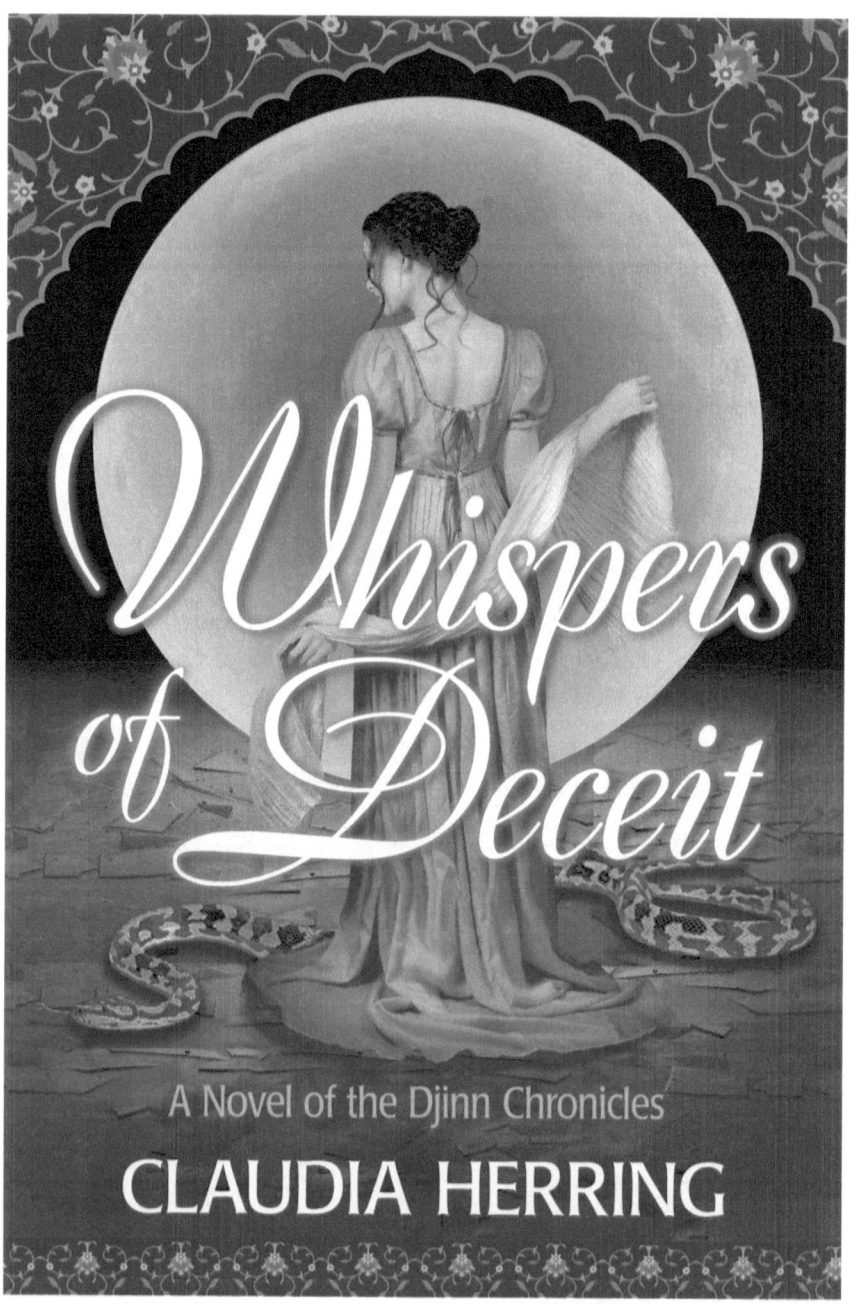

A Novel of the Djinn Chronicles

**CLAUDIA HERRING**

# Thank you!

If you enjoyed this book or received value from it in any way, then I'd like to ask you for a favor: would you be kind enough to leave a review for this book on Amazon? It'd be greatly appreciated!

Click here to leave a review on Amazon.com.

Claudia Herring writes romantic fantasy novels. Her Djinn Chronicles series are set in a world of mysterious powers and tumultuous intrigues fraught with subterfuge. They begin in Regency England where sensible mortals interact in disbelief with djinnis, magicians, sorceresses, and soothsayers.

She would live in a library if she could.

Is afraid of her cat.

If you like Diana Gabaldon or Carol Berg, you'll love The Djinn Chronicles.

For more about her novels, and exclusive content and special previews, visit claudiaherring.com.